THE MOB WAS SWELLING, FEEDING ON ITS OWN HATRED.

The Malays clapped cobblestones together, punctuating shrill screams. A cobblestone arched into the air and clattered against a lamppost as Snow and Connie hurried past. A second stone thudded into Snow's elbow, numbing his arm to the shoulder. He grunted in pain, and his wife turned to help, but he pushed her forward, feeling the first grip of fear constrict his stomach and spread like a stain. His mouth was dry and he didn't trust his voice to give his wife assurances.

They were trapped. . . .

THE
EARHART
BETRAYAL

by
James Stewart Thayer

FAWCETT POPULAR LIBRARY • NEW YORK

THE EARHART BETRAYAL

This book contains the complete text of the original hardcover edition.

Published by Fawcett Popular Library, a unit of CBS Publications, the Consumer Publishing Division of CBS Inc., by arrangement with G. P. Putnam's Sons

ISBN: 0-445-04668-6

Printed in the United States of America

First Fawcett Popular Library printing: August 1981

10 9 8 7 6 5 4 3 2 1

To
John D. Reagh III

Thanks to
John L. Thayer M.D.

THE
EARHART
BETRAYAL

Prologue
July 2, 1937

The Electra's dual Wasp engines filled the cockpit with a comforting low rumble.

Two thousand feet below, the vast emptiness of the Pacific Ocean was blue and chilling and utterly endless. The sky and sea were blurs that met on the horizon in a misted seam. For the hundredth time, the pilot squinted at the distance. Released, and squinted again. Two tiny dots speckled the seam.

"Saipan and Tinian," Fred Noonan, the navigator, muttered angrily. "I still don't like any of this. Those islands are held by the goddamn Japanese."

"All we have to do is pick up the documents. There's no other way to get them out," the pilot said soothingly, then inched the stick forward. The Electra's nose dipped almost imperceptibly. "Imperial Navy plans of some sort. We'll only be on the ground sixty seconds."

"We didn't even put this thousand-mile dogleg into our flight plan. The Brits at Le should've been told."

The pilot laughed softly, "Believe me, Fred, they know all about it on Howland. They've got cruisers and planes ready. They even lengthened the airstrip there to accommodate us. This little detour isn't as spontaneous as you'd like to think."

"I don't like the goddamn Japs or their islands," Noonan persisted, nervously ruffling the chart.

"Has it ever occurred to you," the pilot said lightly, "that 'goddamn' and 'Jap' are separable words?"

"Americans, British, Australians and goddamn Japs. That's how I learned it."

Minutes later, the plane skimmed the coconut palms that ringed Saipan's south airfield, a mud strip hacked out of the jungle. The Electra touched down and the pilot fought against a starboard drift as gravel grabbed at the wheels. The plane bounced to a stop a dozen yards from the wall of vegetation at the runway's end. Noonan flipped off his straps and pressed his head against the cabin ceiling, angling for a view off the port wing where he thought he had seen a metallic glimmer.

It was more than a glimmer. An olive green, flatbed truck pushed its way through the tangle of jungle onto the strip. On its door was a rising sun, and on the bed was a three-foot square crate, solid and heavy, canting the truck.

Noonan turned toward the freight hatch. "I hope the driver is our man." He slid open the hatch. A burst of glittering light and twisting wire slapped at his face, and he reflexively punched at it, ducking his head. The fluttering wire fell away, back to the man who stood under the hatch.

"It's just a pulley, mate. Here, I'll try again." This time the truck driver wound his arm slowly, giving Noonan time to sight on the wire and pulley.

The navigator caught the apparatus and stared at it for several seconds. "We're here for some papers. We won't be needing a pulley, will we?"

"Much heavier than they should be, I must admit." The driver looped the hook onto the crate. He was a tall, rangy man with slightly stooped shoulders and a seamed, thoroughly British face. They had been told to expect a Japanese. "Attach the pulley on an overhead girder, will you? Won't take a minute, and you'll be on your way."

The navigator reluctantly obeyed, cranking the crate off the truck bed to the Electra's hatch. He gripped the crate and grunted as he wrestled it into the plane. "I don't care what your friend in Washington says, this crate is too heavy for documents," he said to the pilot. Quickly lifting a hammer from the Electra's tool kit, he pried open one of the slats and bent close, peering into the box. Blinked, then looked again.

"What is it, Fred?"

"It's an elephant's trunk!" Noonan pushed his arm through the opening. "It's a whole elephant. I can feel the trunk and an ear. A miniature stone elephant, for Christ's sake." Noonan pulled his hand from the crate, then angrily turned to the hatch. "Listen, pal, our deal was to fly some documents out of here, not some elephant carving. If you think. . . ."

Pointed unerringly at his right eye, the pistol stopped Noonan midsentence. In a calm monotone, the driver said, "Climb down out of there. And call the pilot."

Noonan's hands moved away from his body. "Mister, these islands are Jap-owned. If we don't hurry. . . ."

"Jump down. Now." Had there been even a hint of incompetence in the driver's voice, perhaps Noonan would have balked. He one-stepped the wing and hopped to the ground, his eyes never leaving the revolver.

The pilot's face emerged from the hatch's shadow. "What's wrong, Fred?"

The pistol moved fractionally. "You, too. Get down."

The gun followed her movements until Amelia Earhart stood alongside her navigator. Her glance flickered between the driver's face and his crate.

"Back away from the plane," the driver ordered. The high whine of an approaching troop truck filtered through the jungle.

"Mister, we're just here to pick up documents. We're due at Howland Island . . . ," she said.

It was the first time in their long friendship Noonan had heard pleading in Amelia Earhart's voice. It was the last thing he would ever hear.

The pistol barked twice. Two muffled pops that rustled with the leaves were lost in the overgrowth. Amelia Earhart and Fred Noonan slumped to the runway.

The driver quickly climbed up the wing and into the hatch, aware of the scrambling sounds in the jungle. An approaching patrol. Perilously close. But the driver paused at the crate. His hand hesitated, trembling. He slipped it slowly into the crate until the coolness of the stone rested against his palm. His breath caught and his stomach tightened, a carnal stirring.

Only the frantic yells pulled the driver from the stone. With a last lustful glance at the crate, he lowered himself into the cockpit. He quickly tested the ailerons, then pulled the accelerator with a smooth, practiced motion. The Wasps thundered and the plane lurched forward, bouncing into a turn. More throttle, and the Electra gained a steady rhythm as it coursed down the strip, flinging itself toward the palm trees. The pilot pulled the stick, and the plane hesitated only a second before muscling itself into the sky and shooting over the waving leaves.

Three Imperial Navy shore patrolmen struggled through the jungle wall as the Electra's tail disappeared over the trees. One soldier fired, but his target was already too distant. With weapons drawn, they ran toward the bodies on the runway. The patrolmen did not see Amelia Earhart's Electra bank toward Singapore.

I

Two dull sensations: the suffocating, gaseous heat and the wet slap of vomit sloshing across the truck bed. Three days with the doors bolted shut. Jolting days wedged between the bodies of the hopeless.

Amelia Earhart's bones brought them to Singapore, to this Bugis Street café to meet the transvestite. Joseph Snow sipped his Tiger Beer, then stared uncomfortably ahead, directly into his wife's eyes.

"These poor girls have spent hours primping and you won't even glance at them," she smiled, lifting her tea cup. Under the tropical sun her black hair seemed cobalt blue and her smoke-colored eyes paled to a steely noncolor.

"They aren't women, they're men, and you can grin all you want, I still feel like a fool sitting here."

Connie Snow looked flatteringly at several of the transvestites. It was midday, a smothering blanket of a day in May, 1946, and Snow left damp patterns wherever his hands touched. Yet the Bugis Street women sitting in groups around the tables were fresh and unruffled. They occasionally tasted their tonic water, seldom spoke to one another and constantly searched for redheaded devils. A few wore elegant cheongsams, slit to the knees. Others had the latest Western fashions, silk blouses with blocked shoulders. The wigs surrounding the brown faces were of improbable colors: honey and auburn and cinder gray. And the gold. Gold earrings, gold bracelets, gold cigarette holders. One lovely specimen graced her eyelids with gold sequins.

Still locked on his wife's eyes, Snow said, "What do I call the contact? Him or her?"

"He'll be dressed as a lady. Call her 'her.' She'd be offended. . . ."

Gleeful laughs from the next table interrupted Connie's lecture. An Australian sailor—cap and ribbons and spats—lowered himself into a chair between two of the café's spangled and ambiguous patrons.

"Hello, Jack. You buy Betty Grable a tonic?"

The sailor grinned enormously. "Your name's Betty Grable, is it? Well, Betty, you're going to have a good time with this cobber."

"You bet you, Jack." The transvestite's eyes followed the sailor's hand as he reached for his sea purse. "Sodding hot weather, eh, Jack? Any more come with you to see Betty?"

Snow turned back to his wife who had lost interest in the sailor's fleecing. She spread on the table two photographs of Amelia Earhart, one showing her in a nurse's aide uniform, her eyes soft and guileless, her full mouth playfully turned up at the corners. A face of innocence and energy. The second photo was taken years later at Southampton after her first flight across the Atlantic. The Mayor of Southampton supported her elbow. Her mouth hung open with fatigue, and her eyes were glossy and unfocused. The flight suit was rumpled and soiled, accentuating her sagging appearance.

"You know, Joseph, when she wasn't cloaked in those leather helmets and jackets, she was quite pretty."

"Staring at those old photos won't help us. We're after her bones, and bones all look alike, especially when they've been buried for a few years."

"You're being testy," she said, still examining the prints.

"And just because it's ninety degrees, my beer is pisswarm, and I'm under siege by a dozen sexual oddballs gives me no right to be testy."

She looked up to laugh, but one of the oddballs was standing at her husband's shoulder, reaching for a chair at their table. Snow instinctively gathered his feet to rise, hesitated, then dropped back. The transvestite delicately lowered herself into the rattan chair.

"I am Rose," she said, placing a beaded purse on the table. Her voice was neither feminine nor masculine, but a

14

mellifluous whisper that both promised and intrigued. Her satin blouse was the color of her name, and suggestively swelled where no man's shirt would. Her eyes, almond-shaped with deep brown irises and langorously heavy eyelids, were made up for evening, painted in dark, graceful arches.

"Rose?" Snow repeated dumbly, repelled.

"Yes. If you were Australian, it would be Maggie, and if English, Heather. Rose does well with you Americans."

"That's a beautiful blouse, Rose," Connie Snow said, eyeing the curves for signs of a prosthesis, then shifting her gaze to Rose's manicured, blood-red fingernails.

"Isn't it? I found the smartest shop on upper Orchard."

"I'm getting nauseous," Snow muttered.

"What's that, darling?"

"Rose didn't come here to charm us into buying her a drink," Snow said, looking squarely at the transvestite for the first time.

She smiled endearingly, revealing an even row of startlingly white teeth set off by ruby lipstick. She placed her hand on Snow's arm. "A little tonic water would be nice, though. With a lime slice on the rim. After all, you came ten thousand miles just to meet your Rose."

Connie laughed and Rose joined her with a voice that couldn't decide on an octave.

"You've seen the bones?" Snow asked abruptly.

Rose sobered. "No. They are still buried on the Peninsula."

"They could be anybody's. A lot of people died there."

Rose gently shook her head, and the lacquered waves of her black wig tapped against her cheeks. "They are a woman's bones. A white woman's."

Snow argued. "A nurse or a Wac or a missionary. Hundreds never came back from the war. Disappeared in the Pacific rim."

The transvestite dug briefly in her purse to find an inlaid pearl compact that Snow guessed cost two hundred U.S. dollars. She viewed herself approvingly in the tiny mirror, then glanced flirtatiously at the Australian sailor. "I'll bet he would buy me a drink. I'm a favorite of the Aussies."

Only after Snow grudgingly signaled the waiter did Rose continue. "The Japanese soldiers called me their Malay flower. Some of my war friends were very well placed. One of them, Colonel Furusawa, ran the Peninsula camp. He loved to tell me of the American woman under his care. I teased him and said I didn't believe him. One day he brought me proof."

The waiter set a highball glass in front of Rose. Bubbling tonic water. She dabbed the glass at her lips, swallowed for effect, then looked invitingly at Snow. He was a large man with a thick chest and pylon arms that his golf shirt could not conceal. His tapered waist was untouched by his forty-four years. But it was Snow's blond hair Rose abruptly reached for, pushing a strand back into place.

He flinched, then recovered nicely despite his wife's soft laugh. "What proof?"

"How do you Americans say it?" She raised her eyebrows, " 'I'm not in this for the fun of it.' "

From his rear pocket, Snow produced a manila envelope and tossed it contemptuously onto the table. "Five hundred dollars. That's about three months work for you, isn't it?"

Rose sniffed, "It was a transport pilot's license, issued to Amelia Earhart."

"You actually saw the license?"

She nodded, fingering the envelope flap and stealing a glance at the stack of bills inside.

"Anybody could have made up this little story," Snow said, his hand moving to the envelope.

Rose added quickly, "It was issued May 1, 1930, by the Department of Commerce, Aeronautics Branch. Issued to Amelia M. Earhart, age: thirty-one, weight: 118, height: five feet eight inches, color of hair: blonde, color of eyes: gray."

"*Time* magazine had all that."

"License number 5716. *Time* magazine didn't have that."

This was the first indication that he was in Singapore for more than a vacation. His hand retreated from the money. "You saw the license?"

"I held it in my hand long enough to memorize it."

"Because you figured you could someday make some money with the information."

Rose smiled widely and slipped the envelope into her purse. "It looks like I have, haven't I?"

"Not quite yet," Snow countered. "You wrote that you could locate the body. That's part of our deal."

"I never went to the camp."

"Then I want the money back."

"But I can take you there. On Colonel Furusawa's last visit to Singapore before the allies retook the city, he told me that all the prisoners were being marched north up the Peninsula. All those that could walk."

"And Amelia Earhart?"

"She had malaria and couldn't march. Furusawa said she was a spy, so she was shot."

"Her body could be anywhere in the Malay jungle," Snow said.

Rose slowly shook her head. "No, the Colonel said she is buried ten yards north of the camp's icehouse."

"Why would a Japanese colonel tell you that?" Connie inquired.

Rose smiled demurely, "Believe me, Colonel Furusawa would have told me anything."

"How far is the camp?" Snow asked, finishing his tepid beer.

"Across the Johore Strait and twenty miles into the Peninsula near Keluang."

"Can we get there and back by nightfall?"

The transvestite nodded.

Snow rose from the table. "Then we can be on the Pan Am Clipper in the morning."

"I think Howard expects you to spend more than four days in Singapore," Connie said, looking into the street for a trishaw.

"If I get the job done, it's done. Four days or four weeks. Anyway, you know what I always say about Howard Lester."

" 'To hell with Lester.' "

"Precisely."

Howard Lester's title was unclear, as was the location of his office, the name of his secretary, and the color of his hair. Without doubt, he was in charge of the Central Intelligence Group. At least, Joseph Snow had no doubts. Annette Cordez believed he was the third man in the hierarchy. Snow reported to his store-front office near Georgetown University, but Andrew Jay insisted his office was a drab, three-story walk-up on Rhode Island Avenue.

Lester was a man of infinite contradictions and unanswered questions. His agents could agree on only one facet of his personality: he had a vast capacity to annoy. Every time James Payne visited Lester's office, the discussion was endlessly interrupted by the ringing of the telephone in the next office. When Andrew Jay saw Lester, it was sunflower seeds,

17

eaten continuously during every meeting. Payne had never seen a sunflower seed, and Jay had never heard a telephone ring. And only Snow had seen the tic.

One week before his arrival in Singapore, Joseph Snow had been summoned to Howard Lester's office. Snow had been idle for two months and was eager for the meeting, despite the facial contortions he knew he would witness. The secretary ushered Snow into Lester's office.

"Ah, Joseph, it's been a while," Lester waved him to a chair facing the massive desk. "You've been keeping busy?"

"I've been sitting on my butt for months, as you well know."

"I gave you a few weeks off, thinking you could use the time to adjust to your new family." Lester's seraphic face was broadened by a grin.

One fact about Lester could not be disputed. He had a niece, Connie McDaniels, and Snow had met her in this office three months before. Everyone, it seems, has a relative who wants marriage, and the chief was no exception. Snow had been determined to foil Lester's plan, but he failed. Spectacularly. Connie McDaniels and Joseph Snow were married six weeks after they met. Snow's memory of those six weeks was blurred.

"Your niece's marriage isn't the reason I haven't been getting assignments," Snow said.

Lester spread his hands in a gesture of equanimity. "No. I've said this before, Joseph, now that the war in Europe and Asia has ended there is simply less work to be done. Ask Jay or Thompson, they'll tell you they are getting more rest these days, too." Lester's face twitched and Snow cringed.

Lester went on. "I've been inventing make-work assignments for my people. Thompson the Tapper has been over at the cathedral listening to confessions through one of his bugs for two weeks. For the past month, Harvey Lyle has been with Nelson on Two testing RDX chemical fuses. Nelson crimps the fuse, Lyle presses the watch. Nelson crimps, Lyle presses. For a month! You can't complain, especially with what I've got for you today." Another spasm and wink. "It'll involve travel to a sunny climate, not too much work, but it's a chance to get away. A chance to contribute and to earn your money. And there's even a surprise involved. All told, not a bad assignment."

"Out of the country?" Snow asked, already pleased.

"To Singapore. The war is over, the monsoons have passed, and Singapore is once again a very pleasant place to be."

"What needs to be done?"

"Well," Lester cleared his throat and squared several sheets of paper, "you're familiar with Amelia Earhart, of course."

Snow waited.

"Briefly put, her bones have been found near Singapore. I want you to go there and bring them back."

Snow lurched forward in his seat, the scowl already firmly planted. "Bring back some bones? What kind of garbage assignment is that?"

"Joseph, there's a bit more to her story than. . . ."

"Damn it, Howard, I've worked for you for nine years. You've got a file on me a foot thick and it's filled with all sorts of vicious jobs you've had me pull. You've made me a specialist. And now you're going to have me travel to the Far East to fill a coffin?"

Lester held up a hand. "Listen for a minute. You don't know the story on her." Again he tapped the edges of the paper. His pink face darkened. "Amelia Earhart left Oakland on May 20, 1937 on what would've been the first round-the-world flight. She and her navigator flew to Miami, then south to San Juan, Paramaribo, and several other stops, then across the Atlantic to Dakar."

"Everyone knows that."

"Yes, well, she flew east. Gao, Khartoum, Karachi, Calcutta, and so forth. This was in June 1937 when the secret war was heating up. During that month this office learned of a Japanese navy captain who wanted to defect. He was an intelligence officer named Nissho Ito, and he was stationed on Saipan in the Japanese mandate islands, one of Japan's easterly outposts. We let him know that we just couldn't take every defector who comes along, and he would have to prove his worth."

"By producing."

"Exactly. He said he could give us Imperial Navy documents. Contingency plans. All we had to do was get them out."

"And along comes Amelia Earhart and her Electra," Snow said dryly.

"I'll get to that. Remember back nine years, Joseph. Japan was arming herself, marching west, sailing east. We knew nothing about her ambitions and couldn't get any information. The prospect of receiving the documents was exciting, but even more dazzling to us, was the opportunity to have a Japanese intelligence officer working for us. We were salivating."

"And along comes Amelia Earhart and her Electra," Snow repeated.

"Ships were too slow. We had to use a plane. Ito said he and the documents would be at Saipan's south field July 2 and July 3, 1937. No sooner, no later. We had no planes with the necessary range. Earhart and Noonan landed in Singapore on June 20, and that's where we convinced her to alter her plans. She continued the flight, but after she took off from Le, New Guinea, rather than fly directly to Howland Island, she turned north. A short side trip to Saipan, touch down, bring out the documents, and take off."

"Only she didn't take off?"

"No. Ito either changed allegiances again or was discovered. So it was all for nothing." Lester's voice was sour.

"How did her body find its way to Singapore?"

"I have no idea. It may mean that she didn't die on Saipan but on the Malay Peninsula at some later date. At best, you could find out when and where she died."

"And at worst, I'll just be escorting a body bag back across the Pacific."

"Joseph, we've never let it be known that Amelia Earhart did anything but run out of fuel in the Pacific. Sure, there are suspicions, but we scoff at them. Truth is, she died from a Japanese bullet, and I think the least we can do is bring her body home."

"A very nice sentiment, Howard, but why can't one of the new people do it?"

Lester's voice firmed. "The new people no longer work here. Nothing for them to do, so I let them go. I'm trying not to have the same thing happen to my experienced operatives. Put shortly, I've nothing else for you to do. So you're going to Singapore." The tic violently compressed his face. Before each session, Snow swore he would ignore it, but at each successive meeting, it galled him even more.

"Then to Singapore it is," he managed evenly.

"I haven't mentioned the most rewarding aspect of this assignment," Lester said. "There won't be a great deal of work involved, so why don't you take Connie with you? Once in a while we can allow a family junket for a senior operative."

"Well," Snow paused, thrown off-balance by this unprecedented gesture. "That puts Amelia Earhart's bones in a different light."

"I thought it would," Lester smiled. "Put the bones in a box, arrange for their shipment, then forget them and have a good time. Hawaii is enroute, you know."

The Dusun tribesman swung his parang in easy cadence with his short steps. Each arc of the heavy sheath knife left a swath of cleared jungle and a flurry of green fragments. He wore a pair of cotton shorts, stained through with perspiration and flecked with bits of orchid petals and liverworts that had fallen victim to his blade. A *sangkok* kept the foliage from tangling his dark hair. He hummed a shrill accompaniment to his rhythmic parang, a tune legend said guided the blade unerringly to its mark.

The Peninsula highway was a hundred yards behind them, and they were walking on what the Dusun promised was the Leper Colony road, more recently called the Penal Colony road. Snow could occasionally feel vehicle ruts under his feet, but the road had been almost completely reclaimed by Malaysia's *kerangas* jungle. Plank buttressed trees had begun to grow in the tracks, and smooth-barked Borneo camphors were shooting up toward the jungle canopy a hundred feet above them. At work were the liana, the insidious bush ropes which twist around a tree trunk, climb to the canopy, then descend to the green floor to climb another, choking the jungle. The air was humid and dead, trapped under the jungle roof and sickeningly perfumed by wild orchids. A nest of wa-wa's heard the swish of the parang, and these long-tail monkeys began an eery wail, competing with the screeching cicadas. The harsh, hidden sounds of the jungle moved with them.

Snow stumbled over a milkwort vine and cursed under his breath. His eyes were almost useless, confused by patches of brilliant sunlight dappling the obscure jungle floor. Despite her four-inch heels, Rose negotiated the treacherous path with far more skill than either Snow or his wife. She held her satin dress close to her knees, her purse under one arm, while using the other to brush away ferns. She was a graceful counterpoint to the murky, perilous jungle.

Connie followed Rose's path. Snow had argued against her coming, but he had known she would stubbornly insist on joining them. It was against her nature to wait in a hotel room, to be idle. She strained to push aside a vine, then stumbled to one knee. Snow helped her up, and regretted allowing her to accompany them.

"How much further?" Snow asked, struggling to pull his foot from a putrescent sinkhole.

Rose spoke in Sarawak dialect, and the guide grunted an answer without halting the mesmerizing motion of his blade. "He's not sure, but the village *pĕnghulu* told him it was a thousand cuts of the parang."

"How many cuts has he taken?"

Rose conversed again with the Dusun, then said, "He doesn't know. He can't count that high."

For the first time in fifteen minutes, the Dusun's blade stopped. He looked above, then pointed. The jungle had thinned and large blisters of sunlight broke through the canopy.

Rose said, "This is the camp."

Snow turned a full circle. "It's still jungle, I don't see any buildings."

The tribesman's face twisted with concentration as he stared into the foliage. His mouth broke into a golden, gapped grin as he stabbed the parang at the vines. Snow saw only vines and ferns and trunks. He screwed up his eyes, allowing them to focus on a distance not yet visible.

The Dusun was right. Barely discernible through the undergrowth was a whitewashed hut sagging under the weight of bush ropes and moss. The Malay began again with the blade, eager to confirm his find and collect his fee.

The wood-plank building was no larger than a Malay thatch home, and it had once been well tended. The whitewash had only recently begun to crack, rotted by the jungle's perpetual midsummer. The windowsills were still peacock blue, a color achingly out of place in the undergrowth. The door was solid teak, and the brass handle, once bright with the rubbings of a thousand hands, was now weathered to a dull patina. The hut was succumbing to the persistent pressure of the tropics. Banyan roots were loosening the foundation, and epiphytic ferns were eating into the roof. The footpath to the door had been completely overgrown.

"This isn't the icehouse," Rose said without entering the hut.

"They had ice here?" Connie asked, running her palm

22

across her brow, leaving the same amount of moisture as was swept away. She was breathing with difficulty. The sulfurous, sweet air seemed to congeal about the nostrils.

Rose smiled tolerantly, "An icehouse is a camp's punishment block. A prison within a prison."

"Are there other buildings here?" Snow asked, about ready to surrender to the mosquitos. His hand slapped the back of his neck in a last, futile effort.

"At least twenty others. We just can't see them. With the blue paint and the door, this looks like my Colonel Furusawa's office. The icehouse should be thirty paces west of here."

Rose spoke to the Dusun, who began again to sweep away through the green maze. The jungle had been far less successful redeeming the icehouse. The foundation must have been buried deep, for it was still solid. Vines had grown up the side and wrapped around the bars that covered the window. The flatiron door had rusted through near the hinges. The corrugated tin roof turned the torrid Malay sun inward. Confinement in the icehouse had been a sentence of death.

"Her body is behind this building," Rose whispered, as if afraid the jungle would overhear her revealing its secrets. She high-stepped a cluster of poppy blooms at the icehouse corner, then measured ten steps into the brush. "This is it."

"You seem pretty sure of this spot," Snow said as he pulled a hand hoe from his belt.

"She was buried where she fell. Colonel Furusawa took great delight in telling me how he marched her around to the rear of the icehouse, but not far enough away so that the shot would be lost on the other prisoners. He forced a couple of Australian flyers to bury her."

Snow began gingerly swatting the ground with the hoe. "Why was Earhart moved here from Saipan, interned for most of the war, only to be shot?"

"My colonel only told stories he enjoyed. That must not have been one of them." She picked at her silk hose, then pouted, "I've ruined my stockings, and you would not *believe* what I had to do to earn these."

"Joseph," Connie said, kneeling to help, "you're only scratching at the ground. Let's dig them up and leave. The jungle is closing in on me."

The greenery covered the jungle floor with a thick matting. Snow borrowed the Dusun's parang to tear at the liana and the twisters. He put his back to it, aware as Connie said that

23

the Malay jungle was silently approaching them, as it had swarmed over the camp buildings to reclaim them. He could sense the banyan roots descending from the canopy and the orchids turning their blossoms in his direction, seeking him out. The giant leeches had scented him and were inexorably inching toward him.

The earth was wet, heavy humus that crumbled before the hoe. Snow's hands were so damp he had to regrip after every few strikes. He swung fiercely, aware the jungle had made its first inroads on rationality.

The hoe struck something solid, a sharp smack that was out of place in the jungle. With only an instant's hesitation, he dug his hand into the dirt, gripped and pulled.

It was her ilium, the uppermost section of the hipbone. The jungle's accelerated decay had begun to eat into the calcium, giving the bone a chalk softness. Snow bit his lip as he pulled the ilium from the rotting cloth, what once must have been khaki shorts. Decayed strands of ligament held the thigh-bone in place, and when it emerged like a growing thing from the shorts, he quickly dropped it all. Swallowing rapidly against the bile rising in his throat, he murmured, "I can't handle these one by one. Open the bag and I'll rake them in."

As Connie held open the canvas sack, Snow straddled the pit and sank the hoe blade again and again into the body's remnants, shoveling them toward his wife who turned away, unable to look into the hole. Rose stood well away, covering her mouth with a white-gloved hand, eyes fixed on the body bag.

The roots were unwilling to give up their find, and several times Snow knelt into the pit to pull free a bone from the grasping tubers. They gripped the skull with tenacity, and he had to peel back roots from the eye sockets and teeth, almost gagging as he pushed the skull into the body bag. For several minutes, Snow prodded the ground with the hoe handle, then unable to disguise his urgency, he said, "I think we got it all. Let's go."

Connie hastily pulled the bag's drawstring, then twisted away from the fetid hole, gasping for fresh air, but was met by a pungent cloud of cloyingly sweet odor from the spider orchids they had uprooted. Her head wagged involuntarily, shaking off the grip of the jungle. Her knees sagged, and Snow caught her arm, pressing her close, as much to support himself as her. She whispered, "Joseph, we've got to get out of here . . . not thinking . . . I'm not thinking straight."

"Can you walk?"

"Yes, yes. It's my head. The jungle. And the rotten body."

He lifted the bag over a shoulder and turned to Rose. "Tell the Dusun to lead us out."

"Only *too* glad to." She spoke abruptly to the tribesman who backtracked around the icehouse and south toward the Peninsula highway.

An hour later the rented Buick stopped in front of the Bugis Street café. They had been unable to fit the canvas bag into the trunk, so it lay on the back seat. Rose opened the front door and slid out, then spoke to Snow through the window. "You be sure to tell your boss that I'm available for anything he needs in Singapore. I have lots and lots of contacts and could someday do him some favors."

"For a price," Snow smiled.

"Well, a girl must eat. Goodbye, Connie. Goodbye, Joseph." Rose waited until the Buick turned onto North Bridge Road. Then with a speed and purpose that belied her satin dress and silk hose, she sprinted across Bugis Street to a waiting automobile, muttered baritone curses until the starter caught, then drove after them.

II

A blast of light and air, then wrenching pain as a Japanese soldier dragged her from the truck. She and the others were beaten into a single-file line and marched into the camp. The dead were left in a pile near the gate.

Tamils cluttered the traffic divider, sitting on their haunches, filling the languid air with the thin, labial sounds of their language. With charcoal faces contrasting with white swathes, they reminded Snow of a flock of pigeons.

The sun had ended its siege, and for the first time that day Snow's shirt was not clinging to his back. The cool of early evening allowed other impressions of Singapore to settle on him. Even here, in the European district, odors were abusive. Decaying garbage in the Singapore River smelled of rotting eggs and, strangely, the city's rubber processing plants emitted the stench of manure. The syrupy odor of durians and rancid smell of ghee mingled and were almost overpowering.

"Do you think the smells eat into your skin?" Snow asked his wife.

"I've been holding my breath since we left the hotel. Haven't smelled a thing."

"That was fifteen minutes ago."

"I'm tough." She paused, reaching for his arm. "Joseph, can I ask you a personal question?"

"Don't wives have that prerogative?"

"Is your ear congenital?"

Snow laughed, touching the mass of scar tissue that almost

26

filled his left ear. "How long have you been wanting to ask that?"

"That would've been my first question after 'Glad to meet you, Mr. Snow,' but I was tactful."

"It's a cauliflower ear, and, no, I wasn't born with it."

"You never told me you were a boxer."

"If you'll remember, our courtship was a breathless affair, and I didn't have time to tell you much," he said. "I boxed at UCLA, then for the Navy."

She pulled him around and said, "And you never mentioned being in the Navy."

"I wasn't. I only boxed for them. As you know, I was in the OSS during the war, stationed mostly in China. Occasionally, I was flown out to do some boxing."

"I don't understand."

"Well, interfleet boxing rivalries were intense. I was a ringer for the Seventh Fleet. A week before a flight, Admiral Kinkaid would have me sent to his flagship. He'd try to find a bos'n's uniform that would fit me, and one of his staff would remind me how to salute and how to be properly obsequious. I'd fight, usually on a carrier deck with thousands of sailors cheering me on. Then I'd collect my five hundred dollars and slip away, back to the mainland, courtesy of a plane supplied by the Admiral. I don't think more than a dozen people ever knew I wasn't Navy."

"And, of course, it never bothered you that you were cheating, that those fights were supposed to be between Navy personnel," Connie said as they passed a wrinkled Chinese woman making a thank-offering of rice at the precise spot where good fortune had once befallen her. She wore the red medieval headgear and blue samfoo of the San Sui women, the brickhaulers from the Kwantung Province of China. She chanted and swayed her gratitude for the lover or employer she had met here. Connie carefully skirted the woman's sacred spot and asked, "Did you win all your matches?"

Snow hesitated. "I lost one. Against the Third Fleet champion." His voice became surprisingly solemn. "Connie, I'm going to tell you something, and I don't want you ever to repeat it."

She nodded, a trace of fear turning down her mouth.

"I swear to God that the Third Fleet slipped in Joe Louis to fight that match against me."

Her burst of laughter made Snow hastily look over his

shoulder, afraid the San Sui woman had overheard him. His hand firmly gripped his wife's elbow, but she wouldn't stop laughing. He growled. "Listen to me, it makes sense. The guy was big and black and past his prime. I'm telling you, he cut me up. I lasted almost three rounds, and my face looked like the floor of a kennel for the next two weeks."

Connie said, "You can't be serious."

Snow's face was stern. "He had me locked up during the third round, just before he KO'd me, and he said right into my cauliflower ear, 'Look at this face, boy. Remember this face.'"

Connie's was a horselaugh, big and brash.

"Goddamn it, Connie. His face was familiar. And I'm telling you, nobody, *nobody* else could've walked on me like that."

"You're being preposterous. Every sailor on that ship would've recognized Joe Louis."

Snow was silent for several paces. He made a rough noise in his throat. "That's the only part that doesn't fit. They changed his face somehow, then snuck him in."

"There's no doubt you got hit very hard on the head. Perhaps repeatedly." When Snow refused to smile she changed tacks, "Tell me what you did in China."

"I worked for the OSS, for Howard Lester."

"That's about all you've ever said."

"For a while I was a civil affairs officer, then I was sent to Chungking. My job was to assist the anti-Japanese secret societies."

"Secret societies? You mean the opium runners?"

"They engaged in a little of that, but they were paramilitary organizations that raided Japanese outposts. I dealt with the *Ch'ing Pan,* the Green Circle, which had loose ties to Chiang Kai-shek. When I went into China in 1937, the Green Circle was one of the most powerful forces in Central China, and it had over four thousand brothers or officers, and probably four million lesser members. They completely dominated the Yangtze Valley."

"The Green Circle had four million soldiers?"

"No, nothing like that. Most people joined simply so other members wouldn't kidnap or murder their families. It was quite a protection racket, really. But I was involved with the ten thousand or so soldiers of the Green Circle. Arming them, training them, organizing their intelligence, that sort of thing."

"You had a specialty?" she asked as they approached the Polglasa Bridge spanning the Stamford Canal. St. Andrew's rose before them. Built by Indian convict labor, the gleaming white cathedral was an attempt to indelibly stamp Singapore with the British mark. Near the cathedral a crowd of Malays had gathered around a Muslim holy man and were raptly listening to his exhortations against foreigners. Their bleached sarongs hung limply on thin bodies as they bowed to the justness of the holy man's words. Nearby, two Malay children played *sepak takraw*, skillfully keeping the wicker ball in the air with bare feet.

"A specialty? Sure, the Chinese language. Limited Chinese. When I was growing up in San Francisco, our housekeeper was an old amah who took great delight in speaking Chinese to me whenever my parents weren't around. I learned very quickly. Chinese to To-Lin, English to my parents. My Chinese was her way of getting back at my folks. A little sabotage of the family."

"I mean, did you have a skill you taught the Green Circle?"

Snow glanced at his hands. The knuckles were disfigured by scars, red cusps looking like fresh wounds. He flexed his right hand once, stretching the tissue, draining the scars of color. He said in a low voice, "No, not really."

"So what happened to the Green Circle?"

"It took us a while to learn, but most of the large societies were too loosely organized and too easily diverted by their conventional pastimes to be effective fighting forces. So the U.S. Navy and the OSS formed a pro-Kuomintang group of virulently anti-Japanese societies, groups like the Whampoa Cadets, the secret organization of Chiang's old military academy in Canton, and the Blue Shirts, a neofascist organization patterned after Germany's Brown Shirts. After this distilling process, we ended up with an outfit that would fight the Japanese."

"Your role hasn't become any clearer. Are you, by any chance, trying to avoid the question?"

"What question?"

"The one about what you did in China."

"I was a teacher. Let it go at that, all right?"

"All right," she leaned close to him, letting him know that his history didn't matter, and in doing so, observed the crowd

29

of Malays behind them. She said urgently, "Joseph, those people are after us."

"Now you're the one being preposterous." But he turned, and the Malays who had been listening to the mullah were indeed following them. A crowd of perhaps thirty was a half block back, matching pace with the Anglos. Sullen scowls creased their dark faces, and a few raised their fists. Cries of hatred cut sharply the humid evening air.

"What do they want?" Connie's voice cracked, and her nails in Snow's arm threatened to draw blood.

"Don't know. Pick up the pace, honey."

They did, and so did the crowd. One young Malay lifted a cobblestone and waved it menacingly at them, his lips curled back in a primal snarl as he barked an unintelligible oath.

"Joseph, tell them we didn't do anything. We didn't harm them."

"They'd listen with a brick."

"How far is the club?" Her eyes mirrored her fear.

"Couple blocks. We'll make it. They're just trying to scare us."

The growing swarm sent out tentacles. Two or three children skipped ahead, mimicking the shouts of their elders. Sandals slapped against the cobblestones, and the sarongs swished malevolently like the hissing of snakes. Fists bobbed and more rocks were lifted. Faces twisted with hatred.

"Joseph, I'm afraid. They're getting closer."

"Keep walking." He dropped back a half step to shield her.

The mob was swelling, feeding on its own hatred. The Malays clapped cobblestones together, punctuating shrill screams. A cobblestone arched into the air and clattered against a lamp post as Snow and Connie hurried past. A second stone thudded into Snow's elbow, numbing his arm to the shoulder. He grunted in pain, and his wife turned to help, but he pushed her forward, feeling the first cramps of fear constrict his stomach and spread like a stain. His mouth was dry and he didn't trust his voice to give his wife assurances.

For a terrible moment, Snow thought they were trapped. Ahead of them, a second mob spilled around the Capitol Theater, pouring into the street, moving with purpose, closing in on them like a pincer. But these men carried wood riot sticks and many wore pistols. And light blue uniforms. They were Gurkha riot policemen, and they fanned out across the

North Bridge Road, then began a slow, practiced step toward the Malays.

The mob knew the Gurkhas, and it immediately began to splinter. Stones were dropped and the chants died midthroat. Faces were averted and fists unclenched. The Malays melted into sidestreets and doorways, into groups of twos and threes, no more menacing than the brick-laden San Sui women who paused to watch. The Gurkha line parted to allow the Snows through.

For an hour Dillon Synge had stared at the pedestal, the enormous flat slab of polished granite that dominated his office. He sat, brittle in his leather chair, arms flat on the desk, mouth open slightly. Only his chest moved, a dispirited, grudging concession to life.

Synge was surrounded by marks of his success: a thousand-pound teak desk and a beveled glass display case containing jade pieces from four dynasties. Behind him hung a Ming tapestry of willows and blossoms, and under him lay a Gaya rug which had taken four Hindus three years to weave. But his eyes never left the pedestal.

Synge's eyes remained locked on the empty pedestal. The elephant was an acid-stained memory of river-green shades, brushed with delicate swirls of pearl-white so lustrous they transfixed the viewer, daring him to move away. The Kobe Elephant was the largest piece of kingfisher jade ever found. Not lackluster nephrite jade, worn in the earlobes of Chinese peasants. But greenstone. Jadeite. Crystal jade. The most precious.

For five years the Kobe Elephant had graced the stand in Dillon Synge's office. Joyful years when other jade dealers begged him for a glimpse of the elephant, and he had dispensed the privilege with imperial favor. He would point out the delicate, lifelike serrations on its upraised trunk, proudly show the emerald green ears, carved with such skill they were translucent, and would let the visitor marvel at the elephant's bulk, at the sheer impossibility of a two-hundred-pound jewel.

A small, insistent twitch tugged at the corner of Synge's eye and the vision fell away. The Kobe Elephant was gone. Had been for years. But still he stared. Every afternoon he reached this impasse and simply stared at the empty pedestal.

Synge turned his head to the insistent knocking. He blinked

31

rapidly, bringing his eyes into focus, then yelled something unintelligible. The office door opened. His secretary, an Irish gunny known as Flynn, said, "Mister Synge, I've been knocking for two minutes. Your guests are downstairs. Governor Longstreet and Bliss and the rest. They're expecting you."

"Of course, Flynn. I'll be right down."

Synge lifted his tie from the armrest, and strode briskly to the door. Almost to the door. He placed a hand against the elephant—rather, where his memory told him the elephant should have been. He felt its coolness and savored its solidity. And, as always, there came the faint stirrings of arousal. A tugging at his loins. He moved his hand over the elephant's back, then to its flank. Synge hastily left his office.

"It's the teaching of Islam," the governor said, sipping his stengah, a tall, pale whiskey and soda, the only drink Europeans trusted the club's Chinese servants to make. "The Muslims have followed me like that, too. Like frothing dogs after a gut wagon. You're lucky, I should say. A dose of Islam and a dose of communism, and you end up with a *jihad* against the whites. Inevitable." He drained his glass, then turned to a servant, "Boy, bring *satu* stengah *lekas-lekas.*"

"Why against the Europeans?" Joseph Snow asked, scratching his thumbnail against the Tiger Beer label, slowly testing his hand. The feeling in his elbow had returned, but it would be sore for a week. They were in the reception room of the British White Club, formerly known as the White Club, but changed when several Germans applied for admission.

"Europeans are an afterthought." The governor's schoolmaster features were softened by a mass of platinum hair that covered the tops of his ears. His pink face looked untouched by the tropic sun and was bright as paint. He wore a blue seersucker suit, damp with perspiration to the buttons. "It's the Chinese that they're really after. They get a crowd up, then decide to have a go at the Chinese."

"Why?" Connie Snow asked. She had recovered quickly from the sprint ahead of the mob. Her raven hair was again neatly tucked at her shoulders, and her full smile was returning. She had an exaggerated, ensnaring grin that easily spread to those around her. "I thought most people in Singapore were Chinese."

"They are now, but the Malays have long considered Singapore their territory. It became a crown colony in the early eighteen hundreds, and at that time there were just a few Malay fishing villages. Then we imported more Malays to work the plantations. Respectable wages for the time, too, I might add. A better living than tending fish stakes. A few Hindus and Tamils drifted in, and some Ceylonese and some Thais, but nothing to get upset about. But then comes John Chinaman and his million relatives. Now we've got Straits Chinese coming down from Malacca, and Hokkien Chinese who own all the businesses here now, and Teochews who work at the ports, and Cantonese who'll sell you a wicker cricket cage or a diamond ring, and the Hakkas who are the bellboys and the maids. Overwhelming, Mrs. Snow, quite overwhelming."

"And the Malays have gotten frosty as the weather about it," the little man standing at the governor's shoulder said. Terrence Bliss was Governor Longstreet's aide-de-camp with duties, as he had explained on the way in from the airport four days earlier, ranging from policy-making to chauffeuring. He was a dapper Welshman who carried his everpresent briefcase like a badge. His face was miniature; dark, ferret eyes and a chip of a nose. A clerical face, with the yellow complexion of one who has taken an overdose of antimalaria tablets. Weak waves of unctuous hair flowed back to cover a balding crown. "They're beginning to organize, just like we British organize when we get too near the docks, eh, Governor?"

Longstreet's watery eyes glistened with enjoyment of his aide's joke. He drew from the stengah, then said, "There have been riots in the past, of course, all the way back to Stamford Raffle's time. We had flare-ups in the thirties and early forties, but the Japanese allowed none of that nonsense when they arrived. The riots began again as soon as the empire reclaimed Singapore, and now the Malays and the Chinese are carrying on in earnest. Weekly gang fights, I tell you."

Longstreet looked again for a servant, and called, "Boy, bring *ketchil makan*." He confided to Connie, "He can't mix a drink, but his hors d'oeuvres are the tops in town. No idea where he gets his frogs."

"And the communists?" Snow asked.

"We only have suspicions, and they center on the Soviets. Their consulate here is an MGB holiday spot. They mix things up wherever they go, and Singapore is no exception.

Their interest is in our warm-water port. So they stir the cauldron."

The hors d'oeuvres tray was set upon the nearby Bosendorfer. The gleaming concert grand was only one of the European luxuries brought to Singapore by the British White Club and its patron, Dillon Synge. Several Waterford chandeliers were spaced evenly between swiftly spinning fans. He had imported Victorian wing chairs and silver leaf wallpaper. The mahogany and brass bar was an exact replica of one on the Strand. The bartender was a gray-bearded Sikh whose waistcoat was of the same hue as his turban.

"I hate to throw a wrench into your theory, but we didn't hear anybody in the mob yelling at us in Russian." Snow's remark prompted a soprano giggle from Bliss.

Longstreet allowed himself a smile, "No, of course not. But we believe the Soviets are organizing some of the mullahs, instructing them on haranguing a crowd and promising to help them in a final push to rid the island of Chinese influence. The Soviet consul here, Kiril Stasov, is a notorious activist."

"And British influence," Bliss added.

"Yes," Longstreet said. "It seems the Malays are easily confused. Chinese, Indian, and any and all whites. Lately it hasn't made much of a difference."

"The Chinese do nothing?"

"At first, no. But now some of Singapore's secret societies are organizing against the Malays. The Blue Pearls and the Orchid Brotherhood. These are groups with bloody histories, and they'll have their day again, Mr. Snow. Know anything about these secret societies?"

"Only what I read," he replied, and his wife was surprised by the facility with which he lied.

"Centuries-old blood brotherhoods that specialize in murder and protection, in kidnapping and opium running, but when the occasion arises, they can turn in force against a common enemy. It looks like the Malay Muslims may soon be that enemy."

"Anybody keeping casualty figures?" Snow asked.

The governor shook his head, causing strands of white hair to brush against his ears. "When a body is found floating in the Rochore Canal or the Singapore River, who's to say why it's there? We find ten of them daily, most from natural

34

causes, some from murder. There's no way we can assign a cause of death."

Terrence Bliss chirped dutifully, "Tell them about the temples."

"In the past half year, six Buddhist temples have been ransacked by Malay mobs," Longstreet continued, "and two mosques have been looted by the Chinese. These temples and masjids are made of paper and little else, and it doesn't take long for an angry crowd to rip through them, tearing down walls, threatening worshippers, and stealing the idols. In two minutes they are completely sacked. By the time the Gurkhas get there, there's no one to be found."

"And you don't think the riots are spontaneous?"

"I've no proof of anything, only my suspicions. What can I do? Cable London about my intuition? We are half a world away, and the day of the gunboat is gone, believe me. I've sent dispatches to the Foreign Office, of course, and in return I get long winded cables on the heroic British colonial tradition."

The lecture had ended. The governor stared at his whiskey, rethinking Singapore's troubles. Bliss rocked on his feet and frequently stole glances at Connie, who did her best to ignore him. Others were arriving at the British White Club, the bankers and shippers and rubber magnates, each trailed by a Boy who caught the raincoat before it hit the floor. A few wives trailed along, trying to salvage their print dresses from the torrential downpour that had just swept through Singapore as it did daily, scouring the city clean and popping rats from the monsoon drains.

"Tell me, Mr. Snow, what've you found out about the cracks?"

"Pardon me, Governor?"

"The cracks in the bridge. The Clemenceau Bridge."

"Of course. I must admit, Governor, I've been enjoying your city a bit too much, and I haven't even visited the bridge yet."

"I'm sure it won't fall in the next two days. Would you mind sending my office a copy of your report? If there's something terribly wrong with the old girl, I should like to know first hand."

Snow smiled, "I suspect the cracks are superficial. I'm arranging for a cherry picker and a scaffold tomorrow. I'll know for sure then."

A reedy, weathered man wearing a white suit and a black

lace tie stepped into their circle. The hand gripping the glass was adorned with two diamond rings that Snow guessed totaled three carats. His speckled brown hair was combed straight from his forehead. His face was deeply rutted and patches were red and peeling, a perpetual condition caused by the sun and humidity. His gimlet eyes were protectively deep. He would always need a shave.

The Governor said, "Mr. and Mrs. Snow, meet Dillon Synge, Singapore's busiest jade dealer."

Synge bowed slightly from the waist, the artificial movement of a marionette. Snow extended a hand and Synge shook it, but looked at Connie and said, "What brings you to Singapore?" His face seemed to change hue as he spoke, blanching then reddening, giving him the mottled appearance of a decaying apple.

Snow answered, "I'm a structural engineer here to examine the Clemenceau Bridge."

"Yes, of course. I heard you were coming." Synge's voice was a metallic monotone incapable of pleasant inflection.

"You are a jeweler?" Connie asked, smiling at Synge, an effort Snow begrudged without knowing why.

"Not a jeweler, a dealer. I'm the step before the retailer. I gather stones from all corners of the Orient, then have monthly shows."

"Dillon is being modest," the governor added. The compliment sounded forced. "Most of the jade sold in America and Europe goes through Hong Kong or Singapore, and he has a vise grip on the Singapore market. No one else has his contacts and his sources. He can produce virtually any quality or size stone you want. Right, old boy?"

Synge accepted a drink. "I handle perhaps a third of the jade brought into Singapore. No more than that."

The governor laughed, a kindly, professorial rumble. "Yes, but the rest are tiny hairpieces and earrings and good luck stones brought in by the peasants. Worthless stuff. I'm talking about the sculptured pieces, the dynasty treasures."

Synge allowed himself a smile, an empty grimace unsuited to his face. His eyes had not left Connie, but his jaw had firmed and his skin had settled into a consistent patchwork of pink and red. "Well, yes, I do handle quite a bit of that."

"Where does your jade come from?" Snow asked.

With what seemed like an intense effort, Synge shifted his gaze to Snow. "Virtually all Chinese nephrite originally comes from the Khotan-Yarkand area of Turkestan. Jade has been coming into China from this area for over two thousand years, on the asses and camels of the great traders." Synge dug into his suit pocket, then dropped into Snow's hand a smooth, sea-green stone, soapy in appearance and very cool to the touch. "This is nephrite, worshipped in China. Poetry without words, they say. Thrown down from heaven by the Storm God. This touchstone you're holding is a good luck charm, used by Chinese peasants to invoke the spirit of Wei Fan. Even the poorest peasant has one."

Snow turned the jade over in his palm. It almost felt soft. "I thought jade was shiny."

"This is nephrite which is carved to represent idols, put into tombs to prevent decay, and into body orifices to stop the spirit of life from escaping the body. The ancients made bowls and urns and snuff bottles of it. You are thinking of jadeite, what the New Zealanders call greenstone. It's a completely different stone, yet it is also called jade. It wasn't considered anywhere near as valuable as nephrite until about 1880 or so. Most comes from Burma. The Chinese quickly adopted it as the second mystical gift from heaven."

Connie laughed lightly. Snow noticed how her gaze shifted between Synge and the governor.

Synge continued, "I've been a student of jade most of my life, and learned quickly that it has peculiar effects on people. Most immediately adopt a favorite, nephrite or jadeite. From then on, they collect only one kind, wouldn't put up with the other."

"And you?" Connie asked.

Once again, Synge pulled his mouth into a grin. "Unfortunately, I was also affected. My personal collection consists almost exclusively of jadeite, the bright, hard, crystal jade. I trade nephrite, but never hold onto it long."

Terrence Bliss had apparently abandoned his attempt at catching Connie's eye. He held up his empty glass and excused himself. The circle drew together, but Synge kept a substantial distance from Snow's wife. Snow conceded his first civil thoughts regarding the jade dealer.

He asked, "How do you come upon the jade?"

"As the governor said, virtually all the Chinese who come to Singapore carry it. Some more than others. When the war forced the relocation of the entire districts of China, some very wealthy Cantonese and Hokkan reduced their wealth to

37

items they could carry. Jade. They sell it to me for money to start anew. I don't need to send out buyers. The Chinese come to me. So you see, I do very little."

Connie shook the ice cubes at the bottom of her glass, looked for a houseservant, then excused herself and walked toward the bar.

"Is it a secret how you got started in the business?" Snow asked.

"I would like to think I have some sixth sense for jade, but in truth, I was very lucky. My early purchases proved exceptional, and they gave me the momentum to build."

"And build he has," the governor interjected. "He hardly slowed for the war."

Synge's face was immutable, but his voice gained a huskiness like the grinding of an iron winch. White crescents were bitten into the corners of his mouth. "Are you commenting on my war effort, Governor?"

"I'm saying it was a rare man who could move to Sydney on as little notice as the invading Japanese forces gave and commence business again without missing as much as two beats."

The men stared stonily at each other, Longstreet's watery eyes firming under Synge's glare. Snow suspected he was privy to a long-standing feud. Only when Snow loudly clinked his glass onto the Bosendorfer did the governor break the glance, grip Snow's elbow and lead him away.

Dillon Synge's stare continued, first at Governor Longstreet's back, then unblinkingly to the ceiling across the room, above which was the office where his Kobe Elephant should have been.

Terrence Bliss had been waiting a full five minutes. He paced impatiently along the club's rear hallway, then rechecked himself in the hall's dress-length mirror. He stabbed out his cigarette in the sand pot, then immediately reached for another. His hand stopped abruptly when Connie Snow entered the hallway.

Bliss's victorious grin revealed peg teeth. He rocked up to the balls of his feet as she approached, and his smile faltered only momentarily when she reached into her purse.

"This is what you wanted," she said in a low, jagged voice. She handed him an envelope then nervously pulled at a monogrammed scarf her husband had given her.

Bliss opened the envelope, counted the thin sheaf of bills, then said, "And in American dollars, just as I asked. Thank you, Mrs. Snow."

"You said . . . you said you wouldn't be calling me again."

"That I did," Bliss said as he slipped the envelope into his vest. He went to his toes again, almost reaching eye level with her. "And as long as these bills last, you can be sure I won't."

"You promised you wouldn't. . . ."

"I may have promised, I may not have. But either way, what can you do about it?"

She backed away from him as if he were infectious, nearly toppling the sand pot.

"Haven't you forgotten one thing, Mrs. Snow?"

She gripped the felt drapery at the doorway to the reception room.

"There's another condition. Surely you haven't forgotten?" Bliss's voice was flecked with his power over the woman.

"No. I haven't forgotten." A whisper.

"And what is it?"

"I won't tell my husband."

Bliss nodded. "That's right. You tell your husband, and you'll bloody well tear it. We wouldn't want that, would we?"

She fled through the curtains. Bliss laughed, patted his pocket, and said into the mirror, "Yes, that would bloody well tear it."

III

Harsh sunlight bleached the yard, draining the ragged prisoners of color and life. Gaunt faces peered from hut windows, quickly lost interest in the new arrivals, and turned away. Hadn't the nun said the Malay Peninsula?

They returned to the death house on Sago Street in Chinatown. Like all establishments, the Blue Tears was open to the street, but the interior was dank and foreboding, smelling of mildew and rot. The proprietor, Mr. Chin, squatted behind a small wooden podium playing mah jong with an employee. The rigorous clicks of the mah jong tiles punctuated the muffled wheezing and burbling of the dying.

Lying and sitting on stacked shelves were Mr. Chin's clients, the old and infirm brought her by their families to die. It was unlucky to have a relative die at home. Mr. Chin charged according to his eyeball estimate of how long the old person would linger. He was seldom wrong. In Chin's one room were several layers of shelves, spacious enough for the dying to sit and eat. They were separated into groups; those who were dying with spasms, those who were spitting up, and those who were flatulent. Nearby were stacked coffins, waiting.

Joseph Snow nodded to Mr. Chin, then ushered his wife up the Blue Tears' back stairs. She was holding a hand over her mouth, staring wide-eyed at the rows of dying. Snow pulled her up the steps to the translucent glass door adorned with the painted legend SHELBY WATSON, M.D. He knocked several times, heard a distant response and pushed open the door.

What should have been a waiting room was cluttered with medical journals, empty bottles of Bombay Gin and assorted pieces of human bone. Neither a receptionist nor nurse greeted them. Snow shut the door loudly, startling a brown Asian rat, who scurried away, his jaw clamped around a bit of human metacarpus bone. The dead stench of formaldehyde caught in Snow's throat, and he coughed repeatedly.

Shelby Watson emerged from a back room, pushing even more of the chemical odor ahead of him. He smiled weakly and said, "And this is the beautiful woman you told me about yesterday. Hello, Connie."

He extended his right hand. She hesitated for an instant because it was enclosed in a black kid glove. When she grasped it, it seemed to fall away, to change shape under her gentle pressure. Watson, who was apparently accustomed to gaping reactions, ignored it, patted Snow's arm and said, "I think I've got your answer. No trouble at all."

Snow produced a pint of Bombay Gin from his back pocket and gave it to the doctor, who opened it quickly and poured a double shot into a specimen glass. The gin disappeared with one gulp and was followed by a phlegmatic sigh. Watson was emaciated, his once-handsome face cadaverous, and his eyes protruding like a frog's. His face lacked the symmetry of the living. Half of his right ear was missing, and what remained looked much too pliant to cling to his skull much longer. His right cheekbone seemed smaller than his left. Only his thick black hair and clipped mustache spoke of life. Watson wore a surgeon's apron covered with decayed offal.

The doctor swallowed another shot, then said, "I don't see many CIG people anymore, Joseph. All pulled back to the States, I suppose."

"Most of us. But not you."

"Ah, ever since those inside straights, my life has been one of very limited options, Joseph. That damned cheat mucked up my life good."

During a poker game in 1939 Watson had been hearing the quick scrape of an Australian's seconds deal all evening. He had continued to play, using his knowledge to turn a small profit. But when the cheat dealt himself three consecutive inside straights, filling them on the last card, Watson had, without warning or explanation, fired at the Australian. The doctor was sentenced to five years in the Changi Prison or in the Crown Leper Colony, the latter so his skills as a physi-

41

cian would not be wasted. He served in the colony until reprieved by a friend in the OSS to serve in China. Watson carried away more than a memory from the leper colony.

The doctor's gloved hand swept the room. "You can see, Mrs. Snow, that my practice has been failing of late. Several nasty rumors are out about me." He coughed, a long wracking outburst that left him bent over, grasping the Bombay bottle tightly. He stood slowly. "So now I push needles into dying Chinese. Not quite what I was trained for. Follow me into the next room, and I'll show you what we've got."

The surgery was that in name only. The absence of sterilizing tubs and bottles of anesthesia indicated Watson's last operation had not been performed recently. The canvas body bag lay on the floor, and its contents were spread over the expanse of the operating table.

"Joseph, is there any reason why you couldn't take this body to the Singapore coroner?" The doctor drew from the bottle, and the gin pulled his mouth back.

"I don't want anyone in Singapore looking into my business."

"Your business or U.S. government business?"

"Government business. I'm doing this for Howard Lester."

"Lester?" Watson exclaimed. "You mean to tell me that one of his own men hasn't snuffed him out yet?"

Snow laughed. "He's still going strong. Don't worry, there won't be any investigations. Nobody'll be looking into your medical school background, or lack thereof."

Watson grinned, then coughed. "Well, to business. The main way to tell a male from a female skeleton is to look at the pelvis." He lifted from the table the first bone Snow had pulled from the pit in the jungle. "A female pelvis is wider and shaped differently than a man's, allowing her to bear children. You can see that this pelvis is comparatively narrow, and it would be hard to imagine a newborn infant passing through it. The sacrum is narrower, more curved than a woman's would be." He held the bone to Connie, tacitly asking if she would care to inspect it. When she took a step back, he continued. "Also, the female pelvis has a round-shaped pelvic inlet, which we call gynecoid shaped. The pelvic inlet is where the bowels go to the rectum. Here. This is android shaped rather than gynecoid shaped, as it would be on a female."

Connie said, "So this is a male skeleton?"

"Yes."

"Are you absolutely sure?" Snow asked, peering at the pelvic inlet.

"Absolutely. And if this pelvic bone weren't enough, this skeleton has not decomposed enough to erase another clue. The hurtful truth is, Mrs. Snow, that women are more knock-kneed than men. It's called valgus angulation, and exists in women because of their wider pelvis. The knee needs to be more knock-kneed so the feet can rest flat on the floor."

"This body shows no sign of angulation?" Snow asked.

"As you can see, the legs have decayed substantially. I wouldn't be so firm in my conclusion if I hadn't the pelvis to look at. But even here, you can see the straight leg. This is the pelvis and leg of a man."

"Well, that ruins Rose's theory," Connie said, shifting to the end of the table, trying to escape the formaldehyde fumes coming from a draped corpse lying on the floor under the surgery's window.

"Joseph, you asked if this could be the body of a woman who was a Caucasian. No, on the first count, as you've seen, and no on the second." Watson scraped a twisted, decayed substance onto a towel and handed it to Snow. "This is hair from the skeleton. It's waxier, coarser and darker than most whites'. It is certainly that of an Oriental." Watson placed two fingers through the skull's eye sockets and turned it so Snow and Connie could view a small puncture. "A pistol—probably .25 caliber—ended this nineteen- or twenty-year-old's life. He was a Japanese soldier, as evidenced by these, also found in your bag." He pushed three buttons toward Snow.

"Our work in Singapore has just come to an end, Shelby. Can you get rid of these bones for me?"

Watson nodded.

"I owe you one, Doc."

"You've still got the hands?" the doctor asked, glancing at Snow's fists, too large for a man only six feet two.

"Haven't slowed a bit."

"Then some Friday morning I'd like you to be here when my Chinese creditors come banging on the door."

Snow laughed. "You and the sharks. Always, you and the sharks. Goodbye, Shelby."

The clatter of Mr. Chin's mah jong tiles had just faded behind them, overwhelmed by the cacophony of Nankin

Street, when Connie began her argument, a forceful, point-by-point summary of why they should not leave Singapore that afternoon.

The curator led them down the hallway to the armory annex. He was a pear of a man whose wireless glasses were perpetually slipping down and being shoved back up his nose, leaving dual flame-red welts. He walked well ahead of them, broadcasting his authority.

Snow said in a low voice, suitable for the dim hallway, "Connie, tell me again why we're doing this. Try to convince me this time."

"I just think that to go back to the States without looking further would make the entire trip pointless. Howard Lester said the least the U.S. can do is to bring her body back, and that means looking a bit harder than we did."

"Rose obviously didn't know what she was talking about when she led us to the icehouse. What makes you think she knew anything at all? If Amelia Earhart's body wasn't buried where Rose said, we'll never find it. And it means Earhart probably wasn't in the camp at all. Probably never even left Saipan. Rose just made an easy five hundred bucks."

"You're probably right, but it won't take that much time to look here, will it?"

"You like playing detective," he chided, and enjoyed her smile. She had a strong, almost boyish jaw and a quick smile that belied the lines of maturity and experience around her eyes.

The curator, Sergeant Major Wilkes, speared his spectacles with his index finger, then waved the Snows into the armory annex. Against the near wall were several rows of wicker crates. A few were open with their contents spread on the floor before them. Clothes, wallets, several pistols, and many other items were in various stages of disarray. The sergeant major clucked despairingly and said, "You'd think people would put things back the way they found them." He pulled a loose-leaf notebook from a wicker basket, opened it reverentially and said, "Now, this book lists all the items found in the Keluang prisoner of war camp that were worth saving. As you can see," he lifted a worn pair of GI-issue boots, "we went to unusual lengths to fill just four baskets. The prisoners weren't allowed any luxuries."

"Have things been reclaimed?"

"Oh, a few items. Dogtags, for sentimental reasons, a couple watches, that type. We had someone in yesterday, and they plowed through the baskets. Didn't have a thought about putting things back in order."

"Sergeant Major"—Connie accented "Major,"—"how are these things organized?"

"In basket number one are those items the liberating troops found in the mess hall and the latrine shack. Baskets two and three have things found in the sleeping tents, and four here has what was found in the camp headquarters, the things of value. Little value, though."

"Would you mind if we looked?" she asked.

"Of course not, ma'am. That's my job." Wilkes glanced at the motley collection of baskets. "Part of my job. Just part of my job."

As soon as the sergeant major's footsteps had receded in the hall, Connie dug into the nearest basket. Unlike the others, it contained not clothes, but an odd collection of pistols, including a cap-and-ball make Snow didn't recognize, several camp kits, pen and pencil sets, class rings, whatever the Japanese had taken off incoming prisoners. Connie pushed aside several hunting knives to find an oak jewelry box. It contained two paste ear bobs, a dozen aviator's wristwatches and an almost worthless string of chipped and yellowed pearls. She was about to close the lid when reflected light flashed from between the watches. Connie pulled a gold watch from the case.

"It looks a little better than the others, doesn't it, Joseph?"

He nodded, taking the watch. It was an Omega aviator's chronometer, clearly very expensive. Attached to the band by a thin wire was a round metal token on which was stamped a Chinese figure. He fingered the band. "The strap's made of lizard, not leather, like the others."

"And it's much smaller than the others. Try getting it around your wrist."

When he discovered the band wrapped only half his wrist, she said, "Joseph, that's a woman's watch. A woman flyer's watch."

"The chance of this being Amelia Earhart's watch are one in a hundred. One in a thousand. Finding this watch doesn't mean anything."

"Check her inventory."

He pulled three pages from his rear pocket. His eyes

followed his finger down the list. It was a schedule of all the items known to have been on Amelia Earhart's plane when she left Oakland. Snow muttered something inaudible.

"Out loud, Joseph."

"She was wearing a watch, yes. An aviator's watch."

"What brand?"

"Connie, damn it, do you realize how unlikely . . ."

"What brand, Joseph?"

"An Omega," he sighed.

"Doesn't that cut into your odds? A woman's aviator watch doesn't belong in a Japanese POW camp. And the fact that it's an Omega, and clearly a woman's watch—all this adds up."

"To what?"

"We can't say for certain it's her watch, but it could be," she exulted. "It's the only explanation we've got and. . . ."

Snow laughed and held up his hands. "Connie, you're bubbling. I've never seen you like this. You're like a bloodhound who's just been given a whiff of a dirty sock and pointed down the trail."

"Joseph," she said with a visible effort to calm herself, "this watch is something tangible, something we can check out."

Again Snow smiled. "Check out? How? You've got a wristwatch in your hand and nothing to check out."

She held up the stamped metal token. "What's this?"

"I don't know, but I don't want to. . . ."

"There were a couple more in the jewelry box." She dug for several seconds, then extracted three other tags, each with Chinese lettering. "Can you read Chinese?"

"I only speak it, and not very well at that."

"Let's find out what these tags say."

"And when we determine they're meaningless, and that the Omega is meaningless, and this entire journey is meaningless, we'll stop chasing ghosts. Right?"

She nodded.

"Your word on that?"

"Yes," she laughed. "We'll stop chasing ghosts."

The Portuguese brought the distinctly European, two-storied houses with ridge-and-furrow roofs to Singapore. They could not have known the Chinese would move en masse to this steaming flatland between His Majesty's prison and the Singapore River. Now twelve people lived in each room, and

46

their drying laundry was draped from poles stuck out windows, giving the alleys a perpetual and ironic gaiety. Between the laundry poles hung colorful signboards covered with Chinese characters.

The din in these alleys and streets was almost overpowering, for the Chinese largely live in the streets. They move in aimless herds, laboring under bundles of produce or fish or poultry. Women carry their latest child on their backs, and many six- and seven-year-olds are carted around, for they have become as much a part of the women as their fishnet shopping bags. Jugheaded street urchins carry leashed wawa's, stuffing the monkey's mouth with papaya, hoping to fatten them for sale to a Rochore Road pet shop. Other boys carry shoe shine kits, and still others offer Tiger Balm to passersby. Occasionally an elderly woman with tiny, wrapped feet will arrive at the shopping stalls in a trishaw. The mix of bodies and noises and odors is tumultuous and never-ending.

The Snows made sluggish progress along Pagoda Street, stepping around squatting men in striped pajamas and singlets who held rice bowls up to their mouths, rapidly shoveling with chopsticks. Canvas awnings covered food stalls where steam wafted from huge copper pans over charcoal braziers. Hanging from the stall awnings were strings of guts, and piled on vendors' tables were dried cuttlefish, sweetmeats, plucked poultry, and mounds of eggs, noodles, and cockles.

A young boy, naked but for a tattered cloth around his hips, offered Connie a bottle cap in which was a metal washer. He said in sing-song English, "Good luck charm." She gave the boy a dime. Immediately a dozen other youths surrounded the Snows, each proffering a charm. Snow broke through the circle, Connie close behind.

Almost none of the street people looked up as Snow and Connie wound their way to Fat Bird's on Pagoda Street. The shop was named after the proprietor who, like many Singapore Chinese, coveted his collections of songbirds which he kept in wicker cages hung from the awnings of his shop. Fat Bird was on his toes, feeding his yellow swallows and budgerigars and trying to imitate their call by sucking on his golden front teeth. A Chinese merchant, however, is never too busy to be gracious to customers, and he gladly ushered the Snows into his cramped shop.

47

They crowded into the narrow area between shelves of Fat Bird's business. Surrounding them was a bewildering array of jewelry and junk, pistols, and *Pep,* the American comic book. Beads and knives and light bulbs and abacuses, high-ball glasses, ready-made cheongsams and camphor-wood chests. On the shop's rear floor was a scarlet lacquer shrine dedicated to the deities of sky and earth.

Fat Bird's mouth spread to a wide, golden grin as Snow addressed him in Cantonese. The merchant spread his arms to encompass his shop, indicating that whatever he had was theirs, with only a slight mark up. Connie nudged her husband, wanting in on the conversation.

"He says that during the war this was a pawnshop. But now the British are clamping down and more discretion is required. He says he will still make loans if the collateral is adequate, and that's why he's glancing with ill-disguised lust at your wedding ring."

"Ask him about the tokens," Connie said, moving her left hand behind her.

Again Fat Bird and Snow conversed. Connie had never heard Snow speak the language, and she closely watched her husband's mouth as it formed the atonal and seemingly disjointed syllables of the Cantonese language. Snow held out the three tokens, and Fat Bird squinted at each in turn. He hissed in concentration, his gold incisors glistening. Finally, he burst forth with a rush of language. Snow waited for it to trail off before saying, "These are his pawn tokens, all right. After apologizing profusely, he said that he gave this kind of token only to Japanese soldiers who brought in goods to be pawned during the occupation. More respected customers received better, brighter metal chits. He also says that when the Japanese were pushed out of Singapore, he sold most of the pawned items they left behind."

"What kind of pawned goods?" Connie asked.

After another round of Cantonese, Snow answered, "Mostly items looted from conquered territory. A lot of Chinese jewelry, Australian watches, Philippine flip knives, that sort of thing. He suspects the Japanese used the money to gamble, because they seldom returned to reclaim pawned goods. And he complains he had to dump barrelfuls of the stuff after the war, losing much money."

Without Connie's prompting, Snow asked Fat Bird to see if the items pawned for the three tokens were still in the store.

The Chinaman shrugged, then disappeared through an impossibly narrow aisle into a back room.

He emerged moments later, beaming, with both hands behind his back. He handed Snow a token, and shook his head solemnly. Another token, another shake of the head. But then he grinned and handed Snow the last metal chit, and with it, a small cloth satchel. More Cantonese was spoken.

"He says he gave a Japanese soldier five hundred yen for these medals. He has more medals than M'ing has jade, and he can't get rid of them. Medals from everywhere. The only money he'll make from them will be if he melts them down. Those in this bag were pawned by an officer from the Keluang Camp." Snow handed the satchel back to Fat Bird.

"Aren't you even going to look at them?" Connie asked incredulously, reaching for the medals.

"No point. Our inventory of things on the Electra includes nothing like this."

"Think, Joseph. That list was made when she left Oakland. It wouldn't include anything she and the navigator picked up along the way. Didn't I read that in virtually every country where she landed she was given something to commemorate her journey: a straw hat in Puerto Rico, a brooch in Natal, and so forth. And in some of the countries, especially those with British influence, she was presented a medal for valor."

"You're bubbling again."

The satchel contained four medallions, clearly military decorations. Connie spread them out on the only uncluttered surface in the shop, atop a jeweler's case. She lifted the first and read, "Distinguished Air Medal, Burma."

"A thousand of those," Snow said, then translated for Fat Bird, whose pinprick eyes narrowed, sensing the opening gambit of a bargaining session.

Connie said, "She landed in Rangoon, didn't she? It was her stop just before Bangkok."

"Yes, she did. But that doesn't necessarily mean this medal was hers. Connie, I don't mean to play devil's advocate, but you're building a case on implausible coincidences."

She examined another medal. " 'Distinguished Air Medal, Commonwealth of Australia.' Earhart was in Australia. Landed at Port Darwin, didn't she?"

"You know as well as I do that she was there." Snow shook his head with resignation. "Quite the detective," he muttered.

49

Connie turned the Australian medal over, and her face tightened. She blinked several times, her mouth opening slowly. Wordlessly, she handed the medal to Snow. On the reverse side, amateurishly stamped with a letter punch, were the words, "Presented at Port Darwin, June 27, 1937."

"Joseph," she whispered, "when was Amelia Earhart in Port Darwin?"

He stared at the evidence, struggling against its importance. He tried, but failed in his own mind to explain it away. His face flushed, not from embarrassment, but from the building excitement and energy flowing into him from the medal. Snow didn't need to look at his copy of Earhart's flight schedule. He said in a hushed voice, "She was there in June 1937."

"Am I right?" There was not a hint of victory in her question.

Snow nodded, turning the medal over and over in his hand. "You're right. The Omega and these medals must have belonged to Amelia Earhart. She must have been in the Keluang POW camp sometime during the war." He sighed heavily, the exhalation of a man taking his first step up the side of a mountain. "She didn't go down in the Pacific."

One isn't a true Singaporean until he has fallen into a monsoon drain. They are four feet across, six feet deep, and flow with unspeakable filth. Even the rats avoid them. But two men had been standing in one of these drains for an hour. The fetid water had soaked into their pants like a disease, then dried and hardened in the sweltering sun, leaving bits of excrement which now flaked off. Both men glistened with perspiration, and although they frequently wiped their foreheads, sipped from a canvas water bag, and scratched at several species of vermin inching their way up their legs, neither removed his eyes from the drain bridge above them. It was a pedestrian bridge, used primarily by Anglos returning from Chinatown. They had been assured their quarry would cross this bridge.

These men were Straits pirates, men who during the last year of the war had joined a band of freebooters preying on yachts and small freighters sailing the Strait of Malacca. In their courage and ruthlessness, they were identical to the eighteenth-century Malays who had hunted British silk and opium frigates, but these men had had an advantage over their forebears: a stolen U.S. Navy PT boat equipped with torpedoes and .50 caliber machine guns. For a year they had roamed the Straits, until an unsympathetic American Hellcat had put fifteen dozen holes in the PT boat's hull. Now they were at work again, admittedly on land, and for lower wages, but working nevertheless. They were employed waiting for Joseph and Connie Snow.

The taller man was known as the Parrot. He had apparently spent much of his life catching the wrong ends of knives. His right arm was serrated with scars and looked as if a railroad track had been laid on his biceps. At some painful time in his life, most of his right cheek had been torn away, and his jaw was now covered with a thin purple membrane, wrinkled like an elephant's leg, which gave him the rictus of a cadaver. His partner was a stout bullet of a man wearing an Imperial Army kepi above his broad Malay nose. He was named Pinang, after the village of his birth, from which he had been expelled shortly before his twelfth birthday. Like many Malays, he crossed the fingers of both hands whenever an Anglo passed, and he did so now at the first glimpse of Connie Snow's white skirt. The Parrot and Pinang waited until both Snows had stepped off the bridge, then clambered up the drain's iron rungs after them.

"We need to look at Japanese records of the POW camp," Connie was saying, walking arm-in-arm with her husband as they approached the Singapore Cricket Club. Members were taking last sips of gin slings before walking to the pitches.

"I can make inquiries. We shouldn't get our hopes up, though, because most captured Japanese records haven't even been catalogued yet. Howard Lester can find out if the Keluang Camp records exist. I'll cable him this afternoon."

"And until then?"

"I don't know how many people were in the Keluang camp," Snow said, "but if there were Europeans and Americans, some will be in Singapore. We can probably find them. If Amelia Earhart was in that camp—" and at her grin he hesitated and added, "and it appears she was—they would've known about it."

"Do you think she spent all those years, from 1937 to 1944, in Malaysia?"

Snow shook his head. "No. The Japanese had a habit of shunting prisoners around. Maybe she was kept on Saipan for a while, then Tokyo, then Malaysia. Hard to say. The

Japanese didn't control Malaysia until 1942, so she couldn't have been interned there until then."

"Joseph," she put her hand over his, "do you think she could still be alive?"

"If she were, the whole world would know about it. I suspect Earhart and all the other camps' prisoners were marched up the Malay Peninsula toward Siam near the end of the war. Few people lived to reach the end of such a march."

Perhaps it was the tug of intuition, more probably Snow caught the flutter of a shirtsleeve, but something at that moment caused him to thrust his head forward and left, the motion of a boxer in a clinch, shoving his jaw into his opponent's neck to escape an uppercut. Pinang's lead-filled sap whistled, then glanced off the meat of Snow's shoulder. Snow spun, violently shoved Connie away from the direction of the attack, then raised his fists.

Two attackers. The stocky one in the Japanese kepi circled left, menacingly waving his leather cudgel, his face twisting into a dark knot. The taller man wore a permanent scarred sneer. The Malays worked in unison, herding Snow back to the monsoon drain. He backpedaled toward the ditch. Parrot and Pinang moved with him, turning away from Connie.

Snow yelled tightly, "Get away from here, Connie." But she stood, hand to mouth, powerless to move, powerless to help.

The Malays closed in on Snow, backing him up until his heels dipped over the cement edge of the drain. No retreating now, and he put both fists in front of his face and hunched forward protectively.

The familiar elation as the bell sounded the first round swept through him. In the ring, fear was foreign. There were two of them, but there was no question of the outcome of this match. It was of no concern to Snow whether they came singly or both at once.

He even had time to grin evilly before Pinang launched himself. The Malay rushed forward, his sap arcing viciously. Snow's left fist tapped Pinang's incoming wrist, and this light touch bounced the sap inside, where it swished harmlessly by Snow's jaw. Snow's right fist, an enormous scarred hammer, rocketed, seemingly from the ground, cutting under Pinang's sap arm, and exploding into his mouth. Bones snapped, and Pinang's head shot back where it met Snow's left hook, a savage, tight swing that carried the full weight of his body. Pinang flew sideways, then toppled heavily to the ground.

Snow's fist again covered his face, and he spun to the second attacker. But the Parrot had not survived those years in a dangerous profession by being a fool. He stood motionless five feet from the American, his eyes flickering between Snow and his sprawled comrade. The Parrot's hands fidgeted under his blouse.

First elation, then fine madness. The crow of the victor. With Snow, it wasn't a victorious whoop, but a fit of giggles that seized him after the ten count, a snigger of release and jubilation. Always embarrassing. Many times, he had searched out his beaten opponent to apologize, not for the pummeling, but for the insane laughter that seized him after each bout. So it was now, and he looked through his upraised fists for his wife, hoping she was out of earshot.

This time the laughter was premature. From under his shirt, Parrot drew a Japanese Nambu. He waved the pistol for several seconds, letting Snow's eyes fix on it, and watched the American's triumphant grin drain away. The Parrot brought it up level with Snow's nose. Perhaps it was a smile that came to the Malay's face. With the purple scar tissue pulling at his mouth, it was impossible to tell. But there was no question that he was enjoying this moment. His flat, dull eyes pulled tighter, and his finger slowly pulled back the Nambu's trigger.

For a full second, the Parrot stood, frozen in place, not comprehending that a small, perfectly symmetrical hole had opened in his temple and a large, ragged chunk of his skull had been blown out the other side. A thunderous clap sounded from the drain bridge, and its echo rolled away across the padang and into Keppel Harbor. Parrot's body sagged to the cement.

Rose stood on the bridge, having difficulty loosening a heel from the wood slats. One hand was dipped into her purse. Still foolishly peering through his balled hands, Snow saw gray smoke drifting from a scorched hole in her handbag. She freed her shoe and stepped off the bridge toward him. She smiled seductively as Snow lowered his arms, then she pouted as Connie Snow ran to her husband.

Snow cleared his throat, not knowing how to thank the transvestite for saving his life. He settled for an awkward, "Rose, would you mind my asking what you were before . . .

before you became this." Snow pointed directly at Rose's breasts.

Almost imperceptibly, her sensuous smile was transmuted to a masculine taunt. Her voice dropped an octave and gained a hard edge as she said, "I was never one of . . . those." He perfectly mimicked Snow's clumsy hesitation. "My name is Ko Tsukada, from the Japanese Imperial Palace, and I'm your new partner."

IV

One hut was shared by the camp's seven women.
An American, Cynthia Fellows, taught her to make a
sun cap from palm leaves, and told her swallowing
the verminous rice or soup was easier if she closed
her eyes.

They got farther than Snow thought they would. It wasn't
until his hand touched the back of the rattan patio chair that
the doorman rushed up to them. He was a Cockney with lines
of social responsibility holding his black eyes in place. He
wore a white cutaway morning coat. "I'm sorry, sir, but the
club is quite full this afternoon." He studiously avoided
looking at Ko Tsukada, who assisted Connie Snow into her
seat.

"It doesn't look full, Peters."

"But I can assure you, it is. Reservations, that sort of thing,
sir."

Snow dropped into his seat. "Have a Boy bring two stengahs
and a gin sling."

"Sir," Peters said in a stern, obsequiously hushed voice,
"after all, this is the British *White* Club, and. . . ."

"Peters, my wife and I are guests of the governor, and I
don't want to have to tell him that you refused to seat us.
Governor Longstreet wouldn't take kindly to that at all."

Peters paled, pulled uncertainly at his jutting chin, then
muttered, "I'll check with the host, Mr. Snow."

Snow said to Tsukada, "Well, you saved my life and I've
gotten you into the British White Club, so we're even."

Tsukada laughed, exposing teeth as white and even as piano keys. His black hair was raffishly swept back over his ears, and his nose was an aquiline wedge. His angular jaw was marred by a thin cleft. He was as handsome a man as he had been a beautiful woman.

Snow's eyes had been shifting about the room steadily since he entered. Now they looked over Tsukada's shoulders. "A hardcase followed us in here. Wavy black hair, thick shoulders. He doesn't look like a Club member. Know anything about him?"

"I saw him. Sometimes he works as a doorman at the club, but most often he hires out as a bodyguard. His name is Flynn. He's a Bugis Street regular. The girls say he carries a gun high under his left arm."

"What's he doing here?"

Tsukada glanced at Flynn, then shrugged.

"How long have you been posing as a Bugis Street woman?" Connie asked.

"On and off since January 1945."

"Eight months *before* the war ended?"

Tsukada nodded. "It was unhealthy for Japanese in Singapore during those last months. It's still unhealthy. So I employ disguise. I've gotten quite good at it, too, as you saw." He grinned easily. "I get a lot of offers from you Americans and your British allies."

"And you refuse?" she asked too lightly.

Again the laugh. "Yes, although there'd be much more money in it than working for my government."

"But Japan's government is General MacArthur."

"Ah, the Mikado MacArthur." A waiter placed his whiskey in front of him, clucking his tongue with distaste, an inferior serving an inferior. Tsukada sipped the drink. "No, I work for the Imperial Palace, for the emperor."

"The emperor has agents in the field?" Snow was astonished that scorched Imperial Japan could field operatives less than a year after the fighting ceased.

"Only for limited purposes, I assure you. MacArthur doesn't know a thing about it, of course. And to my knowledge, there are only six of us."

"Doing what?" Snow asked, wiping his forehead and beginning to feel the dissipating effects of the Singapore heat.

"Recovery work. We try to find what the emperor owns. . . ."

Tsukada's words grew distant, then more insistent, then

distant again. Snow knew it was his own ears, not the Japanese's voice. Tropic madness, Singapore psychosis, Snow didn't know what to call it. He had known it in his previous trips to the city, and now in the past few days here. Around three o'clock, the sun and the humidity, the perspiration and the squinting, the noise, all began chipping at his sanity, as if he had taken a huge whiff of ether. He inhaled quickly several times, took a long draught of his stengah and stared fuzzily at Tsukada's lips until the distant gibberish made sense.

". . . we lost a lot in the war, most of our cities, a generation of our people. Gone forever. But there are a few things the Japanese people lost that can be gotten back. That's what I'm doing now in Singapore." He rubbed an eye, searching for traces of eyebrow pencil that had escaped his harsh scrubbing. "When it was clear to the . . . forward thinkers that Japan's fate was being sealed by the B-17s, a few of us were called in from the field, and given assignments that had at least some hope of success."

"Yeah, like taking a feather duster to the ruins of Tokyo."

"Joseph, that was crude," Connie reprimanded, watching her husband plant both palms on the table as if fighting vertigo.

It was crude. Also inevitable, it seemed, because after the numbing mindlessness of the three o'clock haze came mounting rage, the product of accumulated irritations, the heat and flies and Chinese chatter and the rest of unrelenting Singapore that seizes Anglos when they broach the tropics. Snow glared at Tsukada, then at his wife. She smiled and touched the back of his hand. The fit lessened its grip.

Tsukada ignored the remark. "For a millennium, the Empire has been collecting treasures. Works of art, jewelry, artifacts, all irreplaceable. Some of them are associated with Japan's religions, others with its feudal history, and still others with the emperor. They are priceless, and many of them were lost in our decade of war. Some of these missing treasures are salvageable and we intend to get them back."

"You've always worked for the Imperial Palace?" she asked.

"All Japanese serve the emperor, but, specifically, no. I was in the army for many years. Military intelligence. In 1934, I spent a year at your West Point, studying military strategy. Your officers were most kind to this heathen, and I came away knowing much more than they thought. I spent

57

the war gathering intelligence, and organizing various operations. That's why I was recruited for this task."

"That biography is a little incomplete," Snow said, and with a speed that startled his wife, his hand reached for Tsukada's lapel, flipping it open to expose a small button resembling a chrysanthemum. "The *Kempai tai*. Still proud of it, I see."

Unruffled, Tsukada replied, "Wearing this button has nothing to do with pride. It still opens a lot of doors, and I use every advantage I can get."

"What's the *Kempai tai?*" Connie asked.

"The Japanese Gestapo."

"That is inaccurate, Mr. Snow. We were Imperial Japan's counterespionage unit. But we avoided German excesses. Unlike the Gestapo, we had the full cooperation of the Japanese people. Our primary purpose was counterespionage, not suppression of our people."

"Counterespionage through fear tactics."

"There's no denying the *Kempai tai* built a myth around itself, a legend of omniscience, but it was myth, nothing more. No loyal Japanese came to harm at our hands."

Snow laughed rudely at what his wife thought was a reasonable explanation.

Tsukada said quietly, "Mr. Snow, I wear the chrysanthemum pin under a lapel, but you can't hide your knuckles."

After a long pause, Snow said, "I was a boxer in the service."

The Japanese smiled caustically. "That, too, perhaps. But those are the hands of a bare-knuckles fighter. May I suggest that your fists were employed in your country's service?"

"Why were you following us?"

Tsukada laughed. "An inelegant change of subject. All right, I'll let it go." He worked on his drink. "As I said, I'm on assignment. Have you ever heard of the Kobe Elephant?"

Snow shook his head, avoiding his wife's puzzled gaze as it alternated between his scarred knuckles and his eyes.

"The Kobe Elephant is a two-hundred-pound elephant carved from jade. Jadeite, the shiny, almost glassine jade, not nephrite. The huge jade rock from which it was carved was brought from Northern Burma to Peking in 1905. It took Chinese master carvers about three years to reduce the stone to the form of an elephant, and it is today the largest single piece of jadeite known in the world."

"How much is it worth?" Snow asked, slipping his hands to his lap.

"How much is the Mona Lisa worth? Or the Pietà? These questions are not answerable."

"How did Japan come to own the elephant?" Connie asked, reaching under the table for Snow's right hand, then irritatingly picking at the knuckle scars with a fingernail. Her questions would come later, he knew.

"It was a gift to the emperor from the people of China, thanking Japan for her role in the Russo-Japanése War."

"How long did it take for the Chinese to ask for it back?"

"A matter of months," Tsukada smiled, "as soon as the Chinese realized we also viewed the mainland as a melon ripe for the picking. Spheres of influence, isn't that the term?"

"Where is the Kobe Elephant now?" Snow asked, peeling his wife's hand away from his.

"It disappeared from a Buddhist temple in Kobe in 1937. Early efforts to trace it proved fruitless, and Japan had more ambitious plans for its agents. But now, the treasures have become a renewed focal point of Japanese pride, one of the few honorable things left, and we are doing all we can to get the missing pieces back."

"You still haven't tied me into all this. Start by explaining why you gave us the false lead on Amelia Earhart's bones. And what have you got to do with Amelia Earhart in the first place?"

The Japanese agent looked directly into Snow's eyes, searching for hints of deception. Finally he breathed, "Then you don't know."

"Don't know what?"

"The fates of Amelia Earhart and the Kobe Elephant are bound together, and have been since 1937."

"I don't know anything about that," Snow said.

"Earhart was lured to Saipan on some pretense, probably to pick up a person or documents. Apparently she had her government's approval, because our sources say that although she flew north from Le, the U.S. Navy was not concerned about her overdue arrival at Howland Island for quite a while."

"I know about her landing on Saipan," Snow admitted. "She and her navigator flew there to pick up some documents."

Tsukada went on. "Apparently there never were any documents. The man, or men, who stole the Kobe Elephant used Amelia Earhart's plane to take it out of Japanese territory."

"What happened to Earhart?" Connie asked.

"Our soldiers found her and her navigator, Fred Noonan, lying on the Saipan runway. They also claim to have glimpsed her airplane as it flew away. Noonan was dead, bullet through the head. Amelia Earhart suffered only a wound in the shoulder. The bullet broke her collarbone, but hit no vital organs. Within two weeks she was well enough to be transported to Tokyo."

"We were right," Connie whispered needlessly, "Amelia Earhart is alive."

Tsukada shook his head vehemently. "I'm not saying that, and it is very unlikely. She spent years in a prison-hospital in Tokyo. Her lodgings were comfortable, I'm told, much more so than American flyers who were shot down. When the fire bombings became too intense, she was moved to a prison camp near Kitakyūshū, on our southern island, and finally she was transferred to the mainland camps, ending up in Keluang, where I took you yesterday."

"You mean," Snow said angrily, "Amelia Earhart was alive, and you told no one for all those years."

Tsukada held a hand up in supplication. "Not me personally, Mr. Snow. Until I was given this assignment, I had no idea she did anything other than go down in the Pacific."

"Keeping her in prison all those years was cruel," Connie said, her eyes cutting into Tsukada.

"Mrs. Snow, your husband has just admitted she was a spy, sent into Japanese territory to steal documents vital to Japanese security. We knew this, too. Under international law, she could have been shot in the field. Keeping her alive was an act of unprecedented leniency."

"What happened to her?" Snow asked, finishing his stengah. His wife's stony glare silently upbraided him for his quick acceptance of Tsukada's explanation.

"We're not sure, but her bones are probably in the Keluang camp. We have no records of the last months of the camp, and no idea what happened to its prisoners."

"Then why the elaborate ruse to get me to come to Singapore, and out to the Keluang camp?"

"The Imperial Palace knows only that her plane was used to steal the Kobe Elephant, and our sources in Singapore indicated her plane, or a very similar Lockheed Electra, landed in Singapore the next day. We're assuming whoever stole the elephant is still in Singapore. It's not much evidence, but it's all we have."

"Again, why bring me in?"

"Simply because your agency knows much more about Amelia Earhart than we do, and your resources are better than ours. For example, until this minute I didn't know whether Amelia Earhart made it back to the United States after the war. Now I know she didn't."

"And what makes you think I'll stay in Singapore?"

"You came here for her bones, and you don't have them yet. It seems our jobs in Singapore could mesh well. I'm after the Kobe Elephant and the man who stole it. You're after Amelia Earhart's body." Tsukada paused, then added in a low voice, "And perhaps the man who double-crossed her. We're looking for the same person."

This time it was Snow who held up a hand. "Wait a minute. I'm not here on a manhunt. I don't have any authority for that, and no disposition for it either."

Tsukada stared at him. "With hands that look like they've been dipped in a meat grinder and that deadly, practiced display against the Malay thug, don't tell me what you've got authority or disposition for."

Snow grunted, "Why were you following us today?"

"I suspected you'd be attacked."

"Why?"

"Because the man who stole the Kobe Elephant and tricked Amelia Earhart doesn't want anyone snooping around looking for her bones, and looking for the reason she never left Saipan."

"Officially I'm here to inspect a bridge," Snow said. "How would anyone know I am looking into the Earhart affair?"

Tsukada's smile was genuine. "You'll forgive me, but after I contacted your boss about Amelia Earhart's bones, I spread the rumor that a vengeful American operative would be visiting Singapore. I knew that if the man who stole the Kobe Elephant was in this city, he would eventually know you were coming and would probably act."

"Next time you use me as bait, let me know," Snow growled.

"Do you have a pistol?"

"Bridge engineers don't need pistols."

"Just because the first attempt on your life failed doesn't

mean there won't be a second. You'd better carry one."
Tsukada drained his glass. "Do we work together?"

Snow brought his wristwatch up. "It's too late to catch the
Pan Am Clipper out of here, so let's work on it, at least until
tomorrow."

"Joseph, how can we leave now?" Connie pleaded. "Mr.
Tsukada has given us our first lead since we arrived in
Singapore. Find the man who has the Kobe Elephant, and
we'll find Amelia Earhart."

"Find her remains," Snow cautioned.

Peters the doorman scurried up. "Mr. Snow, I must apologize for my rudeness." His words oozed distaste. "The Club
would like to buy you and your wife, and your . . . your guest
a drink."

"Kind of you, Peters, but a bit too late. My guest and I have
a little research to do."

"Then you'll be wanting the King's Library. It's about half
a mile. . . ."

"No," Snow said, and for the first time on this assignment
Connie heard muted enthusiasm in her husband's voice. "I'll
be wanting a gun shop. And I know where one is."

For Singapore, the Buddhist temple on Pekin Street was
expansive. The elaborately ornamented, curved roof and the
curled tile eaves distinguished the gray-brick building from
the neighboring shops. Some of the bricks fronting the building had been painted vivid yellow and orange. Too much
color. Near the entrance were two guardian lions, their stone
fangs bared and ever vigilant.

The temple was built around a courtyard, the main shrine
hall facing the gatehouse. Smaller buildings to the left and
right housed minor shrines and the monks' quarters. The
focus of the temple was its massive wood altar on which
rested many carved images of the Buddha and elaborate
banners, altar cloths, oil lamps and candles. To the uninitiat-
ed, it looked jumbled.

The late afternoon rite was beginning, and the bass thunder of an enormous drum called the monks to the shrine. The
nine monks wore jackets and trousers of yellow cloth over
which were long, nearly diaphanous scarves of the same
color. Their shaved heads dully reflected the candlelight. A
dozen laymen stood near the gate and watched as the monks
formed rows, then began the murmured litany which would

last an hour and a half. A few of the monks accompanied the chant with cymbals or small bells. A venerative pulse.

Others in the temple were searching the future. In the side sanctuary, an elderly amah used bamboo sticks to divine her destiny. She carried to the small altar a bamboo tube in which she had placed fifty bamboo slivers. She prostrated herself three times, lit incense, then shook the bamboo cylinder until a single sliver emerged and fell to the ground. She exchanged this numbered stick for a slip of yellow paper bearing a few lines of prose—her prophecy. Still wearing his twist of filthy cloth around his neck, a rickshaw *wallah* cast to the floor a pair of kidney-shaped wood blocks, asking them to foretell the future. The temple was warm with worship and reverence and spirituality . . .

Until the Malays burst through the temple gates, screaming and carrying clubs. Thirty of them spilled into the courtyard and swarmed toward the monks. With shrieks of "There is no God but God" and "Singapore is Malayan," the mob tore into the rows of chanting Buddhist monks, pummeling the worshipers to the floor. The monks offered no resistance, did not even cover their heads with their arms, but continued to intone prayers as they were beaten. The laymen did not show such composure. They tried frantically to escape the Moslem horde, flinging themselves through windows and the gate.

The mob quickly reached the altar, their clubs arcing into the carved images of Man Chu and P'u Hsien, and these embodiments of Wisdom and Perfect Action crashed to the floor. Many small Buddhas were thrown through the temple window and at the icons sitting on the lacquered roof beams. Banners were shredded, then trod underfoot. A dozen incense burners collapsed under the pounding.

In the middle of the temple was a dark-skinned Malay with a hawk nose and fanatic's eyes. He was wearing the dark robes of a mullah, which whipped around his skeletal body as he fanned his arms, directing the rampaging throng. The dervish foamed his hatreds, aiming the rioters as if he were sighting a pistol. But all the while, his livid eyes never left the altar, searching the destroyed idols.

The ranting pack piled into the temple's back hall where men threw themselves at the display of ancestral tablets. Each hand-sized tablet contained the name of a worshiper's departed relative and had been placed in the temple to honor the dead. Hundreds of them were now pulled from their display and snapped in half. Then, not yet satisfied, the Malays tore down the brightly colored display board and flung bronze candleholders at the far wall. The amah was pushed to the ground, her bamboo slivers scattered. The *wallah* was wrestled to the floor by three Malays, while a fourth wrenched open his mouth, pushed a small divination block into his throat, and held a hand over the old man's mouth and nose until he swallowed the block. With raucous laughter and more shrill cries, the mob pushed itself back into the main temple.

Their noses and heads bleeding onto their yellow *cha-sa*, a few Buddhist monks unsteadily regained their feet. The Malays grabbed their yellow scarves and spun the monks like slings. The mood of the rioters had turned from anger to delirious gaiety, and they laughed wildly as the holy men were thrown against the temple walls.

Still bawling his encouragement, the mullah pushed aside the statue of Amida to find a small, stylized tiger of gray-green nephrite, no larger than a woman's fist, which slipped easily into his robe. Cursing and kicking the religious debris, he discovered an ancient gold and glass snuff box. He flipped open the tiny catches and lifted the lid. The box was filled with minute gold nuggets and gold dust, each speck given to the temple over the past year by the devout. It also found its way into the folds of the mullah's robe.

No more than five minutes had elapsed since the ransacking began, but the temple was almost completely destroyed. The dark-eyed mullah glanced about joyfully, then whooped victoriously and marched through the courtyard to the temple gates. His disciples threw their clubs at the monks and followed him out, spitting at the guardian lions in a last gesture of hatred and contempt.

Inside, the monks helped each other to stand. Pausing only to wipe blood from their faces and to search the litter for cymbals, they again formed in lines. Hesitatingly, through bruised jaws and loosened teeth, they began their chant. The monotone swelled to fill the chamber. The temple was again a place of worship.

The Indian's shop on Serangoon Road was a confusing mix. A grainy recording of sitar music sounded from the back room. The heady clouds of incense seemed to further distort the falsetto notes. Mason jars filled with herbs and rock candy lined the counter. In bold contrast, pistols, rifles, and submachine guns decorated the walls.

Godavari pushed a jar across the counter to Connie. "Candy?"

She placed an almond-sized piece in her mouth, and her nose wrinkled at the bitter taste. Godavari said, "My wife makes those in a copper pot. Perhaps she added too much opium syrup this time."

Snow smiled when Connie hastily spit the candy into her palm. He lifted the government-issue Colt .45 automatic off the chamois, held the gun down and away, and ejected the clip. He pulled back the slide to clear the chamber, then peered into the barrel.

"Are you looking for wear, sahib? I personally put a Wesler bushing into that gun. It will shoot better than you can hold it, I assure you."

"How are you going to carry it?" Connie asked after running her tongue along her teeth to remove the sticky opium residue.

"In my belt."

"It looks heavy. Why don't you carry something smaller?"

"I once . . . I once saw someone get hit with a .38 bullet and get right back up from the floor. That doesn't happen with a .45."

Snow pulled out the plug and recoil spring, then removed the slide top, carefully examining each part. His wife absently picked up the clip and said, "You probably don't realize how natural you look with that gun. You handle it as easily as if it were a knife and fork."

"Well, I've had a bit of practice working for your uncle. Mostly on firing ranges. Not much to it, really."

Connie ignored Godavari's low laugh. "You do that a lot, you know."

Snow began reassembling the gun, and only his instant's hesitation with the recoil spring indicated his close attention to what his wife had said. "Do what?"

"When I ask about your past, you offer some lame answer, then trail off with 'Not much to it' or 'It's not very interesting.' Sometimes I feel like I married a man with no past."

Snow busied himself inserting the thick .45 shells into the magazine. "What do you want to know?"

"Well, you've never talked about your first wife. Her name is Janice, and that's the only thing I know about her."

Snow, who had been fumbling for a new lie about his work

for Lester, laughed at this question and said, "Janice is a dull memory. And an unhappy one. If you had any idea how my life has improved since I met you. . . ."

"That's a romantic phrase. 'Improved.' You make me sound like I work for the Salvation Army."

Snow pulled some bills out of his wallet and handed them to Godavari, who produced a box of shells from under the counter. Snow slipped the gun into his belt, nodded goodbye, and followed Connie into the street.

Snow took her hand. "Sometimes I have trouble telling you about the difference you've made."

She laughed lightly. "I'm a *difference*. Joseph, you have such a way with words."

His face didn't reflect her merriment. "I had some tough years, Connie. Years when I didn't feel much. No joy, no despair, and nothing in between."

They walked slowly along Serangoon. She said, "Tell me, and don't say 'Not much to it.' "

He now recognized those four years between his first wife and Connie as the most listless and unhappy in his life. He had finally admitted his first marriage had failed when Janice stopped flushing the toilet, a symbolic summary of the bitterness that drove him from the house. Two weeks after the divorce was final, she married an Arlington dentist.

He quickly recouped the concessions he had made to marriage. He again enjoyed a glass of beer for breakfast, the only beverage that made fried eggs bearable. He hung his speed bag in the front room and worked through his routine, pounding out exhilarating rhythms. He invited a few friends over from his gym days, men with tattoos, broken noses and long pasts. It was all fairly miserable.

Women drifted in and out of his life with monotonous predictability. Brunette or redhead, large breasts or small, all merged into a hazy collage. The longest affair was with a teenage amah in Canton, who wore a black blouse and pants while doing his housekeeping and a revealing cheongsam when she came to his bed at night. She was killed by a Japanese fragmentation bomb, and Snow wondered at his relief.

He found himself pressing his availability for overseas assignments. He didn't care whether it was an intricate, long-term involvement or a short, violent mission. He spent months at a time in Asia. He had rooms permanently reserved at the Peninsula Hotel in Kowloon and the Raffles in Singapore. He did his drinking at the Foreign Correspondents Club and the British White Club.

His frantic pace at the OSS allowed for no emotional anchors and made permanent commitments a risk. At least, he blamed his solitude on his work. But his life began leaving an aftertaste in his mouth. He would return from a month overseas and his house would be precisely as he had left it: same half-filled brandy snifter, same newspaper spread over the kitchen table, same number of eggs in the cooler. When the business slowed at war's end, the artifices propping up his life disappeared. Loneliness enveloped him like a harbor fog.

Connie was waiting for him in Howard Lester's office that day. She was leaning forward in her chair, legs crossed, an elbow on her knee. Lester was staring at a file and waved Snow to the chair next to Connie. After an embarrassing moment—Snow standing with his hands clasped, Connie bouncing her leg—Lester looked up, allowed his face to twitch, then introduced them. Connie extended her hand and displayed her smile as if it were new.

"Connie's from New York, and I want you to show her around," Lester said. "On company time, of course."

Snow's face closed. "You're joking."

"It's either that or sit on your butt. I've got nothing else for you to do."

"I thought you said that business in Berlin. . . ."

"Payne was sent in yesterday. Sorry."

"With all due respect to your niece, Howard, I'm not a tour guide."

Lester sucked on a tooth. "Perhaps you can infer something from the tone of my voice"—it was indeed cold—"a day or two touring D.C. with my niece won't do you any harm. After that, some legitimate work may come along."

"I've got symphony tickets for this evening," she said in a baiting voice. "We could start with that."

Snow had been to the symphony twice in his life and had spent both occasions in a stupor of boredom. He turned to her slowly, giving himself time to prepare an excuse, but was again caught by her smile, the brilliant grin of one testing a new possession.

He struggled with his refusal, "The symphony isn't really. . . ."

"Or I have two tickets to the Mellon-Jackson welterweight fight. Three rows back."

The fight was being held in the Arena, a ridiculously small auditorium for a match between the first and second welterweight contenders. Snow had scoured his contacts for tickets, to no avail. "The fight sounds interesting."

"It should be. Jackson is a three-five underdog because of the soft skin above his eyebrows. He opened up in the Hanks fight. But this time he's hired Red Muller, so we'll see."

Who'd ever heard of Muller, the best cut-man in the business? Snow smiled to himself. He was being set up. Lester had prompted her on his interest in boxing, fed her a few terms and names. He tested, "I'm surprised Jackson would hire old Red. Jackson doesn't like Negroes."

Again with a grin. "He doesn't? Jackson's colored himself. You're testing me, Mr. Snow. Or you're thinking about Frank Harper, the cut-man, who insulted Joe Louis at the Top of the Mark. You remember that story, I'm sure."

Perhaps it was her love of boxing, but more likely it began with her smile, warmly offered that evening. The next evening she changed his sheets—the first time that had been done in months—then stayed with him until morning. Two days later, when she took down his speed bag and tossed it into a closet, he asked her to marry him.

Their lives quickly became one, but Snow knew part of her would always remain hidden. She had been married before, but refused to talk about it. She had been terribly hurt, she said, and to retell it still pained her. Similarly, her family life remained obscure, a wealthy father in upstate New York, and Lester in Washington, few others. Snow detected a desperate desire to begin anew, and she was using him to do so. A healthy *quid pro quo*, he judged.

At some point in his brief story she had taken his arm. He helped her over a monsoon drain. She looked away, and if he hadn't known her, he would have said she brushed at moisture near her eye. But she said, "Is that why you got that reputation at the agency? Because you were lonely?"

He took an exaggerated step, trying to crush a cockroach. The insect scurried to the drain edge and turned to stare malevolently at him. "The world should be thankful roaches aren't as big as dogs." He looked at her. "What reputation?"

"Howard said you would run to your assignments and stay

as long as possible. He said it got to be quite a joke around there."

"Yeah, a great joke." He put his hands on her shoulders. "Let me tell you something. I was sinking during those years alone. If it weren't for you, I might not have pulled out."

She looked into his eyes for a full minute before taking his arm and leading him back to the Raffles.

Dillon Synge marveled at his own control. Across his desk sat his tormentor, the man who had squirmed his way between Synge and the thing he cherished more than life itself. Yet, Synge sat in his office, talking calmly, looking evenly at him, not allowing his voice to waver or his face to flush with anger. And only infrequently did his eyes twitch to the empty granite pedestal.

"Think it went well today?" Kiril Stasov asked softly, following Synge's eyes to the pedestal. The thin smile on his square face remained until the jade merchant looked back.

"We'll know shortly," Synge answered, unable to stop glowering at the Russian's derisive grin.

Singapore's Soviet consul was a barrel of a man with wide shoulders and a trunk which only recently had begun to sag. His hair was a brown that always looked dusty and unkempt. His severe lips were softened by a wide, spreading chin. Stasov wore a gray suit worn shiny with use. His yellowed collar hugged his thick neck tightly and was soaked through with perspiration. He said, "Does your man know what he's doing?"

"He's been working for me for a year and has had a lot of practice. He can give an extemporaneous speech that would set your hair on fire."

"Is he a genuine mullah?"

"God, no," Synge snorted. "No mullah I know is going to voluntarily hand over what he finds. Too smart for that. He's a Muslim, but he works for me. I bought him his robes, and I buy his authority by planting other Malays around him when he begins a speech. Razak can mold a crowd as if it were clay."

"I'm concerned about the frequency of these speeches," the Russian said, running his tongue along the length of his black cigarette before lighting it. "We must have a momentum."

"You yourself have said that with the thousands of Chinese

and Malays arriving monthly, tensions are increasing in Singapore. I think our man Razak is adding to it sufficiently."

Stasov shook his head, the folds of his chin overflowing his collar like paste from a tube. "Not good enough. These things must build. The British aren't going to concern themselves with sporadic flare-ups. They'll brush them under the rug. We need intensity, something that will turn all eyes to Singapore and get Parliament talking."

"I think the British are more resolute than you'd like to believe."

Stasov laughed shortly. "Look at their recent history. Their empire is in decline. A few stones thrown, the Union Jack burned, and the British will sail away, leaving the colony to the natives."

"Russian natives."

This time his laugh was genuine. "If we are here to pick up the reins, so be it. And the Soviet Union will be here, believe me." His grin fell away. "Your part of this is important, more so than you may realize, yet I detect a lack of enthusiasm."

"My enthusiasm for Soviet foreign policy is boundless," Synge said dryly, flicking his eyes to the pedestal.

"Somehow I'm not reassured, Synge. I'll be expecting better efforts from you. You're aware of the price of your failure to cooperate."

He was bitterly aware. He had made Stasov's acquaintance in 1940. One evening, after a numbing combination of gin and vodka chasers, Synge had proudly displayed the Kobe Elephant to Stasov. The Russian admired the jade piece dutifully, but never spoke of it again. A few hours before the fall of Singapore, Stasov arrived at the jade dealer's office to find him almost apoplectic with worry. The Japanese, who had unexpectedly assaulted the impregnable fortress, Singapore, from the Malay Peninsula were about to occupy the city. They would surely remove anything of value. In those last few dizzying hours, Synge had tried and failed to arrange transport for the Kobe Elephant. Synge's beloved jewel was still in Singapore, obvious and vulnerable. Stasov offered a solution. For five thousand pounds he would store the priceless jade in the guarded basement of the Russian consulate. The Japanese and Russians were not at war, and protocol would forbid Japanese soldiers from entering the Soviet building. The price that Stasov asked was so exorbitant, Synge didn't look beyond the money for a motive. A week later, his mind cleared by the Sydney sun, the truth sank into him. Stasov had his priceless jade and it was unlikely he would give it back when the war ended. That fear tormented him day and night during the long war years. When he returned to liberated Singapore, Stasov was willing to return the elephant, but only under certain conditions. For a year Synge had been struggling to meet those requirements.

He sighed, a long, uncontrollable exhale that left him less alive. "Yes, I'll help you all I can."

Flynn opened the door for a Malay, who crossed the office to place a bag on Synge's desk, then silently sat next to the Russian. The Malay's dark eyes were deeply set and his mouth was turned up at the corners. He was confident his boss would approve the catch.

"Did it go as planned, Razak?" Synge asked, fishing into the bag.

"Yes. It was an ugly crowd that stormed the temple. The monks will be sweeping up for days." He cackled gleefully. "If I keep this up, I'll be an imam before the month is over."

With little interest, Synge opened the snuff box. He lifted a pinch of the gold powder and twisted it between his fingers. "Probably four ounces of gold. The box is late Ching Dynasty, made between 1850 and 1900, and worth about the same as its contents." He pulled the jade tiger from the bag, then held it up to the lamp on his desk. Sharp glints of reflected light skittered across the room as Synge rolled the piece in his palm. "This is also from the Ching Dynasty, a bit earlier, around 1700, I'd say. Carved in the K'ang Hsi studio in Peking."

"It sounds valuable," Stasov said in the tone of a gift-giver.

Synge shrugged. "The K'ang Hsi studio was one of the most prolific in Chinese history. This is a nice piece, but there's a lot of it around, and it's relatively young."

"What's it worth?"

"Depends on who buys it. I'd get a good price from a San Francisco importer, not so good from an Englishman." Synge tossed the snuff box to Razak, who caught it easily. "That enough to go around?"

The Malay smiled and nodded.

The jade dealer walked to his office display case. The Ching Tiger dropped onto the felt and tipped to its side. Synge closed the cabinet without righting it. "Did you find anything on this Joseph Snow?"

"A little," Stasov said, pulling a notebook from his coat pocket. "He was born in 1902, graduated from college in 1924, where to the best of our knowledge, he studied prizefighting. He married his first wife when he was thirty, and they were divorced ten years later. No children. He married his present wife only a month ago."

"Skip all this. Why is he in Singapore?"

"Patience, Dillon," Stasov said, pronouncing his name warmly, knowing how irritated the jade dealer became when the Russian implied a friendship between them. "We don't know how he was recruited into the OSS, but we know why: he is exceptionally skilled with his hands. Snow spent much of the war in Asia, ostensibly as a liaison between the OSS and Chinese resistance. Actually he was a silent-killing instructor, and he also participated in a few raids. We know, for example, that he was seen in Kuelin during the Kuomintang's attack on that Japanese outpost. He was with a band of a dozen men dropped into the area hours before the Chinese assault began, to soften up the Japanese."

"Soften them?"

"Kill as many of them in their sleep as possible."

Synge stiffened. His fingers bit into the desk and his knuckles flared red. He whispered, "Why is he in Singapore?"

"I'm not too worried about it," Stasov said mildly. "But you are. Why?" Without letting the jade merchant answer, the Russian added, "It wouldn't have anything to do with our Kobe Elephant, would it? You needn't worry about that, Dillon. It's safe in the consulate basement."

Stasov's mock soothing tone drowned Synge's fear in a wash of anger. He leaped to his feet and pointed a brittle finger at the Russian. "That is not 'our' elephant. It is mine. You reneged on our deal and some day you'll bloody well pay for it."

The consul's smile didn't waver. "You'll get it back, just as I promised. And as soon as you import a few more Malays, you'll get your chance to earn it." The Russian stood, patted down his rumpled suit, and chided, "You're not walking Razak and me to the door?"

But Synge had already slumped back into his seat and was once again staring at the pedestal. His face sagged and his mouth fished open. A faint glow of lust touched his lined cheeks. Stasov and Razak left without his noticing.

He might have remained behind his desk all evening, eyes

fixed on the pedestal. But from the rims of his consciousness he heard a rapid beating, then the toppling of a chair, and a groan. Flynn pushed open the office door, then carried Pinang into the room. The Irish gunman attempted to lower Pinang onto a chair, but his weight proved too much. The Malay fell heavily and would have slipped to the floor had not Flynn pinned his shoulders back.

Synge emerged from his cloud of grief and squinted at the Malay. "What happened?"

Flynn tipped a glass of water to Pinang's mouth. "He's almost potted. Nearly beat to death."

An accurate layman's diagnosis. Pinang's jaw was broken in two places and hung from his mouth like torn cloth. The entire right side of his face was blue-black, and the color was spreading before their eyes. His gasping breath whistled through holes where teeth had been that morning.

"And Parrot?" Synge asked fearfully.

"They found most of him in a monsoon drain."

"And what about Snow and his wife?"

"They were downstairs on the veranda having a drink a short while ago. Calm as you please. Talking to a Jap."

"A Jap? Who?" The jade dealer's voice was tinny and distant.

"How should I know. A Jap's a Jap."

Synge lowered himself into the chair, wiped the beads of sweat across his face with the flat of his hand and starred dully at Pinang. "I am right, Flynn. Stasov shrugs his shoulders, but I'm right about the American. He is in Singapore for me."

"Any proof of that, Mr. Synge?" Flynn asked pulling on the Malay's arm to prevent him from toppling. Pinang's whistling was now a low, stertorous moan.

"You and that Russian are blind. I *know* why he's here." Synge's face was as cold as one of his jade carvings. "Don't contract it out this time, Flynn. Take care of them yourself. Both Snow and his wife. And if I were you, I'd try to stay away from that man's hands."

Flynn surveyed the Malay's smashed face. "Mr. Synge, you can count on that."

V

Her stomach felt full of pus, and she spent hours squatting over the latrine next to Cynthia. Her life was reduced to eating and expelling, or thinking about eating and expelling.

After hours of street work, the location of Wang Yi's shop remained a mystery. Neither Rose's contacts nor Snow's influence in the governor's office had produced the address of Singapore's foremost jade carver. The Chinese knew he was a legendary craftsman whose head was as bald and smooth as his jade. The British knew he paid his taxes. Otherwise, Wang was anonymous.

A shipment of uncut jade had arrived several days before, and the auction was that morning. The importing house on Victoria Street had the rough blocks displayed on tables, each marked with a number. As Rose and Snow arrived in the cavernous hall, the *sin sang* was mounting his stand to begin the bidding. His profession demanded he be a large man, and his enormous gray coat highlighted his size. His hands were hidden by enormous sleeves. Perhaps seventy merchants surrounded the *sin sang*, waiting quietly for the first number. Rose and Snow circled the knot of men looking for a bald bidder.

The *sin sang* firmly planted his feet, then called the number of the first block for sale. Like a startled herd, the bidders suddenly pushed forward, hands high, reaching for the auctioneer's sleeves. In quick succession, he grasped the hands as they were shoved into his sleeve. Each merchant imparted his bid with a finger pantomime. Not a word was spoken. Within a minute, the auctioneer announced the name of the highest bidder, but did not mention the jade block's selling price. Pausing only to straighten his coat and adjust his stance, the *sin sang* cried out the number of the second stone. Again the merchants surged forward, frantically stretching for the sleeves.

Wang Yi was anything but anonymous in the crowd of jade buyers. He was taller than most and his shaved pate stood out like a breakwater beacon. Even legendary figures must push and shove with the mass of jade buyers. Wang Yi used his bulk to practical advantage, nudging aside lesser bidders. Snow detected esteem and deference in the *sin sang's* voice when he called, "The successful bidder is Wang Yi."

Apparently he was here for one stone only, because the jade carver broke from the crowd and was quickly handed a brick-sized block by the auctioneer's assistant. When Wang Yi left the auction hall with the stone under his blouse, Snow and Rose followed.

He moved through the street rabble with surprising agility, swinging his weight left and right to avoid a Chinese wedding party twisting through the narrow street. A traffic policeman with basketwork wings strapped to his back shifted his feet, pulling taut the string connecting his leg to the wings. The red wicker wing lifted and the tide of Asians moving with Wang Yi obligingly halted at the curb. The jade merchant dodged the tiny eight-horsepower Ford taxis that buzzed around him like angry mosquitos. Rose and Snow brushed past pedestrians in Wang Yi's wake.

"Is it possible he isn't guarded, Tsukada?" Snow panted.

"When I'm in heels and lace, my name is Rose," she said testily. "Would anyone walk through the streets alone carrying a rock worth thousands?"

"Will we make it to his shop?"

"Unlikely, so be prepared for some talking."

The jade carver had not looked over his shoulder, could not have known they were behind him, but his pace had accelerated. His bald head floated above the street crowd like a fish bobber. A peddler carrying birds' nests strung to a bamboo pole had to spin out of Wang Yi's path, causing bits of nest to flutter to the street. His curses were lost in the bubbling madness of the Chinatown Street.

Just as Snow complacently decided Wang Yi's head was easy to follow, it disappeared, vanished into one of the murky crevices that rim every Chinatown street. Snow sprinted forward, his head twisting left and right, looking for the carver's hiding place. Rose ran after him delicately holding her lime-green chiffon skirt close to her knees, gripping her purse, the bottom of which had been expertly rewoven.

Snow pulled upright at the point he guessed Wang Yi's shining head had dipped from sight. A dim alley led off the street. Fleeting glimpses of movement could be seen deep in the alley's shadows.

Snow high-stepped over the inevitable litter cluttering the alley floor. Wang Yi's head flashed from the gloom like a ship's signal blinker.

The gun barrel bit into Snow's chin. His head bounced back, but the cold steel moved with him, pressing into his lip as if it had become part of him, a chilling appendage. Snow raised his hands slowly, knowing a quick movement would be his end. The sound of a brief scuffle ended abruptly when Rose groaned. Through the broken darkness, Snow identified the weapon at his lip, a Japanese type .44 carbine. An ugly, venomous little rifle which, when compared to the hard-bitten plug of a man holding it, looked absolutely pleasant.

Snow muttered into the steel barrel, "I'm an American diplomat, and I want to talk to Mr. Wang." He was grateful the gunman didn't laugh outright. He repeated himself in Chinese. This time the gunman did laugh, a coarse burst that did nothing to lessen the pressure on Snow's jaw. "We couldn't find his shop, so we had to follow him from the auction."

Snow's eyes gradually became accustomed to the darkness, and three other bodyguards materialized. Each one carried a weapon.

He repeated, "I must talk with Mr. Wang. All I want is information."

"Mr. Wang knows very little about most things." The lilting soprano voice came from behind the bodyguards. Snow could not see its source.

"He knows about jade."

At first, Snow thought the alley wall was closing in on him, intent on crushing him like a vise. Atop the moving mass was a melon head. Wang Yi's bulk emerged from the shadow.

"What makes you think I know about jade?" He asked in high sweet tones which failed to disguise his strength.

"You just purchased a block of jade and are carrying it now."

Wang Yi's pasty face creased into a broad smile that glittered with wealth. Each of his teeth had been replaced with a gold crown, and even in the alley's diffuse light, his mouth sparkled like a chandelier. "You were not watching closely. When I saw I was being followed, I passed the stone to an assistant."

"We aren't interested in the stone, only in you."

"Why would an American diplomat be consorting with a Bugis Street woman?" Wang Yi asked, pointing a beefy finger at Rose.

"She is not what she appears to be," Snow answered, wondering if a silent command had been given, because the carbine pulled away from his chin and several of the guards crowded around Rose, talking quietly and pointing at her curves.

Wang Yi asked, "What do you want to know?"

"We are looking for the Kobe Elephant."

The confident smile disappeared from the Chinaman's face. "I've never even seen the Kobe Elephant."

"No one in the American government thinks you have." Snow paused, letting the jade carver ponder the force of the words "American government." "I just need to know a little about your business, and maybe you've heard rumors."

Wang Yi nodded, his double chin bulging like a frog's. "Yes, maybe I've heard rumors. Come with me."

Snow followed the dark coat further into the darkness. The bodyguards dropped back to surround Rose. They were giggling like children, pointing at her breasts and thighs and wig. The type .44 gunman quickly pinched her dress where he thought a nipple would be. His finger left a dark smudge. Rose timidly swatted at the hand, causing a spirited uproar. The gunman tried again, but she trotted out of their circle after Snow and Wang Yi.

Wang Yi held up the uncut jade stone he had purchased an hour before. "Tell me what you see."

Snow gripped the rough rock and turned it over in his hand. The feldspar coating hid its worth. "A rock."

"Poetic," the carver chirped, "but inaccurate. Hidden in this stone is a snow lion. It must be liberated and given the qualities of life."

77

Snow followed him across the cutter's yard. In the center of the enclosure was a rectangular stone slab known as the peeling place. Two workmen labored with opposing bamboo handles, guiding a toothless iron saw into the side of a feldspar block. Suspended by a tripod above the saw was a gourd filled with water which a worker frequently tipped, lubricating the saw.

"When the block is peeled, I will use a diamond drill to etch the outlines of the animal," Wang Yi explained. He spread his hands to encompass the entire shop. "I employ thirty craftsmen here, but only I can see the jade figures hidden beneath the feldspar."

All thirty were absorbed in their art. None looked up as Wang Yi escorted Snow and Rose around the courtyard. In one corner a master carver treadled the rocking pedals of a circular saw. Two assistants held a jade block between them as the carver guided the stone under the whirling wheel, following the stenciled pattern. At another table, grinders and polishers smoothed a jade sculpture, using leg-powered grinding wheels and dragon-teeth paste. In a separate compound inside the yard, several polishers employed leather burnishing wheels made of ox hide anointed with finely ground bamboo chips. These men worked for months, and sometimes years, to give brilliance to the carvings.

"The difference between carvers and artists lies in the small touches," Wang Yi said, lifting a nephrite carving of a bear. The small jade animal was walking on all fours, its square nose to the ground. Its ears were transluscent and its tiny claws had been carved with infinite care. "This piece may look finished to you. But it will undergo another thousand hours of polishing. Then, to remove all signs of human industry, the fat from the skin of a bear must be applied to the carving. We do this to all our animal sculptures."

Snow said, "Dragon skin must be hard to find."

Wang Yi slapped his ponderous stomach and chuckled, "Yes, dragons are in short supply."

The tour ended in Wang Yi's cramped office, a kerosene-lit, windowless cubicle decorated with Chinese script painted on butcher paper. He dexterously rolled a thin cigarette and looked relieved when his guests declined the tobacco. Snow guessed Wang Yi had not always been prosperous.

Without preamble, the jade artist began, "Most of what I know about the Kobe Elephant can be summed up in one sentence. It disappeared from Kobe, Japan, during the summer of 1937, and it is no great concern of mine because I loathe the Japanese."

For the first time, Snow understood the necessity of Ko Tsukada's costume. Rose busied herself brushing at a dark smudge left on her chiffon dress by the gunman's fingers.

"That's most of what you know. What's the rest?" Snow asked.

Through a huge cloud of smoke, Wang Yi said, "The rest is rumor and gossip. At first the Japanese blamed the Chinese for stealing the elephant, but that was soon shown to be improbable because a round-eye was thought to have stolen it, and the Japanese didn't think the Chinese would hire an Anglo."

"Are there rumors as to who the Anglo was?"

"None that I've heard, and I hear all the rumors."

"Ask him if he would hear rumors if the thief were in Singapore," Rose said in English.

"I thought you spoke Chinese."

"I do," Rose said smiling demurely at the jade carver, "but if this fat bastard hears my Japanese accent, he'll kick us both out."

Snow asked and Wang Yi nodded, then added, "If the thief were Chinese, I'd know about it."

"Would you hear if the Kobe Elephant were in Singapore?"

"Maybe, maybe not. There is little room for Chinese jade artisans in the white business world. Or the white underworld."

"Do you do business with all the white dealers?"

"All the round-eyes, yes. And I'm aware of most of the large pieces bought for export to America and Europe."

"Most?" Snow asked.

"There are certain deals that never come to light," Wang Yi explained, spitting a bit of tobacco onto the floor.

"Mr. Wang, do you think any Singapore jade merchant is capable of stealing the Kobe Elephant?"

The Chinaman drew thoughtfully on his cigarette, which had burned down close enough to sear his finger. "Capable? I don't know. Willing? Yes."

"Which merchant would be willing?"

"Three months ago a small Buddhist temple on the South Bridge Road was ransacked by Malays. No one was severely injured, but a Ming Dynasty jade dragon was stolen during the riot. I was asked by the monks to locate it, and I failed.

79

But here, too, there were rumors. The jade piece was sold to an Australian collector by a Singapore dealer."

"His name?"

"Singapore's largest jade merchant, Dillon Synge."

Snow switched to English. "My wife and I met Synge at the club today. Heard of him?"

"I've got a little of his biography, as I have for all the important jade merchants here," Rose said, still picking at the ruined chiffon. "Other than that, no."

The American asked in Cantonese, "Do you sell to him?"

Wang Yi nodded. "He pays a fair price, so I do business with him."

Snow thanked the master carver for his time, and Wang Yi displayed his golden grin and promised a reasonable discount if Snow was ever in the market for jade. No middleman. Straight from the polisher's table.

Wang Yi ordered his guards to escort Snow and his guest to the street. Rose was cheered markedly, apparently resigned to her ruined dress. As they approached the gunman at the courtyard's gate, she even managed a seductive smile. The stocky Chinese gunman who had pinched her swaggered forward, assisted by the cheers of his men. Rose's hips began a provocative undulation.

"Don't do anything stupid," Snow muttered.

"I just want to thank these wonderful men for helping us, darling," she cooed. "Won't take a minute."

Rose reached for the gunman's cap, playfully tipping it over his eyes. He laughed, then asked if she were free that afternoon.

She wagged a finger in front of his nose and said sweetly, "No, no. You must come to Bugis Street for that. You come to Bugis someday, you never know what you'll find." Rose placed a hand under her breast, pressing back the sheer cloth to accent her curves. She breathed, "But I know you would like it."

The gunman beamed, and to the applause of his men, reached again for Rose's nipple.

Snow knew most of the moves, but he had never seen this one. Rose's right hand crashed into the gunman's just as it touched the chiffon. His fingers snapped back against his wrist and before his lecherous grin had disappeared, two bones were broken. In the instant before the pain registered, the gunman heard a bass growl from those beautiful lips,

"You come to Bugis Street, and I'll do that to your arms and legs."

The gunman's agonized screams chased Snow and Rose down the alley.

The note read, "Mrs. Snow, I must speak to you about another payment. Terrence Bliss."

Connie Snow sank back into the leather chair of the Raffles Hotel room. She bit her lip and reread the message. She had known the little man would resurface. Wasn't that standard? A blackmailer always calls again. And then again. Two deep clefts formed between her eyebrows. "There must be something I can do about him," she whispered to herself. "I can't have him chasing after me."

How had he known? Who told him? She had lain awake under the mosquito net most of last night turning those questions over in her mind. No answers, just more questions. And now she would have to meet Bliss, try to hold him off, make him understand she couldn't get much more money.

A key scraped in the door, and Connie quickly hid the note in the table, then rearranged her face. Her husband entered, wearing an unusually large grin.

"Has Lester returned the call?" he asked.

She shook her head, then asked about his good humor. He related the incident between Rose and Wang Yi's bodyguard and concluded it with a laughing, "I wonder how long it'll be before that gunny reaches for a pretty woman's breasts?"

Her laugh was hollow and unconvincing and cut short by the raucous jangling of the telephone. Snow lifted the phone off the table, then sat next to his wife, holding the speaker so she could hear.

Howard Lester's voice was tinny and distant, and echoed eerily over the Pacific Ocean cable. "I have the information you need, most of it anyway."

"It didn't take long," Snow said. He pictured Lester in his dilapidated office, his eyes endlessly working. Snow wondered if Lester's face was jumping.

"Two and a half hours, to be precise," Lester said, "I'm taking a personal interest in this, you know. Sort of a hobby. Some people collect stamps, I look for Amelia Earhart's bones." Snow thought Lester was chuckling, but it could have been cable distortion. "We found no records of the Keluang camp, no list of internees or of released prisoners, nothing like that. We think there may have been six or seven women in the camp. Some died. We do know that all liberated prisoners were treated at the Fort Canning hospital in Singapore. Three were women."

"Find anything about them?"

"All nurses. The first was only twenty-four years old in 1945, so she's much too young. She lives in Detroit with her autoworker husband and two children. The second was even younger upon release. I talked with her this morning. Her name is Manning. She's in a tuberculosis sanitarium in San Diego, where she's been since the war ended. She'll be going home soon."

"And the third?" Snow asked, glancing sideways at his wife, whose ear was pressed against his.

"Her name is Beth Johnston, and she told her fellow inmates she was a Wac nurse," Lester said.

"Was she?"

"Not as far as I can tell. No record of her in any of the services, U.S. or Allied. She kept to herself and didn't give her fellow prisoners reason to ask her questions, according to Miss Manning, the girl in the sanitarium."

"Did this Miss Manning say what Beth Johnston looked like?" Snow asked.

"Average height, average weight, you know the kind of description. She does remember that her hair was sandy blonde and that she was older than most of the prisoners. She guessed early forties."

"Well, that doesn't rule out that Beth Johnston was Amelia Earhart."

"No, it doesn't. At the Fort Canning Hospital, Beth Johnston was treated for dysentery and for various external infections, then with a number of other released prisoners, she was flown to a veterans hospital in San Francisco."

"You think Amelia Earhart returned to the U.S.?" Snow exclaimed.

"I didn't say that," Lester answered. "A woman named Beth Johnston returned to the U.S., entered a veterans hospital, was treated for malnutrition and other maladies, and was released six weeks later."

"Any trace of her after that?"

"No. At least, I haven't come up with anything. It seems Beth Johnston disappeared."

"It's been my experience that a person doesn't disappear without a good reason," Snow said.

"Exactly. So we'll keep looking on this end."

"Did you dig up anything on Dillon Synge?"

There was a momentary pause. Snow could hear papers shuffle in Washington, D.C. Lester returned to the phone. "Not much more than you already know. He's a jade merchant, well known among West Coast buyers. No criminal record in any of the Commonwealth Countries. He drives a Rolls-Royce, owns two small freighters, and a motor launch. He has a controlling interest in three Singapore office buildings. He owns a small rubber plantation, one light-cargo airline, and several warehouses."

"An airline? What's the name?"

Another pause. "Singapore-Straits Airline."

"Is he a pilot?" Snow asked, jotting notes on a yellow pad.

"Don't know. I'll check."

"The Chinese jade carver told me Synge sold a stolen jade piece and hinted Synge either stole it himself or is a fence. Any information on Synge's reputation?"

"He's president of the British White Club and is one of its big sponsors," Lester answered. "That's all I know. You think there's a connection between him and Amelia Earhart?"

"Amelia Earhart and her plane were lured to Saipan. The plane left with the Kobe Elephant on board. Tsukada believes it was sighted in Singapore the next day. And Dillon Synge is a somewhat shady Singapore jade dealer. That's all I have."

"That's not much," Lester said.

"But what if it jells?"

"Then we'll stop looking for Amelia Earhart's bones and start looking for Amelia Earhart."

"And Dillon Synge?"

"If he has a connection, deal with him in the field," Lester said cryptically. The dryness in his voice did not seem to be due entirely to cable static.

Connie lifted an eyebrow. Snow shook his head, indicating he would explain it later and hoping he wouldn't have to.

Lester continued, "I want you to stay in Singapore until you've resolved this."

"I still think I'm chasing bones. Beth Johnston or no."

"Then chase them until you find some answers."

* * *

The British brought institutional green to Singapore. Now it adorned the interior of virtually every public building, including the Fort Canning Hospital. Snow and his wife walked down the green hallway of the chronic care ward. It smelled of antiseptic and failing bodies.

Snow stopped at a nurse's station and asked for the resident. He was crisply informed that the doctor was out and was not expected any time soon.

"Was he here in the spring of 1945?" Snow asked.

The nurse, a starched, hair-netted woman with the color long since bleached out of her personality, said, "No. He's just out of medical school. Why?" She apparently could not look up from her clipboard.

"I'm trying to learn the identity of a woman who was in this hospital then."

"It's a big hospital," she retorted dully. Her eyes were shadowed and remote.

"She was suffering from malnutrition and maybe malaria and dysentery," Connie said. "She had been a POW in the upcountry."

"The Keluang camp?" The nurse's voice lifted.

Connie dipped her chin.

"All the Keluang prisoners were treated here in the chronic ward. I was stationed here. We had several hundred internees being treated at once. Wouldn't be able to tell most of them apart. But you say you're looking for a woman?"

"Yes. I understand there were three Keluang women treated here," Snow said, feeling droplets of sweat grow on his upper lip. The ward was oppressive with steamed, dead air.

The nurse offered a long-suffering smile. "I knew the women. Poor dears. All three were thin as rails. We fattened them a bit."

Snow pulled a photograph of Amelia Earhart from his wallet. He passed it to the nurse. "Recognize her?"

"Oh yes." Her smile was genuine. "She had malaria and spent some time in a quarantine room in the west wing. But then she was transferred here and I got to know her quite well. She was discharged in August of last year."

"Remember her name?" Connie asked, breathing quickly with anticipation.

"Sure," the nurse said. "Beth Johnston."

* * *

They had waited on the south edge of the rubber plantation for two hours. Behind them, the cultivated trees spread in a precise pattern that contrasted weakly with the surrounding jungle of Singapore Island's Nee Soon area. A rubber processing plant a mile upwind permeated the plantation with a foul odor curiously resembling that of a barnyard.

The plantation was divided into two acreages, separated by what once had been a service road. The road had been widened into a landing strip, and the deep ruts indicated it was used frequently. At the end of the runway, inserted between a row of rubber trees, was a plank hut that appeared to be a service shop. Gasoline drums were stacked against the hut's north end. One fifty gallon drum stood upright on a push-cart and from the drum's lid a handcranked pump and hose protruded.

Snow dropped back to his knees and said, "We could be waiting here for hours. You sure of your facts?"

Rose plucked a wild orchid and wrinkled her nose at the pungent smell. "A plane takes off and lands at this field daily, sometimes several times a day. That's all I heard."

"It's a cargo plane?" Connie asked. She was wearing tucked and pleated navy-blue slacks that were attracting miscellaneous bits of jungle floor.

"I don't know," Rose said in a voice that dropped to an anxious whisper. She signaled for quiet, then slowly lowered herself to the grass. "Watch the door."

Across the airstrip, the hut's door pulled open and a Malay sentry walked out to the edge of the field, cupped a hand around his eyes, and peered north into the sky. The sentry wore a loose grenadine shirt and ragged shorts. Over his shoulder was an Argentine Mauser. He turned back, but halted midstep and cocked an ear to the north. Finally satisfied, he called into the hut and was soon joined by a second guard.

Not until a full minute later did Snow hear the low drone of an airplane. The indistinct rumble faded in and out like the distant lapping of surf.

"Is that it?" Connie asked quietly, leaning around the rubber tree trunk to look down the runway.

"That sentry knew its arrival time, so he came out to greet it. Yes, it's the Singapore-Straits Airline's one plane."

The drone had become a steady pulse from the north. The guards rolled two fuel drums to the edge of the airstrip and one returned for the hand pump. As they pried on the bung, a surplus U.S. jeep emerged from the access road and bumped along the airstrip until it reached the hut. Snow recognized the driver as Flynn. The passenger was tall and slightly stooped and had skin mottled by the tropical sun. Dillon Synge.

From his position across the airstrip, Snow could not hear Synge's low conversation with his driver or the orders given the Malay sentries. The incoming plane's rumble was now distinct, and Synge gazed at the bright sky, a look of accomplishment settling on his lined face.

"Do you think he meets his plane each time it arrives?" Rose asked.

Snow shook his head. "Not a chance. He must be expecting important cargo."

The plane appeared in the north sky as if by sleight of hand, so close Snow could see the flaps lowering. "It's a twin engine and has a cantilever tail."

The plane came in low as if to avoid detection. It bounced off the runway once, then sank into a familiar rut as it rushed down the strip. The engines' enormous rumble shook the rubber trees. Clots of mud sprayed from the wheels as the pilot skillfully brought the plane to a standstill in front of the hut. The starboard engines roared as the plane twisted around to face the way it had come in.

Snow almost sighed, "It's a Lockheed Electra."

"Same model as hers?" Rose asked.

"Yes, a 10E, but that doesn't mean much. There are thousands of them in service, and probably a dozen or so based in Singapore. And the tail markings don't match. Earhart's were 16020."

"Of course they wouldn't match," Connie said. "That would be the first thing he would change. A little paint and it's done. We need to get a closer look."

The propellers fluttered and both engines coughed and died. Several seconds later, the pilot dropped to the ground and placed in Dillon Synge's outstretched hand a small tin container. They retired to the hut while a sentry climbed onto the port wing and was handed the fuel hose.

"It doesn't look like the Electra is staying long," Snow said. "If we get a look, it'll be a quick one."

For ten minutes, the sentries pumped fuel into the Electra's tanks. They worked quickly, drawing first from one drum, then the other. From the hut came muffled laughter and the clink of glasses. Snow's legs began to ache from squatting, and the thick odor of orchids was making him giddy. Connie was on her knees, looking at the plane through a bush, and the soft ground had begun to suck at her legs, drawing them down.

"How will you confirm it's the plane?" Rose asked. She had been crouched against a rubber tree for fifteen mintes, remaining absolutely motionless.

"Amelia Earhart's Electra was outfitted with Wasp Senior engines," Snow said. "Most 10E's had Juniors. I need to look into the cowling. It'd also help if we could get a look inside the fuselage, because Earhart's plane had fuel tank modifications made in the body which expanded the Electra's range."

"Then you go for the engines and I'll look inside."

"Great plan," Snow responded dryly. "We haven't even figured out how to get rid of the sentries yet."

"Darling," Rose said cloyingly, "once again you underestimate the power of the skirt."

The guards rolled the empty drums to the side of the hut, and one sentry, attracted to the sound of a bottle making the rounds, returned to the hut. The other guard leaned against the Electra's landing gear strut, searched in his shirt pocket, found a bamboo toothpick, and began scraping a molar.

"This chiffon dress is ruined anyway," Rose said as she tore at the clinging neckline. Snow wondered at the Japanese's perfectly exaggerated feminine inflection and her delicate, feline movements. The dressed ripped almost down to her prosthesis. She dabbed jungle mud on her left cheek, then with a forlorn stage sigh, spotted the dress with mud.

Without explanation, she rose from her hiding place, ran several steps onto the airstrip, looked over her shoulder in terror, then frantically hobbled on uncooperating heels toward the Electra. She held out a lacquered and jeweled hand, silently pleading for help. With the other hand, she tried desperately to keep her ravaged dress from falling off her shoulders.

A hand grabbing at his groin would not have had more effect on the sentry. A vision of terrified loveliness was scrambling across the runway in his direction. He instinctively reached for the stock of his Mauser, but then saw her torn dress, the dark smudges, and the fear marring her elegant eyes. A sob escaped from the vision's lovely mouth, the fearful cry of a wounded animal. And when she held both arms out for him, stumbling, about to fall, he could do nothing but spread his arms to catch her.

Rose's open palm chopped into the sentry's throat, and he was unconscious before his knees sagged. She caught him under his arms, hoisted him over her shoulders and carried him to the side of the shack.

By the time the sentry was hidden between the empty oil drums, Snow was prying at the Electra's cowling latch. He had assumed Connie would remain among the rubber trees, but she had followed him across the runway, and while he wrenched the engine cover, she walked the length of the fuselage, moving her eyes along the windows to the radio antenna and the cargo hatch.

Winded and limping slightly, Rose returned to help Snow with the cowling. He glanced nervously at the shack where someone was telling a bawdy story to the accompaniment of Flynn's truncated laugh. The sound of whiskey splashing into a glass carried easily enough to Snow, prompting him to lift the cowling hatch slowly and very quietly. The engine was caked with grease and oil and looked in need of service.

"What kind is it? Can you tell?" Rose whispered.

Snow scraped grease and dirt from a manifold cover. "It's a Wasp Senior." He shook his head. "I just can't imagine anyone brazen enough to try to kill Earhart, then fly her plane all these years."

Rose whispered harshly, "Let's figure it out later. My friend is going to wake up or Synge's party will run out of whiskey soon."

Snow levered the cover back into position, then dropped to a crouch under the engine. "Where the hell is my wife?"

An edge of panic touched Snow as he ran to the rear of the plane, scanning the barrels along the side of the hut. The plane's cargo hatch was sealed, but then with a muttered, "Oh, Christ," he saw the cockpit hatch was open.

He jumped onto the step and crawled up the wing, his hands searching for purchase on the unfamiliar structure. His damp shoes slipped and he fell heavily to his knees. Snow froze. The rumbling clap of his fall echoed in the cavernous wing and must have been audible in the shack, but when the party went on uninterrupted, Snow continued on his hands and knees to the hatch. He gripped the hatch framework with both hands and pulled himself into the plane.

The interior of the fuselage was dark, but he must have been in the navigator's bay because he could feel the back of the pilot's seat. He squinted, as if pressure on his eyes would assist his night vision. The beams and wires of the cargo bay emerged from the grayness. The fuselage was empty. He whispered, "Connie?"

"Right here," came from the pilot's seat behind him. It startled Snow so that his head jerked against the overhead metal strut. His wife was sitting comfortably in the seat and appeared to be reading a magazine or a poster.

"What in Christ's name are you doing?" he whispered fiercely. "We've got to get out of here."

"Were they Wasp Seniors?"

"Yes. Now let's go." He reached over the headrest for her arm, but instead found in his hand the document she had been reading.

"Is that the Electra's license?" she asked, her voice subdued.

Snow held the paper up to the light streaming through the windshield. The document was a printed page with several stamps pressed onto it and with blanks filled with longhand. "It's the certificate of registration, granted by the government of Malaya. It's been given to the Singapore-Straits Airline and its president, Dillon Synge. There's also what looks like a certificate of airworthiness attached to the back of it." He tossed the documents into the co-pilot's seat. "Let's get out of here."

"I found those in the flap near the rudder pedal. And behind them was this." She gave him another document.

It was much older, crumpled with age and the deleterious effects of the tropics. It, too, was a certificate of registration, but it was issued by the U.S. Department of Commerce. And it was issued to Amelia Earhart.

Snow felt the blood warming his face as he struggled to grasp the implications of the certificate. He could not remove his eyes from the aviatrix's name, as if it were a specter reaching for him across the years, pushing aside the rumors, explanations and official pronouncements about her death, and confronting him with an undeniable fact: he was standing inside Earhart's Electra.

"This is her plane, isn't it, Joseph?"

"Yes," he replied lifelessly.

"Why didn't Synge destroy Earhart's certificate?"

"Probably for the same reason some thieves only burgle a house when the owners are home. They get a thrill out of it. Synge has probably used this plane all these years knowing her certificate was in the document pocket and enjoying that knowledge immensely."

"What do we do now?" she asked, rising from the seat.

"It's clear Synge used this plane to steal the Kobe Elephant. We'll cable all this information to Howard Lester."

"I mean, right now. With this plane."

"The main thing is getting away from here. That party in the hut is going to last only as long as the bottle lasts."

Connie shook her head vehemently, "Lester said to deal with Synge in the field, didn't he? Doesn't that mean you have authority to act now?"

"I have authority, but for what?"

"Joseph, this is her plane. It's being used by the man who tried to kill her. We know that now. Isn't it time for us to take the offensive? To strike back, for her."

"You want me to go after Synge?" he asked.

"Not now, not until we find out if Amelia Earhart is alive, and if so where she is. But, Joseph, this plane stands here, mocking her and mocking us. It's of no use to anyone but Synge. Destroy it."

Snow was astounded at his wife's fervor. Her midnight black hair bounced against her neck as she spoke and her fist was wrapped tightly around the pilot's armrest.

"You can't deny Synge is in on it, Joseph. Amelia Earhart spent years in a POW camp because of him. And we'll never know anymore than we do now unless we make our presence known and put pressure on him."

Snow smiled involuntarily at his wife's dancing eyes and firmly set mouth. "How do you propose we destroy the Electra?"

Without hesitation, she said, "Pump fuel on it and set it on fire."

He was shaken. His wife had thought it through, as he should have, as Howard Lester would have. In the business it was called the vise. Unrelenting pressure until the answers squeezed to the top. Make the suspect operate from fear, and he'll make mistake after mistake. Another burst of Flynn's laughter decided it for Snow. "Let's go."

Rose was waiting near the edge of the hut, kneeling below its window and following the progress of the party. When

Snow dropped silently to the ground under the Electra, she ran in a crouch to meet him under the wing. Snow said simply, "It was Earhart's plane. Let's set it on fire."

Rose smiled, one of those beatific efforts reserved for sailors buying her a drink. Wordlessly, they rolled a full barrel under the starboard engine. They moved cautiously, listening for disturbances in the hut. Snow mounted the wing and reached down for the hose. When Rose began a rhythmic cranking of the fuel pump, he aimed the nozzle into the cowling until the gasoline was dripping through to the ground. He splashed gasoline onto the wing and was about to stick the hose into the cockpit when Connie signaled from her post near the empty drums. Snow threw the hose to Rose and jumped to the ground.

As Flynn wound down his last fit of laughter and chairs scraped against the hardwood floor, Rose and Snow rolled the drum between a line of rubber trees at the rear of the shack. They knelt between full barrels near the side of the hut. When the sentry groaned and stirred, Rose quickly put her hand to his throat and he was still.

They could hear the door thrown open and Flynn slap the pilot on the back. The pilot appeared at the corner of the hut, eight yards from them. He threw the empty bottle over their heads into the grove. Behind him was the first sentry, who wiped his mouth with the back of his hand and looked into the trees for his partner. Synge approached the pilot and exchanged a few words. The pilot smiled as the jade merchant placed a small roll of bills in his hand, and he gave Synge an elaborate parody of a salute before turning for his plane.

Rose whispered anxiously, "He's taking off again."

"Do something, Joseph," Connie's voice sounded like a rising wind.

The pilot climbed into the cockpit. Synge's jeep sputtered into life, and Snow heard gravel thrown from its wheels as it darted away from the shack. Muffled by rows of rubber trees, the whine of the jeep's engine faded quickly as it pulled onto the access road.

The pilot flapped the ailerons and rudder. The Wasp Seniors cranked over, first starboard, then port. Their thunder filled the airstrip, and the din increased as the pilot lifted the brakes. The Electra crawled out of the rut and inched forward.

"Can you take out the sentry?" Snow asked over the roar, reaching into his shirt pocket for a lighter.

Rose answered by kicking off her high heels, removing her wig, and launching herself around the barrels to the rear of the hut. At a dead run, her delicate sweat-stained dress pulled apart by her charging legs and her arms pumping like pistons, she rounded the hut's far corner. The sentry was leaning against the shack, lighting a smoke, his rifle resting against his raffia belt. He turned to the sound of trampling from the underbrush and was rooted in place by the sight of the oncoming flurry of green chiffon. Rose's palm clipped the sentry's neck, and she followed through with the heel of the other palm thudding into his ear. She grabbed the sentry's shirt collar and pulled him behind the shack, his legs like sled runners cutting through the grass.

The Electra angled slowly away from the shack, searching for the center of the runway. The light alloy wings bounced irregularly, threatening to snap off the fuselage. A thin stream of gasoline fell from the drenched port engine and splashed into the mud.

The plane was pulling away from the shack. Snow impatiently jabbed a fist at the damp turf and thumbed the spark wheel of his Zippo. The power plants idled as the pilot ran through a preflight check. In a moment, the Electra would muscle itself into the sky.

A flap of chiffon skirt flashed at the hut's far corner, then the dark head of the unconscious sentry was dragged into view. Now, sure his back was clear, Snow sprinted around the barrels and onto the airstrip. The Electra's engines were throttled, and the plane began its ponderous roll down the airstrip. Snow's churning legs carried him roughly over the mire. He came abreast of the plane's tail and almost lost his footing as he entered the props' backwash. He pushed against the gale, digging his heels into the loose earth, bending into the wind.

The Electra rolled forward, fighting the grasping mud. Atomized gasoline blew over Snow, forcing his eyes shut. He spit gasoline from his mouth and kept his legs moving. He was breathing in uncontrollable bursts and his lungs were burning. Four more steps, he thought, no eight. The plane was picking up speed.

Snow lifted the lighter, putting it into the spray of gasoline. His hand found the aileron. The stream of gasoline blowing back from the cowling splashed over his hand. Feeling the wing pull away from him, he thumbed the Zippo. He flipped the lighter again and again. When his hand caught fire, he dived to the ground.

The flame was stunted, blown down by the prop wash, but feeding on the stream of fuel, it climbed the wing steadily toward the cowling. Just as the plane's tail lifted off the runway, the flame disappeared into the engine cover. Lying in the mud, his fist thrust into a puddle, Snow saw the plane's wheels lift off the ground.

Two seconds later, the starboard engine exploded. The cowling blew off and was swept back over the wing. Rockers and pistons shot into the air as flame engulfed the Senior. Almost simultaneously, the starboard fuel tank erupted, disintegrating the wing and sending sheets of alloy twisting into the air. A red ball of flame rolled away, scorching the fuselage before it collapsed back on the wing. The propeller wrenched from the shaft and cartwheeled across the fuselage, leaving stapled tracks in the body of the plane. Suddenly without starboard power, the Electra veered sharply toward a line of rubber trees. A wheel caught in a rut and the starboard landing gear collapsed, dropping the wing to the ground. Still propelled by the port engine, the plane careened into the grove. Its remaining wing slammed into the trees, shearing off at the fuselage. Like a jettisoned torpedo, the fuselage pitched into the underbrush and skidded forty yards before rolling onto its side, coming to rest against several rubber trees.

The cockpit hatch sprang open, and the pilot's hands gripped the frame. With arms shaking like a tuning fork, he lifted himself out of the plane and slid to the ground. He walked unsteadily into the trees.

Rose and Connie joined Snow on the runway. He was examining flash burns on three knuckles. "Now what?" Rose asked.

"My wife is right," Snow said, turning to the Electra's wing. The fire had died quickly, leaving a charred and mangled metal skeleton. "Dillon Synge is our man. From now on, he'll know we're in Singapore."

VI

The Aussies taught a mynah the first ten notes of
"Waltzing Matilda." A relentless annoyance.

Six inches high and cloaked in an opaque sea-green robe, the
Ming Dynasty nephrite carving of Lord Buddha was clearly
the most valuable piece displayed on the table. An iridescent
green and white bowl with ring handles was perhaps the
most exquisite. But there was no question the Los Angeles
buyer coveted the pink phallus.

The phallus had been carved less than two hundred years
before. The penis was of salmon pink nephrite and was
realistically veined and distended. The testicles were of a
darker hue, the left stone slightly larger than the right. The
Chinese were pragmatists, so they not only plugged the
body's orifices to prevent decay, but provided the corpse of a
wealthy female with something she could also use in the
afterlife. The pink phallus had been robbed from a tomb in
Kwantung in the 1870s and had been in a freighter captain's
private collection until Dillon Synge purchased it three months
before. These carvings and eight other pieces were being
offered to the four dealers sitting around the conference
table. The four represented the retail elite of the jade business. Sealth from Los Angeles, Richards from San Francisco,
Palen from Sydney, and Smithers from London—all invited
to Singapore for the viewing. Receiving such a letter from

Dillon Synge was both an honor and an obligation—an honor because less than twenty jade dealers worldwide were ever invited; and an obligation because once refused, for any reason, the invitation was never again extended. And this was tantamount to dismissal from the jade art business.

Synge pushed the phallus across to Sealth, who lifted it delicately, as if picking up a tea cup. Sealth was a broad man whose buttocks sagged like bread dough over his chair. He squinted at the phallus, ostensibly judging the quality of the jade, but Synge saw him glance furtively at the size of the testicles, and as he lowered it to the table, he squeezed it as if it were a living thing. God only knows what he'd do with it if he were alone, Synge thought.

Synge had intended to begin the bidding with the phallus simply to clear it from the table, but seeing Sealth's uncomfortable passion, he said quietly, "Bids are open on the bowl."

The gray-green bowl was passed from hand to hand. Unnecessarily, because the retailers had spent the morning carefully examining each piece. Palen from Sydney said, "We know it's Ching, but do you have a more specific date, Mr. Synge?"

The price would vary greatly on whether it had been carved early or late in the Ching period. Synge said, "I'd like to say it was made at the end of the seventeenth century, but from the shape of the elephant heads holding the rings at each end of the bowl, I think it was carved in the late eighteen hundreds."

Palen nodded his approval of Synge's honesty. The Singapore dealer's reputation was spotless worldwide. Never did he exaggerate the age of a piece or invent a royal history. He had never hired a jade carver to rework a piece, adding an angle or blunting an edge, giving the design the character of an earlier era. If Synge said a statue had no history, the retailers asked no further.

"You can begin, Mr. Palen," Synge said in the tone of a patriarch.

"Eight thousand U.S. dollars."

"Nine thousand," Smithers said.

"Nine five," Sealth added dutifully. His eyes had not left the phallus.

Within sixty seconds, the bowl had been sold to Palen for twelve thousand dollars. A few minutes later, Smithers was the owner of an ornate jade belt buckle carved in the shape of a small dragon. Later still, Sealth purchased the phallus for seven thousand dollars, twice what Synge had been expecting. The auction lasted less than thirty minutes. The buyers placed their jade pieces in lined traveling cases, then used the conference room's telephones to call their limousines and bodyguards. Several glanced expectantly at Synge, who avoided their eyes.

This was the moment he dreaded. Before he lost the Kobe Elephant, he would frequently ask several of the buyers to his office for a highball. Even if they had been there before, or if they had heard what his office contained, they were never fully prepared for the Kobe Elephant, its trunk raised in timeless tribute to its owner. As the buyers stared at the jade elephant, power and authority would flow into Synge. He would casually point out some elegant features and answer a hesitant question, all the while drinking in their reverence for the piece.

But that was before he had given the elephant to Kiril Stasov. *Given it.* Once again, as always, his head lightened at the thought. He planted a hand on the conference table and waited until the blood returned. When he could focus his eyes again, he saw that all four buyers were staring at him.

"Excuse me, gentlemen," he said feebly, attempting a smile. "I've been a little under the weather. Allow my secretary to show you out."

Trading came to Dillon Synge as breathing came to others. From his tenth birthday, he had been aware of his gift at negotiating. At sixteen he opened a pawnshop in Singapore, dealing primarily with sailors needing whiskey money. At twenty his lifelong passion for jade began when he gave an Australian sailor a case of Irish whiskey for five nephrite snuff boxes. He quickly became Singapore's largest jade dealer. He bought a large home in the Tanglin area, became a principal in the British White Club, and built a three-story office building in White Singapore. The accumulation of money was only a side benefit. Synge lived for the deal, for the hours of negotiations and excitement as the deal closed, when he knew he had bested an opponent.

He had been on a jade-buying trip to Japan in late 1935 when he first saw the Kobe Elephant. The elephant was the grand possession of Kobe's largest Buddhist temple and was watched constantly by the temple's two hundred monks.

Synge's first sight of the famed jewel was like a blow to his face. Its massive presence snapped his head back and lowered his jaw. He struggled for breath as his eyes jumped from facet to facet. The *enormity* of it. The perfection. From the altar the elephant seemed to reach for Synge, to taunt him. He took several uncertain steps, and the elephant's eyes followed him, gripping him and daring him to move. The temple's heat and the soft chanting worked on his mind and invited him to enter the celebration. To commit. The elephant demanded as much as it gave. He slowly raised a hand toward the jewel. He made the compact. The bond was sanctified by the holiness of the place. The Kobe Elephant became part of him.

For three days, Synge visited the shrine, standing barefoot in the visitors' area, while the monks performed their rituals and the lay worshippers engaged in assorted religious and superstitious machinations. He knew he must possess the elephant, and he knew that working alone he would never be able to remove it from the temple. For those three days, he struggled for an answer. And it came to him.

For over a decade, bloody insurrections had marred the solidity of the Imperial Army. Now, the spirit of *gekokujo*, insubordination, was at a feverish level in the Imperial Army. Young officers bitterly resented the incompetence and scandal that pocked the military and the government. The Brocade Flag Revolution and the May 15 Incident were quashed and their officer-instigators jailed. By January 1936, over 1400 radical officers had banded together and were prepared to revolt. Their plan included attacks on six Tokyo targets and the assassination of numerous high-level government officials, including Prime Minister Keisuke Okadaar. The rebels' contempt was so open that one unit on maneuvers had urinated in cadence at the Tokyo police headquarters. The War Ministry moved against the rebels by locking up their weapons. Without firearms, the rebellion had no chance of success, and the fire of *gekokujo* would die of impotence.

In early February 1936, Dillon Synge returned to Japan on a tramp steamer he had chartered in Singapore. For a week he made discreet inquiries to enlisted men, plying them with sake, asking for an audience with a dissatisfied officer. The contact was made, and on a bitterly cold evening, he met an Imperial Army captain at a sushi bar. The officer introduced himself as Captain Mitsuo Gota of the First Division.

Maintaining an impassive smile, as he knew he must

whenever negotiating with an Oriental, and using passable Japanese, Synge began with the requisite compliments and niceties. Only upon finishing their second sake did he bring up the subject of the meeting. "Captain Gota, I have come to you because I am in trouble and I understand from your men that you are a compassionate officer."

"My men are kind." Gota wore a tan kepi with a black leather band across the rim. The insignia of his rank was sewn onto the stiff lapels of his uniform. His face was wide, his mouth full. When he smiled only his lips moved. His eyes remained black bullets untouched by the grin.

"If I thought the officers in the War Ministry and the Office of Military Education would understand, I would have gone to them." Thus Synge clearly separated himself from the military establishment in Japan and sided with the disenchanted officers. "I am a trader and make my living looking for objects I can trade for a profit."

"You are an English capitalist, Mr. Synge."

"A Singapore capitalist," Synge corrected. "A month ago, I traded a jade statue of Kuan Yin for three farm tractors. Then, for the tractors, I received six used electric trolleys. For the trolleys, a small warehouse stocked with Persian rugs. A man in my business has very little use for any of these things, so I made one more trade."

Gota nodded his encouragement.

"I now own two thousand Lee Enfield Mark VI rifles and three hundred Webley .455 Mark V pistols. And ammunition."

Gota coughed into his sake. He wiped a drop from his chin, his eyes never leaving Synge. With the peculiar lisp that affects a Japanese's voice when annoyed, he asked, "Why are you telling me about these weapons?"

Synge was very careful. "You are dedicated to the emperor and to the national essence of Japan. You know that the emperor has reigned from time immemorial and will continue to reign to the farthest edge of the future. But recently, many Japanese have neglected their duty to the throne, have amassed great personal wealth and power, disregarding the general welfare of the people. The reign of the emperor is weakened and nothing is being done."

Gota stared stonily at the trader. It was not a Westerner's right to comment on the emperor, even to mention him, but what Synge had said was accurate. He let Synge continue.

"There are groups of army officers who will never betray

the *kokutai* and who seek to correct these grievances, but who do not have the means to do so. I offer the means. My rifles and pistols are for sale."

"Who will you sell them to?"

"You. And your brotherhood."

Gota's laugh was harsh and insulting. "Assuming I had a need for them, I could surely not pay your price."

"You will be surprised at what I am asking."

Gota studied the trader. He nibbled on a string of raw fish, never breaking his gaze. "What is the price?"

Synge smiled and spread his arms. "Let's talk about the goods first. The Enfields and Webleys are in their original packing grease. I have fifty rounds per rifle and twenty per pistol. I also have forty extra cylinders for the pistols. And, perhaps most important, I can have the weapons to you within twenty-four hours."

"The price, Mr. Synge?"

The trader said very softly, "The Kobe Elephant."

His sake cup froze midway to his mouth. Captain Gota stared at Synge for several seconds, then erupted into loud laughter causing eyes to turn toward them. Sake splashed out of his cup and he had to lower it to the table.

Synge waited until the captain had calmed himself. "Let me put it another way. The emperor is being destroyed, Japan is being destroyed. You and your followers can save the throne, but only if you have the tools. I offer you Japan. Is one jade piece too high a price to pay?"

"The Kobe Elephant belongs to the emperor," Gota snorted. "It is a sacred object. To think of even touching it is heretical and traitorous."

Synge shrugged. "To allow the emperor to be betrayed by inept, scandalous military leaders is heretical and traitorous."

Gota's blunt features twisted. He was struggling with himself and unable to hide it. He leaned forward and looked into his cup, perhaps attempting to divine the answers there. Finally, he spoke. "The Kobe Elephant is in a Buddhist temple. How do you propose we get it?"

"Surely there are enough men in your camp to overpower the monks."

"Are you suggesting we use force against the holy teachers in the temple?"

"Once again, balance your priorities. You must have the

Kobe Elephant to save the nation. Isn't that what it comes to? How you get the elephant is no concern of mine."

The son of an illiterate paddy farmer, Gota had not risen to the rank of captain by hesitating to make decisions. His words were brittle. "I will have the Kobe Elephant in twenty-four hours."

"Crated and delivered to slip four of the second dock at the Tokyo shipyard."

"And the weapons?" Gota asked.

"They will be there."

Synge's plan was simple. He knew that Japanese police would cordon all of Japan's docks immediately after the elephant was discovered missing. He also knew that their emphasis would be upon ships sailing to the ports of China and Southeast Asia where the thief would have the opportunity to sell the precious jade piece. But Synge was sailing east to Saipan, one of the dwarf jungle islands that dotted the Pacific. He had paid an enormous bribe to three stevedores and a cement ship's captain. The Great-War-Era ship was part of an armada of supply vessels regularly sailing into the Japanese mandates with equipment, fortifications and soldiers, transforming the Marianas into heavily armed outposts. Once on the island, he would secretly board a monthly supply and mail ship that sailed the Marianas, the Carolines, and Micronesia. That shipping line was owned by a Singapore businessman who had already been paid.

The exchange and loading took place without incident. By the time the *Kempai tai,* the shore patrol, and the Tokyo police were swarming over the dockyard, Synge and his elephant were deep in the hold of a Saipan-bound freighter.

Four days later, native stevedores offloaded on Saipan the Kobe Elephant's crate and the crate in which Synge hid. That night, he and two natives carried the elephant's crate a hundred yards south along the beach, and secreted it in nearby jungle underbrush. It was February 15, 1936. The supply ship that would carry him and the elephant off the island was due in three days.

The three days passed and then another seven. On his tenth day on the island Dillon Synge learned from a native who brought him food that the Imperial Navy, in one of its increasingly xenophobic measures, had forbidden western ships from sailing in the mandates. Synge and the precious elephant were stranded on Saipan.

Synge's hiding place was a thin strip of jungle between the beach and the road connecting the only towns on Saipan, Garapan and Charan Kanoa. The area was heavily patrolled, and Synge knew he would have to move away or eventually be discovered. He could not trust his two natives indefinitely.

So began Dillon Synge's nightmare, a hellish struggle with the jungle that dragged him to the edge of insanity. The crate was only thirty-six inches square, but it weighed two hundred pounds. Lifting it was the work of three men. Yet Synge moved it alone, with the vines and mire of the jungle conspiring against him at every step. It took two nights to push the crate a hundred yards to the railroad that ringed the island, connecting the sugar-cane fields to the Garapan docks. Synge balanced the box on a rail and slid it along, using his shoulders and back, nudging it several inches at a time. He worked from dusk to dawn, never making more than a half mile a night. After a week, he reached the outskirts of Charan Kanoa, then skirted the town on a jungle road. He moved the crate by rolling it over small branches, repeatedly transferring the branches from back to front. Three nights and two miles later, he rejoined the sugar-cane railroad as it rounded Saipan's southern shore.

Pushing endlessly against the crate quickly took its toll. Open blisters on Synge's hands and feet were not given time to heal, and they lay open, oozing pus and blood, a harvest for the numberless insects that surrounded Synge like a cloud. On the second day, the crate slid off the rail, crunching into Synge's left foot and breaking the big toe. Fighting overwhelming pain, he had set the toe and wrapped it with cloth torn from his shirt. Each time he pressed against the foot, a flame of pain shot up his leg almost to his groin. He shoved, then gritted his teeth with pain, pushed, then braced for the pain. His nights were consumed by this terrible rhythm of exertion rewarded by pain.

Synge ate once a day. His rice cakes had been quickly consumed. Now he collected anything that appeared edible along the railway. He piled grasshoppers and rats on the crate, so that at dawn he would have a substantial pile from which to choose. He quickly learned which leaves and roots could be eaten and made only one mistake. A pulpy root that tasted vaguely like mango left him balled in a fetal position, white-faced and sweating from abdominal pain for an entire day. It was his only day of rest during these weeks.

On the twentieth day, he reached the end rail line, in a cane brake near Nafutan Point, Saipan's southerly most outcropping. Another two nights brought the crate into the high ground overlooking Aslito Airfield. Here Synge had no assistance from the smooth steel of a rail line and had to force the crate over buttress stumps and around grasping quagmires toward the small caves that overlooked the airfield. On the last day of his ordeal, twenty feet from the mouth of a small opening in a cliff, his groin popped and sagged, and he slumped in agony to the pebbled ground. Convinced by the balloon hanging from his abdomen that he was dying, he crawled on all fours into the cave, where he dropped, unconscious, into a convenient nest of dried leaves.

It could have been minutes or days, but when Dillon Synge woke, he was staring down the barrel of an 8mm Nambu pistol. The menacing black dot of the barrel hovered an inch from his nose and refused to vanish when Synge blinked repeatedly. The unwavering blue steel was frightening, but paled to insignificance when compared with the savage face of its owner. He was a Japanese soldier, as evidenced by the tan kepi and ragged khaki uniform blouse. The unkempt hair protruding in gnarled tufts from the cap and the uneven grimy beard gave the man a primitive wildness, as if he had returned to the evolutionary past. Synge's eyes ventured to an exposed angry red scar near the soldier's navel, but snapped back to the ominous face when it spoke. Strained through the pain in his groin and the weeks of starvation, Synge could make little sense of the soldier's voice, something about killing Synge outright.

Synge smiled weakly and wondered at his own calm. Perhaps it was the rupture radiating hopelessness and the inevitability of defeat. He couldn't move. He could do nothing about the bullet about to tear his forehead open. Could do nothing about this filthy yellow aborigine who now possessed his elephant. His precious Kobe Elephant. He was dying for his elephant and he maintained the calm of a martyr.

Perhaps flustered by the Anglo's tranquillity, the soldier said simply, "You are in my bed."

Synge coughed then said in Japanese, "I've got a hernia. I can't move."

"Didn't you bring a truss?"

Synge stared at the savage, but didn't answer. The soldier

squatted next to him and said, "You've gone to great trouble to come to my cave. You and your crate."

Synge lowered his hand to his stomach, but was afraid to feel his testicles. Christ, he hurt down there. With a voice fogged with self-pity, he asked, "You're hiding in here. You a deserter?"

The soldier nodded absently and peered out the mouth of the cave. "I'm from Osaka," he said. "And I'm a Buddhist. Almost every Buddhist in that city has made a pilgrimage to Kobe to worship at the shrine and to wonder at the immense jade piece called the Kobe Elephant." He turned to Synge. "I opened the crate before I came in here. You've brought the Kobe Elephant to my cave."

Synge exhaled, a gesture of surrender that echoed with a pain from his groin.

"I'm tempted to end your misery," the solider continued in business tones, holstering the Nambu, "but the fact that the Kobe Elephant is in a cave in Saipan means that you are a man of endless resources and that you hope to make a profit from it. Five minutes ago, you owned the Kobe Elephant. Now you own half of it." He paused significantly. "Understand?"

The partnership was at best uneasy. The soldier's name was Nissho Ito, and he had been an intelligence officer, his euphemism for a clerk who transcribed intercepted American radio signals. He had put in ten-hour days scanning radio bands, searching for indications of warship movements and diplomatic instructions, anything. Ito's English was passable, and he and Synge quickly developed a Japanese-English pidgin.

Ito had been hiding for a month. He was reluctant to discuss his desertion, but Synge soon pieced together his story. Ito's company had long chafed under the autocratic and amateurish rule of his unit's captain, a Tokyo University educated dilettante. Ito drew the short straw and on the first moonless night entered the officer's quarters and slit the captain's throat, ear to ear. Carrying the bayonet, he walked into the jungle. He knelt ceremoniously, holding the bayonet in front of him, recited his death poem, and plunged the blade into his stomach. It had penetrated about an inch when Ito changed his mind. He pulled the blade out, wiped it clean under his arm, then plugged the stomach puncture with his torn shirt. So much for honorable hara-kiri. He walked into the jungle.

In the subsequent months, Ito proved adept at survival. While never particularly tasteful, their food was nourishing and plentiful. Synge gathered the leaves and roots and never asked the identity of the meat Ito found. The streams were disease-ridden, so rainwater was collected in a corrugated tin sheet. Ito occasionally pilfered supplies from the few huts at the airfield. He stole enough leather to make Synge a truss, which miraculously lessened his discomfort. Mutual trust was examined and discarded permanently. Ito slept with the pistol strapped tightly to his hand.

Days slipped by in a numbing montage of scavenging, eating and sleeping. The irony of being imprisoned on an island with a jade statue worth a fortune soon ceased to amuse them. Occasionally they would climb Mount Tapotchau where they witnessed the construction of the Garapan docks. The Japanese were reinforcing Saipan. It meant Ito and Synge were in for a long stay.

Ito was garrulous and resented Synge's week-long lapses into silence. During these times Synge would stare at the crate, silently mouthing a mysterious invocation. At other times, Synge would talk for hours of his early years in Singapore, of his trading successes, of his mansion, of his club. These tales would invariably end with the present reality of Saipan, at which point Synge would become increasingly incoherent until he was sputtering mindlessly. Ito would throw a scrap of food at him and angrily leave the cave.

Synge was most rational in the mornings, and it was then they discussed escape. Endless hours were dedicated to planning the capture of a ship or an airplane. But the boats all required enormous crews and, although Synge said he could fly virtually any aircraft, the planes were heavily guarded. They had been on Saipan sixteen months when the solution finally came to them. They would arrange for the United States government to pluck them from the island.

The airfield on the south peninsula had been carved out of the jungle. Its half-mile long gravel strip was complemented by four service shacks and a dilapidated hangar. It was a subsidiary field and landings were infrequent. Crews were small. The shacks contained little more than cots, tools, and fuel barrels. And a short-wave radio.

In June 1937, Synge spent four days watching the hut. Finally, all four Japanese crewmen serviced a reconnaissance plane at the east end of the field, where its engine had failed. He signaled Ito, who simply walked from the jungle into the hut and carried away the radio and battery.

Synge and Ito installed the radio on the hill above their cliff. A pilfered length of wire was strung between two trees and acted as an antenna. They limited broadcasts to one minute a day, hoping to avoid directional finders the Japanese might be using to locate the stolen radio. The same message was sent every day, repeated in English four times each on eight frequencies. "Imperial Navy intelligence officer wishes to defect with documents. Return signal on this channel in twenty-four hours." Before broadcasting, they would scan the channels, searching for replies to the previous day's radiocast.

Two weeks passed and the only response was static. Each day their hope diminished and their plan seemed less brilliant. Synge sank into despondency. Even Ito seemed grim and resigned.

Finally, one morning during the receiving scan, they heard a distant cackling: "Intelligence officer, can you identify yourself and your location?"

Synge began a joyful two-step, and Ito bent toward the transmitter. On the spur of the moment, he gave himself a promotion. "This is Captain Nissho Ito, Imperial Navy Intelligence Corps, based on Saipan."

There was a momentary pause, and Ito feared the transmission had faded. Then, "Outline what you have and how we can get it and you off the island."

"I have one hundred pounds of documents, transcribed high-level radio communications from the War Ministry to Admiral Hirano on Saipan. All made within the past three months. I suggest a cargo plane pick-up, flying in from the east so it lands away from the hangar."

"Twenty-four hours. Out."

A day later they learned the pick-up would be made in one week at 0900. There would be no further communications, but both parties would be at their radios each morning.

Two days later, Ito took the greatest risk of his stay in seclusion on the island. He ventured into Charan Kanoa to steal a one-ton truck. During that day Synge worked frantically, pulling jungle vegetation from the ground and stacking it in a pile above the mouth of the cave. Ito returned in a Mitsubishi army tonner, which he parked in the underbrush near the airfield. It took them a full day to drag the crate from the cave to the truck.

During his last night on Saipan, Dillon Synge listened closely to Ito's breathing, waiting for it to lengthen to the placid wind of sleep. He glanced repeatedly at the Nambu pistol securely tied to the soldier's wrist. Ito would never have made it as a trader, Synge thought. Too trusting, despite his precautions with the pistol.

Synge guessed it was three in the morning when Ito finally dropped into sleep. Very slowly, Synge crept from the cave, following a path he had carefully cleared of noisy twigs and leaves that morning. He climbed the hill to his pile of dried vegetation, then returned with an enormous load in his arms. He made six more trips, each time returning with an armload of brush until dried vegetation filled most of the shallow cave. As dawn's first light speckled the hill, Synge put a match to the brush.

The fire flashed through the brush as if it were gunpowder, moving quickly into the cave. Black smoke whirled about the cave's mouth, and Synge had to back away from the heat. Through the snapping of the fire came Ito's muted screams. They died with the fire.

Fifteen minutes passed before Synge could enter the cave. Ito was oddly free of burns. Synge guessed he had died of smoke inhalation. He untied the cords and peeled the Nambu from his partner's hand.

The jade dealer was behind the wheel of the tonner when the Electra landed at the airfield that morning. He pulled the truck onto the runway toward the plane. The navigator emerged from the plane and didn't ask questions about the weight of the crate as he helped Synge load the elephant. When Synge ordered the pilot out of the plane, he was dumbfounded that a woman dropped to the ground. It made it more difficult, but not impossible, to fire the Nambu at them.

As the plane lifted from the runway, Synge was exultant. He was once again the owner of the Kobe Elephant. The full owner. It was not until a week later, while reading the *Straits Times*, that he realized he had shot Amelia Earhart.

"I'm sorry, gentlemen," Synge said to the jade buyers as they filed out, forgetting he had already offered an excuse, "but I've got other appointments this afternoon. I've told my secretary not to schedule me so tightly. Next time I hope we can do a little socializing in my office."

Synge walked down the hallway to his office, to the pedestal. The expression on his face could have been a smile as he touched the air where the elephant's trunk should have been. He didn't have the elephant, but he was, nonetheless, a trader. The Japanese had gotten nothing out of the deal. Gota's rebellion succeeded in capturing a square mile of Tokyo in what came to be known as the Two-Twenty-Six Incident. Seven people were killed before the rebels surrendered peacefully. Gota and twelve other rebel leaders were executed. The Buddhists in the Kobe Temple had gotten nothing. Ito had gotten nothing. But Synge had the Kobe Elephant. Or rather, Kiril Stasov had it. Synge flushed and bared his teeth. Kiril Stasov had his elephant. But that would change.

Synge pressed the intercom. "Flynn, send Abdul Razak to my office." By the king's blood, he would possess that sacred animal once again.

VII

Cynthia made herb poultices for their running
sores. They had a dozen infections between them,
open ulcers that festered rather than healed.

Ronald Sealth sat on the toilet in the terminal of Singapore's
Kallang Airfield. The lid was down and his pants were up.
On his knees was one of his three suitcases. They were
identical in shape and size, all of them Samsonite. He had
paid thirty dollars each for two of them. The one open across
his knees cost two hundred.

That was the price the Wilshire Boulevard cobbler charged
to install the false bottom. Sealth had at first laughed at the
idea. No customs inspector would be fooled by a double-
bottomed bag. But this suitcase was a work of art. A small
compartment was concealed by an expanding hinge. All the
angles conformed to a stock suitcase. There were no suspicious flaps and no extraneous stitching. Sealth's jade phallus
fitted the concealed compartment perfectly.

Sealth was a law-abiding American and proud of it. He
paid every cent of his customs tax. He had already filled out
forms covering the six thousand dollars of jade he had purchased in Singapore and Hong Kong for resale at his Los
Angeles shop. The government had every right to tax the
jade he would sell for a profit.

But no right at all to penalize him for adding to his private collection of jade phalli. Taxing profits was one thing, taxing an important art collection another.

Sealth positioned the flap exactly as the cobbler had taught him, then marveled again at the hidden pocket. And at his own cunning. He lifted several boxer shorts from the suitcase, then wiped them in the ordure at the base of the toilet, letting the underwear soak in the green-brown stain. Holding the fouled shorts with two fingers, he carefully placed them over the Samsonite's false bottom. He hadn't met a customs inspector yet who would dig through such vilely abused underwear, especially after Sealth murmured apologetically, "Colonitis. A bit messy, I'm afraid." Sealth folded the suitcase and locked the clasps.

The first blow put a fist-size dent into the stall door and echoed loudly against the restroom's stone walls. Sealth tightened in a spastic convulsion that almost toppled him from the toilet. A second strike ruptured the stall's hasp and the door flew inward, slapping painfully against Sealth's knees. The jade buyer convulsively gripped his suitcase at the sight of the heavy-chested maniac stepping through the stall door, his fists curled into wrecking balls. With one swift movement, Joseph Snow grabbed Sealth by the lapels, lifted him from the toilet seat, tore the suitcase from his grip, and tossed it over his shoulder to Ko Tsukada.

"Taking a long time, weren't you?" Snow asked politely. He was holding Sealth a foot off the floor, and kept him there, in place over the toilet, until Tsukada had shredded the suitcase. Tsukada pulled the phallus through the soiled underwear and wiped it with a towel. He said easily, "Just as we thought. He was doing a little suitcase importing."

"What is it?" Snow asked, slowly lowering Sealth, whose face had turned purple with fright.

"A life-size jade sculpture of a white man's genitals," Tsukada said.

A smile spread across Snow's face. "A white man's?"

"Too small to be Japanese."

Snow pulled Sealth out of the stall. The jade importer's legs were rubbery and there was a damp stain on his pants. His eyes stuttered between his assailant's massive fists and the phallus, which Tsukada delicately held in his cupped hands like a communion wafer.

Standing between the importer and the restroom exit,

Snow asked, "Is there some reason you can't declare this piece of art?"

Sealth's voice was ragged. "Are you customs officers?"

"Answer the question."

"Well," Sealth struggled, "actually I'm returning it to the States. I brought it here for a show and rather than fill out all the forms proving I didn't buy it here, I thought I'd just. . . ."

"Not good enough," Snow interrupted. "You purchased this piece from Dillon Synge today. What's it cost? Three thousand?"

"I wouldn't pay three thousand dollars for that," Sealth scoffed unconvincingly.

"Then you wouldn't mind if we checked," Tsukada said, stepping toward the door. "The customs officials usually know the value of something like this."

"Wait," Sealth held up a hand. "Yes, I paid a bit more." His eyes flickered to the ruined stall door, then to Snow's hands. "If you were going to ask the customs officials, it means you two aren't with customs." Strength poured back into his voice. "And if you were here to rob me, you wouldn't waste your time with pleasant conversation."

Snow nodded. "We're just here for some answers. About Dillon Synge, your jade supplier."

Sealth raised himself to the balls of his feet, to Snow's eye level. Perspiration was running from his brow like a watershed and his hands were still trembling, but he said in a steady voice, "We in the jade business don't discuss each other."

Tsukada stepped into the stall, and at the sound of the phallus dropping into the toilet, Sealth withered. The Japanese asked pleasantly, "Think this will flush?"

"Only one way to tell," Snow replied.

"Please don't. Wait." The jade buyer ran a hand across his face. His eyes riveted on Tsukada's foot as it pressed lightly on the flush button. "I don't know much about him, really. I just buy, buy his offerings. Never much idle conversation." Sealth's words wavered as if in a strong wind.

"We heard that after a session he often invites buyers into his office," Snow prompted.

"Sometimes. That is, he used to. Not anymore."

"Why not?"

Sealth attempted a shrug, but his shoulders were constricted with the fear of losing the phallus, and the gesture resembled a shiver. "I don't know. I've talked about it with

110

other buyers, and none have been invited for a drink since before the Japanese occupation."

"What was in his office that was so attractive, other than the whiskey?" Snow asked.

Sealth was silent for a moment, then equivocated. "Not much really. I . . ."

Tsukada pressured the handle and water began to leak into the bowl.

Sealth's words were suddenly a torrent. "He had the Kobe Elephant in there. I've seen it. So've the others. He would pour us a drink and we would all admire the elephant. Christ, it was a wonderful piece, full of history and tradition. Used to have it right there in his own office. I could tell he got enormous satisfaction from showing it off." The water stopped running, and Sealth allowed himself a breath.

"You seem to be suggesting he doesn't have the elephant anymore," Snow said.

"I don't know for sure. But I think he'd still be showing it if he had it. Synge was a sour man, but, God, he'd light up showing off that elephant. Not anymore. Now he's completely bitter, and I think that means his elephant is gone."

"Could he have sold it?"

"Not on his life," Sealth said. "He loved the Kobe Elephant like a man loves a woman."

"What do you think happened to it?" Tsukada asked, fishing in the toilet bowl with his hand. He wiped the phallus with a towel and handed it to Sealth.

"Synge would never part with it voluntarily. I think it was stolen or lost in the war." The jade importer picked up his ravaged suitcase and squinted at what was left of his hidden pocket. He dropped the bag into a trash can near the sink.

"Did he ever mention how he came to own it?" Snow asked.

Sealth shook his head. "No, and he made it very clear we weren't to ask him." He turned the phallus over in his hand. "Now I suppose I'll have to pay duty on this piece. I have a collection of them, you know. Never paid a single cent duty on my private collection."

"There's a leather worker on New Market Road named Wo Yi who'll make you a new case, trap and all, that'll make this one look amateurish," Tsukada said. "If you tell him you are a friend of Rose's, he'll do it overnight, and you can leave Singapore tomorrow."

Sealth brightened. "Rose? Who is Rose?"

111

"Wo Yi will know."

"Well, I guess I can postpone my departure a day." Sealth stepped to the restroom door, then turned back. "I don't know why I should mention this to you, I certainly don't owe you two anything. But you should be very careful dealing with Dillon Synge. I don't know how he got the Kobe Elephant, but the Japanese Buddhists in Kobe didn't just give it to him."

Snow nodded his thanks, and after Sealth left the room he said, "This makes it a bit more difficult for us."

"For me, anyway," Tsukada said, washing his hands. "The fact that Synge doesn't have the elephant means I can't steal it back." The towel dispenser was empty, so he shook his hands, then ran them along his pants.

"It complicates it for me, too. Synge knew I was in Singapore long before I was aware he had anything to do with Amelia Earhart's disappearance. Those two thugs who jumped us from the monsoon drain must've been his men. He was afraid I'd expose him, so he planned to take me out."

"You can assume he's still planning that."

The three sat at the teak table in the hong. The high ceiling above them was perforated with many windows, allowing the north light to saturate the tasting-room table below. The room was adorned with rotating fans, a luxury that spoke of the importance of the Asia Tea Company. Caged canaries filled the room with their spring chirps.

The table was covered with several varieties of tea leaves. The room's exposure to the north light allowed the merchants to closely inspect color and texture. White cups were arranged around the circular table, ready for the tasting to begin.

Sun Chen was the hong's proprietor, and he would normally have been filling each cup with an exact proportion of tea and boiling water, sipping each variety, then spitting out the tea onto the floor, determining which leaves met his standards. But this morning the water cauldron was quiet and the cups empty. His employees were waiting in the yard, knowing that when Sun Chen met with these two, he was not to be disturbed.

They were the principals of the Orchid Brotherhood, a protective society active in Singapore since the turn of the century and, before that, for a hundred years in China's

Hunan province. The upper echelon of the Brotherhood, these three men represented Singapore's wealthiest Chinese merchants, each of whom owed his position and wealth to his association with the society. The Orchid Brotherhood was a stabilizing factor in Singapore's Chinatown. They donated money to temples and orphanages, they aided widows and students. The Brotherhood's sources of revenue consisted primarily of the profits from murder, kidnapping, extortion, and the extraction of dues from "members." The years of deadly machinations among Singapore's Chinese societies had resulted in the Orchid Brotherhood emerging intact and powerful. The society had matured and grown conservative. But it was still capable of moving ruthlessly in matters of vengeance or money. This meeting at the hong concerned both.

Sun Chen rolled a tea leaf between thumb and forefinger. "Then it is agreed. Something must be done." His gnarled face resembled a tree trunk and was adorned with a white goatee. "Now we must decide what."

"Perhaps if we talked to a few of the mullahs," Li Chia-ping suggested. He had made a fortune running opium into Shanghai in the twenties. He became addicted gradually and had no memory of the years during which his fortune dissipated and his gums turned yellow from eating opium. He left the poppy when his money ran out, emigrated to Singapore and began selling insurance. His business relied largely on arson. Those who refused Li's fire insurance had fires. "Most of the Moslem religious leaders are reasonable men. They will listen to us."

"It is too late to talk," Sun Chen countered. "You know as well as I do that the Pekin temple was sacked two days ago. None of the worshippers or monks was killed, but the shrine was ruined, and three persons are still in the hospital. We need to warn the rioters in terms they will understand."

The third man at the table smiled brightly. His name was Kao Kuei-tze. He was a Teochew from China's Swatow region, and for ten years he had controlled the *swaylos*, the dock workers, most of whom he had coerced into joining the brotherhood. He said jovially, "Then it is my work you want, eh, Sun? A little push and shove, all for understanding's sake."

"Precisely. Our neighborhood will be besieged with row-dies if this is not stopped. Governor Longstreet has been chirping and chirping, with all the effect of a parakeet. What makes anyone think more talk will calm the Moslem zealots?"

Li answered, "Don't you think, Sun, that we are growing out of that? There are many ways to pressure people, and the fist should always be the last resort."

Sun angrily shook his head. "Not so in this case. The zealots are dense and unreasoning and their ferocity is growing. Five temples on Singapore and one on the West Reach have been overrun by them. And it is always the same. Monks beaten, holy icons desecrated or stolen." His hand slapped the table. "This has to stop before our own people are killed."

Kao nodded. "Our people are looking to us for help. The British and their incompetent Gurkha police cannot do anything. One of the monks injured on Pekin Street was from a Brotherhood family, and we've done nothing about it. Our people are beginning to feel we have deserted them."

Li sighed audibly, so uncharacteristic that all eyes turned to him. He said, "You are right, Sun. Our money and safety depend on not letting these riots get out of hand. We must act, but cautiously."

Kao smiled again. "I take it you will want me to handle this?"

The two others nodded. In Kao's employ were certain *swaylos* who had never lifted a box or pulled a line. They were the strong arm of the Brotherhood.

Sun Chen said quietly, "Nothing serious. These people need a warning, that's all."

Again they nodded. Their leave taking was quiet and dignified. Li Chia-ping's limousine was waiting at the door. Kao Kuei-tze disappeared into the crowded streets, as he always did. And, as Sun always did, he waited until his guests were gone, then walked several blocks into white Singapore, to a safe telephone near the Cold Storage. He dialed and waited.

Sun Chen had been a tea wholesaler for seven years and a communist for ten. When the woman answered the consulate telephone, Sun asked for Kiril Stasov.

Bahadur Sak was born in Punjab and raised in Singapore. Like many Sikhs, he was a jaga, a contract watchman who guarded hotels, ships, anything. Sak was an orthodox Sikh who abided by the five k's. He wore Kesh, long hair which preserved God-given form; a Kanga, a comb to keep the hair clean; a Kirpan, the sword to defend the weak; the Kachhaihra, short drawers to ease movement; and the Karra, a steel bangle signifying strict discipline.

Sak was a tall, sinewy man, whose corded muscles were wrapped tightly around his dark arms and legs. His low brows and black beard gave him a ferocious appearance. He was an ascetic who adhered to rigid habits and orthodox belief, a man of little introspection. In the small world of the jaga and the larger sphere of wealthy Singapore businessmen, Sak was renowned. He was the only contract guard in the city who used dogs.

He owned five of them, three German shepherds and two Alsatians, all blindly loyal to their master and all terrifyingly savage. The dogs seemed to be extensions of the Sikh, ferocious but highly disciplined. They were trained to voice commands and hand signals, and two of the shepherds would attack whomever Sak was looking at when he winked his right eye twice. Depending upon the signal, the dogs would charge either for the intruder's arm or his groin, would attack silently or with great commotion, would inflict superficial flesh wounds or leave an arm permanently crippled.

His dogs made Sak the most expensive jaga in Singapore. The Crown had gladly paid the price for protection during the king's visit. During the early years of the war, Sak had guarded American military payrolls going into China through Singapore, and Chinese bullion being shipped away from danger. Twice monthly Sak escorted opium shipments from Keppel Harbor to the refinery in Chinatown. He asked no questions, and his clients never questioned the bill. Dillon Synge was a favorite client, always paying on time, always complimenting Sak's animals. Sak gladly accepted the three-dog, twenty-four-hour assignment of guarding the jade merchant's dock on Singapore's West Reach.

The rented Ford churned through Lokyang, a muddy village southwest of the city. Snow pulled mightily at the steering wheel, but the car had a will of its own, following the ruts in the road like a trolley. He kept the accelerator pedal on the firewall, which resulted in a grudging speed of thirty miles an hour.

"Tell me again how you figure to meet Dillon Synge?" Ko Tsukada asked. Several sheets of paper covered his lap.

"Governor Longstreet provided the list of Buddhist temples in and around Singapore that have recently been sacked. The second list came from my chief, Howard Lester, and shows Dillon Synge's assets. We know that a temple in Kuala Lumpur fell victim to a Malay riot several hours before the Electra made its last flight. Synge went out to the airfield to greet the plane, we think, to receive the items stolen from the temple." Snow slowed the Ford, guiding it around an ox cart loaded with sugar cane. "Longstreet says that early this morning a small temple in Sungaiguntung, across the Strait of Malacca, was looted. I think Synge's men instigated that riot, and that Synge will bring the temple's treasures into Singapore shortly. We've seen to it that he no longer has a plane, and you can see from Lester's list, that he owns several boats, so it makes sense that he'll use the boats to smuggle the stolen goods in. His dock is on the West Reach."

"So what's your plan?" Tsukada asked, folding the papers.

Snow shrugged. "We'll steal the jade treasures back."

Tsukada imitated the shrug and said dryly, "Nice plan. I don't suppose you could be more specific."

"We'll meet the boat when it docks. Any cargo is most vulnerable during those minutes between ship and shore. We'll take it then."

"How?"

"We'll think of something."

"It had better be good," Tsukada warned. "Synge will be alert to all angles. Ever since the Electra burned, he'll have been on his guard. We can expect resistance."

Snow considered for a moment. "If we get the temple's jade and gold back for the monks, fine, but if not, I'm not going to worry about it. Our main concern should be letting Synge know we're on to his racket. If we pressure him hard enough, he'll spurt out of Singapore."

Dusk turns to darkness quickly in the tropics, and as they approached the West Reach, Snow turned the Ford's headlights on. They neared the west coast of the island and Snow reduced speed, looking for the cove. The small island of Singapore has over two hundred miles of coastline, and most of the West Reach section is variegated with inlets and lagoons overhung with jungle canopy. The Reach has been used for two hundred years by Thai and Malay pirates, British gun runners and Chinese opium smugglers. Governor Longstreet had said that Synge made no secret of his small dock in Bryte's Cove, near Point Merawang, the island's westerly tip. Moored there would be a pleasure launch and a converted PT boat. The governor had assured Snow that the PT boat's torpedo tubes and machine guns had long ago been removed.

The road became increasingly narrow and the mud more tenacious as they neared the water. Snow flipped off the lights. Through the trees was the sea, rippling moonlight like a crystal chandelier. When Snow guessed they were within a quarter mile of the cove, he pulled the car onto a turnaround, grabbed two spare clips for his .45 and followed Tsukada down the jungle road.

With every step they sank to their ankles. Snow curled his toes, levering his shoes against his heels, hoping to keep them on his feet. The road was two ruts cut through the mangrove swamp. Snow held his arm up, warding off the liana and spider webs. The dark jungle closed in on them as if they were walking into a cave, blocking out moonlight and the evening breeze. Snow's shin rammed a buttress trunk and he cursed under his breath. He followed the gurgling sounds of Tsukada's footsteps ahead of him.

With startling abruptness, the jungle opened to the cove. Spread before them was a body of calm water no more than five hundred yards across and ringed with drooping mangrove trees that completely hid the banks. Only thirty yards of the cove's shoreline had been cleared. Extending from that bank was a dilapidated dock, its pylons and planks tenuously held together by raffia rope. At the far end of the dock was a Malay *lanca,* a three-masted launch which, from its conspicuous stacks, appeared to have been converted to diesel. The ship was dark and there was no movement on its decks. On the shore near the *lanca* was an automobile. It, too, was dark.

Snow saw the phosphorescent ripple of a wake before he heard the boat. Within seconds, the low drone of its engines overcame the muffling effect of the jungle, and the murmur filled the cove. Snow and Tsukada back-stepped into the jungle and squatted among the ferns. Tsukada drew a pistol from his waistband as Snow pushed aside fern leaves for a view of the incoming boat.

It was Synge's converted PT boat, running with its lights out. The gunboat decks were slung low, and its clean lines made it appear as if it were prowling across the black water, stalking an unsuspecting shore. A deck hand appeared through the forward hatch. With the moon at his back, the man was a smudged silhouette. He walked forward, casting bumpers over the starboard gunwales. The boat glided past the launch and drew near the dock. Snow saw the pilot's head above the bridge windshield. Suffused by the diesel's rumble, splinters of conversation carried to shore. With ghostly presence, the boat slipped to the dock and soundlessly bumped the rub rail.

The hand jumped to the deck and secured the lines to the bollards. A second man appeared from the aft cabin. His shoulders were hunched forward, and his hands were at his stomach holding a heavy object. It wasn't until he had moved to the starboard rail that Snow saw it was an iron strongbox. With difficulty, the man lowered the box to the deck and waited for the other deckhand to swing a small gangplank to the dock.

"I'm going to lift that box," Snow whispered. "We can't do anything to the boat."

"And me?"

"Cover me, but I want your presence known. Loose a shot into the hull. It might prevent them from making a move."

Tsukada stared over his shoulder into the jungle. It was as dark as a raven's wing.

"Did you hear me?" Snow whispered, following Tsukada's gaze.

"I heard something." The Japanese answered almost inaudibly, holding up a hand like a traffic policeman.

"Christ, I hope not," Snow said anxiously, turning to the dock, where the second hand was descending the gangplank. "We've got to move."

"Wait a minute." Tsukada continued to stare into the underbrush, his head cocked and his body rigid with concentration. Thirty seconds passed and he relaxed. "I guess not."

Snow immediately rose from his crouch, his gun hand moving slowly in front of him like a blind man's cane, and edged toward the PT boat. In the darkness, it must have been impossible for the crew to see Snow's face or his weapon, but the men slowly raised their hands above their heads.

Snow pivoted the .45 to the boat and lined it on the midriff of the crewman carrying the strongbox. He said in a hard voice, "Bring the box here." From his loose blouse and shorts, Snow guessed the man was a Malay. When the crewman hesitated and glanced over his shoulder at the bridge, Snow barked, "A stupid move will be your last. Bring it here."

Again he hesitated. A shot from the jungle behind Snow shattered the bridge windshield. The man carrying the strongbox jumped reflexively, and Snow feared the box would topple into the water. The Malay regained his footing, glanced at the other deckhand, then walked down the plank. He lay the box on the dock several yards from Snow. The Malay's hands rose above his head.

Snow scanned the bridge, then the decks. The pilot had disappeared. He backed several steps toward the protective darkness of the jungle and ordered, "Call your captain out."

He was answered with the roar of the twin diesels and the high scream of gear boxes grinding into reverse. The boat churned aft, plowing white water almost over the stern rail. It came within a yard of the launch before the screws reversed and the boat growled forward.

Another shot sounded from the jungle; this bullet thudded into the forward cabin below the bridge. Firing pistols at a heavily armored gunboat was futile. "Let him go, Tsukada. We've got the box." He realigned his pistol on the two Malays.

Within seconds, the boat had disappeared. Its only trace was the cove's water, still white and churning with prop backwash.

"You," Snow jabbed the pistol in the direction of the nearest Malay, "follow me with the box."

A flutter at the corner of Snow's eyes. Then a writhing demon leaped from the center of the earth and tore into Snow's gun arm. White hot lances pierced his arm to the bone. A red eye flashed wildly then fell away behind a curtain of frost-white daggers. The demon kicked at Snow's stomach and groin, pulling down and away, trying to wrench off his arm and to return to the depths with its bloodied prize. In a spasm of pain and fear, Snow yanked his arm to his body, but the devil came with it, screaming like a banshee, its red eyes on fire.

Not until its frothing mouth brushed his cheek did Snow realize the demon was a dog, an enormous German shepherd. Snow felt the sharp teeth grind as chips of bone gave way under the assault. Blood splashed over the dog's head and bubbled out of its mouth. The shepherd twisted wildly, trying to tear the arm loose. Suddenly, Snow's ravaged arm seemed to float away, to become less his and more an ugly extension of the demon's red-flecked mouth.

The animal whipped against the dead weight of Snow's body, causing Snow's free hand to slap against its head. There was a familiarity in that slap, something correct, something protective. Slowly, Snow's training began to return to him and penetrate his terror.

He balled his left hand and swung at the dog's head. The first blow was tentative, searching for the target that writhed insanely in front of him. He struggled to his feet, giving the animal ground to steady its mammoth head. Snow dropped his fist to his thigh, then launched it at the animal's cheek. His strength was draining from his arm and his head was spinning from fear and pain, but the fist caught the head squarely. Without waiting to determine its effect, Snow struck again, and again.

But the howling continued and the fangs kept flashing. The dog's eyes were locked on Snow's, daring him to reclaim his arm. Snow aimed at the eye and like a jackhammer, began a powerful tattoo.

After only seconds of rhythmic pounding, which seemed like hours, the dog's jaw relaxed its grip. Snow's fist worked like a piston, jabbing at the head. Jab, relax, jab, relax . . . comfort.

As suddenly as it began, the attack ended. The fangs pulled out of Snow's arm and the head fell away. Snow struggled for footing, then grabbed his devastated limb with his left hand. The arm was pulpy and damp. Giddy with shock and pain, he turned to the Malay deckhands.

One had disappeared into the jungle, the other had lowered his hands and was eyeing the strongbox. Snow glanced at the mire at his feet, searching for the .45. The dog lay there, a crumpled pile of blood-matted fur. Snow's throat tightened, and his stomach began pumping upward.

He had no time to vomit. Tsukada's fearful call stopped it. Snow looked up. Another dog was coming at him out of the darkness. Without thinking, Snow spun his good hand into a vicious left hook. His fist plowed into the animal's snout, stunning it, stopping it in midair. The German shepherd fell to its feet, shook its head once, and lowered its haunches for another spring at Snow.

The crack of Tsukada's Nambu rolled across the cove, and the shepherd toppled onto the dock. Lying on its side, the dog kicked its rear legs once, prompting Tsukada to fire again. The bullet slid into the dog. This time there was no movement.

Snow rolled his head up and blinked several times, an impossible effort. A brown man in a turban was standing at the end of the dock near the launch's stern. His teeth were bared and glowed like a beacon in his black beard. Near his legs was an Alsatian, frozen at the command of its master. Bahadur Sak's gaze bounced between his dead dogs and Snow.

Ko Tsukada struggled from the jungle, the Nambu pointed at the Sikh. He walked steadily toward the trainer, and his finger was bringing back the pistol's trigger when Snow yelled weakly, "Let him go."

"What about the dog?" Tsukada asked incredulously.

Snow stared at his mangled arm. "I don't care." Tsukada was bringing the Nambu up again when Snow called, "Wait. Let it go, too."

Tsukada waved the pistol at the Sikh. With a few clucked words, Sak back-stepped, blended with the underbrush, and was gone. The Alsatian followed silently. The remaining Malay had fled with the strongbox.

Snow sagged to his knees. His arm was a mass of red. The torn skin was indistinguishable from the shredded shirt sleeve. Only Tsukada's rough hand on his shoulder prevented Snow from toppling.

"Can you walk?" Tsukada demanded.

"My arm's gone." The words were distant and hollow.

The Japanese pulled Snow to his feet and leaned into him as he swayed like a tree in a gale.

Snow stared with glazed eyes at his lacerated arm. "God, I feel like bawling."

Tsukada slung Snow's good arm over his shoulder and guided him away from the cove. "I'll get you to a doctor."

Almost without moving his lips, Snow murmured, "We failed, didn't we? I mean, we never had a chance against the dogs. Another Joe Louis." The words were very faint. Tsukada knew Snow was losing his head. "Joe Louis again."

VIII

The days were blurred by smothering heat and
incandescent light. She would squint her eyes,
and three or four days would vanish, lost forever.

The lorry was dangerously overloaded. As it pushed through
the water propelled by a tiny Liliput outboard engine, it
displayed less than three inches freeboard, not enough to
prevent the small waves of the Johore Strait from spilling
over the bow. Twelve Malays were crowded into that boat,
some occupying slat benches, others squatting above the
lathe false deck. Their tissue cotton *bajus* and ragged shorts
were held together by habit and little else. Most were barefoot,
but a few had rubber tire sandals such as the retreating
Japanese troops had worn. Most carried small cloth bundles
which held all their worldly possessions. Some did not have
even that.

Their similarity extended beyond the shabby clothing.
They were all young men, none over twenty-five. But they all
appeared older, for they wore poverty on their faces like
masks. Sunken cheeks, protruding eyes, blue veins visible
through translucent skin, brittle arms and legs. They should
have sat muted, somber.

Far from it. The atmosphere in the small boat was taut
with expectation. The clipped fragments of subdued conversation suggested a nervousness they were eager to hide.
Their eyes scanned the shoreline anxiously, a black smudge

on a gray-blue sky. The boat was crossing the Johore Strait, the thin band of water separating the Peninsula from Singapore Island.

As they neared the island coastline, several Malays began a slow rocking, as if to propel the boat faster. The pilot stood aft, his hand on the engine arm. He squinted into the soft sea breeze, and when he saw a brief flash from shore, he veered the boat a few degrees starboard. His passengers stopped their movement.

Without shoal beacons or a white line of breakers, the placid shore was indistinguishable from the black water, and the tillerman started when the bow crunched onto the sand. He quickly lifted the Liliput's prop out of the water. His passengers climbed over the gunwales and walked up the beach, quickly at first, then more hesitantly as they approached the rows of rubber trees. Perhaps they had been expecting a greeting party, or at least some congratulations, but the narrow strip of beach was empty.

The boat backed away from shore. Within a minute, the sputter of the small motor had faded, and the only sounds on the beach were the water's quiet lapping, a rustling of rubber tree leaves, and the increasingly erratic breathing of the Malays.

A jeep slipped through the brake near the water's edge. It bore down on them, dredging through the damp sand, whining in low gear. Its headlights cast a bouncing nimbus on the sand. Dillon Synge was at the wheel, fighting the grasping sand. Kiril Stasov held a flashlight, trying to scan several documents on his lap, but the rough ride made it impossible, and he slipped them back into a manila folder. Abdul Razak was sitting in the jump seat, his hands above his head clutching the roll bar.

The jeep pulled alongside the crowd of Malays and Razak called several orders. Synge turned the vehicle into the plantation and drove slowly down a service road. The Malays followed in the jeep's tracks.

Stasov put a foot on the jeep's square fender and asked, "Where do you get them all?"

"The problem is keeping them away. I have a list of hundreds of Malay Moslems anxious to give up the poverty of life on the Peninsula for a chance to live in Singapore. The city of gold streets."

"Why don't they just swim the Strait?"

"The British police eventually catch them and ship them back to Malaysia. If they've got a skill, like plumbing or carpentry, Singapore welcomes them. But if all they are bringing is hunger and the clothes on their back, they don't stay long."

"Ever had any trouble with them?" Stasov asked, looking over his shoulder at the double row of Malays snaking behind the jeep. Their confidence seemed to have returned collectively, and their smiles flashed like fireflies in the darkness.

"Seldom. Our deal is simple. If they follow Razak for one week, doing exactly as he tells them, they'll get their papers. Those are samples you have in the envelope. When we get to the shack, I'll pass them around so they can see what Singapore permanent visa documents look like, so they can envision having a set of them with their names on them. Free and clear in the City of the Lion. Most plan to find jobs, learn a skill, then send for their families."

"And they don't balk at Razak's orders?" Stasov asked. The jeep approached a slat shack tucked between rows of rubber trees. Several latex barrels stood in the grass near the hut.

"They have been led to expect the worst, to be prepared to do anything. They are greatly relieved to learn that Razak isn't going to ask them to kill someone. When all they're asked to do is form a crowd and follow some Anglos for several blocks, shouting insults, they even look forward to it."

"And what about the temples?"

Synge smiled. The moon slipped from behind a cloud and briefly illuminated his face. "Razak watches our immigrants closely. When he sees one who displays enthusiasm in his work, he'll make a little side deal. The men we use to sack the temples get a few dollars for their efforts. I've been using this scheme for a year."

"Untrained people can get carried away in situations like that."

Synge's laugh sounded like sandpaper on rough wood. "What if they do get carried away? What's it to either of us?"

Stasov shrugged. "Not much, I guess."

Synge pulled the jeep into a tight circle in front of the shack. Without being told, the Malays surrounded the jeep. Razak stood so he could address them. The mullah began with whispered words so the Malays had to lean forward. He was smiling, earnest and confidential, a man to be trusted.

He used the lilting Malay language as poetry, letting the truth and wisdom of his words waft to his audience. He seemed to emphasize the breadth of his generosity, how they had been given this one chance to escape poverty. His requirements were simple; he only expected complete loyalty. He talked of Singapore, of its white buildings, green *padangs* and busy harbor, of the money to be made, just waiting for them. Then, in broad strokes, he told them that Singapore was part of Malaysia, had always been, but that the Chinese were trying to steal it from them. The Chinese owned all the shops in Singapore. They made vast fortunes, always sending the money back to China. Soon his audience was nodding and a few raised their fists in support of Razak's words.

Synge and Stasov walked away from the crowd. The Russian lit a dark cigarette and tossed the dead match at the trunk of a rubber tree. He pulled deeply at the smoke. "Are you getting any readings from Governor Longstreet?"

"That old fool doesn't know whether he's coming or going. At a club function the other night, he was frothing at the mouth like a spent horse. He has no idea what's going on. The Malays attack. The Chinese grumble, then threaten. His British sense of order is outraged. That fop who works for him, Bliss, pats him down and smoothes out his feathers, but the governor senses he's losing it."

Stasov nodded. "Think he's sending cables?"

"What else can he do? He has no control over the Malays or the Chinese. His riot police always arrive ten minutes late. The community leaders know he's ineffective, so they no longer communicate with him. Singapore is seething, and the only thing the governor can do is send cables to London." Synge glanced at the Malays. They had closed in on Razak's jeep, and several were examining the sample visas, holding them tenderly, as if they might crumble to dust in their hands. "Longstreet has a new theme, you know." He paused, forcing Stasov to respond.

"A new theme?"

"He's babbling about the communists," Synge said.

"The rebel gunmen in the swamps?"

Synge shook his head. "Our governor has cast about for someone to blame and has settled on the communists. Not the potshots and the stray zealots, but you Soviets."

Stasov stared at the glowing tip of his cigarette. "Does he

have anything concrete? Anything that'll alarm the Foreign Office?"

"I don't think so." Synge paused meaningfully. "At least not until he learns something, which he just might any day."

Stasov's gaze shot to the jade buyer. "Was that a threat, Synge? Are you threatening me?"

Unlike a hundred times in the past, Synge would not break from the Russian's cold stare. "No more than you've been threatening me every day since you took the elephant."

"Took it?" The Russian's laugh was grating. "You forget, Dillon. You gave the elephant to me, and gladly. It was me or the Japanese, remember?"

Synge spat, "I had bloody little choice in the matter."

Much less choice than Synge knew. Kiril Stasov was a survivor of the purges, and that alone attested to his cunning and ruthlessness. A career diplomat, he had been swept into the vacuum created by Stalin's deadly housecleaning and had found himself posted to Singapore as Soviet consul. Stasov was taking advantage of a privilege accompanying his new title, that of attending a British White Club function, when he was introduced to Dillon Synge. Stasov sensed that Synge's cultivated manner was only a veneer, and the Russian determined to discover what lay below. Several more social contacts followed, during which Stasov became unfailingly interested in the jade dealer's business. After a private dinner party one evening, Synge asked if Stasov would like to see his finest art piece. The moment the Russian saw the Kobe Elephant, he resolved to possess it.

The Japanese unwittingly gave him that opportunity. When the Imperial Army lay siege to the city, the British garrison was completely unprepared. Kiril Stasov was not, however. He knew that Dillon Synge would be among the thousands of British subjects attempting to flee with their possessions. In the first week of February 1942, the week of the Japanese siege, transportation out of Singapore was almost impossible to secure unless one was wealthy. Through a contact at the Singapore Line shipping office, Stasov learned the jade dealer had booked passage for himself and a large trunk on the line's last ship scheduled to leave the island, the steamer *Circumnavigator*. Stasov met with Sun Chen who said he would use influence on Kao Kuei-tze, who controlled the dock *swaylos*.

On February 4, as Japanese shells pounded Singapore, Dillon Synge arrived dockside. He escorted his trunk past the sorting area to the dock. Synge waited patiently while the trunks ahead of his were loaded. Then four swarthy *swaylos* approached his crate as if to load it, but suddenly stepped around it and reached for the luggage behind Synge.

"Just a minute, you," Synge said, pointing at his crate. "I believe mine is next."

The dockworkers appeared not to hear him. They chatted animatedly among themselves, like all the other *swaylos* loading the *Circumnavigator*. They were bent muscular men, capable of levering the largest objects.

"Here, you," Synge gripped one of the men's shoulders, "this one next."

The Chinese squirmed out from under the hand and didn't look at him. Others came for the crates further back in the line.

Synge smiled suddenly. "Ah, a little *bakshish*, is it?" He pulled several pounds from his money clip and pushed them at the nearest dockworker. "This should do it."

Apparently he had become invisible. They wouldn't even notice the money. He rushed up to a *swaylo*, grabbed him by the collar, and yelled, "You bloody well better get that crate onto the ship. Now."

An enormous claw grabbed him by the nape of the neck and yanked him away from the dockworkers. Synge's hands tore at the claw as he was dragged on his heels into the maze of crates lining the dock. The claw released. Synge spun to the force behind him. The largest Chinaman Synge had ever seen stood there, hands on his hips, enormous pot belly sagging over the silk sash wrapped around his waist. The giant bellowed, "Take your crate and leave the dock."

Twenty-four hours later he had purchased a seat on a Pan Am Clipper. Japanese shelling had made flights too hazardous. This would be the last one. The seat had cost him two thousand pounds and a Ming Dynasty jade phoenix Synge convinced the ticketing agent was priceless—which was not far from the truth. Buying space for a two-hundred-pound slat crate had cost another two thousand pounds.

Two hours before the flight was to depart, Synge loaded the crate onto a hired lorry and returned to lock his office, a gesture the civil administration said would be futile. The telephone rang, and Synge's face blanched and grew old as the ticketing agent said the cargo space on the plane had been taken by two injured British soldiers on litters. Furiously Synge slammed the receiver down. He didn't hear the knock at his door. Without waiting for a response, Kiril Stasov walked into the office, saw the jade dealer hunched over his phone, and asked, "Something wrong? You look sick."

Synge looked up, his eyes red-rimmed slabs. "You look calm enough, Stasov."

Stasov shrugged. "I'm not like you British. The Japs have crossed the Strait and taken half the island. Mortar shells hitting the city. And I couldn't care less."

The jade dealer dropped into his chair. "They'll probably line you up against a wall like they'll do to the Crown's officials. They're goddamn heathens."

Stasov sat on the empty pedestal. "You forget, I'm a diplomat from a country with strong relations with Japan. My consulate and I will be as secure as if the British were here. I'll hardly notice the difference. Except for one thing." He smiled slyly. "I'm making quite a bit of money out of this panic."

Furrows grew on Synge's forehead. "How?"

"I have a large vault in the consulate basement. A number of people have asked me to store valuable items for the duration. I'm charging them through the teeth, as you British would say."

Synge grasped for the straw. "How large a vault?"

"The size of a small room. It's an old Chubb that . . ."

"Stasov, you've seen my elephant. The Kobe Elephant. I'm having trouble getting it out of Singapore. Something was wrong with the bloody stevedores."

Stasov shook his head. "Can't to it, Dillon."

Synge shot from his seat and was around the desk and almost upon Stasov before he stopped. His mouth worked for several seconds before the words came. "Jesus, Kiril, I'm going to lose the elephant if you don't. You have no goddamned idea what I went through to get it. Why can't you do it?"

"You can't afford it."

Tension seeped from the jade dealer like blood from a wound. His fists slackened. He turned casually to his desk, and said easily, "That's a negotiating ploy. You heard about the stevedores and you're here to rent me space in the vault."

"As I said, you can't afford it. I'm here to have one last glass of your Canadian whiskey before the Japanese confiscate it."

Synge's face twisted into a smile. "Never once did I doubt you would someday turn our friendship into profit. It's in the Russian blood, Kiril. How much for space in the vault?"

Stasov helped himself from the jade dealer's liquor cabinet and returned to his seat. He eyed Synge carefully, like an amah inspecting a carp at the street market. "Five thousand U.S. dollars, and don't bother trying to chisel the price down. It's firm."

"I think that can be done," Synge said lightly, crossing his fingers upright in front of him, forming a chapel.

"No thinking to it. I want the money before you leave Singapore, and I want it in American. None of this bouncing Asian currency."

Like most Anglos preparing to evacuate, Synge was carrying an enormous amount of cash. Producing the five thousand thinned his wallet only slightly. Stasov snapped at the money, and thirty minutes later the Kobe Elephant was in his vault.

Synge and Stasov shook hands solemnly at the consulate's gate, and Synge was in a cab on the way to Kallang Airfield before the Russian allowed himself a laugh. Five thousand dollars, no negotiation, hard currency immediately. The jade dealer had actually thought Stasov was interested in the money. God only knew how many people Synge had killed, how many risks he had taken to possess the Kobe Elephant. Now, with a little money to the *swaylos* and a ticketing agent at the airfield, the elephant was in Stasov's vault. A Japanese howitzer shell screamed into the next block, and the Russian returned to the consulate to cut a white flag from a sheet.

Abdul Razak was playing with his audience, whipping them up like wind on the waves. With demagogic bluntness, he brought them to an angry pitch, then retreated to reason, outlining point-by-point the Chinese atrocities in Singapore. Then, once again, he ployed them with a racist harangue. Synge had heard it a dozen times. Razak knew his lines and seldom strayed from them. His shrill screeching blended with the electric buzz of the mosquitos and the rasp of the crickets. Razak belonged to the jungle.

The tension between Synge and Stasov had passed, at least for the moment. The endless Singapore heat and humidity sapped emotional strength and softened argumentative edges. Stasov's thoughts returned to the plantation, and he caught himself staring pointlessly across the Johore Strait.

One of the Malays had stepped a few feet back from the crowd and was nervously eyeing the dark rows of rubber trees. His head was not bobbing with the others, agreeing to each of Razak's charges. His fists were not jabbing the air. Razak had lost this man.

Dillon Synge also noticed the Malay and immediately high-stepped over the grass to him. He could not allow Razak's spell to be broken by injections of caution or reason by a man who was bothering to think. He approached the Malay from behind. This immigrant was taller than the others, but carried no more weight; his shirt and shorts hung on him like clothes on a line.

Synge grasped the Malay's shoulder with a heavy hand. The man jumped with fright, and spun to the jade dealer, his nose flaring. Synge led him into the trees of the plantation. Curious, Stasov followed.

They marched less than thirty yards into an airstream downwind of a rubber processing plant. The odor was trapped between the rows of trees and caught thickly in Stasov's throat. Darkness was almost total, but he could see white crescents of fear in the Malay's eyes. The man held his arms from his torso, as if waiting to be frisked. Synge said a few words in broken Malay. The immigrant's eyebrows lifted and he grinned widely.

"What did you tell him?" Stasov asked.

"I said he wasn't living up to our deal by stepping away from the crowd, by not listening to Razak, but that he's free to go as long as he doesn't tell any Malay in Singapore that I let him out of the deal."

"This is unusually kind of you, Dillon."

The Malay turned on his heels and walked rapidly away from them in the direction of the city.

"It is out of character, isn't it?" Synge responded. He lifted a revolver from his shirt, lined it on the Malay's receding back, and pulled the trigger. The body was motionless on the ground before the pistol's bark had escaped through the rubber tree leaves.

Stasov refused to let surprise register on his face.

"It's best to leave nothing to chance," the jade dealer said in a mocking tone. "Had he spread the word that passage to Singapore was free, who would follow Razak? Who would storm the temples?"

Synge secreted the weapon and began walking back to the plantation shack. Again the Russian followed. His thoughts were not now on the past, but on the days ahead. This calculated display would force him to take far more cautious measure of Dillon Synge. From now on, Stasov decided, he would guard his back.

The pain had become a shifting haze, an ethereal fog that eased Snow through the passing of time. From somewhere beyond his elbow, an enormous cavern had opened. It seemed to swallow all thought, any attempt to understand where he was being taken. Tsukada's voice could be heard occasionally from the cavern. Snow's shirt stuck to his ribs as his blood dried. It has an odor, Snow decided vacantly. Blood has a smoke odor. The thought pleased him, and he rolled it over and over in his mind until it, too, was sucked away by the cavern.

Had he been in a car? Of course. Back to the city. The Jap was driving. The Jap looked better as a woman. Where does he hide his tits? Slamming car doors. Pulled through a cell of dying. Up some stairs. A Halloween mask peered down at him. Hideous. Mutilated ears, sunken nose. Then the needles.

The haze disappeared. He was on his back on a surgeon's table. Shelby Watson's grizzled face ducked in and out of Snow's view of the ceiling. Snow screwed his brows together and pulled his eyes into line. Watson seemed to be missing more of his right ear than he had two days before. In his gloved right hand was a scalpel. Snow rolled to his right, as if to swing his legs off the table, but Tsukada stopped him.

Watson said, "Kindly notice, Joseph, that you have a needle in your arm, and that if you bolt from the table, you'll rip away even more skin."

"I can't feel a thing," Snow said dully. Visions of the dog were returning, and he knew his arm was shredded, but he was somehow comfortable. He was dimly aware his comfort was drug-induced.

"I've deadened the arm with local anesthetic," Watson said lightly. "Fear not, though, the pain will return in several hours. With a vengeance."

Connie appeared above him. Her eyes were red and damp, but she smiled and said, "Ko said you put up quite a fight."

Snow tried to grin, but his lips were pasty. Watson must have injected his right cheek; it felt as if wads of cotton lay alongside his teeth. His words were a mash. "You should've seen me hit that dog's teeth with my forearm." When his wife's smile faded, he asked, "What am I on, Shelby?"

"A little morphine."

Snow inhaled, a dreamy effort that seemed to last for minutes. "What's the worst that can happen to me?"

"You can suffer a screaming, convulsing death of rabies." Watson was bent over the arm, and each time he held out a hand, Connie placed a cotton swab in it.

"What's likely?" Snow drew out the words, listening to their pleasant, musical echo.

"You'll probably have a full recovery. I've stitched together some muscles in there, so you won't be able to do any push-ups for a while, but barring infection, your arm will be fine. I'm warning you, though, Joseph, I was never a plastic surgeon, and your arm will probably carry reminders of tonight for the rest of your life."

The doctor straightened, dropped a blood-soaked swab into a bucket, took a swallow from a bottle of Bombay Gin and said, "You were telling us about how you met your wife."

"I was?"

The doctor nodded and returned to the arm. "Howard Lester's a lot of things, but he's no *yenta*. I'm surprised at him."

"What did I tell you?"

Connie appeared between him and the ceiling. This time her smile was in earnest. "The morphine is acting as a truth serum, Joseph. You never told me before that your first impression of me was of a rather snobbish know-it-all." Connie laughed, and it sounded to Snow like a Chinese wind chime.

Snow couldn't follow what Watson said next, something about whether he could understand, or whether the morphine was taking hold. Finally, Connie said, "Joseph, we got a call from Howard Lester this evening."

"Lester. He's a pain in the ass even if he is your uncle," Snow slurred.

"He says he found this Beth Johnston, the one the nurse at the Fort Canning Hospital identified as Amelia Earhart."

132

That penetrated the drug fog. "They found Amelia Earhart?"

Connie shook her head. "No, they found Beth Johnston. She lives in Eugene, Oregon, with her husband. She's a registered nurse, was in the Navy during the war and a prisoner at the Keluang camp. But she can trace her Johnston family tree back four generations. Lester said his men never mentioned they were searching for Earhart, but Johnston guessed because she had often been told that she looked like Earhart. Lester's men said she did bear a resemblance, but not much of one. Too short, and her eyes were blue, whereas Earhart's were gray. She laughed the CIG men out of her house."

"Then how did Earhart's medals get into the camp?"

"I've no idea."

Snow felt like slumping, but he was already prone on a table. "Then we're back where we were. No trace of her after the camp. Not even sure she was in the camp."

He hadn't felt Watson's needle enter his arm, but the renewed dosage of morphine took effect rapidly. With a wavering voice, he said, "We've still got Dillon Synge, though."

Watson extracted the needle and said, "From the looks of your arm, I'd say you've got him on the run."

IX

An American wrung the mynah's neck and added
the bird to the soup. He received a field promotion
to corporal.

The Tu twins were born five minutes apart and sentenced to
hang five minutes apart. Their malevolent lives began in-
auspiciously when a day after their birth their mother, told
by an astrologer that her death number was two, held them
under the surface of the Singapore River for a full minute
before being wrestled away from the water by a passing
Buddhist monk. The boat people credited this bitter act for
the fires and broken bones that littered Chao and Chen Tu's
childhood on the sampans of the river.

At age sixteen, the twins left the river, to the vast relief of
the boat people. Almost simultaneously, Singapore's New
Bridge Road neighborhood was seized by an outbreak of petty
crime and vandalism unusual in the orderly affairs of
Chinatown. The Orchid Brotherhood had just decided to act
when the British constabulary saved them the trouble. Searching for his favorite brothel in Sun Alley, an inebriated Dutch
trader staggered into the Tu brothers, who forcibly relieved
him of his wallet. The Dutchman's credit at the brothel was
good, and he died of a heart attack fifteen minutes later while
riding a Malay prostitute. The correlation was sufficient, and
the Tu twins were sentenced to hang.

In a business beset by treachery, loyalty among Kuei-tze's

swaylos enforcers was essential. Nothing breeds loyalty like groveling gratitude. After investigating the Tu brothers, Kao made a substantial payment to Joseph Rantin, the British hangman who drank himself into a stupor at the Savoy before each bout with the rope and trap doors. On the day of the execution, rather than turning left to the Changi Prison gallows, Chao and Chen Tu were led out into the sunlight where Kao's limousine waited for them. Two caskets filled with sandbags were buried in the Chinese cemetery that afternoon. Slobbering with allegiance, the Tu twins quickly became Kao's punishing right arm.

On this suffocating Singapore night, the Tus tipped the cab driver well, for his assurance that he couldn't remember faces. They were unfamiliar with Gelang, a Malay neighborhood of kampongs, the slat houses perched on stilts above the green marsh. The Tus kept to the side of the dirt road, stopping every hundred feet to stare into the darkness. The air was heavy with the scents of frangipani and yellow oleander. A steaming blanket seemed to lay over the entire village, muffling sounds, making movement difficult.

Hunched like stalking cats, the twins ran between a row of kampongs. Chen swung his head left and right, searching for signs of alarm. Most of the windows were dark, the fishermen asleep long before. As they approached the fifth kampong in the line, they slowed, not wanting to stir the damp ground.

Firmly holding the rail of the fifth house, Chen climbed the stairs, letting his weight settle fully on each creaking step before attempting the next one. In the cloud-suffused moonlight, he could see a dozen pairs of sandals near the kampong's door. He moved silently along the narrow porch to the hut's only window. Low laughter and quiet talk escaped through the gauze mosquito netting, and the heady odor of peanut sauce flowed out onto the porch. Chen leaned over and let his head drift across the netting until he had a full view of the kampong's brightly lit interior.

For the new immigrants, the meal was the promise of Singapore. They were gathered around two charcoal braziers in the center of the small kampong. The pungent oil was expertly kept just below boiling. The *satay* were of beef and lamb and were served with rice cakes and cucumbers. A large array of mandarin oranges, muskmelons and glazed carambolas was quickly disappearing. The dozen young Malays

135

were enjoying their first meal since arriving in Singapore earlier that night.

They were aware that one of their number was missing. They had heard the gunshot at the rubber plantation. None had asked Razak about it. They had stayed together, followed orders, and were safe. One of them, who emerged as their leader because he was two or three years older than the others, argued that it was none of their business. Their missing comrade had probably tried to run away or steal something.

The speaker was Datuk Rahman, and like the others in the room, he was from the state of Malacca, a descendant of the Portuguese and Dutch settlers of the sixteenth and seventeenth centuries. Like the others, he knew that the *satay* demanded a certain formality, but he poked the kebabs at his mouth with unceremonious abandon. A woman in a white sarong refilled the platters.

Between mouthfuls, Rahman said, "This meal alone is worth the crossing. But I feel like a *babas* coming here in that little boat."

Squatting on the rattan-covered floor Jalan Batu chided, "You're already talking like a Singapore Malay, calling the Straits Chinese '*babas.*' Remember, you haven't earned your stay yet."

Rahman shrugged. "What could Razak have us do? We're his for one week, after that . . ." He spread his hands.

Around the circle grins widened, but Batu cautioned, "He wants us to run through a Chinese store or home like a rioting mob. Mobs often turn ugly. I don't want to be part of that."

Rahman's smile faded. "Did you have any other way of getting passage to Singapore? This new life isn't free, Batu. I don't mind earning it. The price of one week of our time seems cheap enough—however we are forced to spend it."

"I don't trust Razak," Batu countered. "He wears a *songkok* cap, which I doubt he earned by making the pilgrimage to Mecca. He doesn't have the wisdom or the spiritual force. He's no *Haji*, if you ask me."

"What about his message, though?" Rahman asked. "You don't doubt the Chinese are swamping Singapore, taking all the jobs, sending all the money back to the mainland. They control the shops and the docks. It's even hard for us to find jobs as servants."

Another Malay added heatedly, "Thirty years ago there were almost no Chinese on Singapore. Now look at them. They are everywhere, and more come daily."

"All Razak is asking us to do is to let the British overseers know we Malays are alive. A little yelling, a little fist waving." Rahman wiped his fingers on a towel, then stood and walked to the doorway. "Two days ago all of us were hungry peasants. Not anymore. We've crossed the Strait. We're in Singapore. We'll get our documents. Think of it, Batu. Our sons and their sons will grow up with full bellies."

Batu conceded a small smile. His wife and boy were still in Malacca, but he would be able to send for them soon. Perhaps Razak was right.

Rahman found his sandals at the door and said, "I'm staying with a family down the road. Everyone here remember where they're sleeping tonight?" All in the room nodded, grateful that Rahman had taken it upon himself to look after their interests. "Remember, we're meeting with Razak tomorrow morning at the mosque."

He stepped onto the porch. The Kallang River lay before him like a silk scarf, the glints of moonlight giving the water a spun texture. Beyond the river, the Straits of Singapore and Kallang Harbor stretched into the distance, speckled by the outer islands.

Rahman descended to the path leading away from the kampong. He walked between the homes, then followed the river on the rutted road. His new neighborhood was poor, but not hopelessly poor as in the up-country. And Gelang's new *saurus*, or mosque, was evidence of that. Much of it was made of imported teak and oak. Its minaret, from which the muezzin called the people to prayer, had two balconies and was five-stories high, one of the tallest in the city. A monument to the coming resurgence of Malay Muslim influence in Singapore. As Rahman paused to run his hand along the smooth wood of the mosque, he praised Allah he was here. As it had many times that day, elation welled within him, pulling his features into a joyous smile. Praise Allah, he had arrived.

Two rough hands snapped out of the darkness, throttled Rahman by the throat and choked off his cry of pain. They pushed him roughly into the mosque wall. The Malay's head bounced against the oak, clearing his mind of anything but fear. A forearm plowed into his chin, pushing his face skyward, not allowing him a glimpse of his attackers. Rahman was pinned against the wall like a butterfly in a collection.

Chao Tu spoke in the Malay he had memorized syllable by syllable, "The next time a Buddhist temple is sacked, the iron aims for your head."

These grunted words made no sense to the terrified Malay until Chen Tu lined the sharpened edge of a tire iron against the base of Rahman's fifth finger on his right hand. Chen backed a step away from the wall, planted his feet firmly on the loose ground, then shoved mightily on the iron. Rahman's finger popped, then dropped to the ground, where it curled like a startled worm.

In a feral voice, Chao repeated, "Next time a Buddhist temple is sacked, the iron aims for your head."

Chao released the Malay's neck, and Chen swung him away from the mosque wall, spinning him like a sling. Chen released Rahman's arm and the Malay landed face first in a roadside ditch, sliding several feet before coming to rest in the drainage filth. Without looking at the bloody stump on his hand or at his attackers, Rahman rolled to his feet and scrambled out of the ditch. With his maimed hand balled against his stomach, he sprinted away from the mosque, propelled by terror and pain. Bent on escape, it did not occur to Rahman to warn his fellow immigrants.

Eight thousand miles east, a woman approached the ticket counter at the San Francisco Airport. She attracted attention because she was a handsome woman, but she seemed not to notice the stares.

The ticket agent took her money, then asked, "Do you have any other luggage?" She carried only a small grip, and he had been trained to examine closely those who traveled long distances with little luggage. He took a long look at her. Something was familiar about that face, the wide mouth and sturdy chin. Wholesome and earnest. No fugitive looked like that, he decided. He grinned to reassure her. "Have a good flight, Miss Johnston."

Governor Longstreet was leaning over a Singapore street map as Connie and Joseph Snow entered his office. His bright face was pinched with tension and a hand tapped repeatedly against the desk. A loose wave of white hair hung almost to the bridge of his nose, giving him a boyish appearance that contrasted with his strained features. The Snows had almost reached the massive oak desk before the governor looked up.

He smiled briefly and waved them to chairs. "Mrs. Snow, may I offer you a drink?" Without waiting for her answer, the governor pitched in. "Did you know Singapore has always been considered the second sister, Mr. Snow? Sometimes this office is told of world events, sometimes not. I often feel like I'm running this hodge-podge city with my head in a bucket."

Joseph Snow nodded without knowing what he was approving. His arm was dressed in white bandages, stained red in several spots where the gauze had not stopped the flow of blood.

"Events often swirl around my head. The Foreign Office, the Chinese, the Malays, the communists, you Americans, and the Japs, always the bloody Japs. All swirling." Longstreet lowered himself into his high-backed leather chair. "Do you have any idea what I'm saying, Mr. Snow?"

Snow thought for a moment, then admitted, "Not the slightest."

Longstreet stared balefully at the American. Snow's face was blunt, like the head of a hammer. His sea-green eyes were set back under low, protective brows, and his flat nose had been damaged and suffered a portside skew. Not the face of a deskman like himself. The governor said, "I'm his Majesty's representative on this frothing island. You would think I would be informed of the comings and goings of our allies, wouldn't you?"

Snow was beginning to understand.

The governor continued angrily. "Cracks in the Clemenceau Bridge, wasn't that it? You were going to rent a scaffold and use your enormous expertise in bridge design to keep our bridge from falling into the water." Longstreet pulled a lengthy cablegram from under the map and waved it at Snow. "You are no more qualified to inspect a bridge than I am to crap in the palace."

Longstreet's jaw worked several times, then he read from the cablegram, " 'Joseph Snow. Instructor of Whampoa Cadets.' And here it is. My informant at the Foreign Office sums up, 'Will use his hands at the slightest provocation. Do not get near his hands.' Why would this London clerk think I'd get near your hands, Mr. Snow?"

Snow coughed and avoided his wife's amused gaze.

"Put simply, you are an American CIG agent." The gover-

139

nor spread his hands in a gesture of transparent equanimity. "Now, there are more government operatives in this city than there are flies. But you'd think that our great allies, the Americans, would see fit to inform me when they send someone." Longstreet struggled out of his seat and crossed his office to the liquor cabinet. His voice was even. "Why wasn't I told you were coming in?"

"We didn't think my mission was important enough to bother you with."

"Not important enough? The British hold in Asia is being severely tested, and your agency doesn't think it's important enough?" Longstreet was trying to maintain an edge to his voice. "I would appreciate better cooperation in the future."

Snow nodded and accepted the two-fingers of whiskey from the governor. Connie's shot was favored with a single ice cube that was diminishing before her eyes.

"To be honest, Mr. Snow, I'm glad you're here. I haven't been able to put the kosh on our troubles in the city and any help I can get is appreciated."

"Sir, I think perhaps you've misunderstood. . . ."

"I must say," Longstreet continued, "your government's foresight in this matter is remarkable. After your country bloody well waited until Britain was in flames before joining the war, we thought you Americans were foot-draggers. But here you are. Lessons have been learned, I'm happy to see." Longstreet sipped the whiskey, then placed the glass on a corner of his map. "Let me bring you up to date on our problems. Two nights ago another Buddhist temple was sacked by Malay thugs. A few injuries, a lot of damage to the temple and its icons, and a very valuable jade piece was stolen, along with a small container of gold. The riot was an exact duplicate of the one four days ago, and I think they are planned and executed by someone, or some country, interested in more than theft. I think. . . ."

"Governor," Joseph said loudly, trying to stop Longstreet's enthusiastic lecture. "I think you may be mistaken."

Longstreet looked up from the map and smiled. "I may not be as professional as you in analyzing data, and I don't have your contacts, but I'm certain these spontaneous riots are anything but spontaneous."

"I mean, you're mistaken about why I was sent to Singapore."

Longstreet's smile grew. "I've long been aware of your

organization's ability. You no longer need to work in the dark."

Snow glanced helplessly at his wife, then plunged. "I was sent to Singapore to recover Amelia Earhart's bones. That's all."

For a long moment the governor stared dully at the American. Then he asked in a strangled voice, "You . . . what?"

"Amelia Earhart and her navigator were on a mission for the U.S. when she disappeared. Rumor has it that she was a prisoner of the Japanese at the Keluang camp, and that her body is there now. I came to Singapore to recover her bones."

"You aren't here to help quash the riots?" Longstreet's words were marrowless, and he grew weaker as he said them.

"To be honest, I didn't know anything about Singapore's troubles until I got here a week ago. I've been chasing down one rumor after another and not getting any nearer to Amelia Earhart's bones."

Longstreet slowly folded the map, an effort that seemed to exhaust him. "That sounds like a make-work assignment."

Perhaps Snow should have protested, but Longstreet's opinion accurately reflected his own. "If it weren't for this trip," he admitted, "I'd be searching the archives or bodyguarding. We're a little short of work."

Longstreet waved his shot glass at Snow's bandaged arm. "It looks like your make-work job has turned dangerous. What happened?"

Snow answered with a question. "In each temple sacking some of the more valuable religious objects have not been recovered. Right?"

Longstreet shrugged. "Of course. Even rioters will pick up something that glitters. I'm surprised more isn't taken. Usually only a jade piece or two and the box of gold offerings. Sometimes even the offering tray of coins near the gate is robbed."

Connie Snow added, "But isn't it always the finest jade piece that's stolen? Minor items and newer statues are left behind?"

Longstreet returned to the cabinet where he shuffled in a drawer for a few seconds. He pulled out a manila folder. His eyes climbed the list from the bottom of the page. "Well, yes. It seems that valuable pieces are taken, all right. . . ."

"It takes a knowledgeable eye to pick out an expensive jade

piece in a temple cluttered with idols and lamps and gongs and incense burners," Connie went on. "Some are valuable, some are not. In each of the riots, during all the chaos and confusion of the beatings and destruction, someone coolly picked out the temple's best piece."

"Another thing," Snow said. "Most Chinese Buddhist temples are rather poor. Their idols are carved of rock or even made of poured cement. But all the temples sacked recently had one or two precious pieces, and these were taken."

The office door opened and Terrence Bliss skittered into the room, holding his briefcase like an hors d'oeuvres tray. Beads of perspiration pasted strands of his dark hair to his forehead, and his black eyes flickered anxiously. Bliss would always suffer the appearance of a cornered animal. He withdrew several green sheets from the briefcase and placed them before the governor.

Longstreet ignored them. "You're suggesting that the riots are fomented in order to steal jade?" It was a rhetorical question. He paused for a long moment. "I've been working under a completely different theory, you know. I've assumed the riots were planned, all right, but to create political instability in Singapore."

"If it's political, who's doing it?"

"I mentioned this to you at the club, and you didn't seem too convinced. The Soviets have been trying to get a port in Southeast Asia for years. Their eyes are on Singapore."

Snow smiled. "You think the British would pull out of a colony because of a few riots? You're underestimating your own stock."

"I wish that were the case." He looked at Bliss who was leaning against the filing cabinet, his hands behind his back. "Do these cables contain what I think they do?"

Bliss looked away from Connie's breasts long enough to answer, "The usual."

"Then let me pick a few at random." The governor lifted the first cable and said, "Here's one from the Royal Air Force asking me to assist homeward-bound servicemen. Here's another, this from Sir Benjamin, a member of the House of Lords, reminding me that the British tradition in times of crisis is one of resolute defiance. Here's one from the M6, requesting a study on the feasibility of pulling out fifty percent of their agents." Longstreet shuffled through the remaining cables. His face reddened as he said, "And here, for bloody Christ, is a message from a deacon of the Church of Scotland demanding that I personally dismantle the stained glass at St. Andrew's and ship it home before the cathedral is captured by the damned." Longstreet looked up from the green sheets. "Make no mistake, Mr. Snow, the Foreign Office is gearing up to pull out, and the more racial trouble we have, the quicker it'll be. Retreatism. The Soviets sense it and are more than willing to fan the flames."

"Any proof?"

"Our intelligence reports show the Soviet consulate here is receiving four times the budget it did six months ago. That money isn't sitting in Kiril Stasov's office, it's being used. Couriers arrive every other day at the Soviet consulate. That means the messages between Moscow and Stasov are too hot to trust to the air waves. And twice in the last three months Stasov has returned to Moscow for a few days. Increased activity at a consulate always means something is imminent. In the Soviet case, something underhanded." Longstreet pushed the cables to a corner of his desk, lifted his whiskey, and said, "Back to your arm, Mr. Snow."

"Actually, back to my theory of the riots." Snow explained how the search for Amelia Earhart had led to the jungle airstrip and her Lockheed Electra.

At the mention of Singapore Straits Airways, the governor's brows furrowed, lowering the white wave of hair almost to his eyes. "That's Dillon Synge's airline. Are you saying . . . ?"

Snow outlined his suspicions: that the small bundle handed over to Synge by the Electra's pilot was the plane's only cargo, and therefore was probably valuable; that there had been a Buddhist temple looted on the Peninsula that afternoon, and that the booty was probably what had been transferred. Snow told how he and Ko Tsukada had learned of a temple sacking at Sungaiguntung, across the Straits, and how they had attempted to intercept Synge's incoming boat. He held up his wrapped arm and concluded, "This was the result of that little sortie. My arm looks like cheap mutton, courtesy of a German shepherd."

Longstreet was holding up both hands, trying to push away the inevitability of the American's conclusions. "Back up a minute, Mr. Snow. Are you saying that Dillon Synge had something to do with Amelia Earhart's disappearance? That's too fantastic to be believed."

Snow started again, giving the governor the benefit of

143

Tsukada's investigation. The Kobe temple riot, the disappearance of the priceless Kobe Elephant, how Tsukada believed Synge lured Amelia Earhart to Saipan to hijack her plane. Finally, Snow said, "We don't think he has the elephant now. He lost it sometime during the war."

The governor worked at closing his jaw, then sputtered, "I'm ... I'm dumbfounded. Dillon Synge is ... he's the type we're working to save Singapore for, hard-working, upstanding. He's ... well, British."

"That's the reason I'm telling you this, Governor. We'd like your help. We've run his name through our files and haven't come up with a thing. We'd like you to have your government do the same. Maybe the Foreign Office has something on him showing a tie between Synge and the Soviets."

Longstreet drew a finger along his nose. "I don't mind telling you I'll feel something of a traitor, but. . . ." He turned to Terrence Bliss. "Cable the Foreign Office and M6. Highly confidential. Everything from known facts to rumors about Dillon Synge."

Bliss nodded, shifting back and forth on his heels. He ran a hand through his black hair, then wiped his fingers on his pants.

"And are you suggesting there may be more than one motive for fomenting these riots? That both Stasov and Synge are working for the same goal?"

"And maybe working together," Snow said. "I'm going on that assumption until shown otherwise."

The governor digested this for a moment, then planted both palms on the desk to lever himself to his feet. "Well, if we keep in touch, you may find your answers and I may find mine." The governor's tone had reverted to that of the Crown's representative. "Let me show you to the door."

Before they reached the street, Longstreet asked quietly, "May I have a word with you, Mr. Snow? Alone?"

Connie smiled quickly and moved several yards down the street.

"Mr. Snow, I don't quite know how to bring this up," Longstreet said, clearly embarrassed. "Far be it from me to put my nose in another's business. And I certainly don't mean to imply that I've had you followed, or am particularly concerned about your. . . ."

"What is it, Governor?"

"Well, because you're in Singapore in service to your country, I feel it's my duty to warn you about . . . about the Bugis Street women." Before Snow's smile had time to form, Longstreet hurried on. "You've been seen with a notorious transvestite named Rose and—this is really none of my affair—but I must warn you, those perverts bring misfortune to everyone they encounter. You would do better to keep your mind strictly on business."

Snow nodded solemnly. He didn't trust himself to thank the governor, so he patted him on the arm, and almost caught up with his wife before breaking into laughter.

Terrence Bliss carefully filed the green sheets, then brushed off the governor's desk with his hand. Tobacco crumbs seemed to follow the governor everywhere. He squared the chair, then picked up the crumpled pieces of paper that lay near the wastebasket and dropped them in. The governor expected a neat office, and Bliss didn't mind picking up after the old man occasionally.

Satisfied, he locked the door behind him and descended to the street. He walked for three blocks, then ducked into a shop door. He waited a full five minutes to determine that he was not being followed, then set out again, walking briskly toward the old cemetery on the Fort Canning grounds.

He was already perspiring heavily. But Bliss loved the warm dampness of the city, the heavy, odorous air. He had been raised in Brecon, in the shadow of Wales' Cambrian Mountains, where the elements cruelly conspired against the rock farmers. For as far back as Bliss could remember, his single goal in life had been to escape from crushing poverty. While working in a small print shop, he contracted to forge mine safety certificates, but the shop was burned down by suspicious miners before he could make enough money to leave town. Finally, he did escape when he joined the Royal Navy and was ordered to Singapore. He was in the city when it fell to the Japanese army. Then Bliss and hundreds of other British prisoners were conscripted by the Japanese to build the Siam Railway. Bliss weighed ninety-three pounds when the camp was liberated. After three months at the Fort Canning Hospital, he was discharged from the Navy.

His chronic fear returned. Slipping back into the peasantry, he called it. I will never slip back into the peasantry, he would repeat for hours. Singapore would fulfill this promise. His job with the governor paid adequately. It was also an ideal spot to monitor the rumors and suspicions that swirled around white Singapore society, some of which Bliss had turned to a tidy profit. Unhappy Mrs. Snow, for example. But a penny here, a pound there would never push back the shadow of Wales.

He chose a particular bench on the rolling grass hill in the cemetery. Several mourners walked between the rows of white crosses. Bliss shivered under the tropical sun. Many of those buried here had been brought back from the Siam Railway project. Dug up, bagged, and returned to the empire by the Engineer Corps. Bliss was trying to decide what would be worse, life in Wales or burial in Singapore, when Kiril Stasov sat down on the bench next to him.

"Anything new?" the Russian began without ceremony. His gray fedora was no more out of place in the heat than his everpresent gray raincoat. Stasov's bulk slopped over the bench like pastry dough.

"You have the money?"

Stasov smiled, revealing tobacco-stained teeth. He had been handsome once, but his chin had doubled and his butt had spread. The pouches under his eyes were new and attested to the work and worry he was investing in the Singapore project. He extracted a sandwich from a paper bag, placed the bag on the narrow strip of bench between them, and said, "It's here. Part of my lunch."

Bliss failed to keep his eyes from the bag. "Interesting session at the governor's today. I should be charging you more."

"Incoming?"

"The standard cables, some bordering on hysteria, from the Church, from the gentry. More interesting to you, M6 is asking the governor to determine the effect of pulling out half its people here."

"You don't know how many they have, of course," Stasov said.

"I've told you before, no. I don't think the governor does either."

"Outgoing?"

Bliss attempted to gain control of the conversation by pausing to eye the Russian knowingly. "I've been told to have London look into Dillon Synge's background."

It worked. Stasov's mouth compressed into a thin, perfectly straight line. His eyes wandered for a moment, vaguely scanning the distance over Bliss's shoulder. They snapped back so suddenly Bliss felt as if he had been slapped. Stasov demanded, "Why?"

"Amelia Earhart."

"Don't fuck with me, little man," Stasov snarled.

"This information is worth something," Bliss managed, his hands tightly gripping a bench slat.

Stasov stared stonily at him for several seconds, then pulled a half dozen bills from his wallet and tossed them at the Welshman.

"The Americans have sent an operative here to locate and dig up Amelia Earhart's bones. Joseph Snow is his name. He came to Singapore thinking he was on a mortician's errand, but now he has tied Dillon Synge to Earhart's disappearance. Found him using her airplane. Now he thinks Synge lured her off course, then murdered her and used her plane to bring back the Kobe Elephant." Bliss paused significantly, and his mouth twisted into a daring leer. He added, "Joseph Snow is no errand boy, believe me. I've seen his records. If he decides to take Synge out, I wouldn't put a tuppence on Synge even finishing the course."

Bliss wasn't sure the Russian had heard his last statement. Stasov had drawn inward. His eyes were vacant and his fist gripped the back of the bench tightly. He flexed the corners of his mouth. Stasov turned abruptly to Bliss and asked, "How long can you delay the inquiry cable?"

"Well, not at all, really. The governor asked me to send it off, and he remembers things like that. He'll ask me about the answer soon."

"But can't you wait two days, then backdate it? Or perhaps misspell Synge's name, so the Foreign Office will have to cable back for clarification?"

Bliss pursed his lips. "That would be sloppy of me. More than anything else, the governor appreciates my careful habits. Normally, after I compose a cable, I check it, then recheck it . . ."

"From this day on, your pay is doubled."

Bliss grinned victoriously. "Dillon Synge has just become Dillon Cyne. That little typo will use up several days, if I know the Foreign Office."

Stasov gathered his feet under him. "Don't think this sets a precedent, Bliss. People who try to extort money from me usually find their relationship terminated. That is, their end

147

of it." The Russian pushed off from the bench. A minute later he had disappeared over a hillock to the north.

Bliss refused to let these chilling words mar his self-satisfaction. This was the formula. Milk all the teats, as they said in Wales. With the paper bag in his pocket, he left the bench and wandered among the grave markers. Next, he thought, another visit with Mrs. Snow. Who knows how much she'll be good for. He laughed aloud, a high-pitched chortle, irreverent in the cemetery. Yes, who knows how much dear Mrs. Snow will be good for.

X

At night a candle burned near the hut's window frame, attracting moths and, in turn, the geckos. Her task was to snatch the lizards from the sill and snap their heads back. They flavored the soup.

Dillon Synge's eyes were damp, perhaps in sympathy for the Sikh, more probably from frustration and growing rage. He had been questioning Bahadur Sak for ten minutes, dragging the story out of the taciturn dog trainer piece by piece. What emerged was a garbled tale, dimmed by darkness and hollowed by grief.

Sak hadn't seen the men approach the dock. There were at least two, the one his dogs attacked, and another who fired at his animals from the jungle. He had been patrolling the bay's shoreline with Raipur, his German shepherd at point, perhaps thirty yards ahead. Raipur charged a figure, going in high for a man's arm. The second shepherd, Sirpur, joined the attack, but by that time, Raipur was lying on the ground.

"I cannot understand how it happened," Sak said in his cultured Brahman accent. "The man appeared to be striking Raipur with his fist, but putting a German shepherd down like that is impossible. A dog does not respond to blows as a man does."

"The trespasser killed your dog by hitting him?" Synge asked incredulously.

Sak nodded. "He also knocked Sirpur down once, then a shot came from the undergrowth and Sirpur fell. What both-

149

ers me more than losing the dogs," he slowly flared his hands, "is the unfairness of using firearms on my dogs. It just is not sporting."

Synge waved a hand impatiently. "Did the man have anything in his hand? A knife or a club?"

"Nothing, I'm telling you, he beat Raipur to death with his fist." Sak spoke slowly, as if afraid to test his grief-stricken composure with words.

"Can you describe him?"

"Not very well. He was not so much tall as he was big through the shoulders and arms. A powerful man. And he had blond hair. I distinctly remember his hair."

Synge sank back in his leather chair. "I was right, then. The American knows," he muttered.

"Pardon me, sir?"

Synge pushed himself out of the seat. "What do I owe you for the dogs?"

"Raipur and Sirpur can never be replaced. Only one shepherd in ten has their combination of talents . . ."

"How much?"

"A hundred pounds each." More a prayer than a demand.

Synge pulled the bills from a desk drawer and dropped them into the Indian's hand. Synge walked him to the door and asked, "And if I need your services again?"

"It will be more costly, but I have other dogs. If you expect trouble from the blond-hair, tell me beforehand, and I'll have the dogs go for his testicles. The outcome would have been quite different, you know, had I not made the mistake of sending them in after his arm, of being merciful."

The jade dealer shuddered at Sak's calm statement. And only when Sak had disappeared down the stairs did Synge's groin stop aching. He pressed his call button, then opened an attaché case and began emptying his desk. When Flynn entered, Synge said coldly, "I take it you haven't had any luck."

"Mr. Synge, I know this Snow is staying at the Raffles, I know he's been eating at the Tanglin Club, but I haven't found him yet. At least, not so I could corner him."

"I have been consistently underestimating him, Flynn. So far he has only attacked my property, but soon he may attack me. We're changing address, at least until you've had a chance to meet with him." Synge lifted the photos of the Kobe Elephant off the wall and placed them in a wooden box. He held one in front of him for a moment, then glanced at the empty pedestal. Long-festering anger colored his voice. "I have an appointment with Stasov in a few minutes. He has tentacles all over the city. Perhaps he can locate Snow."

"What do you want me to do?"

"Until you find him, I cannot be without a bodyguard and I cannot move according to any schedule. I'll be using back doors, hired autos, and so forth. No regularity. Cancel all my business appointments."

"Sir, you have got at least a dozen dealers coming in for a show. . . ."

"Damn it, Flynn, didn't you hear me? Cancel it. No shows, no meetings. And no more greeting God-awful society at the club. I can't afford to expose myself."

"What do I tell everyone?" Flynn asked.

"I'm on a rest-cure, a holiday. I don't care."

"Sir, it may be none of my business, but you haven't exactly said why this Snow is after you. I mean, no one just begins a vendetta without reason. If I knew why he was here, it might help find him."

"Suffice it to say he's after me because I have . . . once had the Kobe Elephant." Again his eyes drifted to the pedestal. For a full minute he stared at its polished surface. Only at the sound of Flynn nervously clearing his throat did Synge remove his gaze from the stand. "Bring the car to the alley. After you leave me at the consulate, get Pinang out of the hospital. I don't care if his jaw is wired up. We'll need his services soon."

"You are retreating, aren't you?" Kiril Stasov asked in a mocking tone that affected Synge like a blister.

"Taking a few precautions is far from retreating," the jade dealer protested. "My business was hit again last night. They didn't get the incoming goods, but they came close. It was Snow and an accomplice."

They were sitting in Stasov's second floor office in the consulate. "You wouldn't by any chance be frightened because of Amelia Earhart, would you?"

Stasov's questions caught Synge in the stomach, almost lifting him out of the chair. This was the first time in almost ten years that he had heard that name. The aviatrix had become a distant memory, a piece of history no longer relevant to his life in Singapore. But with the destruction of the

Electra, she had come into focus again. The torturous days spent pushing the crate across Saipan, the months of hunger, the cave, all had slipped from immediate memory. Suddenly, he could see Earhart's terrified face again in the sight of his revolver. Synge blinked her away, then managed, "What did you say?"

Stasov leaned forward. "Finally, I've learned the whole story, Dillon. At least, as much as I care to know. You disappeared for a year and a half back in 1936 and '37. Then you reappeared, gaunt, hollow-eyed, but wealthier by one enormous jade elephant. You somehow tricked the U.S. government into having Earhart land on Saipan, where you were waiting. You left Earhart and the navigator, dead, and used her plane to fly out with the elephant." Stasov folded his hands. "Do I have that right?"

"What does that have to do with our business relationship?" Synge's voice was muted. A bank of perspiration appeared on his upper lip.

"I have to admire you, Dillon. I can only imagine the risks you took for that elephant. Had I known it meant so much to you. . . ." The Russian let his voice trail off, his sarcasm causing Synge's face to redden suddenly.

Synge struggled. "I asked you, how does Amelia Earhart concern *us?*"

The Russian locked his fingers behind his head and leaned back. "Numerous ways. First, it makes your position here much more tenuous. I understand Snow originally came here to escort Earhart's bones back to the United States. The Lord only knows what he intends now."

As red as Synge was, he darkened even more as Stasov spoke. His hands were wrapped tightly around the chair arm and his knuckles showed bone.

"Joseph Snow is just a tool, however," Stasov continued. "His superior heads America's Central Intelligence Group. His name is Howard Lester. Try as we may, we have discovered very little about Lester."

"Then why bring him up?" Synge asked tersely.

"The one fact we have about Lester, gleaned from Soviet Union's experience, is that he is a consummately vengeful man."

Synge stared at the Russian's clouded gray eyes. "What does that have to do with me?"

"Lester will go to great lengths—make that any lengths—

to get even. A long time ago, two people and a plane were lost, which isn't much in this business. But if Howard Lester had anything to do with Amelia Earhart's flight, he will give Joseph Snow orders that will seem irrational and spiteful. Understand?"

Synge had difficulty raising his head, as if the Russian's words had bled him. He worked at spreading a smile, "Why are you telling me this?"

Stasov answered by rising and walking to the office door. He motioned for Synge to follow. The jade dealer moved slowly, bracing himself for what was to follow. He knew this routine as well as he knew the spelling of his own name. Down the stairs, along the hall, past the two plainclothes guards, down the narrow ill-lit stairs and finally, the consulate's basement. His feet moved automatically. Synge had followed this route a dozen times, and another thousand in his mind.

The Chubb safe rested in the center of the consulate's basement. Its plate iron siding had tarnished colorfully during its years in Singapore. At least ten feet high, and as wide as it was deep, the safe's massive door hung on steel hinges and the door's exterior handle looked like a ship's wheel. Four keyholes penetrated the door, but they weren't needed now as the door had been opened for the day. Stasov shouldered the door open further, then high-stepped inside.

A single bulb cast a dim shadow over the vault's interior. Several steel filing cabinets lined a side wall and what looked like an ornate typewriter lay on the floor. In the center, dominating the vault, was the Kobe Elephant.

Even in the weak light, the skin of the elephant glowed as if a source of light came from deep within the jade. The intricate and subtle lines of the skin gave it a startlingly lifelike aura, as if the vault were in fact a cage. The elephant looked as if it had merely paused while raising its trunk, halting only momentarily as it ambled about the vault. Yet it was a glassine jewel. The jade's surface was so pure and clear it seemed almost without substance. Only beneath the skin did the crystal seem to harden into tangible form.

Synge's reaction was always the same. Lightheaded, breathing audible rasps, he leaned heavily against the steel wall. He dry-swallowed several times, trying to generate enough moisture to speak. He raised his hand slowly as if to bless a crowd then lay it on the elephant's flank. He moved his fingers up its spine, then to the top of its skull, pressing his hand firmly on the cool surface, wanting as much of him to touch the animal as possible. He said in a wavering voice, "You always bring me here when you think I'm straying from our bargain, Stasov. Always. I'm aware of this, you know."

The Russian laughed coarsely. "And it always works. Take your hand away from the elephant and listen to me." He waited until the jade dealer complied. "So far you've been doing your part, Dillon. Your man, Razak, has the Malays following him like lost dogs. Anti-Chinese sentiment in the Malay community here is running very high, and the Chinese hatred and suspicion of the Malays is growing daily. It's impossible to read the *Straits Times* without seeing stories of your riots. In short, thanks to you, this city is just a little below the boiling point."

"The elephant is mine, Stasov. You know that."

"And you will have it soon," the Russian promised, stepping left, blocking the jade dealer's view of the elephant. "Listen to me, Dillon. I'm telling you this so you'll know how close you are to getting it back."

Synge took a half step toward the elephant, but Stasov held his ground. He spoke as if Synge were a child. "I know this Joseph Snow has frightened you. I know you feel like running. But if you leave Singapore, if you renege on our deal before I say we're finished, you will never even see this elephant again." Stasov waited until Synge's eyes met his. "The Kobe Elephant will simply disappear. Understand?"

The Boeing Stratocruiser dipping from the rolling rain clouds and approached Singapore's Kellang Airport dead on end. Gray smoke jumped from its wheels as they touched the concrete of the runway. The engines whined, then settled to a steady drone as the Stratocruiser taxied to the terminal.

Portable stairs were rolled to the plane. The hatch opened and passengers began descending. They were businessmen and bankers representing large interests in the States, all wanting a piece of the postwar Singapore boom.

Disembarking midway in the line of gray suits was a man a bit heavier, a bit jowlier than the polished businessmen. This man would be uncomfortable in a tailor-made suit and looked as if he never spent more than four bits on a haircut. His brown wing-tips, tied with black laces, needed a shine.

He was the mongrel in the crowd. Howard Lester was also one of the most dangerous men alive.

The Singapore River was littered with a vast array of Chinese junks. Wenchow fishers, with their flush decks and high bulwarks; Ningpo traders, originally from the mouth of the Yung River, flying three masts of brown and yellow sails; Hangchow Bay traders, box shaped vessels with swim-headed bows and square transom sterns; and Lorchas, originally used by the Portuguese to run guns, invariably painted rust with bright yellow poops and forecastles. All these junks had colorful talismans decorating their sterns. Almost all had eyes painted on their bows because, like fish, the junks had to be able to see their way.

Snow and Tsukada walked briskly along the north boat quay, passed several lighters whose crews were angling the boats under the riverside cranes. Snow briefly held a hand in front of Tsukada, slowing him. "That's his warehouse," Snow said, nodding at a three-story wood structure across the river.

"Are you sure? It'll go badly for us if you've picked the wrong building."

Snow retraced several steps, then looked again at the warehouse. The third story hung over the river and provided covered moorage for two small vessels. Between the berths was a loading dock on which were several dollies and a portable ramp. Two guards could be seen, each with a carbine slung over a shoulder.

"On the side near the top floor is the legend, 'Singapore Traders Association.' That's Synge's building, all right. Who else is going to post sentries in broad daylight?"

Tsukada smiled. "The guards must mean we have Synge worried. What does he store in there that's so precious?"

"Much of it's empty, but the third floor has Indian and Persian rugs in it, remnants of his early trading days. He also leases space to importing companies, and they've got U.S.-made radios, clocks, auto parts, that type of thing."

"No jade?"

"Not that I've heard of. There are rumors he was once a gun runner and that he has a cache of weapons in the building. I wouldn't count on it though. We'll have to settle for the building and the rugs."

They negotiated a narrow ramp to the sampan moorage. Unlike the ornate commercial junks downriver, the sampans were a slatternly lot. Most were less than thirty feet long, two-masted, with rarely used ragged mat sails. Perhaps a few of these sampans occasionally left the river to negotiate the Singapore Straits, but most were homes for the *tan-ka*, the sampan people who live virtually every moment of their lives on the small boats. The *tan-ka* sampans were cluttered with family life. White laundry hung from poles braced in cracks in the deck houses. Canvas tents covered forward sleeping quarters. Water barrels were usually near the bow. Attached to the gunwales hung ceremonial gongs which were sounded loudly to chase away devils of the sea.

The sampans were besieged with children. Most under the age of six wore no clothing, while older children endured shorts. The children played with dice and sticks on the after decks, ran stem to stern, and swung on the tillers. Squatting near the braziers were generations of Chinese families, animatedly talking and laughing. No one looked up as Snow and Tsukada negotiated the narrow mooring plank between the rows of boats, a difficult task for Tsukada because he was carrying a leather suitcase.

Snow's eyes were watering and he said quietly, "How can they stand it here? The smell is killing me."

The stench drifting off the river was indeed awesome—industrial and human waste, combined with rotting fish and the heady aroma of Chinese food. Snow ineffectually waved a hand in front of his nose.

"Which one?" Tsukada asked, carefully placing one foot in front of the other on the narrow planking.

"We're going to be cleaned, so let's have it done by a hungry *tan-ka*." As they approached the end of the planking, Snow added, "We might be able to buy this one."

The sampan he stood near was the poorest of a poor breed. Wood on the hull had warped and shrunk under the tropical sun. The painted eye was chipped through to the wood. Only a child, perhaps five years old, was on deck. He wore sandals and nothing else.

Snow called in Cantonese, "May we come aboard?"

The child scratched his buttocks and answered shyly, "Yes."

"Little boy, is your father on board?"

"What do you want?" The speaker who emerged from the mat shed was a gnarled old man, as brown as an almond. He wore white briefs and a thong around his neck to hold his fortune-telling bones.

"Can we talk business?"

"What business does an Anglo have with the *tan-ka* people?"

"Not the people," Snow answered. "Just you. May we come aboard?"

"Yes," answered the boy, still picking his butt.

"You are welcome on this boat," the old man said, "but not the Japanese."

Snow left his shoes on the moorage plank, then stepped over the low-rise gunwale to the deck, which trembled with his weight. He walked lightly to the aft quarter. A young man climbed through a hatch. He carried a tin cup of green tea which he offered Snow.

"I'm looking for a sampan," Snow said, sipping the bitter drink.

"Congratulations," the old man bowed. "You have found a whole river of them."

"Father, let him talk," the young man said gently. "Our name is Han. This is my father, Ting Lin, and I am Yen Piao."

Snow introduced himself and Tsukada, who was still standing with his suitcase on the moorage plank.

"The Japanese are such an ugly people," the old man said loudly.

Yen Piao said hastily, "Please excuse my father. At his age, he speaks his mind. How may we help you, Mr. Snow?"

"I want to buy your boat."

Both Chinese looked quizzically at Snow. The sampans changed hands vertically, father to son. Only infrequently did one family transfer a boat to another. Selling to a round-eye was a concept outside their experience. The old man said, "Anglos should never try to speak Kuo-Yu."

"This is our home, Mr. Snow," Han Yen Piao said. "I was born on this boat, as were my children. Homes are not often bought and sold in Singapore. We would have nowhere else to go."

"With the price I'll pay you, you can buy another. A larger sampan. There are always several for sale along the river. And you can berth it here. I don't want your slip."

Han Yen Piao said, "I have no idea what this boat is worth."

"Surely you've occasionally priced others."

Han was silent for several moments. Few of the *tan-kas* wanted to leave the river, but they all dreamed of larger,

157

more decorous boats. "Kang Ching-lien is selling his sampan. It is eight feet longer than ours, and at least twenty years newer. It even has watertight compartments inside the hull. He is asking an impossible price for it, though."

"How much?"

Han whispered, "One hundred British pounds."

The old man quickly said, "One hundred thirty British pounds."

"What do you think your sampan is worth?"

"Less than that, but we must have a place to live," Han Yen Piao said, not daring to look at the American. The old man's eyes were searching for Snow's wallet. The boy wrapped himself around Han Yen Piao's leg and continued to gaze at the red-headed devil.

"I'll give you two hundred pounds for it, if I can have it within thirty minutes."

The old man grinned, revealing soured gums. "For two hundred thirty pounds, you can have it in fifteen minutes."

That amount was the price of Kang's large sampan plus a year's pay for the entire household. Both Hans were astonished when Snow quickly said, "Done. I'll wait here while you get your family and possessions off the boat."

"I've heard a lot of talk," the old man said licking his lips, "but I haven't seen any money yet."

Snow peeled the bills off a roll and handed them over the old man's outstretched hand to Han Yen Piao. The son switched to his native Hokkien dialect and called orders to those below, then hurried to the bow to collect what he could in the allotted fifteen minutes. Snow dropped to the moorage plank and lowered himself next to Ko Tsukada, who said, "You aren't really the world's best trader. You just handed those people a small fortune for a floating wreck."

Snow shrugged. "It's Howard Lester's money."

"Is this still Howard Lester's job?"

Snow turned to Tsukada. "What do you mean?"

"You came here to look for a woman's bones. Then you began looking for the woman, then for the man that may or may not have killed her. Rather than going for his throat, you're going to a lot of trouble and expense to ruin him financially. It doesn't sound at all like the task Howard Lester wanted done in Singapore. In Japan we call it building an assignment. From a small task to a large one."

Snow looked again at the sampan.

The Han family was leaving their home single file, their arms full. At least fifteen people, three generations, maybe four, Snow couldn't be sure. Their possessions were wrapped in burlap and canvas. Some of the bundles could have been infants. Han Yen Piao stood near the port gunwale directing his family over the rail to the plank deck. The boat bobbed irregularly as they stepped off. The old man brushed his son's hand away and nimbly lowered himself over the sampan's side. His son followed, glancing over his shoulder for a last look at his life-long home.

Snow looked back at Tsukada. "What's your point?" he asked.

"Your wounded arm may be doing your thinking."

Snow glanced at his bandaged forearm. The pain had largely subsided, replaced by an implacable itch, fed by his constant sweat. Shelby Watson had warned against scratching or pulling at the wrap so Snow suffered every waking moment. "We still don't know whether Amelia Earhart is alive or dead, or what Dillon Synge knows. I don't think he'd be receptive to a polite visit from us. Lester has given me liberty in this matter. I'm going to pop Synge like a boil."

"Now your wounded arm is talking, not thinking."

"Are you with me or not?" Snow asked testily.

"Yes, but I'm out the instant I think you've stopped bringing me closer to the Kobe Elephant."

Rather than untie the lines, Tsukada worked with a knife, and within seconds the sampan was free. Snow held a long pole across his chest and walked the length of the boat, pushing it through the brown water at his pace, while Tsukada remained near the stern, manipulating a second long pole and the tiller. The river flow was almost unnoticeable. As the sampan glided into view of Dillon Synge's warehouse, Snow donned a conical straw cap, then opened Tsukada's suitcase.

It contained two five-liter cans of gasoline. He sprinkled the gas on the sampan's mat shed, then on the fore deck. He opened the second can and showered the boat as he walked aft.

Ko Tsukada stood with the tiller between his legs as he removed his shirt. "We learned during the Tokyo fire bombing to remove all clothing when fighting a fire. The flames won't stick. You won't become a torch."

Snow pointed to an angry purple splash of a scar on

Tsukada's stomach. It ran from his beltline to his left nipple and was the texture of crepe. "It must have been a hard lesson."

"Everyone was a volunteer firefighter during the last days of the war. I was caught in a burning building." Tsukada waved the subject away. "Where are we aiming this fireball?"

"Right into the loading slip."

"What about the guards?"

"Talk some Japanese to them. They'll think we're on business and won't be concerned."

Snow repeatedly pushed the pole the length of the sampan. The warehouse's guards were now plainly visible. They were leaning against a pillar between the two loading berths. They shared a match and drew on cigarettes. One slipped his carbine off his shoulder and leaned it against the post. The sampan approaching slowly from upstream was of no more concern to them than the hundreds of other boats that passed the warehouse daily.

Tsukada whispered, "This is going to be a foul swim." Then he raised his voice and hailed the sentries in Japanese.

The guards turned leisurely toward the incoming sampan. One lifted a mooring line and a bumper from the dock. Snow kept his head low and continued to push against the pole. Tsukada brought the stern about, so the sampan lay cross current as it drifted toward the warehouse.

One of the guards cupped his mouth and called out, his voice carrying easily over the forty yards of water to the boat. Snow said quietly, "He wants to know who we are."

Tsukada answered the guard in Japanese, then raised his hands in a helpless gesture. The silent guard was not completely reassured, for he swung his rifle off his shoulder and held it across his stomach. The other guard motioned them away. Snow waited until the sampan paralleled the loading slip, then began walking his planted pole toward the stern. The boat glided toward the berth.

The guards looked at each other and exchanged a few words. One turned toward the darkened warehouse door at the end of the dock, perhaps looking for his superior. The other lowered himself to his haunches, trying to look under the sampan's mat shed for cargo.

The first guard again called a warning, but he carried the mooring line as he took several steps toward the approaching ship. When the sampan bow nudged into the slip, the guard scratched his chin and lowered the rifle, perhaps believing that now the boat was under the warehouse, confined to a narrow berth, all danger had passed.

He was wrong, of course. With his Anglo face still hidden under the straw hat, Joseph Snow casually pulled his Zippo from a pocket, flicked it once, and tossed it onto the sampan's mat shed. It fluttered on the soaked matting for one second, then threw up a wall of flame between Snow and the guards. Feeding on the gasoline, the fire sped along the wood deck to the bow, billowing enormous waves of orange and red, soaring tongues that scoured the underside of Dillon Synge's warehouse.

Snow tossed away his hat, then followed Tsukada headfirst into the river, screwing his eyes against the chemical and fecal assault of the tepid water. Snow kicked himself along underwater as far as he could, then broke the surface. Tsukada was several yards ahead of him, pulling for the north shore. Snow dogpaddled around for a view of the warehouse.

The sampan was now a cylinder of fire throwing flame skyward. The underside of the warehouse was alive with flame crawling to the building's corners. Flaming pieces of wood fell into the river where they sizzled and threw up steam.

Snow worked against the water for several seconds swimming away from the growing heat of the warehouse. Again he turned, in time to see the guards rush from the warehouse's side entrance onto the riverbank. One of them levered a shell into the breech of his rifle, then stupidly fired into the sampan. He swung the weapon aft and loosed a shot at the tiller. The rifle's report was swallowed by the roar of fire.

Tsukada's hand gripped Snow's shoulder and helped him up the yielding bank. The soft mud pulled at their feet, as if to reclaim them for the river. They had landed on the north bank between two rows of moored sampans. Snow crawled away from the water until the ground firmed, then followed Tsukada's gaze across the river.

The Singapore Traders Association warehouse had become an inferno that spewed ash into the heated air. The building's riverfront facade had fallen, covering whatever was left of the sampan. Only the eye of the tiger remained, and they watched it dissolve into the fire. A surging cloud of flame shot out a third-floor window, and a second later the roof collapsed, sending smoking spars tumbling to the water.

"There go his Persian rugs," Tsukada said, as he wiped brown residue from his face. "And everything else."

Across the river, a hook-and-ladder company and two pumpers arrived, but they stayed well away from the blaze, perfunctorily spraying neighboring buildings and several junks moored at the nearby pier.

Breathing heavily, Tsukada added, "I've seen your list of Synge's holdings. There's hardly anything left to destroy."

Snow brushed river weeds from his sodden pants. "What about the gunman? He's a hard case, but maybe we can get to Synge through him."

"Your fists would be very persuasive in a discussion. But let me have a try at Flynn."

"You or your skirts?"

Tsukada smiled wickedly. "I have a way with men."

XI

A Japanese corporal leered at Cynthia and her for months, and once brought them a jar of salvarsan for their infections. When their hair fell victim to ringworm, the guard lost interest.

Henry Heath had been a maritime sailor for twenty years, and for much of that time, he had been in a rum fog. Heath's memories were of wind and sea, of interminable hours under the tropical sun in eight-knot tramp steamers, of swabbing decks and scraping barnacles. When his ships reached port, his memories ended. He had been married twice and had no recollection of the ceremonies and little memory of his wives. He had found the papers in his sea kit. His tattoos were some of the most colorful and dramatic in the Pacific. Green and gold cobras were wrapped around both arms. A boa constrictor and a mongoose were engaged in mortal battle on his back. His chest was graced by an impossibly voluptuous Geisha whose genitals were meticulously inked around and in his naval. Try as he might, Heath could not remember ever being in a tattoo parlor.

There were a few times ashore, however, when Henry Heath had remained cold sober. On June 21, 1937 he had helped drive a load of airplane fuel from his ship to the Singapore airport to be put into Amelia Earhart's plane. Heath had heard that she always supervised fueling and work on her plane, and he was hoping for a glimpse of her. A sober glimpse.

He was in luck. As he stood on the bed of the truck under the Electra's wing cranking the fuel pump, she walked from under the fuselage. Her light gray eyes followed the fuel hose from the wing down to the truck, where they rested for several seconds on a beaming Henry Heath. She smiled back, revealing the small, entirely attractive gap between her front teeth. She said, "I like the snakes on your arm." Then disappeared under her plane to inspect the aileron wires.

That had been almost ten years ago, but the memory had returned in a rush as Heath sat at a sidewalk saloon on Singapore's North Bridge Road. He lowered his shot glass uncertainly and stared after the red-scarfed woman who had just passed his table. He squinted at the crowd of pedestrians in which she was fast disappearing, then shook his head, trying to gauge how drunk he was. Plenty, he figured, because it just could not be.

If he were sober, he would swear that Amelia Earhart had just passed his table.

Goddamn it, this was only his third shot. That wasn't drunk. But he had to be, because Amelia Earhart had gone down in the Pacific ten years ago, just a few days after she had smiled at him. He rose to a halfstance and peered into the crowd. For a moment, he caught sight of the red scarf bouncing away amid a sea of black hair before it ducked around a corner and was gone.

Heath pushed his rum away. Amelia Earhart alive and walking down a Singapore street. If he took that information to the local authorities, they would accuse him of having drunken hallucinations. He'd be laughed out of the constabulary building.

But what if it were? He had just seen her face. Who else could it be? He had a duty to report what he saw. Didn't he owe her that? Henry Heath pushed himself away from the table, looked forlornly at the half shot he was leaving, then ambled off toward police headquarters.

Wandi Desai owned a flower shop on Serangoon Road in Singapore's Indian neighborhood. She sold garlands used by Indians for welcoming guests and honoring gods. It was an outdoor stall, its only protection a colorfully striped awning overhead. The flowers were displayed on sawhorses and in ceramic pots that Wandi carefully arranged on the cobblestones.

It was common for Wandi to be told by customers that she was more beautiful than any of her flowers. Her features were delicate and refined, and accented by her black braided hair and the small diamond that decorated her nose. At age twenty she displayed the distinctive marks of her heritage: fingers stained yellow with tumeric spice and teeth smeared red with betel nuts.

It was eighty degrees in the shade under her awning, but Wandi Desai was shivering uncontrollably. She rubbed her hands along her forearms, trying to subdue the goose flesh. Ghosts were common in Indian folklore. They were regularly appeased with small offerings. Wandi considered them nonsense. She was a sensible woman. But there was no question in her mind that he had just seen a woman returned from the dead.

Ten years before, when Wandi was the star pupil of the Tamil school, she had won the right to represent the school at the airport reception for the first woman to attempt to fly around the world. Amelia Earhart had emerged from her plane tired, rumpled and hungry. But she had time to smile and thank the schoolgirl in the flaring red sari, who handed her a bouquet of flowers.

Wandi Desai had loved Amelia Earhart for that gesture. When she learned the flyer's plane had disappeared in the Pacific Ocean, she mourned for weeks. Earhart's handsome, strong face returned to her again and again, smiling down at the girl as she accepted the flowers. Wandi had lived with the memory of that face for ten years.

It had just come back to her in the flesh. She had bent to lift a nosegay of lilies from its vase and had given it to an elderly Tamil. She looked up to thank her. Amelia Earhart was passing behind the Tamil. Just a glimpse. Same high forehead and full jaw. Same beautiful mouth and understanding eyes. In an instant she was gone, again leaving only a memory.

Confused and shaking, Wandi sat back against a sawhorse. She had to deny her senses. Her eyes had lied. The American aviatrix had been dead ten years. Disappeared in the Pacific.

And that, too, was a lie, because Amelia Earhart had just walked by her flower stall.

Owen Addison sprinted through the city room, disregarding the "Easy, old chum" and "Where's the fire, Owen?" from his fellow newsmen. Against the wall behind the feature editor's desk were the obituary file cabinets. He yanked two open before he found the correct drawer. He brushed the top of the manila folders, then pulled several out until he found the file he wanted. He spread the contents over his desk.

Amelia Earhart looked up at him from several photographs. She wore a leather flying suit in each photo. Most had been taken at the airport reception in Singapore ten years before. There were also several shots of her plane lifting off the runway, bound for Bandoeng, Java, the next stop on her journey. One shot of Fred Noonan, her navigator. A separate folder held the wire-service reports that her plane was over-due at Howland Island, that the Electra was now presumed missing, that the largest air and sea rescue in history was being organized, how hope for her safety was diminishing. In another folder there were eulogies from world leaders and aviation pioneers, including Charles Lindbergh and Orville Wright. Finally, a paper clip held together the *Straits Times'* own stories about the flyer, most of which Owen Addison had copyread ten years before.

Addison held a large-grained photo of Earhart at arm's length and lowered himself into a chair. He had read some-where that in all the world there are at least thirty people so similar to any given individual that they are almost mirror images. That should have explained what had occurred ten minutes before. Should have, but didn't.

It had only been a glance. She was riding an oncoming trishaw and her head had been lowered to read a newspaper in her lap. Her trishaw was a minute behind him before the face from ten years ago came back. He didn't at all believe his conclusion, but he jumped out of his trishaw and ran several yards before he realized that finding her in the teeming street was hopeless.

Addison had walked slowly past Robinsons, his eyes at his feet as he compared the woman in the trishaw with his recollection of Earhart's face. Something was different. Her hair was darker now or something. But the similarities were striking. And the more he thought about it, the more convinced he became. By the time he entered the *Straits Times* building, he was running full clip.

Now he gathered the file contents and put them back in the cabinet. He went to the open-investigation file and found the folder on Earhart. In it were the records of reputed sightings of Earhart over the past decade. Twenty-eight in all. She was reported to have been tending bar in Manila and to have been seen on the arm of Chiang Kai-shek in Shanghai. One said her head had been shrunk and was in a basket in Borneo. These were the least frivolous reports.

Addison walked to his desk, rolled a sheet of paper into his typewriter, held his hands over the keys, then tore the sheet out. Why should he type anything that would end up alongside a report of Amelia Earhart's shrunken head? But, goddamn, that woman in the trishaw had looked like her. Addison pulled at his mustache before finally deciding to talk this over with Sergeant Tom Alger, his contact at police headquarters.

A gauze bandage covered the stub on Datuk Rahman's left hand, where the night before there had been a finger. The injured hand was tucked into his stomach, as if contact with another part of his body would lessen the pain. Rahman's lips were pulled back in anger as he nodded his agreement with Abdul Razak, the mullah. They were sitting in an outdoor café on Selegie Road, surrounded by a dozen other new Malay immigrants, five of whom wore similar wraps on their hands.

Unlike the night before when words of caution had marked the conversation at dinner, the Malays nodded vigorously at every charge Razak made. Even Jalan Batu, who last night had left the kampong with two others and was thus spared the amputation, voiced his appreciation of the mullah's inflammatory words.

"The Chinese have no sense of history," Razak exclaimed. "No sense of historical justice. How can outsiders act as if this island belonged to them? The Chinese are taking over every business in Singapore."

"Even the food we ate last night was purchased from a Chinaman," Rahman added irately.

"Have you seen maps of Singapore made ten years ago?" Razak ranted. "Chinatown consisted of several dirt streets over on the south swamp. Now look at it. It has expanded tenfold, always pushing back the Malay community. On New Market Road there is even a holy mosque being used as a heathen temple by the Chinese."

A more damning accusation could not have been made. The Malays' mouths tightened in anger, and several fists stabbed the air. One Malay woman standing in the small crowd looked skyward and cursed, an act repeated by her son who was holding her hand. He imitated Datuk Rahman by balling his hand and making jabbing motions.

"Did any one see the men who did this? Anyone get a look at them?" Razak asked.

"Two Chinese, that's all I know," Rahman said. Others agreed.

"Look at you," the mullah commanded. "You're pathetic. One day in Singapore and you've already lost something to the Chinese. Your fingers. Now you run around Singapore with your tails between yours legs."

Razak stared into the eyes of each Malay. "Some day you will find enough courage to strike back. Maybe not today, with your tails where they are, but someday. There'll come a day when the Chinese cannot walk over us Moslems with impunity. We will hit back with hardened fists."

Razak could rouse no more than ferocious nods from the Malay immigrants. But his call to action was not lost on the boy in the audience. He slipped away from his mother, who was rocking back and forth on her heels with anger. The boy was perhaps nine years old, and larger than most his age. His dark hair was worn in a bowl cut, and one of his front teeth was already chipped. In his brief life, he had suffered a broken nose and two concussions, and all agreed he would never reach adulthood. He walked away from his mother with a swagger carefully copied from British sailors.

The boy crossed Selagie Street, where the Indian and Chinese communities tensely mingle to trade, toward several Chinese children who had accompanied their mothers on a shopping trip. The children were working on stick candy while staring at the macaw in a cage suspended from a fish market awning. They weren't aware of the Malay boy until he was two steps away. In Malay incomprehensible to the Chinese, the boy cried, "This is for those fingers," and smacked the nearest child behind the ear with his fist.

The blow was louder than it was painful, but the Chinese child collapsed on the ground with a piercing wail. His mother's reaction was reflexive. She was holding a ten-pound carp by the gills, and she swung the fish in a wild roundhouse at the Malay youth. The fish slammed into the boy with the sound of a firecracker and spilled him backward to the cobblestone.

The Malay immigrants saw only the fish meet the boy's chin. Datuk Rahman and the others were halfway across the street before the boy was on the ground. As Rahman ran, he screamed at the woman, who protectively raised the carp in front of her face. Carrying a gutting knife, the Chinese fish vendor quickly stepped from behind his counter. Rahman grasped for the Chinese woman's arm, but found his hand pierced through with the knife. Rahman leaped back in pain, clasping his injured hand, spraying blood on the vendor and the wild-eyed mother.

Shamed that he had escaped his friend's finger amputation and enraged by the sight of Rahman's blood, Jalan Batu leaped at the vendor, knocking him over the counter. The vendor slashed with the blade as he fell, and Batu's earlobe dropped to the ground near the wailing Chinese boy. The other Malays poured into the vendor's shop furiously tearing apart everything they could reach.

Like volunteers answering a fire bell, Chinese men and boys ran along Selagie toward the confusion at the fish market. When they saw the Malay thugs rampaging inside the venerable Mr. Tai's shop, their run turned into a frenzied sprint. They rushed into the shop, fists swinging.

Standing on the café's table, Abdul Razak stabbed his fists at the brawl and implored fellow Moslems for aid, screaming *"Jihad"* over and over. Moslem strollers and shoppers surged toward the fish market, some pausing to pull legs off of café chairs, others lifting cobblestones from the street. One Malay teen-ager ripped off his shirt, soaked it in a kerosene barrel at a lamp shop, and rushed toward the riot.

Selagie Street soon boiled with violence. Above the seething layer of heads appeared flashes of clubs, fists and broken bottles. Cries of anguish and grunts of pain were punctuated by the sharp sounds of knuckles and stones striking flesh. A few wounded fighters managed to crawl to the edge of the brawl, but were soon swallowed again by the mob as it swarmed to and fro.

A Chinese silk shop burst into flames, and its owner tumbled through the door, his shirt trailing fire. Malays tossed wood planks from neighboring shops onto the blaze, and within minutes the fire had spread to other shops. Shop owners trying to fight the flames were sucked away by the storm of violence.

When the Gurkha riot police arrived in troop carriers, the brawl had moved away from the fish market, leaving a dozen Chinese and Malays on the street, some writhing in pain, others still. Blood and glass shards covered the cobblestones in fine patterns. The neat row of shops had been sacked, and their pillars and awnings and merchandise were strewn about as if hit by a typhoon. The fire showed signs of ebbing as the rioters who had been stoking it began to disperse in front of the advancing wedge of policemen.

The Gurkhas were of the militant Rajput caste of Nepal, and their reputation as ferocious fighters quickly put many of the rioters on the run. The policemen walked in step, swinging their clubs like cane machetes. Those Malay and Chinese who continued to pummel each other soon found themselves on the street under Gurkha boots. Within minutes, the rioting factions had disengaged and had melted into the alleys and streets off Selagie Road. With the road cleared of combatants, the firefighters and ambulances moved in.

The governor would not see a report of the riot for a full day. It would show that two Malays and three Chinese had perished in the street fighting. One of the dead Malays had recently lost a finger. Fourteen people were admitted to hospitals with injuries ranging from split lips to broken ribs. Six shops had been ransacked, and another ten were destroyed by fire. The Chinese fish vendor, who the investigators believed may have sparked the incident, was back in business by nightfall.

Joseph Snow threw the sheet that covered him to the foot of the bed. It was seven in the morning and his back was already covered with sweat. He rose to his elbows and looked at his wife, who was sleeping on her stomach, as she always did. He gently placed his hand on the small of her back and ran it toward her buttocks, collecting the dampness in a small puddle. She murmured and turned her head his way, but did not open her eyes. Her lips parted as she slipped back into sleep.

Connie wasn't aware that each morning Snow gazed at her for long lingering moments. He ran his eyes from her hips, along the lovely curve of her spine, then back to her sable black hair. It had been four years since anyone had regularly shared his bed, and he had compensated for that lost time by memorizing every freckle on her back. His fingers followed her spine lightly, pressing into the muscles that formed firm ridges on both sides of her backbone. His thumb came to rest against a small red welt just under her shoulder blade. He

170

had asked her about it once, and she told him it was a birthmark, but she didn't laugh when Snow suggested that "birthmark" was a happy euphemism for a congenital defect. His hand moved to the soft down on the nape of her neck. He was about to wake her, when he heard a soft scraping at the door.

Snow swung his legs to the floor. His feet pressed into the seeds the Chinese maid threw around the bed each day. She believed that if the sleeper's soul left him during the night, it might fly back down to peck the seeds and thus enter the body again. Snow brushed the seeds from his feet, then crossed the room and reached for the envelope that had been shoved under the door.

In it was a handwritten note from the governor. "I still think you're chasing ghosts, but you should know about these." Stapled to the message were three Singapore police green sheets, each written by a desk officer, and each describing in humorous terms an encounter with a citizen who claimed to have seen Amelia Earhart in Singapore during the previous day. Snow groaned and lowered himself into a chair near the bed. He scratched at the wrapping on his arm as he leafed through the sheets.

One report said Earhart's hair was brunette, not blonde. Meaningless. The reports were riddled with comments from the interviewing policemen: "Officer asked if Earhart was floating or walking by." "Constable Latham asked the sailor what he was putting in his rum." It made for a jolly time at police headquarters.

Snow dropped the green sheets on the floor and began picking at his bandaged arm. He was drawing away from his assignment, he knew. Finding Earhart's bones or, improbably, Earhart herself, meant less and less to him. Finding Ko Tsukada's Kobe Elephant had become more immediate. Cornering Dillon Synge was their method, and that was a task more suited to Snow. As he flexed his wrist, trying to chase the itch from under the bandage, Tsukada's words came back to him. Perhaps his wounded arm was doing his thinking. Maybe a new man, one who hadn't been shot at near the monsoon drain or attacked by a dog, would do things differently. Or maybe a new man would just leave Singapore.

Connie rolled to her side and tucked her knees under her chin. Snow knew Singapore was affecting her, too. In their few weeks of marriage, he thought he had discovered the entire range of her emotions, from laughing delight to somber reflection. But he had never seen her irritable and sour. She had never snapped at him before this trip. He leaned back in his chair and smiled. He had warned her how Singapore shortened fuses. She believed him now.

The telephone rang. Snow picked up, knowing who it would be. Howard Lester's voice crackled from the speaker. "Good morning, Joseph. How goes it in Singapore?"

"Fine, sir."

"Couldn't be better here in Washington, either. Fair skies, sunny weather. But we've got a bit of a problem."

"At this end?" he asked, watching his wife sit up in bed and mouth Howard Lester's name. Snow nodded.

"Well, this is a bit embarrassing. You reported to me that a nurse at the Fort Canning Hospital remembers treating a woman in 1945, right after her release from the Keluang camp. When you showed her a photo of Amelia Earhart, she identified her as Beth Johnston."

"I remember all that, sir. You don't need to summarize."

"Bear with me, Joseph. We checked this Beth Johnston out. She was single, lived in Eugene, Oregon, was a Navy nurse. And she was in the Keluang camp. But she proved to us that her name had always been Johnston, grew up in Oregon and so forth."

Snow made room on the chair so Connie could sit next to him with her ear on the phone. "I remember that, too."

The weariness in Lester's voice was audible despite the ocean cable. "Joseph, this Beth Johnston has disappeared. She was last seen at the San Francisco Airport. We're not certain which plane she caught, but she arrived at the airport a few minutes before the Pan Am Clipper departed for Honolulu."

"And then perhaps to Singapore?" Connie asked.

"Hello, favorite niece. Yes, perhaps to Singapore."

"And you rechecked Beth Johnston's background?" Snow asked.

"Of course. It fell through. Beth Johnston is a recent creation. There are no records of this particular Beth Johnston anytime before 1946. Her birth certificate, her social security card, her Oregon driver's license, were all obtained fraudulently. It seems the woman appeared from nowhere, created her own background, lived a year in Eugene, and has disappeared again."

"Right after your men talked to her?"

"That's right."

"You think this woman is Amelia Earhart?"

"Joseph, that Amelia Earhart had been living in Eugene, Oregon, sounds so implausible that I'm not going to say yes. But have you got any other solution?"

"The Clipper arrives in Singapore once a day. I'll be there to meet anyone who looks like Earhart."

"She's probably already there. She left Eugene three days ago. Our men told her about the investigation in Singapore, so if this woman went anywhere, it's your direction." There was a long pause as the telephone static roared, then subsided. "We keep grasping at shadows, Joseph. I'm still not convinced that Amelia Earhart didn't go down in the Pacific."

Connie turned the phone her way. "Howard, we know from Japanese records that she was in Tokyo, then in the Keluang camp. And this woman in Eugene was in the camp. What more do you want?"

"I want to sit over a roast beef dinner and talk to her here in Washington. Or I want to see her bones."

Snow laughed. "I'll try to arrange for you to meet this Beth Johnston, or whoever she is."

Lester rang off. Connie went to the closet for a light blue dress. She put it on in front of the dresser mirror. "Does Howard Lester always deny the facts?"

"You're his niece. You know him better than I do," Snow said, and his eyes fell on the police sheets. He lifted them from the floor, and flipped through them again. "Connie, this woman from Eugene is already here." He held up the police reports. "Yesterday, three people reported seeing a woman who looked like Earhart. The Singapore police thought they were talking to crackpots, but this sailor and the other two must have seen this woman."

She smiled. "Do I actually hear excitement in your voice?"

"Calm, deadpan me? Certainly not." Her grin was infectious, and Snow allowed himself to share it. "A woman who's a dead ringer for Amelia Earhart is walking around this city."

"Or Amelia Earhart herself."

"I'm of the Howard Lester mold, Connie," he cautioned. "I tend to think her remains are underwater or underground. But I'll find this woman from Eugene."

173

"How?" she asked as she pulled her purse off the dresser and walked to the door.

"I know this city. I'll find her." He looked up from the green sheets. "Where are you going, Connie?"

She grinned again. "Joseph, what does every normal visitor to Singapore do?"

"Sweat?"

"No, shop. I'm going to do just that."

Flynn had been chased out of Ireland by the British militia who suspected him of sympathizing with the Germans. He had been indignant about it. He certainly had no sympathy for the krauts, although on occasion he had rowed out to one of their U-boats to transport a crate of Schmeissers to the Republicans. The pay was good.

In his two years in the city Flynn had become intimately familiar with Singapore's dark underbelly. When he wasn't working for Dillon Synge, he prowled the murky paths that lead from one iniquitous enterprise to another. From the pirates who docked in small coves on the West Reach to the opium smugglers who plied their armored junks on the Gulf of Siam, from the gun runners who sold weapons to Communist insurgents to the white slavers working the Singapore–Saigon–Hong Kong circuit, Flynn knew their methods and people. In the shadowy bars near the Empire Dock, Flynn traveled inconspicuously among his outlaw friends.

Flynn occupied a stool at the Weeping Girl Bar, and he was working on his third shot. The bartender, a weathered Chinese with wood dentures, had left the bottle of unblended mash on the bar, knowing Flynn would otherwise occupy too much of his time. The Chinaman, well paid as a shaker, circled the small room every ten minutes to reach behind curtains and into booths to jostle the opium smokers. The authorities ignored the patrons as long as they remained conscious. If, the morning after, the smoker was still in the booth and not in the city's drunk tank, he tipped the shaker substantially.

Flynn topped his shot glass and waited for the bartender to return. "How many kids you got, Lin?"

"Eight, no counting the girls."

"You said they were all bartenders?" Flynn threw back the glass, letting the harsh alcohol chill his mouth. He chewed on nothing for a moment, feeling the blood rush to his head.

"You bet. They pretty savvy. They bow low and the jacks tip."

"Tell you what, Lin. I want your boys to look for a man for me. He's an American. Thinning blond hair. Good looking if you like them tough. He's got one ear full of scar tissue and his nose has been busted. He's got hands that look like he uses them for anvils. Twenty British pounds for you, and twenty quid for your boys, if you spot him."

Lin pulled his mouth back in an imitation of a grin. "You bet you. With ten pounds in front, we look real hard."

The Welshman pulled the bill from his wallet. Lin snapped it up, then walked quickly down the bar. "You, get out. This is a class place. Not for you."

Flynn turned to watch the bartender shake his fist at a prostitute who slid onto a stool and crossed her legs, giving the gunman a tempting view. She ignored the bartender to look at Flynn. Her smile was strictly a business proposition. An attractive one, though, thought Flynn. Her sugar-brown hair was certainly a wig, but nicely kept, unlike the Malay hookers in the alleys. Her features were refined, not Chinese or Malay, something else. Her lips were painted deep red, almost a purple, and her languid eyes slowly rose and fell.

"Ease off, Lin. Let me talk to the lady." He picked up his glass and bottle and moved along the bar, then motioned for another glass. He filled both of them and immediately emptied his. He drew his tongue along his lower lip and blatantly stared at the prostitute's silk-covered breasts. "I've seen you before on the streets."

"And I've seen you, too, talking to your boss, the jade dealer. You must be a good man to work for him." Her thick and sensuous voice cut through Flynn's increasing whiskey fog.

"That guy isn't my boss. I just work for him sometimes." He splashed more whiskey into the shot glass. "I'm thinking of quitting and going back to the old country."

The prostitute lifted her purse and put a foot on the floor. "Well, if the money isn't good enough, I doubt you can afford. . . ."

Flynn roughly grabbed her wrist. "I make plenty." He released his grip and ran his hand along her arm to her shoulder.

"So why leave Singapore? Your boss too tough?" Her voice was taunting. Flynn smiled broadly.

"His name is Synge, and he's the biggest wheel in the jade business. But he's going barmy. Slowly going up the flue. I walked into his office this morning and he was muttering something about the ghost of a woman he killed." Flynn laughed.

"You Anglos all have bad dreams." She poured whiskey into Flynn's glass. "Tell me, does he have a lot of money?"

"More than the king, and that's a fact." Flynn lay his palm on the prostitute's knee and slowly brought his hand up her leg. His fingers disappeared under the silk dress; only when they were an inch from their target did the woman close her legs, trapping the hand. She smiled teasingly. "A woman has to pay the rent. I haven't seen any money yet."

Flynn produced five pounds and tucked it into her blouse, letting his fingers follow the line of her neck. Her mouth puckered. "You must think me ugly," she said, leaning into the Irishman's shoulder, letting her lips flutter against his ear lobe. She nipped his ear with her teeth, then smiled suggestively and pulled back. "I don't even get off the bar stool for five pounds," she said.

Flynn hastily opened his wallet, holding it away so she could not see its contents. He swore silently.

This time it was her hand traveling along his leg. She paused just short of his groin and began to knead the heavy muscle there. Then her fingers lightly touched the swelling near his zipper. "I tell you what, mister," she whispered, "I'm new in town and I don't have many friends. Paying friends. Maybe if you'll tell me where I can reach your big boss, I'll give you a little credit tonight. And I'll charge him double to make up for it."

Flynn jumped at the offer. "He's at the British White Club. He has an apartment there."

She pursed her lips, then nudged his crotch again. "If his name is Synge, he has left the club. That's what my friend says."

Flynn's eyes went from her probing hand to her eyes. "Your friend?"

"My friend, Sari. She's a little bitch"—the prostitute waved her free hand in contempt—"but your boss is a regular of hers. And she says he's no longer at the club."

Flynn laughed. "I'll be goddamned. I never thought that bastard had it in him."

The prostitute closed her fingers around Flynn's crotch,

bringing his thoughts back to her hand and his empty wallet. "Sari says he's a big tipper. I'd like to get a little of that."

Flynn's breathing had become charged and his eyes repeatedly traversed the prostitute's arm from his pants to her alluring face and back again. He said, "Yeah, Synge moved out all right. And he won't even tell me where. So I meet him on Crawford Street near the bridge whenever he calls. He's on the run. Shaking like a leaf. You won't be getting any money from him. He's probably too nervous to get it up."

"But I've got five pounds from you, don't I? And I don't think you are paying for talk." Her words were exotic and guttural. With a parting squeeze, the prostitute left the stool and sauntered to the door.

Flynn took her elbow, and as they climbed the steps to the street he asked, "What's your name, lass?"

"Rose," she whispered.

They walked quickly through a parking lot. Flynn repeatedly glanced at Rose's breasts, and she let her hips brush his leg.

She waited until the walkway was wedged between a stucco building and a monsoon drain before she put an arm on his shoulder, turning him to her. Her cheek brushed his, letting her fragrance settle on him. "Crawford Street? You're sure of that?"

Flynn muttered indistinctly, his mouth searching in her long wig for the nape of her neck. Her arms enfolded his shoulders and she pushed against him. A low sound rumbled in Flynn's throat as his hand molded her buttocks, then slid around on the silk to her thigh, and finally to the front of her dress.

The back of his neck stiffened when he felt the unexpected mound there. In that second of confusion, Rose laughed lightly, then savagely pumped her knee into his groin. Flynn heard the hollow crunch before the pain registered.

Rose said in a deep voice, "Crawford Street, it is." She shoved her palm into Flynn's face, and stiff-armed him toward the monsoon drain. Hunched over and gripped by waves of agony, Flynn could not prevent his wobbly progress to the edge of the drain.

"And thanks for the five pounds." Rose pushed the gunman over the ledge. He fell four feet into the fetid water and coughed into the sludge. Finally he screamed, and the sound covered the receding flap of Rose's heels.

177

* * *

Connie Snow left the Raffles and walked north along Bras Basah Road. She moved quickly, brushing by several elderly Chinese strollers and almost tripping over a Tamil who was squatting on a curb. She repeatedly ran a handkerchief along her forehead and nervously chewed on her lower lip. She had difficulty controlling her eyes as they darted into every doorway, searched every passing face. She dug her hand into her purse and felt the envelope. She opened its flap and ruffled the contents like a dealer squaring a deck of cards. She turned left on Victoria Street and passed the American Embassy.

On Hill Street near the Armenian Church, she turned a full circle and began to wait. Not long. Terrence Bliss walked from the entrance of the church, his eyes flitting between her bosom and her handbag. He pushed his hand through his hair, then held it out for Connie. She backed away a half step.

"Nice of you to come, Mrs. Snow," Bliss said lightly. He had worked hard to rid his voice of the Welsh accent, but outside the governor's office, it slipped back, twisting his words. "And I trust you brought a little something for me?"

She nodded, a palsied dip of her chin.

Bliss waited a moment, then said impatiently, "Well, let's have it."

"I . . . I can't give it to you here. Someone might see."

He laughed shortly. "The Armenian worshippers could care less." He held out his open hand. "Hand the money over."

"No." She backed another step. "I think my husband is suspicious. He might have followed me."

The Welshman's face turned color so quickly he looked ill. He took a short, rasping breath, then turned to face the crowd on Hill Street. He shakily opened and closed a hand as his head clicked back and forth. He managed, "I don't see him."

"They never see him. At least, that's what he tells me."

That was good enough for Bliss. He gripped Connie's elbow and fairly dragged her away from the church. "Maybe we shouldn't stay in the open. Who knows who could be watching." Every third step his head turned for a view of the rear. He had read the governor's report on Snow. A maniac.

"Mr. Bliss, I've lived up to my end of the bargain. Now, how do I know I'll never hear from you again?"

They were passing the central fire station and, surrounded

178

again by pedestrians, Bliss's shallow confidence returned. "You don't."

"Well, I can't give you the money unless I know you won't be asking for more. I had to go behind my husband's back to get this, and I can't . . ."

Bliss seized her shoulder and spun her around to face him. Connie yelped with pain, but he kept her shoulder in his grip. "I may call you again. I may not. But you can count on one thing, Mrs. bloody Snow, the minute you stop cooperating with me, I tell all."

"You promised . . ."

"I might visit the constables. I might write your family. I might call your husband. There's no way of telling what I might do. So I don't want any more talk of what I can or can't do. You understand?"

She held a handkerchief tightly to her mouth to subdue a sob. Bliss should have noticed her eyes were dry.

"Let's get this over with," he growled. "Your blubbering is getting on my nerves."

Again she dipped her chin. She, too, must have wanted to end their business, for she stepped ahead of the little man and looked into several shop doorways. She took another few steps, until she came to an alley that angled off Hill Street. It was one of hundreds of dark holes cut into Singapore's vibrant face. In these dank, smouldering cavities was Singapore's second life.

Bliss peered into the alley and saw nothing but overturned crates and a mound of oily rags. "Why here?" he asked nervously.

"It's close. I want you out of my sight as soon as possible," she said bravely, as she moved into the alley. She began digging in her purse, but fumbled long enough for Bliss to snatch the bag from her. He turned it upside down, dumping its contents onto the cobblestone. Her compact splintered and coins rolled out of her wallet. Bliss bent for the envelope.

He tore it open. It contained a half-inch thick wad of cut newspaper. Bliss's face twisted with rage. "What is this?" he screamed, and his hand went for her throat.

For an instant Bliss thought he had struck the wall. His hand had been stopped midair, six inches short of her neck. An iron band seemed to have been thrown around his wrist, making it impossible for him to move it. Terrified, Bliss squinted at the form attached to his arm.

Howard Lester moved out of the shadow. His beefy hand was wrapped around Bliss's wrist. Bliss yanked frantically, but Lester pushed him back against the wall. His other hand cupped Bliss's chin, pinning his head against the brick. In a low, menacing voice, he addressed Bliss. "Tell me what you know about Mrs. Snow."

Bliss's eyes were enormous with fright. He panted into Lester's hand for several seconds before he could squeal, "Who are you?"

"Answer my question or I'm putting you on the ground."

The Welshman's eyes jumped to Connie, who was watching the scene impassively, as if she were viewing a play. Bliss's gaze twitched to the man pinning him against the wall. He was just an inch or two taller than Bliss, and he was carrying a paunch under his shirt. He had a double chin and his hair was thinning. The Welshman found strength in his antagonist's innocuous appearance. He snarled, "I'll tell you what I know, you bastard. This woman. . . ."

Howard Lester's hand shot from Bliss's chin, grasped his arm in a vise and brought it down over his knee. The Welshman's arm cracked loud enough to echo in the alley.

"Now, once again, tell me what you know about Mrs. Snow." Lester's voice was devoid of threats. It was a simple order.

Aghast, Bliss stared at his arm which hung at an odd angle. His entire body below his shoulder seemed on fire and the fingers of unconsciousness tugged at him. He blinked away tears and tried to bring the madman's face into focus. "You . . . you don't know what you're doing," he stammered. "This woman, this woman . . ."

For an instant Bliss thought his ordeal had ended, for the hand unclamped his jaw, but just as suddenly, his other arm was clenched in the pincers, raised high above his head, then plunged downward across the madman's upraised knee. The hand simultaneously slammed into Bliss's mouth, blocking his screech.

"Tell me what you know about Mrs. Snow."

Wild-eyed and awash in agony, Bliss sputtered, "Nothing. Nothing."

Lester decreased the pressure on Bliss's neck. "And how did you break your arms?"

The Welshman slipped down the brick wall, his legs folded

under him. His head was light and he had difficulty forming the words. "I . . . I got hit by a car."

"That's right." Howard Lester took Connie's arm and was several steps away from the crumpled Bliss before he said, "I'll go to the nearest call box and send for an ambulance. I don't imagine Mrs. Snow will be hearing from you again."

Indistinguishable from a nearby pile of soiled rags, Terrence Bliss groaned, and his conscious mind collapsed.

XII

The camp's men and women grew to look alike. Sunken eyes, protruding cheekbones, cracked skin. They walked with hunched gaits, swollen legs, and shuffling feet. Her friendship with Cynthia was her only link to sanity.

White Singapore was withering. Eighteen thousand Anglos had lived in the city before the war. Half of them were chased away by the Japanese, and the remainder had their eyes on Australia or the old country. The howitzer smoke had cleared, but an uneasy pall still hung over the city.

The social circle was closing. Playing soccer around the antiglider trenches on the Cricket Club's *padang*. Snooker and stengahs at the British White Club. Dancing on the vast veranda at the Raffles. Sipping gin slings and singing "There'll Always Be an England" at the Seaview Hotel on Sunday mornings. The old life was slipping away.

All of which made Joseph Snow's task easier. In a city of a million swarthy inhabitants, places a white woman from Eugene, Oregon, would go were few. He had been standing at the Kellang Airfield cab stand for over thirty minutes. Most of the drivers were Sikhs who grunted begrudging answers to his questions about Beth Johnston. Fewer than ten taxis were licensed to ferry airport passengers and if the woman from Eugene had already arrived in Singapore, she must have taken one of these cabs.

Snow hailed the next in line and climbed into the rear seat, an almost impossible task in the tiny Ford. The bearded and turbanned Sikh asked, "Where you please, sahib?"

With his knees under his chin, Snow struggled to remove the photograph of Amelia Earhart from his shirt pocket. He held it over the seat. "I'm looking for this woman. She arrived in Singapore within the past two days. Maybe you've seen her."

The Sikh's dark eyes moved to the photograph. If he recognized the woman, Snow couldn't read it in his granite expression. "I carry many from the airport."

"Surely not many white women."

"Are you paying for a ride?"

Without waiting for Snow's answer, the Sikh pulled his cab away from the curb. He reached over his shoulder for the photograph, then held it on the steering wheel, glancing at it during the less hazardous stretches of road. "I am not certain, sahib. I have had several women passengers yesterday and today."

"She would have been traveling alone, probably with not much luggage," Snow said. Rickshaws and trishaws, delivery vans, bicycles, and a swarm of pedestrians crowded the right-of-way. The taxi's progress was fitful, and Snow found himself tightly gripping the arm rest.

"I am not sure, but I believe I picked this woman up yesterday morning. She had light hair and a strong face, but I didn't get a good look at her. She was alone and seemed very nervous. I do remember that."

"Where did you take her?"

"Where I take most whites. The Raffles Hotel."

Fifteen minutes later, Snow had tipped the cab driver and was standing at the hotel's reception desk. He and Connie had been guests at the Raffles for a week, and the deskman recognized him and was cordial. "Morning, Mr. Snow. What can I do for you?"

"My sister checked into the hotel yesterday. She's left a couple of messages for me, but I'll be damned if we can find each other. I'd like to put a note on her door." Snow held up the photograph of Amelia Earhart.

The deskman took a pair of glasses from his pocket, flipped them open, and shoved them onto his nose. "That's an old picture, isn't it, Mr. Snow?"

Snow laughed. "Well, yes. It's one I've carried for years. I didn't think I'd ever be using it to identify her with."

The deskman joined in the laughter. "I know what you mean." He turned the register back a page. "Here it is. Miss Johnston is in room 202. Are you sure you wouldn't rather leave a note in her box? No trouble at all."

"Thanks, no. This way I'm sure I'll catch her."

The lift dropped Snow off on the second floor. He knocked on room 202 and received no answer, then pulled a celluloid tab from his wallet and inserted it into the jam of the door. He jimmied it several times before the door swung open. He stepped through and gently closed it behind him.

Other than an open suitcase on the bed and a few perfume bottles on the dresser, the room could have been unoccupied. The bed was tightly made and not a piece of furniture was out of place. Snow opened the closet and ruffled through the lightweight cotton dresses hanging there. Feeling like a voyeur, he pushed aside several bras in the suitcase. A pair of sandals, a small make-up kit, a pair of white gloves. He pulled open the dresser's top drawer and found a leather traveler's purse. He opened it and pulled out its contents.

Topmost was a photograph of Amelia Earhart, identical to the one Snow had just shown the deskman. However, this was not a reproduction like the one Snow carried, but the original print. He flipped it over. No notations had been made. Next was another snapshot on Kodak paper, this of Beth Johnston, or Amelia Earhart, whoever. On the reverse was a developer's stamp. Snow brought the photo close to his nose and read, "Blessing Photo. Eugene, Oregon." It was dated a month earlier. Last was a U.S. passport issued to Beth Johnston, birthplace, Oregon, U.S.A., birthdate, December 5, 1905. Snow stared at the photograph of Beth Johnston. Amelia Earhart plus ten years? He held his picture of the flyer next to the passport photo and imagined her with a few wrinkles. Hair was the same color. The jaw was firm and the mouth wide. All of Snow's training and basic common sense argued against what his eyes were telling him. A woman as world-renowned as Amelia Earhart could not have lived anonymously in Oregon since the war. But Amelia Earhart and Beth Johnston were the same woman.

Snow refilled the purse and placed it in the drawer. He scanned the room to assure himself that the drawers and doors were positioned as when he arrived. On a hunch, he lifted the telephone and asked for his room. When Connie answered he said simply, "Meet me in the lobby."

She was there, in the same cornflower blue dress. Snow frowned when he saw how pale she was, and he pulled a handkerchief from his pocket and dabbed the dampness from her forehead. He squeezed her and asked, "You all right, honey?"

She nodded quickly and ran her tongue along her upper lip. "The heat." She waved the complaint away. "What did you find?"

Snow grinned. "She's checked into room 202."

She gripped his sleeve. "Beth Johnston?"

"Connie, I got into her room, found her passport, and stared at it for a full minute. I won't swear to anything, but it looks like Amelia Earhart."

Connie's smile was slow in coming. "Amelia Earhart is staying in a room down the hall from us." She laughed shortly. "Do we wait here for her?"

"She came to Singapore immediately after she learned from Lester's men that there was an investigation taking place. She's here for a purpose, and I think it's to stop us. She's lived in Eugene for a year or so and she may have been happy there. She's here to insure we don't dig her up."

"What could she do?"

"She'll anticipate us by finding and destroying evidence that she didn't go down in the ocean." Snow led his wife through the teak doors of the Raffles Hotel into the glaring sunlight. "A starting point is the Fort Canning Armory where we found the things Earhart left behind at the Keluang camp."

During the brief cab ride to the armory, Connie asked, "What do we do when we find her, Joseph?"

"Ask a lot of questions. After that . . ." Snow shrugged.

"Any chance she could return to Eugene and live quietly?"

"Unlikely."

The cab pulled up to the armory. Snow handed the driver a bill and asked him to wait. They walked quickly up the grass embankment past a tall hedgerow to the curator's office. Sergeant Major Wilkes looked up at them through his bottle-bottom spectacles. "Back again, Mr. and Mrs. . . . ?"

"Snow."

"I'm afraid nothing has been turned in since your visit three days ago."

"Sergeant, we're trying to find a woman who came to

Singapore yesterday. She's about my wife's height, but her hair is much lighter. Name is Johnston." Snow held out a photograph of Amelia Earhart.

"Yes, of course." Wilkes poked a finger at the bridge of his spectacles. "Miss Johnston just came by to look through the baskets of the Keluang camp articles."

"How long ago?"

Wilkes glanced at his watch. "She left two or three minutes ago. No more than that. I'm surprised you didn't bump into her. She's wearing a white dress. Handsome woman, really."

"Did she mention where she was going?"

"No, that's not really any of my business."

"How did she get here?" Connie asked, her voice strained.

"Walked, I suppose. I didn't see a cab or a trishaw." He pushed his chair away from the desk and leaned back to peer out his window. "Well, she's got a cab now. She's getting into one right out there. If you hurry . . ."

Snow was through the door and sprinting down the lawn before the Sergeant had completed his sentence. The woman in white was opening the cab's door. Startled, she turned to the sound of Snow's steps. Her eyes widened and her hand jumped to her mouth.

Snow was covering the ground fast, passing the hedge where the woman must have hidden as he and Connie approached the office. The woman's hair was sandy blonde, and as he drew near he could see her broad mouth. When her lips pulled back in fear, the small gap between her teeth was exposed. Snow was twenty yards away when she spun into the cab's rear seat and slammed the door after her. The cab lurched forward, and Snow's legs pumped to keep pace. He hunched forward until his knees were almost beating against his chest, trying to glimpse the woman through the low window.

For an instant their eyes met, then her head turned away. The taxi sped through the grounds gates, leaving Snow in a wake of thrown gravel. He called desperately, "Miss Earhart. . . . Amelia . . ." The car disappeared around a row of trees.

There were only five seaworthy passenger steamers in Japan's fleet at the end of the war. One of them, the *Meiyomaru*, had just docked at the Singapore pier. The first two men down the boarding ramp walked with a businesslike intent that distinguished them from the tourists that followed. They carried small grips and walked briskly past the luggage area. Both wore dark suits with high-collar shirts and narrow black ties. One was a reflection of the other.

They stopped in front of the small desk that served as Singapore's car-rental agency. After scowling at the two Japanese, the Malay clerk processed their rental papers as slowly as he could.

In Japanese, Shigero Imada asked his partner, "Are we going to run into this surliness during our entire trip?"

Kanau Kondo replied, "There's no love lost between the Malays and us. This journey is going to be unpleasant and I want to get it over with as soon as possible."

"How do you propose we do that?" Imada asked, leaning over the desk to fill in the rental-car forms. "We have absolutely no idea where the elephant is."

"But we do. It's in the hands of a jade merchant in Singapore."

"That narrows it to fifty or so people," Imada said, scratching his signature with a pen. His suit was ill-fitting, failing to disguise his disproportionately large shoulders and thick neck.

"So we go from one business to the next knocking on doors?" Kondo asked. He shared the large physical presence of his partner. Kondo wore his competence up front, in his economical movements and his alert eyes, which flicked from passenger to passenger as they disembarked. Kondo signed the rental contract with his left hand, an awkward movement. His right arm ended at the wrist, where an angry purple stump gave evidence of recent surgery. "If it's in Singapore, why didn't the emperor take it back when we occupied the city?" he asked.

"The Army had no idea where it was. A battalion of men searched for two months and turned up nothing. If the elephant had indeed been here, it slipped through our nets, or had been removed from Singapore before the city fell."

"And now it's back?" Kondo asked, reaching for his bag and following Imada out of the terminal.

"So the Palace believes."

"If it took a battalion two months, how are the two of us supposed to search the entire city?"

"What the Singaporeans patriotically refused to tell the Japanese Army, they will tell us—when prompted with enough cash. We will work in and among the jade merchants. I doubt it will take us long to learn of the Kobe Elephant."

"Your confidence is reassuring. I hope it's justified," Kondo replied as they walked into the rental lot. Another Malay, as sullen as the first, tossed them a set of keys and pointed to an automobile, a dilapidated black prewar Renault that looked as if it had fought on several fronts.

"Remember," Imada said as he climbed behind the wheel, "our main objective is not to make waves. The people of Singapore have had enough of the *Kempai tai*, the Imperial Navy intelligence, and the others. We don't want any horror stories reaching MacArthur's office. In fact, we don't want anything reaching his office."

The Renault pulled to the rental lot's driveway, and Imada craned his head left and right, looking for a break in the chaotic traffic. His clutch foot jerked repeatedly as he tried and abandoned attempts to join the flow.

"You know, Shigero, it's good to be back in business, even if it is only looking for statues."

Shigero Imada's head was still twisting left and right as he gauged the oncoming traffic. "Yes, it is." He smiled. "When the war ended, I thought our careers were through. And our lives. I honestly thought the Americans would shoot us, and all the other agents."

"But here we are, back on the payroll, less than a year after the fighting ended. We can thank. . . ."

A brisk tapping on the driver's window stopped Kondo midsentence. He leaned forward and was astonished at the lovely vision standing there.

"May I have a ride into town?" the woman asked. She bent to look into the cab and her brilliant smiled ensnared Kondo. She was wearing a lime-colored blouse that swelled suggestively below a string of pearls. Her sable black hair, tucked in at her neck, highlighted her golden skin. She puckered her lips, as if sending a kiss through the window, then asked again, "A ride into town?"

Kondo rasped, "Let her in, Shigero."

Shigero Imada's hand was going for the rear door lock, but he paused. "She looks like a whore."

"A simple ride into the city," his partner said, his voice vibrating with excitement. "What harm could there be?"

Imada's hand inched toward the lock, but again he hesitated and said weakly, "Women have no place in this assignment."

"Shigero, she speaks perfect Japanese and, look, she's pressing her tits against the window. Let her in."

Something about her perfect language rang a faint warning bell in Imada's mind. Abruptly, he decided, "No, we can't risk this."

His foot was releasing the clutch when Rose smashed the driver's side window with the butt of a Nambu Automatic, held the pistol against Imada's ear, and, in a voice that dropped two octaves, snarled, "Unlock the rear door."

Imada moved with alacrity. Rose slipped into the rear seat, carefully keeping Imada's head aligned with the Nambu's barrel. She brushed a few glass splinters from her dress, then pushed the barrel into the nape of the driver's neck. "Driver, keep both hands on the wheel, and, you," the gun moved fractionally toward Kondo, "both hands on the dashboard. Pull out into the traffic."

Imada's face was the color of a pomegranate and his knuckles were ivory white against the steering wheel. In a voice choking with anger and embarrassment, he managed, "What is this?"

"The British and the Americans would be interested to know that the Imperial Palace has agents in the field," Rose said lightly.

"Who are you?" Imada demanded gruffly.

"Turn right at the corner. And with one hand, very slowly knock your rearview mirror out of alignment." Rose increased the pressure of the barrel against Imada's neck. "Now, using two fingers, remove your pistol. If more than two fingers touch it, it's over."

Imada did as ordered, lifting the automatic from a shoulder holster. Rose lifted it over the back of the seat, then slapped her Nambu into Kondo's ear. The ear immediately filled with blood that trickled down his neck over his collar. "I said, keep both hands on the dashboard." Rose transferred her gun to Kondo's neck. "Hand yours over. Remember, two fingers."

Out came the pistol. Rose tossed both out the shattered window. "Let me make myself clear. I know why both of you are in Singapore, and I know the training you've had. Those innocent little movements you may be tempted to make that

189

would mean nothing to someone not aware of your ways will result in your being killed. You understand?"

Both men in the front seat nodded, grudging movements more suggested than real. Imada said in a steeled voice, "Tell me why we are in Singapore."

The Nambu moved back to the driver's head. Rose said pleasantly, "The Imperial Palace has sent you to retrieve the Kobe Elephant."

Imada sputtered, "How can you possibly know that?"

"I have friends in Tokyo. Take the next left."

They turned onto the Johore Causeway Road, and the car sped north, paralleling the Malayan Railway. The buildings soon thinned, replaced by rubber plantations. They passed the Singapore Race Track on the right.

For twenty minutes, as the Renault crossed the island toward Malaya, no one spoke. Finally, with a slight turn of his head, Imada asked, "You are Japanese?" When an answer didn't come, he continued smoothly, "Yes, you are Japanese. We are on a mission for the emperor. In stopping us, you are directly countermanding his wishes. Your actions today will be a matter of eternal shame for you and your ancestors if you. . . ."

Rose angrily jabbed the pistol forward, bowing Imada's head. "One more word about the emperor, and I'll drive."

They crossed the Johore Strait Causeway in silence. Rose squinted against the water's glare. On the banks Malay fishermen worked their nets, stringing them between upright poles. The brown odor of the rubber refineries was thick. Rose's eyes moved at irregular intervals between the two agents. Never did she ease the pressure on Imada's neck.

Ten minutes up the Peninsula, Rose leaned forward to glance at the jungle that lined the road. She said, "Start slowing down. Up another hundred yards is a dirt road off to the left. Take it."

The road's entrance was hidden by several buttressed trees. It appeared suddenly, a temporary slash in the jungle. Imada pushed the brake pedal almost to the firewall trying to make the turn. Rose gripped Imada's neck with her spare hand, letting him know the violent turn was not distracting her.

She said, "Drive for twenty yards, then follow me out of the car."

The car sunk almost to the axles as it negotiated the sodden road. It ground to a halt. Rose backed quickly out of the car. One at a time, the Japanese agents climbed out of the car. They placed their hands on the car hood and splayed their feet behind them.

A Dusun tribesman emerged from the undergrowth followed by four others. All carried war parangs in scabbards on their backs. One had a Japanese carbine over his shoulder. They arranged themselves in a loose circle around the Japanese agents.

Rose dropped the Nambu into her bead purse, then pulled her skirt close to her knees and slid into the car. She pushed the ignition pedal and leaned out the shattered window. "The Dusuns will keep you in the jungle for one week, then they'll release you." She smiled widely. "The Kobe Elephant may or may not be in Singapore at that time, but I wouldn't count on it." She backed the Renault toward the highway, then called out, "One last thing. Those blades the Dusuns carry are called parangs. They are not ornamental."

In the past two days Flynn's contacts had meant nothing. He had put word out that he wanted to locate two Americans, Joseph Snow and his wife, and that he needed to find them in an isolated spot. No tips had come, so Flynn had resigned himself to waiting. His groin still ached, making walking difficult, so he waited on the leather ottoman in the Raffles lobby. The Snows had crossed the lobby several times that morning, but never together. At ten o'clock they both left the elevator and crossed to the doors hurriedly, his arm at her elbow. Flynn tossed aside his newspaper and limped after them.

His cab had remained a full block behind theirs. When the Snows pulled onto the Fort Canning grounds, Flynn left the cab and followed them on foot. He had been fifty feet away when the woman in the white dress darted from a hedgerow and climbed into the Snows' cab, and he had ducked behind the trunk of a fan palm when Snow sprinted out of the armory office toward the cab. Flynn had no idea why the woman in white was running from Snow. And it wasn't his job to figure it out.

Flynn took advantage of the situation to take measure of his man. He was taller than the American by two inches, but not as thick in the trunk. Connie Snow joined her husband on the armory's driveway and reached for his arm. Flynn's eyes went to the American's hands. Synge had said to stay away from them. It was advice Flynn planned to follow.

Out the East Coast Road, the Masthead Tavern stands as a sentinel for maritime sailors laying over in Singapore. In its close confines, men of the sea find company, commiseration and an occasional loan. The Masthead was decorated with collateral left behind by busted sailors. Strapped over the low door was a Japanese 7.7 mm heavy machine gun, the tripod protruding from its base like welcoming arms. The tavern had the finest collection of Waterford crystal on the island, each piece pawned by sailors over the past twenty years. The exquisite crystal was used to hold candles and honey, pretzels and *ketchil makan*.

The Masthead's walls were covered with the sea's castoffs. Narwhal tusks, seal traps, manacles and chains, several cutlasses arranged around a breastplate of Portuguese armor, and the enormous jawbone from a tiger shark. Mosquito netting covered all windows, smudging the view of the Singapore Straits. The bar itself was eighty years old, a mammoth, solid oak affair brought from Billings, Montana. It displayed the largest collection of rum in Southeast Asia.

The tavern's owner was Stump Schmidt, an expatriate German who had lost his foot a decade before when it became wrapped in an anchor chain. Stump never had much luck with prostheses, and eight wooden legs were nailed to the Masthead's back wall. Stump Schmidt limped to Joseph Snow's table, lowered two schooners of beer, and asked, "You running a chit, Joseph?"

"If you're asking if I'm going to be here all night, no," Snow smiled. "I don't want to be trapped into hearing any of your lectures on how General von Paulus fouled up Stalingrad." He gave Stump a coin, then pushed a beer over to Shelby Watson.

The doctor wrapped a gloved hand around the schooner and drank deeply. His lower lip came up to remove foam from his mustache. "Tell me about your wife."

Snow's foot tapped against a brass spitoon, and he pushed it away from the table trying not to look at its contents. "I didn't know too much about her when we got married. Still don't."

Watson smiled unevenly, accenting the irregular cast of his face. "So tell me how it happened. A whirlwind romance? The stuff of a two-act play?"

Snow picked at his bandage. "I tell you, Shelby, I don't really understand it. I've thought back on the time before our marriage, and I think I was attracted to Connie because she was so purposeful. She decided to marry me the first time we met in Howard Lester's office and worked unrelentingly on it until it happened."

Watson leaned back in his chair and laughed. "Quite a flattering interpretation."

Snow shook his head. "No interpretation to it. Suddenly Connie was a huge presence in my life. I no longer had to buy groceries. I no longer ate canned tuna every night. I no longer called up the Tapper or John Crown for a beer a couple times a week. Suddenly there was someone watching my weight and feeding me eggplant and all the other things I hate. My apartment smelled nicer, and there were *Vogue* magazines alongside my boxing sheets."

"Utterly touching." Watson pulled the empty glass from his gloved hand and replaced it with the new schooner. "Are you sure I can be of any help with your assignment here?"

"No, I'm not. But thanks to my stupidity there won't be anymore chance encounters with the woman in white. The way I ran after her, like a dog in heat, I'm sure I scared her."

"You keep referring to her as 'the woman in white.' Why don't you just use her name, Amelia Earhart?"

Snow leaned forward over his beer. "I've seen all the evidence that she's alive, Shelby, everything from a nurse who says she was with her in the Keluang camp, to a passport issued to a Beth Johnston with Amelia Earhart's photo on it. And when I was sprinting toward that woman in white and she looked at me, there was no one else she could've been. Amelia Earhart had returned from a sea grave and was climbing into my cab. Even though I know all these things, I can't get used to referring to her as if she were alive."

"How're you going to find her now?"

"That's where I need your help. I'm not going through the governor's office. He has his hands full with the riots. I don't have contacts in Singapore any longer. You do. I want the word out that I need to find her. Sandy blonde hair, five feet eight, gray eyes, athletic build. There can't be too many Caucasian women in Singapore that fit that description."

"Not more than a couple hundred," Watson said dryly. "If I find her, what then?"

"She's not going to sit down over tea while you summon me. Have her followed until whoever spots her can get to a phone and call you or me. . . ."

They didn't see Flynn until he was lowering himself into a chair at their table. His hand came up from his lap, and the solid knock on the underside of the table wasn't flesh. "I want you to come with me, Snow."

"Do you know this person, Shelby?"

"Can't say I do."

"What do you want?" Snow asked, keeping both hands on the table.

"You heard me. Get up and walk out of here. I'll be behind you."

Snow looked at Watson. "It doesn't look like I have much choice. For my own information, are you working for the same person who sent those two Malays at me out of the monsoon drain?"

Flynn nodded, his mouth turning up. "You almost killed Pinang with your hands. That's a warning to me, Snow. If I see those hands of yours ball into fists, I'll pull this trigger. I don't care where we are."

"You've been sent to take up where Pinang left off."

A flicker of fear touched Flynn's eyes. He didn't feel the advantage the Mauser he was holding should have given him. Both men were talking as if he had joined them for a beer. Far too casual. But Snow's hands were still on the table. Flynn bumped the table with the pistol again. Snow stared at him as if he were a naughty child.

"Tell me, friend, who do you work for?" Snow asked. When Flynn was silent, he added, "Telling me can't make any difference, can it?"

Flynn worked his mouth into a smile. "No, it can't. Dillon Synge pays my way. And Pinang's too. I was told to take out you and your wife, but I couldn't find you together anyplace where I had a chance. So one at a time it has to be."

"My wife?" The humorous inflection drained from Snow's voice. "I have a lot of enemies in this part of the world, I imagine, but what would Synge want with my wife?"

"I just follow orders, Snow. Now get up."

"Mister, you may have wondered why I just didn't beat Pinang to death. I held off because Pinang was stupid. And, friend, you're stupid, and I'm going to help you out, too."

"Snow, if you don't get up. . . ."

"I'll tell you why you're stupid. No one with any sense would sit down at a table where his victims are sitting across from each other. We have you surrounded, you see. You can't watch both of us at the same time. Dr. Watson here may not look like a hard man, but I know better."

Flynn was clearly frightened, for reasons he did not understand. He had the weapon and it was trained on Snow's belly. He tried to sneer. "I've heard of you, Dr. Watson. The leper who calls himself a surgeon."

Snow counted quietly. "One, two, three."

When Flynn's eyes snapped back to Snow, Shelby Watson's gloved hands came out of his lap. The scalpel blade reflected the room's light for an instant before it sank into the skin above Flynn's left ear. With a surgeon's dexterity and speed, Watson ran the scalpel down the Irishman's cheek to his chin. The skin flapped open, exposing white jawbone before the gap filled with blood.

Flynn screamed and tried to jerk his gun across his lap to the doctor, but Snow's knee rammed the weapon against the underside of the table. Simultaneously Snow's fist shot to Flynn's face, aimed at the gushing wound. The sound of the crunching impact filled the tavern. Flynn flew backward from his chair and collapsed to the floor, toppling a spittoon. The Mauser rattled between the legs of the chair and came to rest between the Irishman's legs. The spitton's brown spill stained his sleeve.

"Do you want another beer?" Watson asked. His scalpel had disappeared.

"What business does Dillon Synge have with my wife?" Snow's fists were still clenched. Flynn's blood oozed between his fingers.

"Synge just threw her in. 'Him and his wife,' he said."

"Goddamn, that upsets me."

Watson glanced at the motionless Flynn. "I can tell."

None of the other patrons left their seats. Stump limped to their table and bent to right the spittoon.

Snow leaned over the arm of his chair to wipe his hand on

Flynn's pants. "Shelby, don't waste any time on this. I want to find Amelia Earhart, find that goddamn Kobe Elephant, then get my wife and me out of Singapore."

"What happens to Synge when you find him?"

Snow stepped over the Irishman, who groaned and began to stir. "Figure it out, Shelby. Unlike Pinang and his gunny, Dillon Synge isn't stupid."

XIII

Cynthia Fellows died of malaria.

Snow had been slumped in the leather chair in the Raffles' lobby for over an hour. The same chair that Flynn had occupied that morning. Snow swallowed rapidly several times trying to generate saliva. He shouldn't have had those beers with Watson. Too early in the day. His mouth was suffering from dry rot and the tall iced tea he was working on didn't help.

He had been staring at the Raffles' doors, waiting for the woman in white to return to her hotel. Little hope of that, but Snow had a few other leads. He had asked Ko Tsukada to spend the morning at Synge's airstrip. Perhaps Amelia Earhart knew who had waylaid her and would try to find her plane. Connie was posted at the Fort Canning Hospital on the chance Earhart would return there.

The assignment's loose ends cluttered his mind. He was sent to find her bones and found himself searching for *her*. Now that she was in Singapore, was it still necessary to chase after Synge? Snow glanced at his bandaged arm. Yes, he decided grimly, it was. What was the tie-in between Earhart and Synge? He double-crossed her on Saipan, yet she lived. Could they have been partners in a scheme to steal the Kobe

Elephant? Improbable. There was nothing in Earhart's background to suggest she could be tempted by such a deal.

Lester's suspicions made sense. She was lured to Saipan to pick up Imperial Navy documents. Synge and his pistol were waiting for her on the island. She spent years in Japanese camps, survived, was treated at the Fort Canning Hospital, then moved to Eugene, where she went to great lengths to live anonymously. She had only returned to Singapore to protect that anonymity by trying to destroy the clues to her fate.

Snow finished the tea and was about to rise to stretch his legs when Governor Longstreet lowered himself into the chair on Snow's right. He was carrying a highball. He took a grateful swallow before turning to the American. His face was florid from the tropical sun. A network of burst capillaries mapped his nose, suggesting the governor was a morning tippler. Beads of sweat clung to the white hair that hung almost to his eyebrows. The governor sighed heavily, as if it were his life's last breath.

"Iced tea, Mr. Snow?"

Snow nodded. "It's a little too early for a gin sling." Or more beer.

Longstreet stared dolefully at his drink. "I used to wait until teatime, but not any longer. It's easier to read my London communiqués through a bit of a fog."

"Are your communiqués the same as usual?"

"Worse. The riots here made front page of the London *Times*. Labour has called for a full-scale evacuation of Singapore. The Prime Minister doesn't agree, but he has ordered me to make concessions to the local populations. That's his phrase. 'Make concessions.' " Longstreet snorted. "What concessions? What do I have that I can give them? A franking privilege? Free tours of the harbor?"

"Any way you can guarantee the community's safety? Keep them off each other's throats?"

Governor Longstreet shook his head and several drops of perspiration fell into his drink. "I don't have enough police. I'm meeting with moderate Malay and Chinese community leaders this afternoon. I'm told there are fewer moderates after yesterday's fracas at the fish stand."

"Any idea what caused the riot?"

"A young chap was hit in the face with a carp, so I hear. I'd laugh if five people hadn't died." Longstreet's face purpled.

"Good bloody Christ. Five dead, fourteen hospitalized because of a bottom fish." He pulled at his drink. "I've a mind to leave this ragged city myself. I'm swamped, Mr. Snow. Even my secretary has been hospitalized."

"He was caught in the riot?"

"No. He had a bit too much gin and walked in front of a trolley. Broke both arms. Now he has plaster casts from wrists to shoulders, and he can't even pick his nose." Longstreet laughed shortly. "It isn't funny, really. Poor Bliss. I've asked the newspapers to play down the riot and what has followed."

"What's followed?"

"Dozens of sporadic street fights, involving anywhere from two to ten Malays and Chinese. Last night and this morning. A number of small fires. I'm telling you, Singapore is close to the edge. The markets in white Singapore are running short of tinned goods because the housewives have begun to hoard, thinking that the next riot may hit the stores. The bomb shelters dug in 1942 are being reopened in the event the whites need to hide from a mob. The gun shops have sold out. It's impossible to book passage out of the city. Even cargo ships are taking passengers. You can buy a home in the Tanglin area or Holland Park for a pittance. And on and on."

"How are you holding up?"

The governor's smile thanked Snow for the question. "My authority is crumbling. The Gurkha are a force unto themselves. They do as they please. The British military command has been further separated from my office, and the colonel seems caught in the same quandary Parliament is. He refuses to engage his men. Says they are soldiers, not riot police. I don't blame him, actually."

A waiter in a starched white coat approached, placed another drink in the governor's hand, then said, "Mr. Snow, telephone at the desk."

Snow excused himself and crossed the lobby. He lifted the phone to his ear. Shelby Watson said briskly, "We may have found her. A bartender I treat thinks he saw her in front of the Orange Hotel about three minutes ago. She was just standing there, still wearing the white dress. She was looking up and down the street, as if watching for someone."

Snow barked his thanks into the phone. He rushed out of the lobby, raising his hand to the governor. The Orange Hotel was two blocks away, on Stamford Road near St. Andrew's Cathedral. Snow ran on the curb, avoiding the crowded sidewalk and the anarchic street. He adroitly dodged telephone poles and fireplugs. Tamils and Chinese jumped out of his way.

By the time he sprinted onto Stamford Road, his shirt had become a second skin and his shoes seemed filled with water. Snow pushed himself toward the hotel, his lungs sucking the simmering air like a great bellows. Sweat fell into his eyes in a cascade, and he wiped it away to see the Orange Hotel sign hanging over the intersection of Stamford Road and Victoria Street. He slowed, searching among the cheongsams and *bajus* for a white dress.

She was there, rocking back and forth on her feet in front of the hotel door. Same sandy hair, same white dress. Amelia Earhart, Snow exulted. She stepped to the curb and went to her toes, looking up Victoria, all the while twisting one hand in another. A yellow taxi pulled up to the curb near her.

Snow had taken three more steps toward her when a thickset, crew-cutted Anglo emerged from the tiny cab. The man had difficulty negotiating his bulk through the narrow cab door, and the woman in white stepped forward to take his arm. They embraced. Big man, crumpled suit, wide face. A familiar face. A sudden, ominous realization brought Snow to a dead stop forty feet from them. He had seen that face fifty times in Washington, D.C. Howard Lester and the woman in white disappeared through the lobby doors.

The bandage covered the entire half of Flynn's face below the eye. Each time the truck bounced into a chuckhole his face knotted with pain and the stitches tugged at each other. Sixty sutures which the physician said would leave a permanent jagged scar from scalp to chin. Flynn angrily clenched the wheel.

Sitting on the passenger side, Dillon Synge said, "What did I tell you about getting close to his hands?"

"Snow's hands didn't move. It was the man sitting across from him, the leper."

"That makes no difference. You got too near and you paid the price. I just can't imagine why you didn't walk into the Masthead and fire at him. Why the need for talk? Why the need to see fear?"

Pinang sat between them, his mouth wired shut by an elaborate brace that ran from his jaw to the back of his neck. It looked like a squirrel cage. He glanced at Flynn's wrapped face and tried to grin. "That would have taken the fun out of it."

"Take the next left," Synge said, idly waving his hand at the corner.

"I know where the consulate is," Flynn snapped.

"Remember what I've told you. Every time I've been in the building, two Russian plainclothesmen are standing or sitting in the hallway. I'm sure they're armed. Stasov is usually upstairs behind his desk, but don't go anywhere near his office. Just clear a path to the basement, and do it quickly before anyone can push the vault door closed."

"You should've done this a year ago when you got back to Singapore," Flynn said, pulling on the wheel of the truck. It was an army surplus two-ton Dodge, still in its green and khaki camouflage. It had been a tow truck, but the crane and winch had been replaced with a cargo box. A heavy-gauge push-bar still protected the radiator.

"Things are different now," Synge said quietly.

"Yeah, they sure are," Flynn said, steering the truck around a Klentong man and his wagon of housewares. "We've moved out of the club. Our plane is gone. Our river warehouse is gone. You've called off further jade shows, and as far as I can tell, your business has ground to a complete stop. You've got your motor launch ready to leave. In other words, we're in full retreat."

Synge chewed his lip, working to check his temper. It wasn't Flynn's place—not anyone's place—to criticize how he ran his business. But now was no time to anger him. "Maybe so, Flynn. Right now the pressure is too much. A maniac is after me, so I'm getting out." Synge flicked the safety off on his Mauser pistol. "Pinang, I want you to stand at the bottom of the flight of stairs to the second floor. No need to go up there, just keep Stasov from coming down. Flynn, you'll go downstairs to the vault with me."

Pinang sucked air between his teeth. "Shouldn't you consider leaving Singapore without the elephant? Maybe coming back for it when things are a bit safer?"

"I will never leave this city without the Kobe Elephant. I did it once and it was the biggest mistake of my life."

The truck turned onto Middle Road, and as it approached the Soviet consulate, it ground down through the gears. Flynn missed a gear when the stick slapped into the shotgun standing between his knees. He opened and closed the truck door several times, insuring it was clear. With this knowledgeable movement, control of the operation passed to him as clearly as if there had been written orders. He said, "I want both of you to cover your faces with your arms when we go through. I don't expect any trouble with the windshield, but it'd be tough running up and down those stairs blind. Another thing; open your door, but stay behind it until I give the clear signal. The doors on these trucks are armored, and nothing they've got will go through them."

A block away from the consulate the crowd thinned, as it always did near white Singapore. Fewer shopping amahs, fewer street vendors, less rabble. The truck accelerated in low gear, and its whine reverberated between the white colonial buildings. They approached the Soviet consulate with its wrought-iron fence and barred windows. Flynn brought the truck to a halt, waiting for a clot of schoolchildren to pass. He lifted the shotgun to his lap, cracked it and touched the bottom of the twelve gauge shells, then snapped it closed. Pinang drew the British Colt .455 from his shirt and held it near his wired chin. Flynn whispered, "Let's go."

The engine roared, and an enormous plume of diesel smoke shot from the exhaust pipe. The truck lurched forward ponderously, gaining speed for thirty feet before sharply veering across the oncoming lane. Its deep-tread mud tires rammed the curb, almost throwing Flynn to the cab ceiling. He pushed the accelerator pedal to the firewall, and the truck leaped across the sidewalk into the iron fence. The gate sprung open with such force the hinges tore from the frame. The padlock and chain flew into a shrub alongside the building. Both sides of the gate rebounded to slap at the truck's flank. Still accelerating, the Dodge bounded up the two steps to the consulate's enormous door.

The push-rod tore into the door, splintering it as if it were balsa. The shattered door crashed inward and a ceramic umbrella stand caught between the door and the wall disintegrated. The truck rushed into the consulate's hallway, pushing the reception desk ahead of it. The two astonished plainclothes guards gaped at the truck that had suddenly smashed into their lobby. The guard nearest the stairwell recovered first. He pulled a revolver from his belt, but he was too late.

With a fluid, practiced motion, Flynn swung the truck's door open and pushed the shotgun's barrel through the window. Crouched on the runningboard, shielded by the heavy plate in the door, he squeezed the first trigger. The shotgun jumped reassuringly against his shoulder. He moved it slightly to the right and emptied the second barrel. The pounding rattled the consulate's walls, and the immense crystal chandelier over the stairwell shivered.

Both Soviet guards had been blown back against the rear wall, where they slumped in spreading pools of blood. Their shirts were red rags, and their faces and hands were pocked in red, as if from a sudden disease. The gun-pulling guard's revolver had landed near a potted palm. A bank of leaded windows above the two dead men had been shattered.

Flynn rose from his crouch, broke the shotgun, and slipped new shells into the chambers. With his pistol at arm's length in front of him, Pinang stepped over the Russians and posted himself at the bottom of the stairwell.

Dillon Synge looked neither at the dead guards nor up the stairs to Kiril Stasov's office. The jade dealer immediately descended to the consulate's basement. Flynn followed Synge closely, guarding his back.

The vault door was partially open, as it was each day until Stasov left the building. Synge walked across the basement, passed the ponderous Chubb door to the light switch, as he had seen Stasov do so many times. He waved Flynn over, and both men pulled against the inertia of the massive steel door. The hinges filled the basement with an unearthly squeal. Synge strained against the door until it was doubled back against the safe.

The Kobe Elephant was framed in the safe's door, bathed in the artificial light, a perfect painting. For the first time in five years, Kiril Stasov was not standing between Synge and his elephant. Synge's legs felt as if they were made of rope, and he found himself panting. He held a hand out to the safe wall to steady himself. Flynn caught his other arm. A few more breaths and the jade dealer nodded he was all right. He looked again at his elephant, *his* elephant, turned to Flynn and smiled, the grin of a man freed from chains.

Synge bent to enter the safe, his hand outstretched and trembling. He took the three steps he knew so well. His fingers touched the Kobe Elephant's ear, and he pressed his palm onto the cool trunk. Flynn stepped over the safe threshold. He had suffered through a hundred of Synge's descriptions of the Kobe Elephant, but they hadn't prepared him for the treasure in the safe. He gazed over his boss's shoulder at the luminescent, sea-green elephant.

Kiril Stasov's Tokarev jabbed into Flynn's shoulder and exploded. The roar sounded like a blasting cap detonated inside a barrel. A small hole showed on his shirt and bits of bone and tissue splattered against the far wall of the safe. Flynn dropped first to his knees, then sideways against the safe's steel wall. His shotgun clattered beside him. His hard eyes dropped to the wound, then raised slowly to Stasov's pistol. His mouth opened, but only a whispered moan escaped it.

Stasov had simply stood in the safe's corner, knowing Synge's eyes would never leave the elephant. They did now. Slowly, the jade dealer turned to look down the pistol's barrel. His shoulders slumped in defeat and his jaw sagged open. His palm remained on the elephant's trunk. As if Stasov's hand were at his throat, his whisper was cracked and dry. "This is my elephant, Kiril."

The jade dealer's nose was in the Tokarev's notched sight. Stasov replied evenly, "Have I ever said otherwise, Dillon?"

Synge swallowed quickly, but said nothing.

"I've got some dead men upstairs, don't I, Dillon? You must be getting desperate. And less and less cooperative." Stasov waited for an answer, but again Synge was silent. "Give me a reason I shouldn't end your struggle here and now."

Synge touched his tongue to his upper lip, and drew in a long breath.

"You don't seem to understand why we are indispensable to each other, Dillon. I need your Malays, and you need the elephant, which only I can give you." Despite the reassuring words, the Russian's pistol had not lowered. "Listen to me this time, Dillon. You'll get your elephant, perhaps within the week. Look at what's happening in Singapore. It's ready to split open like a rotten palmetto. Once we learn the British are abandoning the city, once we change the minds of a few more British MP's, you'll have it."

Stasov waved Synge through the vault's door. The Russian followed, keeping the jade dealer's spine down the barrel. "If you have other men upstairs, call them off."

Synge hesitated until prodded by the Tokarev. "Pinang," he yelled, a weak, tremulous effort. "Leave the building."

The Malay's footsteps were heard crossing the lobby. Wood

204

splintered loudly as he tore a pathway through the ruptured door. The Russian waited a moment, then spurred Synge up the stairs with the pistol. Both men pulled at loose fragments of the door until a wider opening was made alongside the truck.

Synge stepped through them down the steps to the walkway. He turned back to the Russian and said, "A week, Stasov. I'll have the Kobe Elephant in seven days, one way or the other."

The Orchid Brotherhood had many imitators. At the Brotherhood's last count, there were five other Chinese protective societies in Singapore. The Yellow Nightingale recruited many Teochews, and the Black Pearl consisted of Singapore's Cantonese, but these and the others were largely repressed by the Orchid Brotherhood, whose strength among the city's Hokkein Chinese overshadowed rival tongs. On occasion, Singapore's Malay and the Indian populations attempted to emulate the Orchid Brotherhood, but without the Brotherhood's instincts for murder and extortion, these loosely knit organizations quickly reverted to community clubs and charity fund-raisers.

Without question, the most virulent imitators of the Orchid Brotherhood were the sons of the Brotherhood. The youth packs recruited nine-year-olds. Usually, by age fourteen, the boys had outgrown them. For those few years a child could find an organized channel for his destructiveness.

The master of Singapore's *swaylos*, Kao Kuei-tze, had been blessed with two sons, Chu and Tung, who because of their respectable sizes were the moving force behind the Red Daggers, a Chinatown street gang of toughs waiting to become old enough to join the Brotherhood. The Red Daggers specialized in petty theft, vandalism and bullying. They collected daily at dusk and prowled Pagoda Street and Temple Street, cutting what they thought a wide swath.

Chu and Tung and the other Red Daggers were caught up in the nationalistic spirit of the past weeks, during which Malays and Chinese seemed to be struggling for control of Singapore. The fish market riot became a rallying cry for the Red Daggers. Imaginary scenarios of vengeance were told and retold. Chu and Tung promised massive reprisals.

On this early evening, with the sun disappearing behind Mount Faber, members of the Red Daggers met on the South

Bridge Road near the Elgin Bridge. After the customary hooting and jostling, the fifteen or so boys formed ragged double-file columns and marched along the South Boat quay above the hundreds of sampans moored on the Singapore River. None of them had been on Selagie Street during the fish market riot, but all knew precisely what had happened: how a Chinese infant had been stoned by ranting Malays, how members of the Orchid Brotherhood using mystical martial arts retaliated swiftly, washing the street in Malay blood. The Red Daggers continued the massacre by chopping the air with fists and feet, cutting down untold numbers of imaginary Malay interlopers.

The police investigation would conclude that the Red Daggers had not intentionally headed for the fishing pier that jutted out into the Singapore Straits just south of the river mouth. Rather, the gang drifted that way, propelled by exuberance. They ran onto the beach and wrestled and splashed for a while, unaware of the seven Malay children fishing from the pier.

The inspector could only guess how long the two groups of children remained oblivious to each other. But at some point, one of the Kao boys pointed at the pier, then led his gang up the beach onto the wharf. The Chinese boys ran along the pier, screaming obscenities and anti-Malay oaths. Several Englishmen walking along Fullerton Road reported that the Malay children froze, their bamboo rods hanging over the pier's rubrail. The Red Daggers crashed into the Malays and with loud laughter and curses began shoving them toward the end of the dock.

With cries for revenge, the Kao brothers threw the poles and fishing gear into the water. Several Red Daggers grabbed a Malay child and swung him back and forth like a sack of rice, then hurled him into the water. Next, a six-year-old girl was cast over the end of the pier. For five minutes, whenever the Malays tried to climb back onto the wharf, several Red Daggers would walk on their fingers or pry their arms from the pillar, forcing them to drop back into the water. Finally, when all the Malays were in the sea at once, Chu emitted a battle cry and with a raised fist, led his troops off the pier. Invigorated by the victory, the Red Daggers whooped and danced. They promised each other that this was just the beginning.

All but one of the seven Malay children would regain the

dock. Because the tide was going out, the little girl's body was never found. Confused reports of the incident—variously called a drowning, a murder, and a riot—reached Governor Longstreet's office within the hour. He immediately ordered the Gurkha police into the streets to form a human barrier between the Malay and Chinese neighborhoods. Singapore would spend a sleepless, fearful night.

Snow had spent an hour standing on the curb near the Orange Hotel's door. Again and again he had reviewed what he had just seen: his boss Howard Lester and Amelia Earhart met on the sidewalk, then entered the hotel. He tried to analyze everything, every gesture, every nuance. She had been waiting impatiently, obviously knowing Lester would arrive. They had quickly embraced, the hug of friends reunited after a short absence. Lester carried a small suitcase, meaning he wasn't staying long. And he wasn't with his omnipresent bodyguard, indicating this wasn't official business.

Snow leaned against the building. He touched his damp forehead with a handkerchief, then shook his head at a Chinese boy offering to shine his shoes. Those clues meant little, he knew. They were an axis around which his mind could work, could chip away at the straitjacket of suspicion that had been suffocating him for an hour. Never in all his years with Howard Lester had he been assigned to cross purposes with the boss. Lester had always been straightforward, carefully outlining all he knew about an assignment, doing his best to see his agent got in and out alive. Hidden information only meant hidden dangers. Annette Cordez, Thompson the Tapper, Andrew Jay, all agreed that despite his array of irritating habits, Lester could be counted on for complete candor.

Yet, for Christ's sake, Lester had sent Snow to Singapore on a bogus assignment, one that had already imperiled him and his wife. Lester had even *insisted* that Connie accompany him. An angry bile rose in Snow's throat. He ran the calloused knuckles of his left hand along the side of the building. His mind flashed a vision of the two Malay thugs running at them from the monsoon drain and the casualness with which Flynn was going to put a bullet into him. All because Lester was playing games. The more he dwelled on these thoughts, the angrier Snow became, until he found himself walking toward the hotel door, intent on confronting Lester straightaway.

Snow was a dozen feet from the door when Lester and the woman in white emerged. Instinctively Snow flattened himself against the wall, his resolve quickly overwhelmed by curiosity. Like a tourist, Lester hailed a trishaw, and the woman in white handed him a flat leather book before climbing in. Lester got in beside her, then leaned forward to give the *wallah* directions. After several false starts, the trishaw edged its way into the flow of traffic.

Snow frantically searched for another trishaw, repeatedly rising on his toes to follow the course of Lester and the woman in white. A cab pulled up to the Orange Hotel and an elderly Dutch woman was part way out when Snow's hand circled her wrist and pulled her free of the door. She opened her mouth to protest, saw the size of the man jumping into her taxi, and thought better of it. Snow tossed her suitcase through the door where it bounced to her feet. He gripped the cabdriver by the shoulder and said, "Follow that green trishaw."

"But, sahib, . . . the woman's fare? She . . ."

Snow's hand clenched the Sikh's shoulder. His eyes bulged with pain. "Get going. I'll pay for everything later."

The Ford taxi buzzed away from the curb and was quickly in sight of the trishaw, which was moving at a leisurely pace through the stream of pedestrians and vehicles. Snow tried to relax, but the cramped rear seat of the taxi would not allow him to stretch out and acted to bottle his increasing anger. When he muttered "Goddamn Howard Lester," the driver looked around to inquire, saw Snow's hardened face, and quickly turned back.

For twenty minutes the taxi trailed Lester and the woman in white. They left white Singapore and crossed the Singapore River into Chinatown. The Sikh bleated the horn at an elderly amah carrying plucked chickens hung from a pole over her shoulder, and her shuffling slowed further. He waved his fist at the old woman and she returned a gesture Snow had never seen before.

Their eyes had been on the amah, and the taxi was almost up to the trishaw before Snow tapped the Sikh's shoulder and pointed. The driver pulled the cab to the opposite curb. The trishaw had stopped in front of a book vendor's stall where a

Chinese scribe was squatting on the sidewalk with a board across his lap. Next to him, a young woman dressed in a flower print cheongsam dictated a letter to her family on the mainland.

Snow squeezed himself from the cab and dropped a few dollars into the Sikh's hand. The cab rolled away from the curb and Snow followed it, using it as cover for several yards until a fruit truck stood between him and the trishaw. Between pedestrians, Snow glimpsed Lester giving the leather book to the scribe, who rose, walked under the awning, and carelessly tossed it on a pile of newspapers. Lester slipped something into the scribe's hand, perhaps money, Snow couldn't tell. Lester and the woman in white climbed back into the trishaw and the *wallah* strained to pull away from the curb.

Snow had to choose between running after the trishaw or trying to look at the book Lester and the woman—no, Snow resolved to call her by her name, Amelia Earhart—had left behind. He chose the latter, simply because the trishaw had already rounded the corner. He stepped around a group of six-year-old beggars who clutched at his shirt and crossed quickly to the book stall. He kneeled next to the scribe, who automatically placed a sheet of paper on his writing board. He dipped the pen in a bottle of India ink and turned to Snow. His eyebrows went up at the sight of the Anglo, and rose even higher when Snow spoke to him in Cantonese. "I want to buy a book."

The scribe's dark hair was knotted in leather thongs that reached the ground behind him. His smile was toothless. "I have a lot of books and I'll write you a letter if you can't do it yourself."

"Just a book."

"Or I'll carve you a chop and sell you lucky red ink. They guarantee your letters arrive safely."

"A book." Snow rose and walked to the leather book deposited by Lester. He turned it over in his hands. The brown calfskin was well-worn. Several dark stains, perhaps engine oil, marred the binding. Imprinted on the front cover was the word "Log." Flipping to a random page, Snow examined the tight, controlled handwriting squeezed between blue lines. He held the log closer and read, "Departed Dakar, 2-10-37 shortly after dawn." He turned several pages. "6-20-37, climbed to 8,000 feet to rise above a squall. Clear above the cloud level."

Snow felt the blood rising to his face. He knew what he held before he turned to the front page to read her name. He was holding Earhart's flight log. The last entry read, "Saipan, Tinian on horizon. Starboard engine throwing a little oil. Fred nervous. Me, too." The handwriting was familiar. Snow felt as if he already knew Amelia Earhart, as if she had become part of him.

And he felt betrayed. Howard Lester was planting clues that Amelia Earhart was alive. The medals and wristwatch had been plants designed to convince him she hadn't gone down in the Pacific, to prevent him from leaving Singapore. The pages of the log were shaking as if brushed by wind. His hands were trembling with anger.

He slammed the log shut and returned to the scribe. "How much for this book?"

"That book isn't for sale. I was paid a dollar just to hold it for three days."

"Well, Honorable Gentleman," Snow said, "I'm walking away from here with this book, and you can either take five dollars or take nothing."

The scribe looked up from the chop he was carving. "I'll take the five dollars."

Snow pressed the bill into his hand. By the time the scribe had tucked the money under his board, Snow had disappeared into the mass of passing people.

"Tapper? I can barely hear you," Snow yelled into the phone. He was crowded into a booth in the Raffles' lobby.

"You're coming in all right. Go ahead." Thomas Thompson the Tapper's voice rode on a crest of long-distance static.

"Are you on a clear phone?" Snow said loudly, gripping the receiver tightly. Lubricated with sweat, the receiver felt as if it would shoot from his hand like a banana from its skin.

"Yeah, it's clear. How's your vacation going?"

"Tapper, I've got to call in a few favors from you."

"You want me to tap your wife's phone?" The Tapper laughed. "Christ, that relationship went downhill fast."

Thomas Thompson was the best in the business. He could extract a conversation from an office or an automobile or, his favorite, a bedroom. He could wring the words from telephone wires or pluck them from the air. The Tapper was a conversation thief.

"Tapper, do you have any idea what a week in Singapore does to you?"

"No jokes from this end, right?"

"Right," Snow breathed deeply, then tested the Tapper. "How's Howard Lester doing?"

"Haven't the slightest. He's on vacation or something. Haven't seen him in days." The Tapper laughed from nine thousand miles away. "You're the first person I've ever heard ask after his health."

Snow exhaled slowly. Lester hadn't set Thompson up. He wasn't in on it. "Can you run a few checks for me?"

"Sure, no problem, Joe." Thompson's voice faded in and out as if carried by the wind. "Who do you have in mind?"

"Tapper," Snow said carefully, "I think Lester is setting me up."

A long dead silence. "You know what you're saying, Joe?"

"You're goddamn right. Lester sent me and my wife to Singapore on a phony mission, and he's working to keep me here. He's put blinders on me, and there are some very tough people looking for me. I'm under the long gun, Tapper."

"What do you want me to do?" Even accounting for the static, the Tapper's voice was tentative.

"Run a check on Lester. See what his connection was to Amelia Earhart's 1937 round-the-world flight."

"Are you shitting me, Joe? Amelia Earhart?"

"You heard me. Can you do the check outside the organization? Lester can't be warned."

"Well, the British owe me. I could have M6 take a look. And I could do a little prowling around here myself."

"There're other names, Tapper. I trust you're recording this?"

"Always, always."

"You never change." Snow forced a laugh. "I want a ground-up check of everyone I've come into contact with here in Singapore, and whether they have any connection with Amelia Earhart. The names are: Ko Tsukada." Snow spelled it, then continued, "Dillon Synge. A thug named Flynn with an Irish brogue. Governor Grayson Longstreet. Beth Johnston from Eugene, Oregon. Shelby Watson, a sometime M.D. who used to be with the agency. And above all, Lester. Call me at Watson's in four hours." He gave the doctor's phone number.

There was a pause at the other end. Finally, the Tapper

said, "Joe, you said a ground-up check of everyone you've been involved with in Singapore. Do you really mean that?"

"Of course. What do you mean?"

"You want me to run your wife's name through?"

Snow yanked the receiver away as if it had branded him. It must have been a full minute before he could push it back to his ear. He swallowed. "Sure, Tapper. Run Connie's name through."

XIV

Dengue bloated her joints so she couldn't walk
and gave her a rash that appeared as if her first
layer of skin had been peeled away. She halluci-
nated about the mottled face of the man peering
down the pistol barrel.

Shelby Watson held the ball-peen hammer in his gloved hand
and idly swung it into the human skull. Bone shards burst
away sprinkling the operating table. The cranium rolled to
the edge of the table, but Watson deftly hooked an eye socket
and returned it to the center of the table. The hammer arced
into the jaw. Several teeth snapped off and rattled around in
the brain cavity. Watson lifted the skull, turned it over, and
shook the teeth out. Again, he began his tattoo with the
hammer, slowly demolishing the skull.

Joseph Snow opened a can of Tiger Beer and said, "I'm
probably asking you to violate physician-patient confidence,
but why are you demolishing that head?"

Watson ran his palm along the table to collect the fragments, then scooped them into a small wooden box. "A
Chinese merchant paid me fifty pounds to make this skull
and a few other parts disappear, then issue a legal death
certificate. He brought the bones here in a sack. I don't ask
questions. He'll get his certificate saying the man drowned,
and I'll end up with a lot of bone powder."

"You put those sacks out for the wagons?" Snow asked,
draining half his beer in a long swallow.

"No profit in that. I sell it as rhinoceros tusk powder. Best aphrodisiac in the world, so the Chinese think. I get twenty pounds a pouch."

Snow tossed the can into the wastebasket and reached for his second beer. "Tell me, Shelby, you do surgery anymore? You used to be pretty good."

The hammer's tempo increased. "Don't do too much now. The hand, you know. And the Chinese are funny people. They don't mind me having misplaced my medical school degree, but they want a pretty face. Mine doesn't quite fit the bill."

"So now you pound skulls into rhinoceros powder?"

"I also wrap friends' arms without asking many questions." Watson topped his shot glass with gin. "Joseph, you're a bit on edge. Singapore does that, you know. But is there some other reason?"

"I may have a reason." Snow's voice was tight. "I'm on my own for a while."

"You look like it. You show up here out of breath, like you've run from the Raffles. You usually have someone in tow, your wife or the Jap, but not now. And you haven't told me why you're here."

"I'm moving for a while and I needed a phone where I can be reached."

"You on the run?"

Snow punched open a third can. "Just waiting for a phone call."

"Joseph, if you're in trouble, get hold of Howard Lester. He has resources everywhere."

Snow said quietly, "Lester has crossed me. He may have me under the long gun."

The hammer stopped in midair. "I don't believe that."

Snow's enormous hand balled up a beer can as if it were paper. "Hired gunnies have taken after me twice. You were there the second time."

"That doesn't mean. . . ."

"Howard Lester sent me to Singapore to look for Amelia Earhart's bones. Yet Lester is in Singpore this minute escorting Earhart around."

"Joseph, that's insane."

"Goddamn it, I know what I saw. He's arranged a forwarding hookup, so when I call Washington, I still get Lester, even though he's here."

"That's not the way Lester operates, Joe. He's a square dealer, always has been. I can't imagine. . . ."

Watson was interrupted by the ring of the telephone. He pulled it from behind a stack of bedpans and handed it to Snow. "Must be your call. Most of my patients don't survive long enough to make phone calls."

Thomas Thompson the Tapper's voice crackled into Snow's ear. "Joseph, I've been running my ass off, but I think I got most of what you want. Who do you want me to start with?"

Abruptly, Snow pulled his .45 automatic from his waistband and leveled it at Shelby Watson. "Start with Watson."

Watson had looked down the barrel of a gun before. He froze. Then his eyes widened. "What in bloody hell, Joseph?"

Snow's voice was brisk. "The surprise play doesn't work with me, Shelby. You've already pulled your scalpel from somewhere. Put it on the table. Slowly."

The blade glinted in the dim light before coming to rest on the operating table. Watson held his hands away from his body. Snow's eyes never left the black glove covering his corroded hand.

Tapper's voice came clearly from nine thousand miles away. "Watson? Nothing new on him, Joseph. He hasn't been employed by the service since the war. No connection whatever. He was booted from the service because of a fondness for gin and because he refused treatment for his disease."

Snow returned the .45 to his belt. He tried to smile as he looked at Watson. "I'm sorry, Shelby. I had to be sure. You'd have done the same thing."

"I probably would have been a bit more subtle, Joseph. That Colt's got an ugly front end." He passed his gloved hand over the scalpel and the blade disappeared.

"What else, Tapper?" Snow lowered himself into a wicker chair.

"Your friend Ko Tsukada. I don't know what he's been telling you, but it probably isn't what I've found out. He was a regular Army Japanese dogface, no trouble, no commendations, no ripples, until early 1937, when he killed an officer."

"An accident?"

Tapper's voice merged with the static and was barely audible. "The killing of an Imperial Army officer is considered murder whether it was or not. I imagine they would've lined Tsukada up against a wall had he not gone on the lam."

Snow pressed the receiver against his ear and held his free hand over the other ear. "Tapper, can you talk louder? Did you say 'on the lam'?"

"That's right. He deserted to save his neck."

"Tsukada wasn't a member of the *Kempai tai?*"

What Snow heard could have been laughter, could have been cable distortion. "Shit no. You give him too much credit. He's a deserter."

"And you're sure of your facts?"

"I had to kiss the butt of a very high-and-mighty MacArthur adjutant to get this. Before I do that, I make sure it's going to be good information." Tapper's voice washed in and out. "The Imperial Army waited the required twelve months, then declared Tsukada dead. Nothing heard from him since."

"He's alive and well in Singapore, and I owe him a couple of favors," Snow said, rubbing his bandaged arm against the edges of the wicker chair. Watson saw the motion over the rim of his shot glass and drew a pair of scissors from a glass-front cabinet. He rolled up Snow's sleeve and began cutting the swathing. The arm resembled the surface of a mincemeat pie and Snow looked away as it emerged from the bandage.

"Anything on Governor Longstreet?" he asked.

"Long suffering. Hard working. Nothing interesting."

"Dillon Synge?"

"You must know more about him than I do, Joe. All I can find are hearty recommendations from his jade business associates. He's either straight or he covers himself well."

"He's anything but straight. What about Lester?"

"Ah, here we get a bit more interesting. I have to admit, when you asked about any connection Lester might have with Amelia Earhart, I started to laugh and didn't stop until I found out about our involvement with her flight. Christ, she was flying to Saipan for the OSS . . ."

"I know about that, Tapper. Tell me what Lester had to do with it."

"My British contacts say everything."

"What does that mean?"

"It was Lester's operation from the beginning. He dreamed it up, and he planned it down to the last detail. Apparently he was obsessed by the coup. It was to be the first major leak in Japanese military intelligence. A Japanese network could be possible. He was on Howland Island July 2, 1937 waiting for Earhart and Noonan. His ass was chewed by everyone from President Roosevelt to his own wife. The boys at M6 are still laughing about it, or so they said when they gave me this information. If embarrassment could kill, M6 said Lester would've left Howland Island in a box."

"That explains why Lester's in Singapore," Snow said, more to himself than Tapper.

"You bet it does. You know how he is. I've done a few clean-ups for him, and I imagine you have, too. He makes up some big story, but he uses us to get even. I've never decided whether his penchant for revenge is a deliberate warning to his antagonists, or whether he's just ornery."

"So he sent me to Singapore to find the man who duped him, and now he's come to finish it."

Tapper's voice faded, then surged back. ". . . sounds like it. I found something else, Joe. Lester disappeared for three or four months after Earhart's plane went down. M6 thinks sheer humiliation drove him into hiding. One of the boys here thinks it was confusion abetted by alcohol. He emerged from hiding and spent the next few years pushing low-level paper back and forth. Only after the war began did he begin his rapid climb in the organization."

"Tapper, is there any reason why Lester would keep me in the dark?"

"Can't think of it. But you'd better find out whether he's working for or against you."

"Let's hope it's for me," Snow said darkly.

"Christ, yes." Thompson paused, then said, "Other finds: that woman you wanted me to check out in Eugene. I had Harvey Lisle do it on the QT. To sum up, there is no Beth Johnston."

"I know that. Lester said she fabricated her college degree, that sort of thing. She appeared in Eugene out of thin air a year ago."

"That's not what I mean," the Tapper explained patiently. "There wasn't then, and isn't now, a Miss Johnston. She never appeared in Eugene, never worked as a nurse there. She doesn't exist."

"Are you telling me Lester lied about Beth Johnston, to make me think it was Amelia Earhart?"

"All I'm telling you is that there is no Johnston."

Snow crossed his brow with a hand, and beads of perspiration rolled down his fingers. There was a long pause. Finally, Thompson the Tapper's brittle laugh came through. "You haven't asked me about your wife. I put her name through, too. Your wife is from Schenectady, New York, born in 1912.

217

She went through the Scotia Girls School in only seven years, then went on to prep school, an exclusive all girl boarding school in. . . ."

Snow let his head roll back against the wall, a wave of relief eased the tension that had kept his neck tight all during the conversation. "Is that all you've got?" he interrupted.

Another laugh from Washington, D.C. "No. There's another page, all of it uninteresting, except for a little episode at Radcliffe where she was suspended for a week because the dorm marm found a bottle of Pims under her mattress."

Snow smiled widely. "Good work, Tapper."

"Joe, it might be the connection, but I doubt it. You sound a little tight. Are you going to be all right?"

Snow nodded, as if the Tapper could see him.

In a tone Snow appreciated, Thompson said, "I've been picking my butt in D.C. for months. I could be in Singapore in three days."

"Thanks, Tapper. You'll get a call if I need you."

The receiver was back on the cradle for only ten seconds when the phone rang again. Snow wearily lifted it to his ear. Ko Tsukada's voice was strained with excitement. "Snow, Flynn talked, and I've found Dillon Synge. He's walking north on Crawford Street, and I'm a half block behind him. I figure he'll be at the Crawford Street Bridge in ten minutes."

"I'll be there." Snow clamped down the cradle and handed the phone to Shelby Watson. "And when I get there, our Japanese deserter will answer some questions."

The stone caught Kiril Stasov behind the right ear. He staggered to one knee and clutched his head. Warm fluid seeped between his fingers, and in a painful daze he stared at the blood dripping from his hand to the cobblestone. The Russian shook his head, trying to clear it, and struggled to his feet.

Jeers pierced the ringing centered behind his eyes. Ragged young Malays, their melodious language turned to ugly taunts, set Stasov's knees quivering. He planted a palm on a light pole and slowly turned in the direction of the catcalls.

A gang of fifteen boys had gathered. They were led by a tall youth whose torn *baju* hung from his gaunt shoulders like laundry from a pole. The others mirrored this boy, and when he raised his fist and shook it at the Russian, the gang followed. Stasov blinked rapidly, trying to chase away the pain. He said feebly, "You men must be mistaken. . . ."

Stasov's sudden smile broke off his words. They weren't mistaken. These boys had the correct target. Anything non-Malay. Their focus had broadened from the Chinese to anyone foreign. Fed by Dillon Synge's man Razak and by increasingly alarming rumors, the Malays' poisonous hatred had grown to such a pitch that their target made little difference. These boys sought a release from his carefully concocted choler. Their rage was confirmation that Stasov's plan was working.

His victorious grin was a mistake. Furious at the insolent, smiling foreigner, the pack's leader reached down for another cobblestone. Immediately the other Malay youths picked up heavy stones. The first caught Stasov squarely in the stomach. He lurched, more in surprise than pain. Stupidly he swatted at the rock as it fell to the ground. Another missile bounced loudly off a billboard. His smile had soured to a grimace and he strained to right himself. The boys were coming toward him, one cautious foot at a time, as if testing jungle sand, but their words were brazen and several held their arms cocked.

Stasov turned on his heels and sprinted away from the gang. Several rocks skittered on the sidewalk near him, one slapped into his heel, almost buckling his leg. He kept his legs pumping. He passed several Malay women who carried the day's produce in net baskets. Most laughed at the frantic white man, but one raised a slim fist in the air as Stasov ran by.

Breathing in huge gulps, the Russian turned onto Middle Road near his consulate. Only then, where most of the pedestrians were Anglos, did he slow his pace. He glanced over his shoulder, saw only the predictably chaotic condition of the street, and pulled a handkerchief from his rear pocket to sponge his face. Stasov laughed into the cloth. The city was turning into an enormous racial and religious bomb. When it was detonated, the British would be blown from Southeast Asia.

The sight of his consulate sobered Stasov. Repairmen were replacing the fractured door with one of case-hardened steel. An embassy guard overseeing the operation idly saluted his superior as Stasov came through the gate. When Stasov replaced the handkerchief, his hands began to shake, as they had for a full day since Synge's truck burst through the door.

It was blind luck that he had been in the basement, he knew. Had he not been down there with the code book and transmitter key, Synge could have shot him, or worse. After scraping parts of his two consulate guards off the hallway wall, Stasov knew how trigger-happy the jade dealer had become. Synge was losing his sanity.

Stasov wondered at the jade dealer's sudden decline. True, the Russian's possession of the Kobe Elephant was maddening, but Synge had lived with that fact for years. He had become increasingly testy, but not irrational. And the pressure the American was applying must also be unnerving, but Synge possessed an animal cunning. In the past he had dealt swiftly and mercilessly with jade pirates. Yet a single American had him bluffed. It was uncharacteristic for Synge to have gone into hiding. Either he knew more than he was telling the Russian or he had become addled. Probably the latter.

The Russian pushed his way through the heavy doors into the consulate hallway, leaving a smear of blood on the handle. An Indian carpenter was plastering the bullet holes in the far wall, another was puttying glass into the window. The guards' replacements, flown in from Kuala Lumpur that morning, were setting a Degtyarev light machine gun on a bipod in the center of the hallway. The new guards had scoffed at Stasov's orders to post the gun in the hallway, as they had questioned assigning another man to the basement near the Chubb safe. Stasov had opened the coffins for them, and they had since been silent.

Stasov stood over the Degtyarev and watched the guard oil the bolt lock and firing pin slide. The machine gun did little to assuage Stasov. He was not a veteran of war, or a man accustomed to violence. His tools were deception and artifice, promises and pressure. Snaring Dillon Synge and creating his Malay riot machine had been a triumph of these tactics.

He needlessly reminded the guard that he wanted a man on the weapon twenty-four hours a day, then climbed the stairs to his office. Stasov's pressure was no longer keeping Synge in line. The mercurial jade dealer had become violent. Should Synge try the door again, violence would be met with violence.

* * *

Snow was stationed on the Crawford Street Bridge less than five minutes after he had left Shelby Watson's office. He leaned over the bridge railing looking at the sampans lining the river below. Hokkein Chinese wearing black and white samfoos streamed past Snow on the bridge's catwalk. The women wore their hair in knobs, pulled back so tightly that many of them were partially bald. Two Sherpas wearing sash-tied overcoats, their hair plaited with ribbons, almost bumped into Snow. They quickly apologized and resumed their crossing, nervously searching the crowds. The Sherpas were heavily armed gem traders from Nepal, who carried sapphires and turquoise in leather pouches wrapped around their waists. Snow hunched lower over the rail.

Dillon Synge's mottled face bobbed above the wave of dark faces. Snow rose from the rail to risk a glance. Synge was wearing a white linen suit with a blue tie. The starched collar of his shirt seemed to be choking him, as his face was flushed and damp. The jade dealer was trying to move quickly, rudely shoving aside the amahs and Hakka women that clogged the bridge.

Snow turned back to the river, giving Synge time to pass on the opposite catwalk. His gaze returned to the oncoming horde. Snow's next task would be more difficult, finding Tsukada's amber face in an ocean of Oriental faces.

Tsukada was angling toward him on the catwalk before Snow saw him. The Japanese caught his sleeve in an amah's shopping net and shook himself free. He didn't break step as he said to Snow, "Synge is fifty feet ahead of us. We can catch him at the end of the bridge. . . ."

Snow jabbed a hand under Tsukada's shoulder, almost lifting him off the catwalk grill, and spun him into the railing. The crack of Tsukada's backbone slamming into the metal guardrail was clearly audible above the clatter of the passing horde. Tsukada's reaction was instinctive. He jerked his right leg viciously at Snow's groin, but the American had anticipated the standard defensive move taught all Imperial Army soldiers. Snow's fist drove into Tsukada's rising leg, violently stopping it two inches from Snow's testicles. The leg went limp and dropped to the catwalk as Snow pushed Tsukada further back over the rail.

Snow's voice was feral. "*Kempai tai*, my ass." His hand moved swiftly from Tsukada's throat to his lapel, where it tore off the *Kempai tai* chrysanthemum, taking most of the

221

collar with it, and tossed it into the Rochore River below. "You'll follow that button down there if what you say in the next ten seconds doesn't make sense."

Tsukada struggled to twist his head. His eyes were wide with anxiety, not fright. "Snow, we'll lose him."

"That makes no difference to me," Snow said, oblivious of the stares from the passing throng. "You made up a story about trying to reclaim the Kobe Elephant for the Imperial Palace. All bullshit."

"I'll explain that," Tsukada gasped. "But let me do it while we catch up with Synge. It'll make sense, I swear it."

Snow increased the pressure on Tsukada's adam's apple. "For all I know, you've had a hand in setting me up with the Malay thugs and with Flynn."

Tsukada's eyes were still on the crowd, trying to follow Synge's head as it became less and less distinct in the sway of the crowd. "I killed the gunman. Think, Snow. I was the one who saved you and your wife."

For a moment, there was no reaction. Then Snow allowed Tsukada's feet to return to the grating. The American's face was still creased with anger. Tsukada stared after Synge, but sagged into the railing on the second step. He grunted, "My leg is numb. It feels like you hit it with a wrecking ball." Again Snow shoved his hand under Tsukada's arm, this time helping him to his feet and acting as a crutch for a few steps. "Just keep after Synge," Tsukada pleaded.

Tsukada rubbed his thigh to work feeling back into his leg. They increased their pace along the catwalk to the foot of the bridge, then onto Lavender Street. Snow asked, "You see him?"

Tsukada took three running paces, craning his head frantically. "No. I can't make his head out. . . ."

For an instant, the crowd parted as if blown leeward by the wind, and Synge's white suit appeared at the end of a long tunnel of Singaporeans. Tsukada sprinted fifteen steps until the jade dealer's form was fixed firmly in his view. Snow's hand caught his shoulder. He demanded, "Before we get any closer, I want your story."

"It's simple," Tsukada answered without turning his head away from his prey. "I want the Kobe Elephant."

"So you've said." Snow skirted a Chinese fortune teller who had set up her teapot and destiny cards on the curb. "I don't buy that. You're an army deserter. The Imperial Palace had never heard of you, much less assigned you to return the elephant."

"I admit that I even waylaid the Imperial Palace agents that were sent. They're vacationing in the jungle right now."

"Why? And make sense."

"The Germans would call me a freebooter," Tsukada said easily.

"A freebooter?"

"I intend to find the Kobe Elephant, then sell it to the highest bidder."

"You're nothing but a thief," Snow said incredulously.

"An inelegant word," Tsukada grinned. "But accurate, I suppose."

Snow stopped so suddenly a rickshaw *wallah* who had been using their path through the crowd collided with him. He muttered what might have been an apology or a curse, then negotiated his vehicle around them. Snow said, "I'm not in Singapore to help a thief."

The anxious scowl returned to Tsukada's face as they lost ground to Synge. "No, but you need to talk to Synge to find out about Amelia Earhart. I must talk to him to discover where he has hidden the elephant. Our purpose is the same; to confront Synge."

"That elephant belongs to the government of Japan."

For a moment, Tsukada's eyes left the back of Synge's head to stare hard at the American. "Are you telling me you owe Japan anything?"

Snow's mind flashed to the years he had spent fighting those slant-eyed bastards. "No, I guess I don't."

"Then why does the elephant's fate matter to you?"

After a moment, Snow's mouth turned up. "Come to think of it, it doesn't."

"Then let's get to Synge."

With renewed purpose, Snow covered the ground they had lost. Finally they closed in. Snow could see Synge's head crank left and right at irregular intervals. He was quickening his pace. At the Kallang Road intersection, Synge plunged into the traffic, causing a trolley to lock its rear wheels, showering the street with sparks.

By the time Snow had crossed the Kallang Road, they were less than ten yards from Synge. Snow sprinted the last three steps to the jade dealer, viciously clamped one hand around his mouth, and whirled him around, using his own body as an

223

axis. The Chinese continued to obliviously throng past them. Snow and Tsukada both grabbed an arm, lifted Synge off the ground and turned him into a lot siding a warehouse. Synge yelped as he was thrown against the wall, then slowly sank to a squat. His head rolled back against the bricks and his fogged gaze rested on Snow.

Snow snapped, "You're going to answer some questions."

From the corner of his eye, Snow could see Ko Tsukada's transformation. As he stared down at Dillon Synge, Tsukada appeared to be seized by a malevolent, primitive passion which distorted his face into an evil mask.

Snow turned to the Japanese. "Ko, let's find out about Earhart before. . . ."

Tsukada's hand rose slowly in front of Snow's chest. His voice was a hollow whisper, like wind through a canyon. "Let me ask the questions, Joseph. It will save Mr. Synge some time."

Snow nodded and took a half step back, as if ceding the spotlight. He saw the muscle cords rippling the back of Tsukada's neck.

The Japanese spoke evenly, as if addressing a small child. "This is the end of a nine-year search, Dillon. Because of you and the Kobe Elephant, I've wandered for all those years, visiting a dozen countries, traveling the jade routes, always searching for the tall Anglo rumored to have Kobe's precious statue. I enlisted in the Imperial Army a second time in 1941, using a false name, so I could be in the first wave to liberate Manila and Singapore, hoping to find your scent." Tsukada's words were flat, as if he had memorized them, "It's been a long struggle, Dillon. I've been jailed, beaten and shot at. I had malaria twice, and I almost starved to death in Manila, for lack of money. But here we are, Dillon. You and I, face to face. Again."

Synge's words were calm. "You'll never get the Kobe Elephant. I don't have it."

A bitter smile twisted Tsukada's face. "The elephant means absolutely nothing to me. It never has."

Synge glanced at Snow, then back to the Japanese. The jade dealer's mouth opened, but he remained silent.

"Look at me," Tsukada demanded, his voice ringing. "Imagine my face covered with grime and a beard. Imagine me in the tattered uniform of an Imperial Army private."

Synge's face was blank. He looked again at Snow, as if seeking clarification.

Tsukada pulled his shirt tails from his pants, exposing the rippled, crepe-textured scar across his stomach. His voice was a brittle staccato. "Remember, Dillon? You awoke that morning, piled dried bushes at the mouth of the cave, and set a torch to it. I am Nissho Ito."

Synge's jaw sagged open and his brows climbed his forehead. He began shaking so violently that he slid further down the brick wall. He coughed, *"You're dead!"*

"I should have been. I raced frantically around the cave, searching for a gap in the wall of fire. There was none. You had seen to that. Finally, I lay on the cave's floor, so I'd be below the smoke and fumes. My last conscious thought was one of pain, the torture of lungs filled with smoke, of fire eating into my belly."

Synge's eyes had locked onto Tsukada's, the rodent mesmerized by the cobra.

Snow stepped forward, "If you don't want the Kobe Elephant, then why . . ."

He was cut off by Tsukada, whose voice had acquired a sing-song quality as he struggled to control himself. "I have no idea how long I was unconscious. I awoke surrounded by ashes. And I was a deserter, remember, I couldn't use the Saipan infirmary. I was ill for four months, couldn't breathe, couldn't eat. Later, I stowed away on a supply ship headed for Japan. It was a year later, but I began my search. It has ended today, Dillon."

Snow didn't see Tsukada pull the Nambu pistol from his belt. As the pistol lined up on his nose, Synge squealed in fear, and churned his legs, trying to push himself into the warehouse wall. Tsukada's finger tightened slowly around the trigger. He whispered, "Nine years of searching, just to put a bullet into you." The trigger came back.

Snow's fist smashed into Tsukada's gun hand just as the Nambu fired. The hand shot skyward, and Snow stepped under the Japanese's arm holding it aloft with both hands. He yelled, "Not until we ask him about Amelia Earhart."

A cry escaped Tsukada. He pulled desperately on the pistol, his feet leaving the ground. "No," he cried. "Synge is dead." This time, Snow's hand wasn't free to stop Tsukada's knee. It plowed into his thigh, and Snow immediately lost all sensation in his leg. Snow fell into the wall, carrying Tsukada with him, and he thrust the pistol against the bricks. It remained in the Japanese's grip. Leaning precariously on his one leg, Snow repeatedly smashed Tsukada's hand into the wall. The hand slackened and the Nambu dropped to the ground. Pain climbed from his leg and through clenched teeth. Snow said, "Just let me talk to him." He released Tsukada's hands. "Christ, try to calm down."

With a practiced motion, the Japanese chopped Snow's chin with an open palm, then stared dumbfounded as the American shook it off, and launched his right fist. The scarred knuckles careened off Tsukada's ear, spilling him backward onto the gravel of the vacant lot. Snow felt his own chin and muttered weakly, "Goddamn, that hurt."

Tsukada rolled to his feet, staggered briefly as if drunk, then sank to his knees. "He's gone," he said quietly, defeat eviscerating his voice.

Snow spun to the wall where Dillon Synge had been a moment before. Only the Nambu leaned against the bricks. Mindlessly, Snow patted the wall, then slowly, carefully, he lowered himself to a squat. He repeatedly opened and closed his mouth, testing his jaws. He coughed and spat, then said, "What an asshole you are."

"We'll find him again." Tsukada's voice firmed as he spoke.

"I think you've broken my face." Snow coughed again.

"He's in Singapore. He doesn't have his elephant, so he'll stay. We'll find him again."

Snow sank back against the bricks. "There's no 'we' to it. I'm on my own. You're an asshole."

"We'll find him." Ko Tsukada said, apparently not hearing Snow. "Dillon Synge can't hide from both of us."

XV

Days of weeping. The lost years. Oh, the lost years.

A number of gentlemen on the British White Club's veranda must have noticed Shelby Watson insert his hand into Joseph Snow's mouth. But Singapore had prepared them for the unusual, and no one commented.

"If you've fractured your upper maxilla, your teeth will slip in and out, but it doesn't look like it," Watson said. He ordered Snow to open and close his mouth several times, then asked him where his jaw hurt.

"All over."

The doctor put his finger under Snow's ear and murmured absently, "If anything is broken here, I'll feel the crepitus, the soft grating as the broken bones rub against each other." He moved his fingers along Snow's face. "But I don't feel it. Now, I'll press on the cleft of your chin. Anything? Thought not."

"Why did Ko hit you?" Connie asked, following Watson's fingers with his own.

"He went crazy. He wanted to do Synge in without letting me talk to him. The scowl of hatred that overcame him was frightening. For those sixty seconds, he was insane."

"Now I'll check for a blow out fracture. Also unlikely." Watson held his gloved hand in front of Snow. "Follow my hand with your eye. Don't move your head. If the eye socket has been ruptured, you won't be able to look upward. But I see you can. Lastly, the nose." Watson pinched Snow's nose and tried to push it left and right. "If your nose were broken, you'd have jumped out of your seat when I did that. Joseph, I can't find any bones broken."

"Then why does my head feel like it's inside a bass drum?"

"You've got a bruised bone and some soft tissue trauma. Your cheek will change from its pleasant blue color, to brown, then pale green and yellow. Very mild concussion, maybe. You'll live."

"So Ko was on Saipan with Dillon Synge?" Connie asked. She caught her husband's nose between her thumb and forefinger and wiggled it long enough for Snow to be embarrassed.

"He filled me in on the way back to town. Tsukada was a *jotohei*, the rank above Pfc. He killed an Imperial Army officer on Saipan, then fled into the jungle, where Dillon Synge appeared a month later with the Kobe Elephant. They stole a transmitter and used it to summon American assistance. Synge double-crossed Tsukada, left him in a flaming cave, and flew the plane out of Saipan."

"Amelia Earhart's plane," Connie said.

Snow nodded. "Synge thought he killed Earhart on Saipan. But she lived, and she's in Singapore now."

"Teamed with Howard Lester?" Connie asked with less energy than the question deserved. She removed her tea bag from the stainless-steel pot, then poured the green tea into Snow's cup.

"Working together," he said, then glanced at his wife. She was moving slowly, too carefully, as if afraid she would lose control of the teapot. Exuberance was the hallmark of his wife's personality, and Snow was enormously attracted to her spirit. But lately, she seemed to be losing that vivacity. At first Snow thought she was becoming a casualty of Singapore's oppressive heat. Now he blamed it on the emotional strain of looking down a gun barrel. It was his fault, he knew. It had been easier to ignore, rather than accommodate the fact that she had never before seen a man gunned down, had never before seen her husband beat a man almost to death.

And there was another factor, he knew. Constant scheming is a malignancy. Living with duplicity is debilitating and leaves the novice chronically fatigued and increasingly despondent. Connie's long afternoon naps, her absence of an appetite, and the gin sling hastily drunk just before bed were all symptoms. She wanted out.

Snow put his hand on hers. "You know, darling, I've just figured out that there's nothing keeping us in Singapore."

She looked up at him, then swatted at a fly determined to land on her nose. "What do you mean?"

"We could be on tomorrow's Pan Am Clipper, back to D.C., away from this heat and everything else."

"What about Howard Lester?"

Shelby Watson answered. "Lester sent you to collect Earhart's bones. She's alive, so there are no bones. The assignment is over."

"And secondly," Snow added, "Lester is playing me for a fool. I don't need to sit here in Singapore and have him play deadly games with me. And with my wife." He unconsciously gripped Connie's hand hard enough to make her wince. "He knew he was sending me into a combat zone, yet he blithely urged me to bring you along."

"Joseph, one of the things I learned about you is that you don't like unanswered questions. I think if we left Singapore now, you'd always wonder: where had Earhart been since 1937, why is Howard Lester in Singapore, and why did he send you here?"

A waiter approached, but Snow waved him away.

"Answers to questions aren't worth endangering you . . . or me, for that matter," Snow said. "Especially questions that don't mean anything to me."

Connie ran her hand along his pocked and scabbed arm. "Another thing I've learned is that you and Howard Lester are very much alike."

"Great."

"You don't want to return to the States until you've paid back whoever did this to you." She picked at an infected scab on his forearm. "If you went home now, your whole body would fester, not just your arm."

Snow looked from her hand to her eyes. "You use 'paid back' very lightly. Do you know what you're suggesting I do?"

"Only what you've been planning to do since that dog latched onto your arm. Get even."

Her words carried a virulence that startled Snow.

"I don't think you know what you're suggesting," he said, trying to sound casual.

She smiled, almost a pre-Singapore grin. "I do. Maybe I'm tougher than you think."

Snow signaled a passing busboy for a telephone, and within a minute it was on their table. He asked for the overseas operator, then gave Howard Lester's Washington, D.C. phone number. He put a hand over the phone. "It was easier than I thought it would be. Lester didn't cover his tracks this time. I've paid a few dollars to the operator."

Three minutes later, Lester's voice strained through the telephone. "Joseph, it's about time you checked in."

"Sorry, sir. How're things in Washington?"

"It drizzled all day and I'm not in a good mood. I've got something on this Ko Tsukada." It took Lester sixty seconds to outline Tsukada's history, almost exactly as Thomas Thompson the Tapper had done the day before. He concluded, "So he's not *Kempai tai*. He's a deserter."

"What do you think he's doing in Singapore?"

"No idea, but watch yourself, Joseph. How's my niece?"

Snow handed the phone to Connie. Her gaze never left her husband, and anguish turned down her mouth. She held a finger at the corner of an eye as if blocking tears. Finally she managed, "No, Howard, I won't forget. Send father a card. . . . Bye bye." Slowly she lowered the phone to her lap. "He said he saw my father this morning. Reminded me it's his birthday in four days. Joseph, he's lying to me, too."

Snow took the phone from her and muttered, "Come on, ring."

Five seconds later, the phone rang. Snow snapped it to his ear. "Got it. Thanks." He slammed the receiver down and turned to Watson. "Lester's at the Savoy on Orchard Road. Let's go."

The Savoy is a large, shabby bar in the ground floor of an apartment building on upper Orchard. A tobacco stand crowds the doorway and Chinese children vie for space near the windows to peer inside. The barroom is vast and dimly lit by tropical sun strained through coarse pink curtains. The room is dark and hushed near the back wall, where several booths are lit only by the pale offering of a single light bulb and are reserved for guarded conversation and intimate exchanges.

Howard Lester's bulk filled most of the booth nearest the lavatory. On the table before him were two plates, one filled with *dim sum*, the other with *röst bratwurst*. He alternated between them, using chopsticks on the Chinese delicacies and a fork on the sausage. He shoveled his food mechanically, chewing large mouthfuls, pausing only when the toilet flushed, as if the sound of gurgling water disrupted his cadence. Lester stared without blinking at the seat opposite, letting the food find his mouth automatically.

Joseph Snow abruptly slid into the booth. Lester's hand froze midway to his mouth, and his eyes grew. Snow seized his boss's wrist, increasing the pressure until a sharp sound escaped from Lester's mouth and his hand sprang open. The fork dropped from Lester's hand and his lips flared in pain.

Snow's voice sounded like cloth tearing. "There's a good chance you won't be leaving the Savoy alive."

Through clenched teeth, Lester pleaded, "Just let go of my wrist. For Christ's sake, Joseph, you're breaking it."

Snow released his grip while Lester, just as slowly, pulled a Smith and Wesson from his belt with his free hand under the table. The pistol was almost to Snow's crotch when Lester yelped in pain and the revolver tumbled from his hand to the floor. Intent on Snow, he had not seen Shelby Watson approach, nor had he seen the flash of the doctor's scalpel under the table. Snow kicked the revolver across the floor.

Sucking the webbing between his thumb and forefinger, Lester grunted, "I thought you died, Shelby."

"Not yet."

"You've got a lot of explaining to do in a very short time," Snow rasped.

Howard Lester glanced at Watson, then back to his operative. "It's simple. I want Dillon Synge dead."

"I figured that out," Snow said. "Keep talking."

"You don't understand all of it." Lester took a deep breath, "In any operation there is sheet after sheet of boilerplate. If the ax falls, the blame is always spread thinly over a large number of organizations and people. Not so in June 1937, Joseph. I originated the Earhart mission and those around me stayed clear." Lester pushed the plates to the wall so he had room to gesture with his good hand. "It should have been perfect. We received radio messages from a turncoat Japanese naval officer on Saipan. He wanted to be picked up, along with his documents. He wanted out immediately. By complete coincidence, Earhart had the only plane that could do it. Her Electra had been modified so she could make the long

231

flight across the oceans. Added fuel tanks, better communications gear. Her plane had more range than any other in the world."

Lester's voice was edgy and a strand of sweat beads grew under his hairline. "During her stop in Rangoon, we asked Earhart to volunteer. I talked to her for two hours, long distance from Washington. She wanted to talk to my superiors, but for this scheme, I had no superiors. That had been made very clear to me. It was my head on the block. Earhart finally agreed, but only to pick up the documents. The Jap was going to be left on the island."

"Why? Too much weight?"

"That was her reason. Mine was that, as far as we knew, this Nissho Ito wasn't a deserter. He was still doing his radio duties on the island. My idea was to pick up the documents, but keep him away from the plane, with a pistol if necessary. Earhart was to bring his papers to Howland Island."

"What about the Jap?" Watson asked.

"I knew the documents probably wouldn't be worth much. Top secrets don't often reach Saipan from Tokyo. But with the documents as proof of Ito's treason, we could've blackmailed him into our service. An Imperial Navy radio operator *working for us*. In 1937, with war on the horizon, that was a blinding prospect."

"Your ticket up the OSS ladder," Snow said dryly.

Lester put both palms on the table. "I begged for this plan. Begged Earhart. Begged my superiors, begged the Navy, and prostrated myself before SeaBee second lieutenants to get them to lengthen the Howland Island landing strip a hundred feet. I used up ten years of favors. I laid my career on the line."

"And you blew it."

"By the time Amelia Earhart began the leg to Saipan, I was on Howland Island. I had interpreters there to read the documents. The Secretary of War was standing by his phone in Washington in the event we found something startling."

"But she didn't arrive at Howland."

"No. We lost her, and we never heard from the Jap radioman on Saipan again either. The mission was a complete bust, and I paid for it. I left the service and drank gin for four months in Honolulu. An entire physical and mental deterioration. Only when I ran out of money did I return to Washington. They gave me a job as a supply clerk."

"And for the next eight or ten years you worked your ass off to rise in the organization again. An inspiring little story."

"You're goddamn right it is. And I'll tell you one of the reasons I've been able to do it: I never forget, and those people that caused me all that grief are going to wish I had."

"So why did you send me to Singapore blind?"

Lester coughed, then patted the corner of his mouth with a napkin. "Amelia Earhart's flight has been an embarrassment at the agency for a decade. Nobody talks about it, and there's an undiminished fear that the American public might find out how we . . . how I sent Amelia Earhart to her death. My chances of getting men and money to search out Earhart's killer were about equal to my chances of being elected Pope. There was just no way to do it."

"So you set me up. Why didn't you just come to Singapore yourself?"

"We all have our specialties, Joseph. Mine is organizing, yours is . . . implementing policy."

"And why go to such trouble to leave clues suggesting Amelia Earhart is alive?"

"To keep you on the killer's trail. Joseph, when I sent you to Singapore, I had no idea who duped Earhart and me. Searching for Earhart's body, you quickly discovered it was Synge. Now I'm asking you to help me see this through."

"You ask a lot for someone who just aimed a .38 at my balls."

"Christ, I thought you were going to murder me as I sat with my mouth full of *dim sum*. You'd have done the same thing." Lester wrapped his hand with a handkerchief, and wiped up the small pool of blood that was threatening to drip into his lap.

"Why didn't you simply tell me what you wanted done?" Snow asked.

"Ask yourself: would you have come here to help me avenge a ten-year-old drubbing, come here unofficially, outside the agency's auspices?" The right side of Lester's face convulsed.

Snow winced. "No, I wouldn't have."

"Well, so I fixed it so you wouldn't have a choice, wouldn't even know what your real task was."

Snow unfolded his hands. They had been clenched with anger so long his fingers moved only in painful protest. "How about Earhart's body?"

"We knew something was happening in Singapore only when the transvestite contacted the agency saying she knew where the bones were. I figured that anyone who made up the story about the bones wanted us in Singapore for some reason."

"But there never was a body."

Lester examined his fingernails. "No. Amelia Earhart is alive."

"And she's in Singapore."

"Yes." Almost inaudible.

"And you've known for almost ten years she was alive?"

"I thought she was dead until she walked into my office three months ago. Joe, you've already discovered she was in the Keluang camp, was freed in 1945, and was treated at hospitals in Singapore and San Francisco. She knew that if the fact she was alive ever became public, she would never be able to confront the man that left her for dead on the Saipan runway."

"And you've been working together on this?"

Lester nodded.

"I want to talk to her."

"Not yet. She's not ready for it."

"Because of her, I've been eaten by dogs and shot at. Don't tell me she's not ready."

"Until this moment, I was the only person in the world who knew she was alive, knew she survived seven years of hell in the camps. She's just not ready."

Snow chewed on the inside of his lip. "What's keeping me in Singapore?"

"Being eaten by dogs and being shot at." Lester allowed himself a small smile. "You now have the same motive as I have, and we're after the same person." Again, his face twitched.

Snow bared his teeth. "Things have worked out pretty well for you, haven't they?"

"Not yet," Howard Lester answered dully. "Not until I meet Dillon Synge face to face."

Terrence Bliss hammered on the governor's office door with his right cast. The casts came down to his thumbs, and vivid red rings had grown around his hands where the skin had been rubbed raw. The sleeves of his suit coat had been

234

slit to the shoulders and were held together around the casts by safety pins. The plaster would not quite harden in the tropical heat, and the sleeves had become mired in the paste, giving the casts the appearance of a tideflat.

Bliss backed away from the door to find the correct angle, twisted the knob by rising on one foot and tilting his trunk at the waist, then kicked the door with his foot.

Governor Longstreet was bent over a map of Chinatown and his eyes were following his finger as it traced a line. "What's the name of the temple?" he asked without looking up.

"The White Garden Buddhist Temple. It's on Tew Chew Street near the river."

Longstreet lowered his head. "Here it is. You've got the police reports?"

"Issued just thirty minutes ago. It doesn't look good. It's the third temple this week."

The governor braced himself on the arm rests before slowly lowering himself to the chair. "Let's hear it."

"The Gurkhas arrived at the temple at 12:30, and the sergeant says the riot had been in progress for about ten minutes. He thinks there were about forty Malays, most using wooden staves and cricket bats. They ransacked the temple. Five Buddhist monks are in the hospital, one isn't expected to live. There is very little salvageable. The icons were smashed, the altar was set on fire and the ancestor tablets were pulled off the wall and shattered."

Longstreet sighed. "And the monks just sat there and took it?"

"Not quite, sir." Bliss's miniature face split into a smile. "There were a number of Chinese toughs at the temple. Apparently, they were there without consent of the monks. They tried to defend the temple, but there were only about five of them and they were overwhelmed."

"Was it a *tong?*"

"Orchid Brotherhood, the sergeant thinks."

Longstreet's head swayed back against the rest. "They bloody well wouldn't stay out of it, would they? I don't suppose the Gurkhas made any arrests?"

"Here's a surprise. They did." Bliss held both arms in front of him like a derrick, lowered the green sheets to the desk, backed away to allow his arms space to drop, then hunched over the sheets. He bent lower and wrinkled his face. After a moment, "Sorry, sir, but would you help me with my specs."

Longstreet settled for a brief, wistful gance at his liquor cabinet, then struggled out of his chair to reach into Bliss's coat pocket. He opened a pair of wire-rimmed glasses and pushed them up Bliss's nose.

"Yes, here it is," the Welshman said brightly. "There were six Malays arrested. None of them had papers or permanent addresses. The sergeant thinks they arrived illegally a short time ago."

"If they just came to Singapore from the Peninsula, what are they doing rioting in a temple? No reason, unless they were put up to it. It's that sod Kiril Stasov." Longstreet's palm slapped the desk top, fluttering the green sheets. "I *know* it's the Russian."

"Two more things, Governor. Missing from the temple after the riot were the carved box of gold offerings . . ."

"Always the same."

". . . and a small, but apparently exquisite jade dish decorated with five hydras. The plate was from the Sung Dynasty, and was the temple's only valuable jade piece."

"Always the gold, always the jade. No spontaneity to it, Bliss. None at all. So-called spontaneous riots, planned down to the last whoop. The Soviets have a history of this, you know."

"And, lastly, the sergeant wanted me to draw your attention to this and tell you he had no idea what it means: Three of the detained Malay rioters were missing fingers." Bliss tried to hold up a finger, but the cast would not cooperate. "All had lost the little fingers on their left hands, and very recently, at that."

Longstreet groaned. "Now what in Christ could that mean?"

Bliss shrugged, a difficult task. "No idea."

"Compose a formal request to the Military Commander, that idiot, requesting in the strongest terms that he release two hundred troops to this office. Send a copy to the Foreign Office. And tell the Gurkha sergeant that I want some answers from his Malay prisoners, and I want them on my desk tomorrow morning."

"Anything else?"

"No. Should there be?"

"About the order to Pan Am?"

"That still stands. They're to hold open those seats until ten minutes before take-off every day, unless they hear otherwise from us."

"You think we'll need them?"

The governor swiveled to the window. "The chances of a mob moving into white Singapore are remote. Quite small, I believe. But going down with this ship is something I'm not prepared to do. Just not prepared to do."

Connie Snow pulled open her cosmetic pouch. She twisted up her lipstick, decided it was too high, and lowered it. Still not right. She repeated the procedure, taking her time. She leaned over the dresser and applied the lipstick. Very slowly, trying to use up another minute. She was convinced that because of Singapore's proximity to the equator time passed more slowly than elsewhere, that the world took longer to go around. Time passed like Singapore River sludge.

As she did each day, Connie stared into the mirror, searching for fading or irregularities in her tan. Occasionally her cheeks would wash out or her chin would appear pale under artificial light, as it did now. She pulled two bottles from her case, poured a spoonful of each into a hotel glass and stirred them with her finger. She dabbed the clear liquid onto her chin and cheeks and spread it evenly, puckering her mouth to avoid smearing her lips. In ten minutes, her dark tan would be renewed.

She pulled her mouth into an affected smile to see if the lotion would gather in her dimples. The thin metal retainer across her upper teeth glimmered in the light. She opened her mouth and ran her index finger along her palate to dislodge the orthodontic retainer. She smiled again, this time broadly to admire her teeth. They were, as Joseph had insisted many times, strong, even, and remarkably white. Her beautiful smile didn't look real to her. Too perfect. But Joseph loved it, and saw nothing else when he looked at them. He had never even seen the retainer, which, the dentist had promised, would keep her teeth in line if she wore it two hours a day. She renewed her smile. Someday she would tell him about her visits to the orthodontist. She squeezed some toothpaste onto a finger, then washed the retainer briskly and put it into its case.

Connie lifted the phone off its cradle before its first ring had ended. She cupped her ear as if surrounded by noise. "Yes, I'm fine, Howard. I'm holding up. . . . I don't think it's possible to adjust to the heat."

She lowered herself into a chair near the bed. Her hand found a white cotton towel on the bedstead, and she awkwardly dried her free hand. "No, I haven't heard from Terrence Bliss. Howard, was it really necessary. . . . I suppose so, but I . . . No, Joseph refers to her as 'the woman in white.' Doesn't seem to be able to call her Amelia Earhart. . . . Yes, I know you're looking out for him. . . ."

The doorknob turned partially. Connie looked to the door and called, "It's locked, Joseph. I'll be right there." She lowered her voice. "He's here. Goodbye."

She had returned the phone to its cradle and was almost to the door when a fist exploded through the wood above the lock. Splinters burst away from the shattered wood. The fist shook violently, clearing away the wood shards. Her eyes wide, Connie watched as more of the arm pushed through the jagged hole and the hand gripped the inside lock. The deadbolt was thrown. The hand disappeared.

The door flew open, bounced against the armoire, and was on its way back when Pinang spilled through the door. In two steps he reached Connie, grabbing her hair with one hand and whipping the back of a fist into her jaw. Her knees sagged and she opened her mouth to scream, but the Malay jammed his hand over her mouth and dragged her to the bed. He shoved his meaty fist into her chest, pushing her into the mattress. He held her chin in a viselike grip, allowing her only a view of the ceiling, which swam in tears of pain.

Dillon Synge appeared above her. His face was sunset red and sweat fell from his forehead onto her face. His voice sounded like water splashed into a sizzling pan. "I couldn't get your husband, but you'll do." He backed away from the bed. "Bring her, Pinang."

The Malay bounced her out of the bed and with an arm tightly around her throat pushed her toward the door. She tried to drop to the floor, but Pinang grabbed her skirt belt and propelled her out of the room.

Dillon Synge turned a slow circle in the room. He lifted Connie's cosmetic case off the stand and dumped its contents onto the bedspread. He dug into his coat pocket for the jade piece, a finger-size nephrite touchstone and tossed it onto the bed near the vials and bottles. "Just a warning," he whispered. "Just a warning."

Synge followed the gunman and his captive out the door.

XVI

Heat lay over the camp like a heavy hand, but she
trembled. A chill of hatred for the man on Saipan.

Yahya Bandar was understandably nervous. At the end of
two more blocks, he would meet Pali for the first time and
five minutes later they would be married. He tried to move
his feet in time with the kumpang drums paddled by his
father and brothers as they marched to his bride's home, but
worry overcame his sense of rhythm and his older brother,
Tam, had to constantly prod the small of his back.

Two months before, Yahya's father, a prosperous Malay
shipper, had announced at dinner that Yahya was to be wed
to the daughter of an even more prosperous warehouseman.
Yahya's father had already contracted to give Pali's family a
large amount of *belanja kahwin*, wedding expenses. Malay
tradition allowed no protest from Yahya, but during those
two months, he had desperately tried to determine what his
fiancée looked like. But during the engagement, Pali's family
carefully hid her in their home, as befitted her requisite
timidity and chastity. Yahya begged one of Pali's brothers for
a photograph or even a description. To no avail. Yahya was
marching to his wedding without a clue to his wife's
appearance.

The kumpang drums stopped near the door of Pali's home.
Yahya was escorted into a room full of Pali's male relatives

and guests who were chanting Muslim verses. With more prodding from Tam, Yahya sat on a mat facing the *kathi*, who firmly grasped his hands. With one last fervent appeal, Yahya silently beseeched Allah not to have given his fiancée the snout of a boar, then he haltingly repeated the marriage vows. With trembling hands, he signed the marriage register and had to be nudged out of the way so Pali's father could do the same. As of that moment, Yahya was legally married to a woman he had never seen.

Like a man being led to the scaffold, Yahya was pushed toward the next room where the women of both families parted to form an aisle to the colorfully decorated *pelamin*, the throne where his wife waited. Perspiration fell into Yahya's eyes in a constant stream, clouding his attempts to appraise the figure in white lace on the throne. As he approached, Yahya's breath caught in his throat, throttled by his first two wonderful impressions: very fair skin and slenderness, the two most important aspects of Malay beauty. Her face was the color of the sky just before dawn, pale gold blended with subdued orange. A true Malay, with none of the mongrel Portuguese blood. Pali shared the luxurious dark hair of all Malay women, but hers framed secret eyes, languishing sloe eyes that shyly lowered as her husband approached. Carefully taught modesty would prevent her from glancing at Yahya until she was sure his attention was elsewhere.

Yahya halted in front of her throne. He held his right hand over her head for several seconds, lowered his arm to shake her hand, then turned to march to the next room where the men would celebrate with *satay* and *ketchil makan*. The groom could not see his wife until the next day.

An hour later the brothers walked in the afterglow of the wedding celebration, oblivious to the heat, unmindful of the respectful stares from the occasional Malay passerby who knew from Yahya's henna-stained hands that he had just been married. The brothers were also unaware of the black Ford coupe that had been following them for two blocks. The coupe maintained a distance of a hundred feet and accelerated only when a pedestrian came between it and the brothers. The glaring sun reflected off the Ford's windows and his the driver. As the brothers entered a residential neighborhood and the pedestrians thinned, the coupe gained a few yards, closing in on Yahya and Tam.

Immersed in tales of married life, the brothers did not see the black coupe until it was abreast of them, until Pinang emerged from the Ford like an Asian moon rat from its burrow. The brothers' eyes were transfixed by needles of light dancing off Pinang's jaw brace. A nickle-plated revolver appeared from Pinang's shirt. With the light stutter-step of a stalking animal, he rushed toward the brothers.

Their hands cemented together in terror, Yahya and Tam turned to run. Pinang's revolver arced viciously into Tam's skull, sounding like brittle kindling snapped over a knee. Tam's knees buckled, and he pulled his brother down as he fell. With wild eyes, Yahya stared at the deep red stain quickly matting Tam's hair. He frantically shook his hand free, stood for one agonized second of indecision, then twisted, churning his legs, trying to free them from his brother's arms.

Pinang's first shot tore into Yahya's shoulder just under the collarbone. Propelled forward by the force of the bullet, the second bullet tore into the small of his back as he fell. Yahya was lying motionless on the ground before the clap of gunfire had faded through the trees.

Pinang tucked the revolver into his pants, then with both hands dragged both brothers into the coupe. The car pulled away from the curb, leaving only a few drops of Yahya's blood on the cobblestone.

The emptiness of the hotel room sucked air from Snow as if he were drowning. His wife was always where she said she would be. Never an exception. Yet, she was gone. The gauze curtains fluttered across the headboard, a suitcase lay open on the desk, and her cosmetics were scattered on the bed. The room screamed with her absence.

He forced air into his lungs, hoping the deep breathing would allow his mind to come up with a reasonable explanation. Connie was orderly. She would no more dump her purse onto the bed than Snow would clear his pistol's chamber with the barrel at his stomach. Blood rushed to his head, and he tried to push his thoughts through it. Connie was missing. *She was missing.*

He stared down at the cosmetics, keys and note pad which were strewn on the bed. He had seen everything a hundred times before. Except for the oblong green stone. It was resting on the bedspread apart from Connie's belongings.

Intentionally apart, Snow knew instantly. He lifted the jade piece with thumb and forefinger. It was a touchstone, just like those owned by hundreds of thousands of Singapore Chinese. Its bottle-green shade was peppered with gray flecks, and it had been rubbed so smooth it seemed malleable. No Chinaman would willingly depart with his talisman. And an amah hadn't forgotten it as she cleaned the room.

Sudden knowledge swelled up from Snow's stomach like a sickness. Synge had kidnapped his wife and had left the jade piece as a message. With urgency fueled by hatred, Snow crossed the room to the phone. He tried twice before his knotted throat would allow him to tell the operator the number. Each ring seemed perpetual. Finally, Shelby Watson's listless voice offered a greeting.

"Shelby, what happens if you shoot a man in the shoulder?"

"You break his acromion or his clavicle, probably the former. Why?"

"Does that put him in the hospital?"

"You bet. It doesn't require a cast, though. We use a figure-eight bandage around both shoulders. . . ."

"Shelby, meet me at the Fort Canning Hospital in fifteen minutes." Snow hung up without waiting for a response.

Those minutes were a blur. Dodging automobiles and rickshaws, brushing past the agile pedestrians, Snow bounded for the hospital. The normally indifferent Chinese turned to stare at the sight of this madman churning down their congested street. The relentless sun had driven another *Gwailo* insane.

Watson was waiting on the steps of the hospital. Snow tried to explain through bursts of air. ". . . got Connie . . . Synge . . . no idea where . . . but I heard his flunkie Flynn . . . is in hospital . . ."

"Flynn in the hospital, here?"

Snow nodded rapidly, his lips pulled back and his nostrils flaring.

"And he's got a broken clavicle?"

". . . think so."

Watson's unstable smile spread across his face. "Let's talk to him."

Shelby Watson's official tone quickly produced Flynn's floor number from the hospital receptionist. Snow two-stepped the stairs and waited with dancing impatience for the doctor

243

to catch up with him. They walked to the orthopedic floor's nurse station.

A weary nurse carrying a fouled bedpan greeted them with an indifferent smile which soured when she saw Shelby's withered ear and misaligned cheeks. "I'm sorry," she said, her voice professional, "you gentlemen want the communicable disease section. It's two floors up, west wing."

Watson matched her tone. "We are looking for one of your patients. Name is Flynn."

"Mr. Flynn underwent surgery last night. The surgeon reconnected a broken clavicle and patched up the wound. He's resting comfortably right now, but he's not to be disturbed."

"We want to talk to him for a few minutes. Won't disturb him at all." Watson's voice was as reasonable as the nurse's.

She shook her head, displaying a measured, tolerant smile. "I'm sorry. Perhaps tomorrow the doctors will let visitors . . ."

Snow's Colt appeared in his hand. He stabbed its barrel into her right breast. "Tell me his room number. Now."

The nurse's eyes widened at the metal suddenly clamped to her breast. Her eyes slowly rose to Snow's face. It was as pitiless as the Colt. She whispered hoarsely, "Three-twelve."

Snow and Watson burst into Flynn's room. The gunman was propped up on several pillows, cigarette in one hand, a tattered copy of "Yank" in the other. He shared the room with three other patients. Indefinable lumps under rumpled sheets. The pistol was resting on Flynn's forehead before he was aware of his visitors. Snow's voice was dead. "Tell me where Synge and my wife are."

The Irishman's voice was remarkably stable. "Or you'll blow my head off? In a hospital in front of these witnesses? You'll have to do bloody better than that."

His harsh laugh was cut off abruptly when Snow gripped both of the gunman's wrists and pulled them to the side of the bed. Snow grated, "I don't want any more discussion from this bastard. Understand, Shelby? I just want the location of my wife."

Watson's scalpel slashed through the elastic bandage and the gauze over Flynn's wound in two swift cuts. As Flynn's eyes jerked to his shoulder, the doctor brushed aside the frayed dressing. The scar from that night's surgery was six inches long, paralleling the broken bone. The closed gash was seeping and angry.

Like a striking snake, Watson's scalpel lashed out, sinking into Flynn's shoulder just above the point of the closed incision. With one smooth, powerful downward stroke, the doctor sheered through the stitches, opening the shoulder to the bone, just as it had been on the operating table the night before. Flynn's scream filled the room, bringing two of the other patients up from their pillows.

With his gloved hand, Watson reached into the wound, firmly gripped the shattered clavicle, and wrenched it away from the shoulder. The bone snapped, its second break in twenty-four hours, and the doctor held it up for Snow's inspection.

An irritated patient in the neighboring bed called, "Don't you have operating rooms for this sort of thing?"

Snow bent low over the ghostly white Flynn. "Where's Synge and my wife? Or the Doctor works on your other shoulder."

Flynn's mouth opened and closed like a fish out of water, then his voice kicked in. "The Smythe Building," he choked in agony, his face ashen.

Snow looked at Watson. "Know where it is?"

Watson was examining the bone in his hand. "Not far."

Snow released the wrists, Flynn Fell back onto his mattress, unconscious. Snow was through the door before the doctor tossed the bone onto Flynn's chest, looked at his work with faint disapproval, and turned to follow.

Abdul Razak swung his fist into the air, then dropped it almost to his knees, a fighting gesture exaggerated for the benefit of the Malays in the rear of the crowd.

For ten minutes, Razak had been ranting against the Chinese, accusing them of everything from usury to incest, from gambling to piracy. His audience, perhaps four hundred men and boys, swayed with his words and indignantly shook their heads and balled their fists. The Chinese deserved the wrath of Allah, a *jihad* must be waged.

Razak's transition was skilled and subtle. The Chinese were the enemy, but they, after all, were merely puppets of the British regime. The British had landed on Singapore in 1819, purchased it for a pittance from the duped Sultan of Johore, and had been cheating the Malays ever since. The

British allowed the Chinese into Singapore, the British allowed them to own shops, gave them preferential tax benefits and let them send their earnings back to the mainland. British troops were at that very moment pushing back Malays who sought to cross the Johore Strait into Singapore. The crowd nodded in unison. Young Malays shouted anti-British epithets.

Razak abruptly ended his tirade and jumped off his fruit crate to disappear into the crowd. As he had planned, his Malay listeners were caught with their oaths in their throats, their anger at full throttle with nowhere to go. The mob spontaneously rushed forward, but in the small square, they quickly rammed into each other and the surge clotted. Without a director, the crowd could not focus its anger and it began to break up.

One block from the square, three Malays leaving the harangue saw what they at first believed were two drunken English sailors collapsed in the basement entrance to a theater. But the head on top of the mound was clearly Malay. Thirty minutes later, virtually every Malay in Singapore knew that the bodies of Yahya and Tam had been found, dumped in a stairwell. A Chinese jade touchstone was discovered in the mouth of the groom.

Three lighters beached near the godown were belching huge clouds of acrid smoke. The lighters are hollow boats, no longer than fifty feet, resembling empty walnut shells, and are routinely beached on the riverbank. Fires are set from stem to stern to chase out the vermin that make the lighters home. Smoke from the three boats rolled with the idle wind, enveloping a nearby godown, a one-story warehouse on the bank. The godown's walls and roof were made of plaited coconut fronds rapidly succumbing to green mildew.

Snow and Tsukada stepped into the smoke, light-footing toward the south corner of the godown. Snow palmed the building's corner and peered around to the street-side loading bay. A delivery van was parked opposite the bay. He hesitated until he was sure workmen were not loading the truck, then signaled Tsukada to follow.

Tsukada had been grateful for Snow's call ten minutes before. Snow had assured him that there was no longer any reason to talk to Synge, that Snow didn't give a damn what happened to the jade dealer—all he wanted was his wife.

246

Their division of labor was agreed upon immediately; Tsukada would enter the Smythe godown first, taking out Synge, and Snow would look after Connie.

Tsukada moved several short strides ahead of Snow and reached the loading bay. He kept the Nambu pistol in front of him. He leaned around the loading-bay corner, saw nothing but the dark opening from the building, and in a crouch sprinted up the ramp into the loading bay. Snow waited until the footfalls stopped, then hurried after him.

The godown's interior was palpably dark and smelled of mildew and grease. Regularly spaced support pillars broke the expanse of floor. A small section of the warehouse floor had been enclosed in plywood to make an office. Snow traced Tsukada's steps to the office.

A thin band of light streamed from under the closed door. Where a knob should have been, a short length of knotted raffia rope acted as a pull-chord. Silently Tsukada positioned himself a yard away from the door. He took a long breath, and with a shoulder-high heel-punch, sprang the door open. Tsukada was through the door before it hit the wall. Snow was on his heels.

A dilapidated oak desk, a filing cabinet, three wood chairs, and little else. The door from the office to the river was open, but Snow was drawn to the desk, where a faint green light radiated from a silk square. He lifted the oblong jade piece from the cloth to uncover his wife's monogrammed initials on the scarf he had given her. A second warning. He clutched the charm until his knuckles were white. Synge had his wife and he was powerless. *Powerless!*

The retort of a pistol brought Snow out of his paralyzing rage. He lunged through the door leading to the riverbank, where Tsukada must have gone while Snow was staring at the jade. He ran along the bank in the direction of the shot, his shoes sinking into the mud.

Ko Tsukada was squatting just around the corner, holding his pistol with both hands, pointing it at a Ford coupe that was spinning gravel forty yards down the road. Three heads were visible in the small rear window, including Connie's, her raven hair flowing. Snow immediately swung his Colt to Tsukada's head.

Through tight jaws, the Japanese said, "Don't worry. If I were going to fire into the car, I would've done so already."

Snow realized his mistake and turned his gun away.

Tsukada's voice was thick. "I want you to know that I had another chance and didn't act because Connie was in the car."

Snow nodded, his eyes following the Ford as it turned onto a paved street a hundred yards away. Tears of frustration and anger blurred his sight, and he turned from Tsukada and made a production of returning this pistol to his belt.

"I can't get up." Tsukada's words were uneven.

For the first time Snow noticed the pool of blood growing under the Japanese's buttocks. "Jesus, Ko, are you hurt?"

He looked balefully at Snow. "No, I'm bleeding for the hell of it."

Snow muscled Tsukada to his feet. Pinang's single bullet had creased his buttocks, leaving a four inch furrow. Tsukada's eyes misted when he tried to put weight on his right leg.

"I can walk on it." He took a hobbled step, leaning into Snow's shoulder.

"A lot of good you'll do me with another hole in your ass," Snow said, jamming his hand under Tsukada's arm. He squeezed Tsukada's shoulder a bit more tightly than needed to help him walk. "I know you wanted to fire, and didn't. I appreciate it." He helped him around a pile of railroad ties. "Shelby Watson will sew your butt up in no time."

"Not him," Tsukada replied weakly. "He's scalpel crazy."

"He's also good with a needle and thread. He'll do."

The needle entered the ridge of flesh smoothly, passed across the gash and into the skin again. Watson worked with a quick rhythm, stab, pull, stab, pull, lacing together Tsukada's right buttock. The Japanese occupied himself by loading his Nambu, extracting the shells from the clip and reloading it. He lay on the bed in Snow's room, with Watson kneeling over him. Near the doctor's feet were a bottle of disinfectant and the syringe he had just used to numb Tsukada's backside.

"It's obvious, isn't it, Joseph?" Howard Lester asked. His gray jacket was stained through, forming a damp cummerbund. "Synge has taken her to keep you and Tsukada away from him. He figures you won't do anything rash if he has her. It's already worked. Tsukada would've fired blindly into the car had Connie not been there."

Snow gazed out the window, not seeing anything. "He can't believe it'll work indefinitely. I mean, he's not going to just go about his business for years using my wife as a shield."

"No, this is a stopgap measure, to buy him time, only a day or two. He knows the caliber of people looking for him, and he knows he won't last long in Singapore." Lester leaned back in the chair, "In the next day or two, Synge will attempt to retrieve the elephant, then he'll leave the city."

"Where's the elephant?" Tsukada asked, playing with the safety on the pistol.

"No idea," Lester replied. "But he knows and he'll move."

"Then what happens to my wife?" Snow's voice was heavy with emotion. "Goddamn it, Howard, then what happens to my wife?"

"We'll find her before then." Lester assured him, and failed to sound confident.

"Tell me how."

"You forget, Joseph, but I have contacts in this city. I made more than fifteen phone calls this morning. A white man cannot disappear in Singapore. He stands out like a flag. There are a hundred pair of eyes looking for him at this minute. Waiters, cabbies, policemen, the lot. We'll find him. . . ."

The phone interrupted Lester. Snow snapped it off the cradle. "Yes . . ." He sighed with disappointment. "Hello, Tapper."

Thomas Thompson's voice was thin and reedy through the phone. "Joe, I've made a mistake. An amateurish mistake you can chew my ass for."

Snow took a deep breath. "What is it, Tapper?"

"I gave a clear signal regarding your wife, and I think she still is, but I found an irregularity that I can't explain."

Snow's eyes closed slowly, as if to shut out whatever bad news, whatever further complication, the Tapper was going to tell him. "Go ahead."

"I didn't have anything to do back here, so I did a little more digging, just for the hell of it. Joseph, I can't find Connie's father, Benjamin Lester. He doesn't exist in Schenectady."

"Christ sake, Tapper, of course he exists. He owns a small shoe manufacturing plant, he's a member of the golf club, and all the rest. He sends Connie a little money every month."

"You ever met him?"

"No, he couldn't come to the wedding because he was in Europe. . . ."

"Joe, this man doesn't exist. I checked and rechecked. Believe me, I wouldn't give you news like this if I weren't sure."

"He's Howard Lester's brother," Snow protested.

"There is no Benjamin Lester. Period."

Snow held the phone so tightly against his face a red bruise formed under his chin. He whispered almost inaudibly, "Thanks, Tapper." Slowly he lowered the phone.

Snow crossed the room to Lester. He stood so close over him it could only be interpreted as threatening. Watson paused with the needle and Tsukada twisted to watch.

"Thompson the Tapper just told me your brother, my wife's father, doesn't exist. Once again, you'd better talk."

"Thompson's working for you, is he? I was under the impression he was my man."

"Talk." A high flush rose on Snow's forehead. Tension pulled at his scalp and the back of his skull seemed to be on fire.

Lester smiled easily. "You weren't supposed to know this, but I've got a hunch if I don't tell you, it'll go hard on me." Lester's grin broadened. "Connie's father works in the clean-up department of the CIG. Has for years and years. In fact, he's the same level I am. When things go awry—usually my jobs—his men go in to salvage what they can, smooth over the populace . . ."

"I know what clean-up does."

"And you know our policy, too. My wife thinks I work in the postal service. Connie thinks her father owns a shoe company. Her father was instrumental in getting me back in the organization after I washed out with the Earhart debacle. He also helped me climb again. Connie knows nothing of this."

Snow turned on his heels angrily. "You never play it straight, Lester."

"Call the Tapper back. Ask him to look for Benjamin Lester in clean-up. He's there in D.C. Or he might be in his office in Schenectady." Lester laughed in his irritating way.

Snow struggled into his linen jacket, his moves choppy with anger and pain. "And where's your Miss Earhart during all this?"

"In a hotel room," Lester answered, searching for his Pall Malls. "Don't try to find her. You can talk to her all you want when this is over. Where're you going?"

"To check the jade sellers. Again. Just like I did three hours ago. Maybe Synge has contacted one of them."

"Why would he?" Lester asked, scratching his chin.

"He probably wouldn't, but it's better than doing nothing. Which is what all four of us are doing. Absolutely goddamn nothing." Snow pulled furiously on the door knob, then remembered to turn it, and rushed out of the room.

Snow crossed the Raffles' lobby swiftly, propelled by a furious energy. A man hurrying to nowhere. A businessman standing at the check-in counter saw his grim look and stepped out of his way. Snow circled a sand-filled ashtray and a middle-aged woman sitting on a trunk. By the time he reached the Raffles' doors, he had slowed considerably.

He looked up for the door handle. Through the glass, he saw a white skirt, gently tugged by the tropical wind. The woman in white, Amelia Earhart, was standing on the other side of the door, holding a white bead purse. She was smiling at the bellhop and handing him a tip. Without thinking, Snow called her name and flung himself at the door, just as the bellhop entered from the other side. Snow struggled for several seconds, pushing the Tamil bellhop out of his way. The woman in white saw Snow's open mouth and raised hand, and turned to run.

Snow burst through the door into the heat, fifteen yards behind the woman in white. "Amelia," he called, as if he knew the aviatrix. To hell with Lester, he thought. Answers, now. He dug in his heels, rapidly closing the gap between them. As his legs pumped, a small smile came to his face. He would be the second man in the world to talk to Amelia Earhart since her presumed death. He lengthened his stride and leaned forward to grasp her shoulder and pull her to a stop. A gasp of fright escaped her as Snow turned her to face him.

She had the sandy-brown hair, the gray eyes, the strong chin, but the woman in white wasn't Amelia Earhart. Snow squinted, as if he could resculpt her face into Earhart's. But it simply wasn't she. The woman stood, wide eyed, as Snow's thumb delicately pushed up her lip to reveal her teeth. At first glance, the small gap was there, like Earhart's. He bent close. The gap was artificial. Two thin strips of black adhesive were attached to her upper front teeth. This woman had been made up to resemble Amelia Earhart.

With his hands still resting gently on her shoulders, Snow asked, "Why are you doing this to me?"

The woman finally met his eyes. "I'm sorry, Mr. Snow. Howard Lester ordered me here from San Francisco. I work for him. I just do what he tells me."

XVII

Others weakened and died, but she began to
recover, feeding on her hatred as if it were a ration.

Like a corpse left too long in the tropical sun, Singapore
decayed and bloated. At first the Malay community had been
paralyzed with disbelief. For all of an hour, Selagie and
Serangoon streets were at a standstill as small groups of
Malays compared versions of the news. The murders of Yahya
and Tam were magnified and distorted, embellished with
rumors and exaggerated by lies. Abdul Razak's men orches-
trated the confusion: Two Malays had been murdered by the
Chinese death societies. Strangled. Decapitated. Three Malay
men and a child. At least twelve Chinese involved. Orchid
Brotherhood thugs. Unspeakable depravities with the bodies.

For that hour, tension lay on Singapore like the scent of
fire orchids—thick and sickly. In the Malay bazaars, crowds
gathered, talking in hushed voices, trying to digest the
increasingly outrageous stories of Chinese atrocity. Tales of
past Chinese crimes were recounted and confirmed. The
Chinese were compared unfavorably with the hated Japanese and with smallpox. An unspoken suspicion grew: that
Yahya's barbarous murder would be the end of Singapore.

Word of the murders spread almost as quickly in Chinatown.
Streets and shops emptied as the Teochews and Cantonese
and Hakkas prepared for the inevitable retaliation. Small

groups of Chinese bent low to exchange their fears, and heads turned anxiously north, toward the Malay area. Kempong men left the sidewalks, vending stalls closed, street cafés disappeared. Funeral processions were postponed and lighter-men pushed their boats into the center of the river. Chinatown braced itself for a blow.

The first police report of the murders was on Governor Longstreet's desk twenty minutes after the bodies were found. The haggard Gurkha riot squads were ordered into the streets. Their commander, unsure where the first stone would be thrown, spread his men thinly along a no-man's-land dividing the two communities. Extra rounds were issued and a new shipment of riot shields was quickly distributed.

Longstreet dictated a stream of orders to Terrence Bliss. With encrusted arms, Bliss diligently transcribed them. The governor wanted messages sent to the Malay and Chinese leaders, asking them to come to his office immediately. He also asked Bliss to find Sun Chen, a master of the Orchid Brotherhood, with whom the governor had traded favors before. And he wanted the Sultan mosque searched for Telok Ipoh, a mullah known for his responsible, peaceful attitudes. Perhaps these men could help diffuse the city. Longstreet ordered extra soldiers posted around the government building and the radio stations to broadcast calming messages. He ordered a curfew that night at ten o'clock. Anyone found carrying rocks or clubs would face imprisonment. And the licenses of the inflammatory Malay and Chinese newspapers—always full of racial harangue—were suspended as of that moment.

Fifteen minutes later, Longstreet's fury of orders ended. He pulled a bottle of Canadian whiskey from his liquor cabinet, offered a shot to Bliss. Calmed somewhat, Longstreet returned to his chair to stare out the window, a posture that had dominated much of his time in the past few days. Bliss assured the unhearing governor that he would immediately see to his orders and excused himself.

Bliss returned to his office and scanned the sheets. With difficulty induced by the casts, he pulled open his wallet to thumb once again the sheaf of bills Kiril Stasov had given him that morning. Two thousand British pounds. He smiled his ferret smile, then dropped the orders and memoranda into the wastebasket.

* * *

254

When Abdul Razak screamed "God is great," tore a leg from a card table for a club and ran from the crowd, the bloating corpse of Singapore burst. He had been agitating a crowd of youths, several with missing fingers, and they followed Razak across Serangoon, scooping up cobblestones as they ran. Razak allowed his followers to overtake him. When they reached the fish stall—the same one—Razak was in the rear of the charging throng, screaming encouragement.

Ah Ping Yueh, a fish vendor, had joined the Orchid Brotherhood ten years before, paying exorbitant dues for protection. After the first sacking of his business two days before, he had called on the Brotherhood for insurance against another riot. That insurance was in the form of seven Brotherhood toughs who loitered near his stall. At the sound of Razak's war cry, they formed a phalanx in front of the shop and met the Malay charge with chains and *chungkols*. Bilious hatred was no substitute for experience. Within seconds the Malays had fallen under the swinging saps.

The brawlers' screams sounded through the neighborhood. The Malays were the first to respond, sending another wave of men to the fish market. This time the Brotherhood soldiers were overrun and went down under arcing bamboo staffs. Returning from the docks a band of *swaylos* rushed into the melee with pipes and cobblestones. Like gasoline splashed onto a fire from two sides, Malays and Chinese swarmed to the fish market. The rioting spread rapidly along Serangoon, enveloping bystanders and shops. Within minutes the first flames shot to the sky as the tinder-dry stalls exploded. With the names of Yahya and Tam as a battle cry, the Malays set shop after shop on fire, then blocked fire wagons as they tried to reach the spreading conflagration.

Sun Chen and the other Brotherhood leaders conferred minutes after the riot began. The hesitation and moderation of their earlier meetings were gone. At stake was the Orchid Brotherhood's painstakingly built reputation for guarding the interests of Singapore Chinese. Dues-paying businesses were being sacked and owners would look to the Brotherhood. Kao Kuei-tze's solution was immediately agreed upon.

A dozen *swaylos* were sent in a flatbed truck to Redin Street in the Malay district. They stopped in front of a sundry store, backed the truck almost to the facade, and pumped gasoline from a barrel through the door. A lighted match followed. Flames engulfed the shop within seconds. The truck

255

drove another block, pulled up to a rice wholesaler's building, and repeated the procedure. Like a string of firecrackers, buildings along Redin exploded, one after another, until the street was pocked with raging fires. Kao Kuei-tze had made certain that none of his relatives were on the truck. With good reason, for after the sixth fire an outraged horde of Malays congealed around the truck and turned it over, rolling it over the *swaylos* who had been riding on the truck bed. Gasoline spurted from the crushed barrels and was ignited by a spark, trapping the Chinese in flames. Unknown to Kao, the Tu twins had volunteered for this enjoyable assignment. Their identical charred bodies were found under the burned-out truck.

The Gurkhas arrived on Serangoon, where the riot was spreading in a tidal wave of violence. They unleashed their batons and levered cartridges into chambers while still a block from the fighting. Their commander ordered them forward, a precisioned line of blue uniforms and wicker shields. First to turn on the Gurkhas were the Malay youths, who screamed that they were puppets of the British and hurled tiles from the rooftops. Two Gurkhas fell, and their comrades, ignoring the command to hold fire, loosed volleys at the roofs. A ten-year-old Malay boy spun over the roof railing and toppled to the ground. More shots were fired and tear gas cannisters were lobbed into the frenzied crowd. The mob ran in all directions to avoid the spewing gas, many of them into the advancing police line where batons and rifle butts fenced with sharpened bamboo staves and stones.

Block after block of Singapore was consumed by the riot. Muffled explosions, sharp retorts of rifles, screams of agony, and angry shouts could be heard above the steady hissing of the advancing fires. Sirens and police whistles shrieked in the distance, never close to the confusion. Plumes of black smoke bellowed up from Serangoon Road, clouding the sky with ashes and warping the tropical sunlight with waves of shimmering heat. Seething with hatred and anger, Singapore was destroying itself.

White Singapore, with its cricket pitches, columned buildings, its shaded tea rooms and massive cathedral, was in the eye of the storm. Standing on the *pedang*, white-gloved ladies swatted ashes from their straw hats and clucked at the irritation of living in a barbarous city on the edge of the

empire. Men in limp white suits impatiently signaled for
their stengahs and, carrying serving trays above their heads,
Chinese boys rushed across the *pedang*, scattering thousands
of Java sparrows. Blame for the unrest was distributed
equally among the communists, the trade unions, and His
Majesty's government back home. What could be expected,
many asked, holding the tall glasses at stomach level, rocking up on the balls of their feet, and nervously searching for
flames above the rooftops. What *could* be expected with John
Chinaman, not truly British, and bloody cheeky at that? And
the Malays, with a militant religion that rendered them
incapable of learning simple English syntax. Nothing would
come of this latest skirmish, they believed. But seeing a
renewed surge of black smoke roll over St. Andrew's Cathedral, several Brits began pulling discreetly at their testicles
to dissipate their fear, an action their Japanese guards had
taught them in prisoner-of-war camps.

The riot soon began nibbling at the edges of white Singapore. A tattoo parlor that had served sailors for two decades
fell to a Malay charge. The peg-legged Irish proprietor bluffed
his way to safety with a fearsome tattoo needle. *Tuan* John's
cab stand was burned. Sporadic gunfire crackled from the
Tanglin area as British homeowners used souvenir Japanese
weapons to defend their homes against looters. Families in
the white district began retreating to the center of the city.

Dillon Synge slouched behind the wheel of the van. In his
rearview mirror was the Soviet embassy, a full block behind
him. He held a shotgun across his lap. Little good that would
do him, he thought. He had been a fool to rush the consulate.
Put a good man in the hospital and it had warned Kiril
Stasov. God only knew what that bastard Russian had waiting in the foyer this time. Synge's mouth pulled into a
malicious smile. In his plodding Soviet way, Stasov would be
prepared this time, but surely not for what was coming.
Synge craned his head out the window to see ashes bubbling
up from a building two blocks away. Yes, it was coming.

It all depended on Abdul Razak's momentum, Synge knew.
Razak and his men—four or five nine-fingered Malays—would
guide the frothing mob in a mindless pack. Anyone shouting
loud enough and running fast enough would lead. Timing
was critical. Razak's screaming prods would turn the mob at
the precise moment. The damage inflicted would depend on

the example set by Razak. The mullah had promised it would be catastrophic. He had also promised Stasov's head.

The first rioters began to appear in Synge's mirror. They were soiled and battered, some carrying torches, others rocks. The street was dug up on their way as cobblestones were requisitioned for missiles. Hedges were trampled underfoot, autos rolled over and set on fire. A homeowner was beaten to his knees as he attempted to scramble into his Mercedes. The doors were ripped off the automobile and thrown onto his front lawn. His house was torched, as was the next one. Strident yells fed the flames.

The crushing, frenetic mob was abreast of the Soviet consulate when the Malays began yelling anti-white, anti-imperialist oaths and launched stones at the consulate windows. Abdul Razak gripped the iron gate surrounding the yard and began shaking it like a madman, cursing the Soviets in a screeching falsetto. With renewed fury, the mob pitched itself at the fence. A shot was fired from a second-story window, and a nine-fingered Malay slumped against the iron grill, but the press of those behind pinned the body upright. The mob surged and the fence slowly bowed inward, the metal posts bending as if melting in a forge.

Dillon Synge shifted into reverse and slowly backed the van toward the consulate, not fast enough to draw attention, but steadily, so that he would be across from the consulate two minutes after it was broached. The consulate's metal door was assaulted by the throng. Another shot spurred the mob and the door buckled inward as the frames snapped. With an exultant cry, the Malays gushed forward.

And were blown back by the first burst from the Degtyarev machine gun. The bullets ripped into the first wave of Malays, tearing them open and cutting through to the second and third rows. The jammed procession staggered and trembled, its front layers peeling away as the dead Malays sank to the ground. Now at the rear of the mob, Razak rasped frantic commands and encouragement, screaming "God is Great" again and again, until the mob took up the cry, and fortified by religious fervor pushed forward again. Using their dead comrades as shields, the screaming column coursed through the consulate doors. The Degtyarev's thunderous pounding mixed sickeningly with the hollow thud of bullets slamming into upright corpses. Within seconds the machine gun was overrun, its firing silenced. The two Russian gunners disappeared under the rushing mob. A delirious Malay raised an arm, torn from one of the guards' shoulders, and waved it victoriously above the crowd.

Kiril Stasov had fired the shot from the window, praying a casualty would sober the horde. He had heard the door crumple and the hinges pop. He leaned out over the window-sill, hoping to jump to safety, but the Malay throng was below. A cobblestone burst through the window, sending glass splinters across the room. When the machine gun abruptly stopped and a whooping cry soared up the stairwell, Stasov knew he had only seconds.

He ran to the office door, trying for the coding room. A leap from there into the garden wouldn't kill him. He was two steps from his office when the first Malays streamed up the stairs, bloodied fists raised, and bearing clubs and bottles. The Russian was cut off. More and more of them streamed up the stairs to Stasov's floor, wild eyes fixing on the Russian, teeth bared in hatred.

Stasov flicked off the safety on his Tokarev, yelled an order to halt and immediately saw it was useless. He pointed the pistol and fired all eight rounds into the mass as it flowed around the bannister rail and surged toward him. The shots were ineffectual. Fueled by fury, pushing the wounded and dead ahead of them, the rioters rushed toward Stasov's office.

Stasov's last impression was one of admiration of himself, for his preparation, for his remarkable calm. He had taken every precaution, planned every contingency. But this one. He was serving the motherland to the last. His family would get a medal, or something. He stepped into his office, closed the door and threw the bolt, then sat behind his desk, his hands went to his lap, and he lowered his head. Stasov could have been asleep.

The thin office door had no braking effect on the mob. It sprang away from the frame. Shouting men climbed over the desk and yanked Stasov from his seat. He was dead before any part of him touched the ground.

Synge's instructions to Razak had been specific: be the first to the vault and prevent the mob from damaging the Kobe Elephant. He sprinted along the consulate's hallway, throwing open doors, searching for the basement stairs. Three of his men followed, one carrying a tarpaulin. Behind them were the splintering noises of destruction.

In the past weeks, Abdul Razak had been as careful as he

was demagogic. Always the first to cry for revenge, never the first to enter a door. This time he made a mistake. With the goal so close, Razak plunged down the basement steps, rushing for the Kobe Elephant. When his hand batted the light switch on, he found a Soviet guard standing at the mouth of the Chubb safe. Razak wheezed with fright and desperately threw his hands in front of his face. The dum-dum bullet entered his chest, spinning him backwards into his men. The first Malay, a ruggedly built man with nine-fingers, had already that day learned the value of a human shield. He lifted Razak's body by the arms and propelled him into the guard. The Russian fired again. The bullet spent its fury on the dead mullah. The body slid off the guard and he fought to align the pistol, but the big Malay's hands were around his throat, pushing him up the side of the safe until he was dead.

The three Malays entered the safe. The Kobe Elephant stood mute on its pedestal, oblivious to the ransacking above and the intruding Malays. Its placid, sea-green presence arrested the three as if hands had simultaneously gripped their collars. Synge had told them of its size and beauty, but his lustful descriptions could not have prepared them for this confrontation. The meager light filtering through the vault door rippled across the elephant's back, giving it the illusion of motion, and its eyes seemed to glow, to follow them as they stumbled into the safe. For several moments they stared at the elephant. Then the tarpaulin was thrown over the Kobe Elephant, and after several attempts, the three found their grips.

By the time they reached the hallway the rampage was ebbing. The few remaining Malays were stripping the building. One boy filled a napkin with crystal from the fallen chandelier. Another tore an Indian mat print from the wall. A child no older than six was loading his pocket with Degtyarev shells. Little else in the building was left to salvage.

The Kobe Elephant was carried over Malay bodies, slowly pushed through the remnants of the iron door and escorted down the steps to the street where Dillon Synge's van waited. Pinang jumped from the running board, levered the truck's rear doors, and helped muscle the elephant into the cargo bed. He waved the Malays away, then climbed into the truck, stepped over Connie Snow's bound form, and pounded on the forward panel. The truck lurched away from the curb, and turned right into King's Street as it sped away from the riot.

* * *

Black bag in hand, Shelby Watson pushed his way through the Raffles' door, swatted at a gray ash that threatened to land on his jacket, and scanned the boiling horizon. Sections of the city were glowing orange and red. Without money for a cab, he stepped across the Raffles' driveway and again peered through the fan palms at the distant fires, searching for the safest route to his office. A familiar voice called his name. Watson turned to the vigorously waving hand. Snow's hand.

Watson smiled as best he could and approached the American. For a moment he thought the woman standing near him was Connie. Same sturdy build. But the woman's hair was much lighter than Connie's, and . . . Watson stopped twenty feet from them. He worked his face into a squint. "Jesus, Joe, that's. . . ."

"That's what I thought, too." Snow held the woman's hand tight enough to make her cringe. "She's another one of Howard Lester's games."

"You work for Lester?" The doctor stepped closer, his eyes never leaving her.

Snow answered. "This is the woman I've been chasing around Singapore. Her name is Barbara Durant, and she works out of San Francisco."

"What happens next?"

"They've got my wife." Snow's voice carried panic Watson had never heard from him before.

"I know that. What're you going to do?"

"Lester is working with Dillon Synge."

"That's absurd."

Snow turned to the woman. "Where's Lester's room?"

She hesitated an instant too long. Snow's fingers dug into her hand, and something popped. Her face tightened. Only after several seconds could she open her eyes. She whispered, "The Orange Hotel. Room four ten."

They made sporadic progress, Snow dragging the woman and Watson limping after them. Stamford Road was clotted with automobiles, many with wicker trunks strapped to the boots. Brits gathered around taxis, bidding frantically for service. Pedestrians carried grips and baskets and seemed to be scurrying randomly, looking at the blackened sky, listening to the distant rumble of the fires. The sidewalk in front of the Orange Hotel was covered with tourists, suitcases and sea trunks. The tourists scattered before Snow and his cap-

261

tive and stared after the doctor, who followed, breathing in huge asthmatic gasps.

Snow simply ran through the room's door. It cracked open, its bolt falling to the floor. Snow had pulled open all the drawers in the dresser before Watson struggled into the room. He sank onto the bed to watch Snow frantically search Lester's possessions. Snow fumbled with a suitcase for a moment, swore loudly and ripped it open, tearing the latches from the leather. The contents spilled to the carpet. The woman in white cowered near the closet. Snow brushed her aside and began ripping pockets from Lester's clothes. A steady stream of shirts and pants flew from the closet, until Snow emerged carrying a leather notebook. He flipped through the pages, then handed it to Watson.

"Ever seen anything like this?"

The doctor leafed through the notebook. On each page was a photograph of a woman, beginning with a photo of Amelia Earhart taken just before she disappeared. Several others were of women Watson had worked with during his years with the agency. There was also one of the woman in white, Barbara Durant, who had lowered herself into a high-backed Malacca chair near the closet. Watson turned a few more pages, stared for several seconds, then handed the notebook back to Snow. "You'd better have a look, Joe."

Connie Snow stared from the page, sable black hair, strong chin, wide, purposeful mouth. Snow gazed dully at the photograph, then brought it to within inches of his eyes, canting it to the light. "Shelby, I hope this doesn't mean. . . ."

"What else?" the doctor cut in. "Your wife is on the payroll."

Snow's voice was tinder dry. "Why?"

Watson ran a gloved finger under his nose. "Figure the worst, Joe. Lester has been setting you up. Connie must be in on it. Lester has lied to you every step of the way, and your wife knew about it."

Snow took two angry steps toward the doctor, and Watson's gloved hand moved with that peculiar twist. Snow arrested his movement and his face slowly unknotted. "Sorry, Shelby. I just. . . ."

Watson held up his good hand. "I know. I'll ask you again. What are you going to do?"

Snow pinched the bridge of his nose, as if trying to prevent a thought from forming. His words were blurred. "Shelby, with her picture in Lester's notebook, I don't even know if my wife is worth . . . is worth going after. If she's been manipulating me, where does that leave me?"

Watson pushed himself off the bed. "So she works for Lester. She's still your wife, and Dillon Synge is going to kill her. You can count on that."

The desk phone rang. Snow looked at the woman in white, who haplessly shrugged her shoulders. Snow lifted the phone to his ear, listened, then snapped, "How did you know I was here?"

Howard Lester replied, "When Barbara Durant didn't meet me, I figured you'd found her. I also figured you'd head for my room."

"Lester, you've been leading me around. . . ."

"We don't have time to talk. One of the pairs of eyes I said I had all over the city was watching the Soviet consulate. It was ransacked a few minutes ago by a Malay mob. After the gunfire, three Malays emerged from the building carrying a large, canvas-covered object. The wind lifted the tarp, and my man saw a flash of brilliant green. It's the Kobe Elephant, I'm sure of it. A man matching your description of Pinang helped push it into a truck."

"The elephant was at the Soviet embassy?"

"Yes, and Synge has it now. He knows he's under the gun, so he'll be leaving the city right away. And I can think of only one way he'll get out with the elephant: on his motor yacht. I got hold of Tsukada, and he's on his way to the West Reach. I'll be at the Orange Hotel in three minutes. Meet me out front."

Snow followed his boss into the Ford. Howard Lester's bulk completely filled the space behind the wheel. The car pulled into the traffic, most of it oncoming, as Singapore's white citizens withdrew to the center of the city. The Ford had crossed the Singapore River onto New Bridge Road before Snow could trust himself to talk. His voice was rigid. "I ought to strangle you, Lester."

"I wouldn't be the first, would I?" His jowls twitched.

"How long has my wife worked for you?"

"Couple years. The two of you made a pretty good team tracking down Dillon Synge."

"I've gone to a lot of trouble to keep my work history from Connie."

Lester laughed. "Work history. That's a happy phrase for

what you do. She knows it all. Every nasty little job you've ever pulled."

"She doesn't have a father in clean-up?"

"Hell, no. And I'm not her uncle, either."

The air had thickened with smoke as the car drove south into Chinatown. The auto churned a wake of ashes that had settled on the road. Shops and stalls along the road had been torched, and many small fires were still burning. Ragged merchants pulled salvageable items from the culls of their shops.

Twisting to view the wreckage, Watson said, "I think we're driving into it."

"I don't want to try the roads further east where the shots are coming from," Lester said. "If we dawdle around, Synge'll be in Jakarta before we get to the West Reach."

Lester slowed to wind around the blackened carcass of a horse. An elderly amah, her face smeared with soot, was cutting strips of flesh from the horse's flank. A rock rattled against the fender.

"You're still holding back, Lester," Snow said, leaning forward in the seat.

"You'd better hear it from your wife, Joseph. It might make some sense. . . ."

A fist-sized rock smashed into the Ford's windshield, exploding glass shards into the cab like a fragmentation grenade. Snow's hand jerked up. Glass splinters caught in his forearm. Others bit into his forehead below the hairline, and beads of blood streaked his skin like dripping paint. Snow blindly pulled the .45 from his pants.

An inch of Howard Lester's cheek lay open, distended like a dog's tongue. The glass splinter was still implanted at the fork of the cut, and his cheek was running with blood. Shelby Watson leaned over the back of the seat and deftly pulled the shard from Lester's face. Lester's hands were still on the wheel and he was eerily still. Snow was grabbing a shoulder to shake him out of it when the rear of the car lifted from the ground. Snow turned to see six or seven Malay youths crowding the back bumper, trying to overturn the car. He yelled a warning and raised the Colt, but his threat was lost in the screaming and the ferocious pounding on the Ford.

To the sound of glass pulverizing, the Ford settled onto its side. Snow braced himself between the seat and the dashboard and tried to climb up through the open window. His foot glanced off Howard Lester who yelped in pain, his first sound since he had been slashed by the glass. Lester coughed, waved his hand at something invisible in front of his face, then ordered in a weak voice, "Get us out of here, Joe."

Snow's foot found purchase on the steering column. A piece of glass dug into his hand as he gripped the window frame. Most of his body had emerged from the window when a stone bounced off his chest. He doubled over, gasping. A second rock careened off an ear, and he slumped back into the Ford's cab.

Snow peered up at the window. It was covered with a mass of tan limbs, some of them groping into the cab, slithering like a knot of snakes. He took a deep breath, raised the automatic above his head, and loosed four shots through the window. The thunderous retorts were followed by screams of pain. Blood and bits of tissue dropped into the cab. The limbs peeled away. With Lester bracing his leg, Snow again climbed out of the cab, his Colt at point.

The street swarmed with rioters. The injured were being passed back into the crowd. Snow leveled the Colt at the nearest Malay, who backstepped quickly until the press of the mob stopped him. Snow tried to grip the roof, but his hand slipped in blood. Lester pushed from below and Snow lifted his legs out, then slid down the car's roof to the street level.

Bracing his back against the Ford, he swung the pistol in a rhythmic arc toward the rioters, encompassing as many Malays as he could. They were chanting harsh words, eyes alight with hatred. When those in the back pressed forward, the circle closed several feet. Only the thin perimeter of Malays who could see Snow's pistol kept the mob from rushing the car.

Snow braved a glance upward. Lester's arm was hanging over the top of the car, searching for a hold. His head appeared, and a moment later he dropped to the ground. The Malays increased their shrieking and inched forward. Snow raised the Colt higher and soundlessly mouthed a warning. A rock was lobbed from the rear of the crowd and it caromed off the grill.

Shelby Watson hit the ground and his left leg gave way. Snow braced the doctor's arm and leaned into him and in that second of inattention, the Malays took another step. Lester pulled a Smith & Wesson from his jacket and the circle paused again.

"What do we do?" Lester asked. He spit blood, then drew back the revolver's hammer.

"I'm pissing my pants," Watson answered in a brittle voice.

Like a hand closing around a throat, the circle of furious Malays drew closer. Six feet separated them from the barrel of Snow's gun. He said, "We dig a tunnel out of here."

"How?" Lester coughed.

"Follow me." Snow stepped away from the car. Lester grabbed the tail of his shirt to be led out. At first the crowd parted in front of the slowly advancing Snow. Fists waved, but the Malay line opened. The three whites stepped into the breach.

The Malays froze, those in the rear would not allow any more retreat. Snow yelled in English, "I'll fire," then futilely repeated himself in Cantonese. The human vise began closing. Arms reached for them.

Snow fired at the nearest Malay. The mob howled, first in fear, then rage. The Malay dropped to his knees and sagged into the legs of another rioter. The crowd melted back, opening the tunnel again. Lester yelled an order, but it was lost in the mob's shrieks. Snow walked steadily. The crowd parted before him. The three men moved in a seam which quickly locked behind them.

Snow yelled, "At the first break, we start running. Shelby, can you run?"

"Faster than hell if . . ."

A brown hand shot from the crowd, latched onto the doctor's hair, and yanked him into the line of Malays. Watson disappeared into the mass. The Malays swarmed around him like wasps to an intruder. Watson's cry sounded above the Malay curses. His black glove was tossed into the air, then a handful of his dark hair. Snow fired three times randomly into the seething mob, seemingly with no effect. He stepped toward them, but Lester's hand caught his arm. Lester yelled, "Watson's gone and the line has broken. Run, Joe."

In the maniacal attempt to lay hands on Watson, the Malay wall had parted. With a last look at the boiling mob, Snow sprinted from the pocket with Lester at his heels. Two youths carrying bricks moved to intercept them, but Lester fired a shot and they veered away. Lester's hand was still gripping Snow's shirt as they turned onto a side street. A

266

bottle shattered near them, but the rioters were quickly left behind.

A block later, they slowed to a walk. Snow ran a sleeve across his brow, leaving a red stain. He gulped air and said, "What about Shelby? Maybe his body is. . . ."

"He's beyond caring. But your wife isn't. Let's go."

A quick flush of embarrassment crossed Snow's face. For all of ten minutes he had forgotten Connie. And Dillon Synge. With renewed energy, he sprinted toward an automobile he was about to appropriate.

XVIII

A Japanese guard opened the gate to a U.S. Army sergeant carrying a submachine gun. The G.I. felled the guard with the gun butt, then called, "You men are free. Your war is over." For her, it had just begun.

Ko Tsukada left the car wedged between two buttress trunks a few yards off the road. He pulled the bottle of water and the box of lye from the passenger seat, and began high-stepping across the jungle floor toward Bryte's Cove. Sunlight sprayed through the jungle canopy, dappling the undergrowth. Through the Borneo camphors he could see the flickering blue water. A family of wa-wa's followed him, marking his progress with shrill cries.

He approached a row of bamboo trees which grew so close together they looked like the stockade of a fort. He found an opening in the wall that would lead him to the cove. Tsukada crushed the lye tablets between his palms, letting the powder fall into the bottle. He stirred the mixture with a bamboo shoot, turning it into a gray-white paste, then splashed it onto the jungle floor between the trees, leaving a sticky puddle where he had just walked. Should the Sikh's dogs find Tsukada's trail, they would also find lye eating into their pads or into their tongues if they tried to lick it off. Tsukada had never liked dogs anyway.

The Japanese worked his way through the mangrove swamp to the water's edge, fighting the sand that sucked at his feet, pulling him down. He moved slowly, carrying the Nambu in one hand and gripping the exposed trunks and bush ropes for support with the other. He waded into the murky water and almost immediately his arm began to burn. He lifted it. Two leeches had attached themselves to his forearm, their black, doughy heads disappearing under his skin. Tsukada had lived with leeches on Saipan, but had never overcome his instinctive revulsion to them. He looked away and swallowed several times. He would deal with them later with splashes of paraffin.

The swamp bottom sank away and Tsukada kicked into a one-handed sidestroke, keeping the pistol above the small waves. The water quickly turned from black to blue as he churned away from the tentacles of the swamp. Several moments later he rounded the last outcropping of plank trees and swam into the cove.

Dillon Synge's motor launch was moored at the pier a hundred yards across the inlet. The deep rumble of its twin diesels rolled across the cove, and water near the stern bubbled from the exhaust. Tsukada stopped kicking, and let all but his eyes slip beneath the surface. The stark sun fluttered across the waves, and Tsukada squinted against the flashing. Standing near the stern rail, a rotund Chinese deckhand was toying with a hauser, idly swinging it against the gunwale. His other hand was occupied with a cigarette. Tsukada scissored his legs. Dogs and Chinese. He had never liked either of them.

The Japanese's hand struck a deadhead, submerged six inches below the waterline. The sunken log's bark had been replaced with barnacles which scraped away the skin on the back of his thumb. He shook his hand under the water and again began to paddle.

The Japanese steadily drew near the deck. The converted PT boat's lines were sleek and low, giving the illusion of movement even when the boat was docked. The forward gun mount was empty, and the torpedo tubes and depth-charge launchers had been removed, but the boat still wore the white U.S. Navy numerals. It was painted slate gray, a noncolor that contrasted dully with the brilliant blue water.

Tsukada slowed to a shallow breast stroke, not breaking the water, moving silently. The dockhand flicked the cigarette butt into the water, and immediately drew a pack from his shirt pocket. He scratched the match several times along the aft rail before it caught. He glanced over his shoulder at the shore, then returned his full attention to the glowing cigarette.

A moment later Tsukada was dog-paddling against the side of the PT boat, the barnacles tugging at the cuffs of his pants. He pushed against the water, moving toward the bow. His hand loudly splashed through the water's surface. He froze, listening for the deckhand. A full minute passed before he continued to the bow, and then around the sharp prow to the slip of water between the port freeboard and the dock. Tsukada planted both feet on the boat's side and braced himself against one of the dock's oiled pylons. He dropped the Nambu's safety and waited.

The van bounced along the rutted service road under the jungle canopy. When it pulled into the clearing near the dock, Dillon Synge pushed a pair of aviator's sunglasses up his nose. He negotiated the truck along the turbid ground, guiding the wheels on a trail of liverworts to avoid sinking to the axles. When the van was thirty feet from the dock, he pushed the brake pedal to the firewall and heard a hollow thump as Pinang bumped into the partition.

The Malay had already spread the doors when Synge reached the rear of the van. The jade merchant signaled for the deckhand and nervously scanned the jungle wall until the Chinese appeared alongside the truck. Synge and the Chinese each held one of the Kobe Elephant's rear legs, while Pinang grasped its thick neck. The elephant was carefully lowered to the muddy ground.

Synge tore at the tarpaulin like a small child opening a gift. When Pinang lifted one of the elephant's legs, the tarp came free. Synge stared vacantly for a moment, his body shaking as if chilled. Then he pressed his palm onto the elephant's flank and sucked at the air as if it were his last breath. His hand glowed in sea-green light reflected from the elephant's jade skin, blurring the distinction between the jade and his flesh. His other hand tenderly touched the Kobe Elephant's ear, lightly stroking the finely carved ridge. Synge's mouth parted and his nostrils flared.

Pinang glanced nervously at the deckhand, then said through his wire brace, "Boss, the sooner we get to Bengkalis, the better."

Synge's head jerked back as if he had been slapped. "Yes. There'll be time for this later." He peered into the van, could

270

see nothing because of the contrasting light, and said, "We'll load the elephant, and I'll come back for the woman."

They moved cautiously, one tentative step at a time, making sure each foot was firmly planted before shifting their weight. Synge murmured encouragement, perhaps to his men, perhaps to the elephant. They carried it across the gangplank. Pinang stepped over the gunwale and took most of the elephant's weight as it was lowered to the deck. Synge's hand was almost touching the elephant's flank again, when he stopped himself, ran his tongue along his lower lip, and returned to shore.

Before entering the van, the jade dealer pulled a stainless steel Weiss knife from his belt. Double-edged and gleaming, it looked perfectly at home in his hand. He climbed back into the back of the van, pausing to let his eyes adjust. Connie Snow cowered in the corner, blood seeping from her nose to the gag. She pushed against the panel as Synge approached, but the metal wouldn't give. Her eyes closed in resignation as he yanked her to her feet. He bent to slash the manila rope around her legs, then pushed her to the door. He took a fistful of her hair and jumped from the van bed as she tumbled after him, her knees hitting the ground first. Her cry of pain was muffled by the gag.

Synge jerked her head back and snarled, "You thought you'd just come to Singapore with that killer husband of yours. . . ." He stopped abruptly and turned to the boat to locate the Kobe Elephant as if it were an apparition threatening to disappear. Finding it where he had left it he continued, "Just come to Singapore to do me in, is that it? And now look at you, on your knees in the mud." Synge lifted his hand, and Connie closed her eyes, preparing for the blow.

The steady grumble of the diesels had provided a comfortable backdrop to the loading. But suddenly their deep bellow was altered, not substantially, but they had gained a tenor echo. Again Synge glanced at his elephant. He cocked his head and held his breath. His face darkened as he realized that another engine had been added to the chorus, this one coming from the jungle.

"Your *husband!*" He pulled Connie to her feet and held her by the nape of the neck as he backed to the gangway. The car rolled into the clearing.

Joseph Snow was on the ground in a crouch before the vehicle stopped. He held the Colt with two hands, and the heads of both his wife and Synge danced across his notched sight. Howard Lester ran to the front of the car. Needlessly he ordered, "Keep your finger light."

Synge's hands were twitching uncontrollably as he stumbled onto the gangway. He pinned Connie against his chest. The blade dug into her side and a thin stream filled the blade's blood gutter. Synge backstepped. His mouth narrowed to a thin crease as the pudgy man and Snow fanned out in front of him. A dog's painful howl cut through the diesels.

Ko Tsukada pushed against the slippery pylon and gripped the edge of the gangplank from below. He kicked away, using the momentum of his body to swing a leg onto the plank. His heel jabbed into Dillon Synge's leg. The jade dealer flinched with surprise, his arm again raking the blade along Connie's side.

Synge stared dumbly at Tsukada trying to lever himself onto the gangway. A leg shot up from below, wrapped itself around the wood plank, and was followed by an arm. Tsukada's head appeared, and their eyes locked. For five seconds, neither man moved, each was held immobile by hatred and fear. Then propelled by a vengeful oath, Tsukada swung his body onto the narrow plank.

Synge risked a glance at Snow, but all his eyes could see was the ugly black hole at the end of the Colt's barrel, still thirty yards away, but frightfully large and centered between Synge's eyes. Tsukada scrambled to his knees and had one foot under him when Synge tugged Connie to one side and lashed at the Japanese with the knife. The blade caught the flesh of Tsukada's shoulder, leaving a jagged path along his collarbone to his neck. The Nambu dropped into the water. He toppled forward, his hand snaking between Connie's feet to find the jade dealer's ankle.

Synge grunted as the Japanese's fingers dug the bones of his ankle. He screamed for Pinang and struck viciously at Tsukada's wrist with his other foot. Connie Snow backed between them, trying to block the jade dealer's legs with her own. Synge's heel found Tsukada's wrist twice, smashing it into the plank. Pinang ran along the rail to the gangplank, then swung at Tsukada with a belaying pin. The first strike missed by inches, slamming into the plank as the Japanese pulled in his arms. Synge's ankle broke free. Pinang raised the pin again, but a bullet slapped into the gunwale three inches from his knee. He ducked, dropping the pin. Howard Lester cursed himself for the missed shot.

Synge dropped over the gunwale to the deck, tugging at Connie's hair, bending her, using her as a shield. He called, "Wan, release the lines."

The Chinese deckhand moved to the port rail. Snow shifted the menacing Colt and shook his head. The Chinese stopped and slowly raised his hands. Synge pulled Connie behind him toward the line that secured the boat. He passed in front of the Kobe Elephant and just as his hand went for the mooring line, Snow's Colt spoke again, the peculiarly flat clap of the Issue .45 rolling out across the cove. Almost simultaneously, the slug tore into the boat's cabin three inches from the Kobe Elephant. Synge's face turned the gray color of death.

Snow yelled from the shore, "Synge, I don't want you to have any doubts about where my next bullet will go. Your beloved elephant will shatter like a light bulb. Lower that knife."

Synge made spastic lurches of indecision. His eyes batted between the Kobe Elephant and the ragged hole in the cabin so very near it. He wrenched his gaze away to find Snow's Colt now clearly aimed at the jade sculpture.

A sheet of blood pouring from his shoulder, Ko Tsukada inched along the gangplank toward the gunwale. The deckhand remained with his arms outstretched. Pinang had disappeared into the cabin and Howard Lester, holding his Smith & Wesson with two hands, was scanning the bridge and afterdeck with the pistol. He waded a few steps into the water, but Pinang was not on deck.

Snow was about to force a decision on himself—perhaps realign the Colt on Synge, hoping for a clear shot—when the engines roared. Still tied to the dock by a single line, the boat churned white water and lurched forward. Caught unaware, Synge and Connie toppled to the deck. The Kobe Elephant slid several feet aft. The line tore the bitt from the dock's rotted wood and skipped after the boat as it shot away from shore. Snow waved the Colt at the boat, his eyes narrow with helpless rage.

Ko Tsukada had almost reached the gunwales when the ship accelerated. He grabbed blindly for the boat railing and screamed in agony as the boat pulled away, dropping the gangway into the water but yanking him along with it. His wail of pain was drowned by the engine's thunder, as was the sound of his body colliding with the freeboard as he dropped toward the water line. As the ship rushed to the center of the cove and began its port tack to the West Reach outlet, Tsukada hung from the port rail, his feet skidding along the water.

When the boat was a hundred yards offshore, Snow lowered the weapon, the most painful movement he had ever made in his life. The sweet taste of blood spread in his mouth, and Snow realized he had bitten almost through his lower lip. He exhaled, a long sigh of surrender, and said faintly, "Shelby's dead. And now my wife's dead."

Snow's face hardened and the Colt came up again, this time sighting on Howard Lester. "You killed her, Howard, just as sure as if you'd been holding the knife."

Tsukada's arm was ripping off. Already damaged by Synge's blade, small ligaments and tendons were giving way as he tried desperately to hold onto the rail of the speeding boat. His arms shook with the vibrations of the engines through the thin hull.

He tried to kick his leg up the railing. His first effort was so agonizing, he sank his teeth into his tongue to prevent himself from screaming. He launched his foot again. He shook his head to will away the agony of his shoulder, and found that his heel had caught on the port rail.

Tsukada jackknifed his knee and brought himself up the freeboard. His right hand was almost useless, so he gripped the rail with his legs like a saddle. He pushed himself over onto the deck. His eyes misting with pain, he looked fore and aft along the port walkway. He was alone. Pressing his back against the trunk cabin wall to avoid being seen from the bridge above, Tsukada stepped aft. The Chinese was coiling a line, wrapping it around his hand and his elbow. Three quick steps brought Tsukada to the deckhand's back. He lightly clipped the man's ear, then pushed him over the rail. A few seconds later the deckhand emerged in the frothing white water to shake his fist, but his yell of alarm was lost in the steady drone of the diesels.

Holding his injured arm close to his chest, Tsukada took the stern ladder two rungs at a time. His head emerged above the bridge deck, and he saw the squat figure of Pinang at the wheel. Dillon Synge and Connie had apparently gone below. Tsukada scrambled up the last few rungs onto the deck.

Alerted by animal instinct, the Malay turned when Tsukada was two steps away. Pinang reflexively raised an arm, but Tsukada's open palm smashed into the jaw brace. The wire crushed against the Malay's cheek. A second chop slammed the wire sideways, rebreaking Pinang's jaw and preventing him from opening his mouth to scream. Tsukada struck again, but the Malay's arm blocked the blow, giving Pinang two seconds to shake off the pain. He backed into the wheel, then slipped sideways across the bridge.

Without a helmsman, the boat veered to starboard, away from the narrow mouth of the cove. The Japanese glanced over the wheel. The boat was approaching the cove's north shore at twenty knots. Tsukada feinted right and came at the Malay from the left. His hand hit the base of his neck. When Pinang's knees gave way, Tsukada gripped the jaw brace and pushed him over the bridge rail into the sea.

Tsukada leaped to the wheel. He tried to turn the speeding boat, but with only one hand at the wheel, the boat veered only a few degrees. He tugged again, with the same result. The shore approached with frightening speed. Without the slightest clue as to what he was doing, Tsukada pulled back several levers on the control panel. He took his first full breath in minutes, when the engines faded to a low chug. Leaning his weight into the wheel, he brought the boat about. It came within a dozen yards of the outstretched trunks of the buttress trees on shore. Tsukada rode the wheel until the boat's prow was aimed at the dock. He thought he saw Snow and Lester planted where he had last seen them. He pushed the accelerator forward, forcing the engines to wind up again, then locked the wheel and turned to look for Dillon Synge.

The jade dealer had climbed the bridge ladder and was standing ten feet aft, holding an ancient Enfield Mark 1 revolver. Synge's voice sounded like the hiss of escaping steam. "You always wanted my elephant, Nissho. You never fooled me on that. That's why I left you in the cave." As he spoke, Synge's eyes dropped briefly to the Kobe Elephant, which was misted with sea spray, its intricate facets shimmering like a thousand miniature suns. Only when Tsukada took a threatening step could Synge force his eyes away from the sculpture. His gun returned to the Japanese.

Tsukada was out of moves. His deadly hands and feet were useless within the range of Synge's revolver. He half-stepped left, but the bore of the enormous pistol followed him easily. Not since the day he had walked away from his dead captain into the Saipan jungle had Tsukada felt so numbed by helplessness. In all the years of rage since then, never did he envision this end, that his last sight would be the end of Dillon Synge's revolver.

The boat's hull tore into the deadhead twenty feet from the dock. A second sunken log followed immediately, tearing a jagged furrow in the hull a foot from the waterline. The boat abruptly pitched starboard and the stern skipped away from the shore, launching a wall of water into the air.

Synge was thrown forward as the Enfield fired. The bullet coursed into Tsukada's shoulder, spinning him back against the wheel. Blood splattered against the spokes, and he slid onto the deck. The diesels sputtered and died, and the boat became motionless on the water. The prow began to sink as the forward compartments flooded.

The Kobe Elephant slid aft twenty feet, its trunk hanging out over the deck edge. Its blocky rear legs lifted momentarily from the deck, and the trunk dipped toward the water, but then settled back with a hollow thump.

Joseph Snow ran to the east end of the dock, and threw himself into the cove. He flailed at the water, his enormous hands catching huge quantities of water as they propelled him to the sinking boat. He kicked furiously, oblivious of the deadweight of his shoes. Panicked seconds elapsed before his hand hit the bow. With one powerful motion, he lifted himself from the water and swung over the gunwale to the deck.

Snow knew Synge must still be on board, but he didn't check his back. He took a few steps down the increasingly canted deck to the forward hatch and dropped into the cabin. He splashed in the foot of water which covered the interior catwalk. The hatch on the first bulkhead was open, and he bent low to pass through it. The sound of water rushing into the boat from several directions followed him up the catwalk as the boat slid further underwater.

The torpedo boat's conversion to a motor yacht had not been complete. Belowdecks was strictly functional, with wood bulkheads and low hatches. Snow moved quickly aft, calling for his wife. He held a hand in front of his face to ward off unseen protrusions. The interior was dark, made sinister by the rush of air pushed out of the boat by the incoming water. The boat shuddered. Snow lost his balance and grasped a hatch. He estimated the boat had dropped another foot.

The galley hatch was secure and wouldn't give when he pushed a shoulder into it. He stepped back and sprang it open with his foot. Behind him, the black cove water crawled up the gangway. He yelled his wife's name again, but heard only the ominous sound of water boiling into the boat. He grabbed the galley spigots for support as he worked aft. Another bulkhead was latched, and he cracked it under his foot, then crawled through it to the crew's quarters.

"Connie?" His voice accented the low whistle that echoed eerily in the ship. The boat keeled starboard as the deadhead scraped against the shattered hull. "Connie?"

He was running out of boat, he knew. Had he missed her? Was she underwater in one of the forward compartments? Fear dug at his throat, and his breath was labored and shallow. The water followed him like a dog, lapping at his heels, urging him on.

He scanned the bunks and was about to spring the next hatch when an object on the lower bunk hit his leg. Snow started, cocking his fist. The water had just reached his wife's ink-black hair, lifting it from the bunk. He found her shoulder, his hand brushing the knot of cloth over her mouth. He braced a leg against a stanchion and pulled her to her feet. Because her arms were bound behind her, she couldn't stand upright. She leaned into Snow who slipped the gag over her chin. He quickly untied her hands.

He started to speak several times before he managed, "You all right?"

Her mouth opened and closed, and blood dripped from the corner of her lip where the cloth had gnawed into the skin. Her voice was ragged. "Oh God, Joseph." Her arms found his neck. "I thought. . . ."

The edge of a bunk roughly scraped Snow's neck, as the boat keeled further starboard. His knees sunk below the waterline while he tore at the raffia rope on Connie's hands, then bent to release her legs. Snow touched her wrists lightly, looking for the cuts that were dripping blood.

"Joseph, this water is getting higher."

Snow quickly stepped around her and waded to the bunkroom hatch he had just come through. The hatch was completely submerged. Their retreat was blocked.

"We've got to go aft," he said, pulling her behind him. They stepped through to the engine room as the ship trembled. An unwilling cry of alarm escaped Connie as the water touched her elbows for the first time.

The engine room, the PT boat's aft compartment, resembled a dark mausoleum, its enormous diesel engines lying like caskets. They threw off steam as the water climbed the heated blocks. Snow duck-walked between the two engines, looking for the overhead hatch in the cramped low-ceilinged compartment. His hands bounced along the wiring and the pipes. "Connie, you there?"

"Right behind you."

He groped for the opening, continuing to work his way aft. "Where the hell is the hatch?"

Water climbed his chest, and it closed off the engine-room hatch.

"Joseph, I'm frightened." Her words tumbled out. "Once when I was a kid, my sister held me under a rain barrel until I almost drowned."

His hands came off the ceiling. "Your sister? Is she like your father in Schenectady, who doesn't exist?"

It was too dark to read her face, but her voice was again level. "Let's get out of here first. We can talk about it later."

"You're goddamn right we will." His hands returned to the pipes. "If we don't drown first."

As if on cue, the PT boat listed and dropped, rolling the water in the engine room into a wave. It caught Connie with her mouth open and pushed her against the engine block. She rebounded into her husband, coughing and spitting. A thin film of oil from the engine covered her face.

"Joseph, we've got to get out of. . . ." Another wave choked off her words.

He moved further aft in a crouch, one hand above the other searching for a grip on the engines. He dragged his hand along the wiring and pipes until it finally found a smooth square of wood. His fingers searched for a latch, but found only nail heads.

"It's nailed shut." He shoved with both hands. Pain coursed through his bandaged arm. The hatch didn't move. "Give me some help."

Connie inched up the increasingly steep gangway between the engines until she was pressed against her husband. Her hands also found the hatch and they strained together. Still no movement. The water reached her neck.

"We're going to die here, Joseph. I've been through too much to die here." Her voice trailed off, and her chin sagged into the water.

Snow's fist slammed into the hatch. He repositioned his foot and struck again. And again. His hand and arm were transformed into a mammoth piston, dipping into the water, then launching at the hatch. The sound of flesh meeting wood filled their small space and rippled the water. Connie's head was pressed against the ceiling to keep her nose above the waterline. The force of her husband's blows rattled her head, and she closed her eyes against the oily water.

Snow's middle finger broke at the second joint as he continued striking the hatch, his fist taking on the rhythm of a metronome and the force of a jackhammer. Another pop and the second finger fractured. And yet another snap, but this was wood giving way. A needle of sunlight flashed into the compartment. Snow uttered a low wail of pain which filled their shrinking space. Sunlight pierced the rough opening as splinters fell into the water and Snow continued to pound. The circle of light grew until Snow's fist shot through the opening. He clenched the wood and tore it down. Bubbles came from his wife's direction.

Snow ripped at the hatch until the opening was shoulder width. He planted his palms, and a fierce sound escaped from him as his broken fingers were bent back with his weight, then he lifted himself through. He thrust his hands into the water and fished for several seconds before finding his wife's hair. He pulled her through in one motion, and lay her on the deck. she fell back on her elbows as saltwater ran from her nose and mouth. She gulped air in enormous draughts. Finally, her eyes opened.

Snow grunted, trying to gather his legs under him. "Where's Synge?"

At that name, his wife came alive. She was standing before her husband could wrestle himself upright. Cautiously they stepped around the trunk cabin to the port rail.

A frantic sight met them there. Dillon Singe was pushing the Kobe Elephant up the deck, away from the water which claimed increasing portions of the deck as the boat sank. His feet churned ineffectually against the wet walkway, but the elephant moved only by inches. Snow knew it was the pain radiating from his fingers and his overwhelming exhaustion, but it seemed to him that the jade elephant was leaning away from the water, helping Synge, encouraging him. The waves lapped at Synge's legs and a frightful cry escaped from him.

"Joseph, give me your pistol." The sheer force, the raw virulence of his wife's words compelled him to release his grip when she reached for the Colt. The boat lurched starboard again, and Snow braced himself against the gunwale. Connie was steady though; she raised the gun to sight on Synge and called his name.

Synge snapped upright. His face paled so quickly he appeared to be dying. His eyes batted between the elephant and the pistol, but his hands remained on the elephant's flanks. His words rambled. "You keep coming back. Keep coming back." He pressed his loins into the jade, but the animal slipped back, drifting inch by inch with the cant of the deck. "Sent Pinang, sent Flynn. But you keep coming."

Her whisper was a deathly rattle. "You kept me alive all those years, Synge. Hatred sustained me. And now, killing you doesn't seem enough. It isn't enough."

Synge saw the Colt angle away from his face. He whimpered, "Please, no. Not my elephant. . . ."

The pistol jumped in her hand, and the Kobe Elephant's skull burst into a crystalline cloud that rained jade chips onto the deck. Synge's eyes fell to the ragged crater blown out of his jewel. The trunk and an ear still hung tentatively from the elephant's body. He moaned, "No, no. . . ."

Again the pistol barked, and the trunk and a leg disintegrated. The elephant began to topple, but Synge desperately righted it. With tearing eyes he looked up from the remnants of the elephant. "Miss Earhart, please, no . . ."

Those words stunned Joseph Snow and ensnared him, preventing him from moving, from thinking. Miss Earhart. His mind was a void, incapable of understanding.

Her arms were still rigidly extended, the Colt unerringly pointed at the maimed elephant. The pistol roared again and more jade shards erupted from the wounded animal. "It just doesn't seem enough," she whispered, and fired again. This time the elephant's round belly fragmented, and jagged green chips skittered along the deck.

Only the elephant's haunches remained intact. Dillon Synge lifted his hands from the jade. His face was pulled into angles of disbelief and grief. He gasped, "I recognized you that first day at the club. Amelia Earhart, oh Jesus . . ."

The .45 thundered again and the remnants of Synge's elephant lay about him like litter. Sea water lapped at the fragments, and the sun glittered back from both the water's rippling surface and the jade chips.

In those few moments, Dillon Synge had grown old and died. Now he raised both hands toward Amelia Earhart, as if he were prostrated before a shrine. "Please . . . please finish it," he pleaded.

The colt's last bullet tore into Synge's chest, blowing him back against the cabin. His body rebounded, slipped on the jade pebbles, and rolled over the gunwales into the sea.

Joseph Snow saw none of this. His eyes were locked on Connie. Her black hair, her even teeth. His wife of two months. Amelia Earhart.

They sat on the dock watching the radio antenna of the PT boat slip beneath the surface. Bubbles and white water marked the boat's passing. Concentric rings rippled away from its grave, then the cove was still.

Snow had not said a word since diving from the boat. Howard Lester had struggled with Tsukada's limp form, dragging him from the bridge through the water, and finally onto the dock. Tsukada had regained consciousness sometime during Lester's struggle and now leaned against a pylon, blood running from his shoulder. Amelia Earhart climbed to the dock. She wouldn't look at her husband.

Snow seemed incapable of digesting the last few moments. Synge and the elephant were gone. He was on the dock. Amelia Earhart. He couldn't understand.

Lester began quietly. "Imagine her hair much lighter, sandy-blonde, and much shorter. Imagine a small gap between her front teeth and her skin much lighter. I changed her, Joe. With the help of a dentist and a hairdresser. And that little pucker on her shoulder you like so much, that's three sessions with a plastic surgeon who tried to erase the scar from Synge's bullet."

Tsukada coughed and touched the puncture on his shoulder, then the knife gash just above it. The bleeding had stopped, but Tsukada's face was haggard. He tried to sit up, but fell against the pylon. He said weakly, "You knew about me?"

Lester shook his head and blood sprinkled from his cheek. "We thought Nissho Ito died on Saipan. When Rose tipped us off about the supposed bones at the Malay camp, Amelia and I knew someone else was after the Saipan hijacker, someone who was in Singapore and wanted to draw us in. Fine with us. Anyone with information was welcome."

Snow's face was open and vulnerable. "Connie, you've been using me all along."

She bit her lower lip, then moved her eyes to Snow. "Joseph, you have no idea what those years in the camps on Saipan and in Malaysia did to me. They ate away everything that was human, everything that was compassionate and caring. For all those years the only thing that kept me alive was the memory of Dillon Synge's face above the pistol barrel. I'll live forever with that face. And I couldn't live at all until it was extinguished."

"Extinguished," Snow repeated dully. He looked at her face as if trying to see through a misted window. "You used me to extinguish Synge. Pushing me along with your enthusiasm. Goading me into following him." Snow's face tightened. "No wonder the handwriting in Earhart's flight log was familiar. No wonder . . ." His voice trailed off.

"When I arrived back in the U.S. in 1945, I pleaded with Howard to help me find the man who shot me on Saipan. He gradually convinced me it wasn't possible, not through the agency. For him, Amelia Earhart couldn't be mentioned, couldn't even be talked about. The 1937 flight had made him a laughingstock and to bring it up again would have ended his career."

"So you *used* me."

Amelia Earhart glanced at Lester. "You'd better tell him all of it now," he said.

She took a deep breath. "It was mostly my idea, Joseph. I had Howard introduce me to you, a man, he assured me, who was as good as they came at what I needed."

"A tool," he spat.

"Someone to help me kill the man who left me on Saipan. I did everything I possibly could to make you marry me, and quickly. And when Howard sent you to Singapore, I came along as your wife."

"And you kept your identity from me, knowing that I'd blindly chase after a man."

She nodded, searching his eyes. "Joseph, you were ready to

fly back to the States, and I had to keep you in Singapore. So I left those medals in the Fort Canning armory. I paid the Chinese pawnbroker to say what he did about them. I left my flight log, and was going to let you discover it. I had to keep you here, had to keep you after Synge. And no one recognized me; not you, not the hospital nurse, not Governor Longstreet. Nobody."

"Except Terrence Bliss," Lester reminded. "He threatened to tell you, so I fixed it so he'd keep his mouth shut. And when you got too close to discovering who Connie was, I brought in Barbara Durant, a ringer you chased for days. It was a delicate balance, keeping you after Synge, but not allowing you to find out your wife's identity."

"All to find and kill Dillon Synge." Snow's words were hollow, the shock wrung out of them.

She reached for his hand, but he yanked it back as if hers were electrified. She said, "Joseph, I knew one day you'd find out. And I knew, too, that whatever explanation I could give would be inadequate and would hurt you. The more we lived together and shared our lives, the more worried I became."

"But never worried enough to tell me." Snow pushed himself to his feet and looked down at her. "I loved you. I loved Connie Snow."

"And now you love Amelia Earhart. The difference is only in the name. I'm the same person you met in Howard's office, who took down your punching bag and who suffered through those ringside seats with you. *Look at me.* I'm the same person you love." She reached again for his hand, this time not allowing him to pull away. "Joseph, you gave me a new life these past few months. I began to feel things again, things I left on Saipan. I'm your wife and I want to stay your wife. No one will ever learn I'm anyone but Connie Snow."

He looked into her eyes for a long moment, then shook his hand free and walked away, down the ramp and toward the car. She looked helplessly at Lester, then ran after him. She called his name, then said something else that didn't reach the dock.

Howard Lester said to Tsukada, "You got anything planned?"

"Synge is dead and I'm going to start healing."

"You want to work for me?"

"Snow said you're an ass."

Lester shrugged. "But the money's good. From now on, you're on the payroll."

They turned back to Amelia Earhart, who had reached her husband on the sand. She turned him by the shoulders, then gestured with her hands, arguing, convincing. Even at that distance, they could see Snow's shoulders slump, see him clasp his broken fingers in front of him. A moment passed, and Lester smiled when Joseph Snow slowly reached for his wife's hand.

ABOUT THE AUTHOR

James Stewart Thayer, author of two widely acclaimed novels, *The Stettin Secret* and *The Hess Cross*, lives in Seattle, Washington, where he is at work on his fourth book.

NEW FROM POPULAR LIBRARY

GREAT ADVENTURES IN READING